The Trusted

Michelle Medhat

Mindblowing Books Ltd © 2019

THANK YOU FROM MICHELLE MEDHAT

Now you've picked this up, I'm sure you're going to want to know what happens next. There's a direct link to The Dominant (part two) can be found at the end of this book.

Also, at the end of this book you can find details on how to get the free eBook **Operation Snowdrop**. This book is only through sign up to my newsletter *'Fearless Spies, Amazing Realms and Ice-Cold Villains'*. It's not available anywhere else. Operation Snowdrop is the mission that is cited throughout *The Trusted Thriller Series*. Together with this free eBook you'll get early bird discounts, the latest news on this series and access to incredible free thrillers bundles to keep you entertained.

But for now....

Dive in, hold on tight and enjoy!

Chapter 1

21 March, 2017

Ellie Noor sighed with satisfaction and gripped the leather steering wheel, turning it sharply to the left and into the lane. Ellie loved to feel the power of her Porsche Carrera 911 beneath her fingertips. Knowing she had control of something so magnificent and fierce gave her such a buzz. After the day she'd had of tough negotiations, she needed to unwind and let go. She flipped on Bluetooth and her music blasted out through the windows.

Ellie pressed down on the accelerator and hedgerows vanished in a viridian blur. She could see the traffic lights at the end of the lane, which widened into a single carriage way. The T-junction approached fast. Ellie slammed down on the brakes. The traffic lights flickered to amber, but Ellie didn't stop. She toggled the drive mode to manual, dropped down to second gear and swung a hard right across the road, just as the light flashed to red and traffic started to move.

Exhilarated, adrenalin pumping, Ellie smiled broadly and yelled, "Yeah!"

She shifted up the gears until the six-cylinder turbo engine purred contentedly underneath her feet.

It was Friday. Sam might be coming home today, and perhaps then, she could put some fun back into her life again.

Ellie glanced in the rear-view mirror. She'd been working non-stop that week with little sleep. But the deal with PalmerPharm, one of the pharmaceutical giants she had on her radar, was finally coming through. But everything came at a cost. Her skin had a pale translucence and her face seemed gaunt from a poor diet and lack of daylight.

She'd burnt the midnight oil, putting the finishing touches on her virtual warehousing application with her programmers. The application integrated block chain capability, giving her clients better flexibility, immediacy of distribution and, most of all, unrivalled cybersecurity in their supply chain management.

That was why the pharms were getting interested. She just had to close that deal and the rest of the lucrative life sciences market would follow.

Ellie glanced again in the mirror. A morning in the spa tomorrow was her indulgence. It would be time that should be spent running the final tests on the software. She flicked a look into the mirror again. Hell, I've got testers for that job. I deserve a bit of pampering. I've got to look great for Sam.

The second Ellie thought of her husband, her phone vibrated, still on silent from her last meeting. She swallowed deeply as she looked at the face on the on-screen display and inside, she fluttered with anticipation. Although just a thumbnail image, the dark captivating eyes, chiseled jaw and high cheekbones were unmistakable. She hit the pickup button.

"Hello sweetness," she cried, as she turned the car onto the ramp and glided smoothly into the flow of traffic on the M3.

"Hello darling," responded Sam, her husband. "What are you up to?" In his voice, Ellie could discern a slight chuckle.

"Oh, just driving back to London. I've decided to have a break tomorrow. We're almost there with the software launch. Alpha and beta testing have all gone through fine. We've just got one more testing set with some critical friends. I don't need to spend another weekend in Winchester for that. My team can handle it."

Ellie checked all around for signs of the authorities and then maneuvered the 911 quickly into the fast lane, pushing the accelerator up to her usual knuckle-whitening speed.

"Good. You're giving them a bit of latitude at last, sweetness. You've been like a mother hen for too bloody long."

Ellie detected a touch of bitterness in Sam's response. That's rich, coming from him. After all, he'd gone his own way when the Foreign Office called about their 'great job'.

"Sam, you're not still annoyed about me pursuing my dream, are you?"

They'd been together too long for Sam to harbor any feelings he didn't express to her. Communication was key in their marriage. Anything not right was brought out into the open. They had no secrets. It had been the very foundation on which their relationship was built.

"You're not, are you?" pressed Ellie.

But Sam didn't answer.

The silence grew. Ellie breathed heavily, feeling uncomfortable.

"Sam, love, don't be like this."

Sam sighed. "It's ok, sweetness. I'm happy for you. But I think you've given that place too much. I know it's your baby, but you need to know when to pull back a little."

"Oh, and you haven't devoted all your bloody time to the FCO? I never see you, Sam. You're always away."

It was Ellie's turn to feel hard done by about her husband's career choice.

"Of course you never see me. I'm in London and you're always in bloody Winchester."

"Not always!" retaliated Ellie sharply. "Sometimes I am in London. But you're always somewhere else."

Silence floated between them. Ellie heard Sam breathing gently. He wasn't getting riled, but she was.

"Sam, don't you understand? I love you. I need you. Just get back from wherever the hell you are."

"I'm in Oslo," said Sam. "I'm due to stay a bit longer, maybe two or three days. Then I'll be back."

Ellie heard what she didn't want to hear. She really wanted him back. She needed him back.

"Fine. Stay a few more bloody days," Ellie snapped.

"Look, Ellie-"

"It's your job. Just finish it!"

"Ellie!"

"It's fine, Sam. Really."

Ellie stared at the road and pressed down harder on the accelerator. The speed flew past 130 mph. Cars were leaping out of the way as she tore down the road toward them.

"Ok, sweetness. I'll cut short my business here and come back tonight."

Ellie's eyes dipped down to swiftly snatch a glance at Sam's thumbnail image on the touchscreen panel. She smiled. She'd got her way. As always.

"Thank you, darling."

"I do love you, Ellie. You know that."

"Of course I do," said Ellie. After a beat, she added with a touch of visible reluctance to keep Sam in check, "And I love you too."

Chapter 2

Sam closed the connection and Ellie's voice vanished, but her demanding, powerful cadence still rang in his ears. Even after twenty-three years of that bubbly and often argumentative tone, he knew he'd never get tired of hearing it.

She was right. She did deserve more.

Sam lifted his head up and glanced out of the rigid square windows of the British Embassy's administration building on Thomas Heftyes Gate. His view had some greenery, thanks to a proud, white eighteenth-century residence opposite that was replete with beautiful gardens. He considered himself far luckier than other colleagues who only had a concrete car park to enjoy.

Rain pelted relentlessly against the pane and the faintest tinge of a draft hit Sam's cheek as he moved his head down to concentrate on the files. The name at the top of the file 'Stor Spill', meaning Great Game in Norwegian, spelled out the company he was evaluating.

Sam had been sent over to check out a new potential gazelle firm that had experienced extremely rapid growth, and to test the temperature with them on expanding into the UK, if the incentives were right. The company's new augmented reality platform, which they used for their gaming environment, had many industrial applications beyond the entertainment industry. It was Sam's job to analyze whether Stor Spill could be a good future investment for UK PLC.

Recalling his earlier engagement with Stor Spill's prickly, twenty-something managing director, Sam wondered whether they were worth his effort.

"What do you think, Dr. Noor?" asked Stor Spill's MD.

Sam shrugged, keeping things neutral until he had a chance to run the proposition over with his boss. "I believe your technology offers interesting opportunities."

The MD scoffed, clearly annoyed. "Interesting opportunities? A bet on the horses at Ovrevoll Racecourse is an interesting opportunity. What I'm offering to the UK government is a dead cert, as you say."

Sam didn't give anything away. "As I say, consideration of various options is being undertaken. I will get back to you once decisions have been made."

The MD retorted, "You may come back, but we may not be here. We may have taken our 'interesting opportunity' to another country."

Sam smirked slowly. "And that is your choice."

Sam glared at the file, turning the pages over until he arrived at the potential for investment section. Working with companies meant partnership. Sam didn't feel that the MD wanted to play straight. The technology was good but not unbelievable. He'd seen other examples around the world.

After picking up the 'Reject' stamp, he then hesitated. The tech could be useful in other areas, especially the Ministry of Defense. Yes, the MD was an upstart, but he could be brought around. Sam put down the 'Reject' stamp and picked up the 'Pending' stamp. Then he slammed it down on the file.

Sam pulled out a drawer out and took out a file. It was completely different to the others piling up on his desk. It was foolscap, beige and marked up 'Rikard Allan.'

Sam moved his hand over to pick up Rickard's file, but his mobile rang.

"Yes," said Sam with a terse inflection.

"Need you back Sam. Meeting tonight. Debrief on everything."

"Understood sir."

"And Sam, we need to talk about Kinley," added the caller.

Sam gritted his teeth hard, and said, "Yes, sir. Ok."

By the end of the conversation, Sam was enraged. They were making the wrong decision, but they couldn't see it. Sam breathed deep and concentrated on something else in a bid to quieten his overflowing anger.

He picked up Rikard's file again, scanned inside and shut it abruptly, scowling.

Then, unexpectedly, Ellie's face popped up in his mind. Her beautiful grey-blue eyes were enticing him to make his move. Sam breathed in. For God's sake Ellie, not now thought Sam, feeling a desperate need to compartmentalize better.

He pressed the intercom on his phone.

"Helga, get me on the next plane out of Oslo."

Chapter 3

A woman, svelte and stunning with long dark hair blowing in the wind, joined an equally handsome and tall man. Both were in their early forties. They smiled, linked arms and walked together. The man flashed a smile to his partner that showed perfect white teeth shining from a chiseled face bursting with wholesome goodness. She returned the smile with a traffic-stopping ruby red grin of her own.

They could have been new lovers wrapped in the radiance of each other's love. They could have been actors from a rom-com film set. They could have been top models promoting the latest fashion or fragrance. What they couldn't possibly have been were international terrorists. At least, that's what a casual onlooker glancing their way would say. But they'd be wrong.

The man was Dr. Salim Al Douri, leader of Al Nadir.

The woman, Dr. Sabena Sanantoni, was his second in command. Although beautiful, she was colder than an Antarctic glacier. Known within the Al Nadir collective as The Slayer, her reputation afforded her the right to stand by the side of the man who was soon to be the most powerful force on Earth.

Chapter 4

The drive had been longer than usual. A four-car pileup just before junction two left Ellie stuck in a five-mile tailback that ended up lasting over two hours.

Ellie tried to call Sam, but his phone was on voicemail. She left a couple of messages and then gave up trying. You're never where you should be, thought Ellie, resenting the fact he was not with her.

The heavy rock music she'd blasted earlier had lost its effect. Tired from the drive, or lack of it, Ellie switched to a classical music channel on the radio. Scheherazade by Rimsky-Korsakov gently tickled her senses. The hypnotic music was accentuated by the power of the car's Burmester surround sound speakers, and she calmed down. The music soothed away her frustrations.

By the time the accident had been cleared away, she'd hit rush hour. Traffic coming out of Brentford and Twickenham made the rest of her journey a slow crawl. The red tail lights of the cars blurred in front of Ellie's eyes and her lids started to close. Her concentration was waning. The classics that had calmed her were now turning the interior of her car into a soporific bubble. Ellie breathed deeply, pulled her back straight, shoved a chewing gum in her mouth (chewing always helped her concentrate), and pressed Bluetooth again. Rock music jumped out. Ellie jolted back as the notes assaulted her weary brain. She flicked on another artist. A strong, pounding ballad enveloped her. Throughout her body, Ellie could feel the harmonic energies of the music and her own energy level rose just enough to continue the laborious drive home.

Ellie turned into the driveway of her apartment, Silent Waters in London's Chelsea Wharf. The automatic gates sensed the RFID on her windscreen and opened. Nearly four hours had passed since Ellie had spoken to Sam back in Winchester, and exhaustion was now setting in.

Ellie parked next to Sam's C63 AMG Merc, grabbed her Mulberry tote, and headed for the lift.

Halfway across the car park, a little vibration shook against her shoulder. Ellie swung the tote around and dived into the pocket housing her phone. It was Sam.

"Hiya, gorgeous. Where are you?" she asked.

"Just touched down. I'm going into a meeting now but it should be finished soon."

"Oh! Ok." Ellie breathed despondently. "But I thought we…"

Ellie's voice wandered off, and between the beat, Sam replied with a curt, "Bye."

Ellie stared at her phone for a few seconds, hoping Sam would call back. But he didn't. The phone stayed inanimate of vibration. Ellie sighed with annoyance, threw the phone back into her tote, and finished her journey to the lift.

Chapter 5

A few miles away from Ellie, Sam ran across the tarmac at RAF Northolt to a waiting Jaguar. He climbed into the back seat beside his boss, Sir Justin Maide. The car moved as Sam closed the door.

On seeing each other, they issued convivial greetings. Neither spoke about the heated conversation they'd had several hours earlier. Sam could see Maide wanted to bury it and focus on business. And just forget it happened.

Maide handed Sam his tablet. Sam took it and scanned through the reports, shaking his head.

"A lot's happened since I've been away?" said Sam, reading at speed.

"You're telling me. The PM wants a debrief."

Sam looked up as Maide's eyes hooded, and his voice dropped in timbre.

"You know the summit's almost upon us."

Sam nodded. "Yeah, I know. But we've got more problems."

Sam reached into his pocket and took out a package. It was small, silver, and shaped like a solid molded pen case. Sam flipped it open to show a single phial of orange liquid.

"I got this from Rikard. Dr. Wang, who couriered this package, had rerouted flights, bumping from Beijing, Mumbai, Lagos, Madrid, and eventually Oslo. We'd have missed it if the tech guys hadn't been scanning on tail call signs. This has got to be something big. See if you can get that analyzed before the meeting."

"Tonight?" exclaimed Maide.

"No, of course not tonight. Can you square it with the PM, and we'll meet tomorrow? By then, you'll most probably have analysis on whatever the hell it is." Sam waved around the silver case.

Maide scanned Sam's face. Sam knew he was under inspection.

Ellie's beautiful blue-grey eyes surfaced in his mind again, and he could hear the pain in her voice. 'You're always somewhere else'. It was true. He was always somewhere else. She never really seemed that bothered before, but when he'd spoken to her earlier, he could feel something. Maybe she was just tired after all the work she'd put in on her new product. But he sensed something was different.

He didn't want anything to break the love they had. He couldn't risk them going down a path that led to resentment and animosity.

"You're off duty tonight, and not just because of the analysis, aren't you?"

Sam looked down and tried to stop the tidal wave of emotions he could feel building, swallowing up any enthusiasm he may have had for a meeting. The compartmentalization that he always used had failed to engage. Maide had read him. He looked in front of him, trying to avoid Maide's eyes.

"It's just with K-" Sam held back, almost at the brink of mentioning Kinley. Maide's eyes narrowed. Concern rippled through him.

"Sam!"

Sam shook his head like he was getting his thoughts in order.

"I need to be with Ellie tonight. God knows I never see her."

Sam suddenly dropped his head into his hands. He was aware of Maide glaring at him.

"It's been ten years. And she still doesn't know."

"Ellie…?"

"Yes, she doesn't know anything…"

Maide leaned in toward Sam. "Do you *want* her to know?" he said slowly, pointedly.

"God. No!"

Maide smiled, reassured. "So what do you want?"

"I want…"

Sam's voice trailed off and he stared past Maide at the curtain on the side. The folds in the curtain took on the layers of his life. Underneath each neat turn lay another crease of lies and deceit. Sam thought of everything he'd seen. Everything he'd done.

What did he want?

He wanted his life back. He wanted to live it again, the way he should have done. That's what he wanted.

The driver turned into Silent Waters and Sam made to exit quickly from the car. Then he turned around.

"Look, I've got what I want. You can be sure of that. Sorry about changing tonight but I have to sort this. I'll see you tomorrow," said Sam, embarrassed and acutely aware that he'd revealed a side of himself that his employers never should see.

Chapter 6

Treeborne stared at his desk. The papers for tomorrow's state business lay in front of him. But he had other thoughts on this mind. He pushed his leather captain's chair back. The feet made deep grooves in the carpet. Then he stood, circled the desk and walked with haste to the door. He locked it and pressed a button to close the drapes around the room. Once all external links to the outside world had been suspended, Treeborne walked with reverence to his hidden safe.

He took out a memory stick from his pocket and stuck it into the underside of a console table beneath his own portrait. The front dropped down, revealing a keypad. He punched in his code and waited. Above him, the painting seemed to sink several inches into the wall, making room for a small shelf that rose up inside. On the shelf lay his treasure. Smiling, he took out the contents.

It was small in his large hand. It was cold, hard and seemed to resonate, although he'd never been able to establish how this happened. As his hands clasped around the object, his mind took him back. Back to when it first began.

Treeborne had been eight years old when his parents had relocated to the Middle East. Both were chemical scientists working for a petroleum corporation engaged in oil exploration in Uruk, Iraq. Their contract had been two years and it had been his parents' intention to return to the US once their spell in the Middle East had ended.

Treeborne had turned ten just a few days before they arrived back in the US. His birthday had been uneventful, but his parents promised to take him on an exploration dig for his birthday treat.

That day was the day of the dig. His parents bought some new books on geology for him. They'd told him the books were 'cool' and 'exciting', but all he could see were diagrams of rock strata. They really didn't do much for him. But he persisted with reading the books, as he knew his parents meant well.

After taking him to one of the exploration sites and showing him around, they had to get back to their work and undertake their geological tests. Treeborne was left with a local guide to keep an eye on him. By midday, the heat had sucked the energy out of everyone and his guide, being no different, had fallen asleep by 1 p.m.

Bored with his 'cool' geology books, Treeborne had wandered off, deciding to explore on his own. He'd travelled only a short distance when he found a stocky pyramid. Its upper levels were in ruins but the lower half was intact. He recognized the structure as a Sumerian ziggurat from ancient history books. Stumbling around it, he found a fissure between two massive blocks. His frame was small for a boy of his age, and without a thought, he slid through the crack.

The fissure led into a tunnel. Although small in diameter, he fitted it smoothly and crawled along, tentative and wary. The sand under his hands and knees shifted for the first time in 6,000 years. Finally, he reached a chamber, which was far higher than the tunnel.

Treeborne had scrambled to his feet. A flush of cold hit him. But he dismissed it and walked inside the chamber. The farther he walked, the greater the flush of cold. A sinister aura reached out to grab him. But he was unafraid.

He held up his oil lamp to see the chamber, but the light went out. At first, he thought it was a draft causing the light to extinguish. But as he moved deeper into the darkness, he could see the flame didn't want to stay lit; it was going out deliberately.

His last attempt to shed light through the chamber lasted for a few short moments. In that instant, he noticed that an area on the far side of the wall appeared much darker than the rest. Drawn inexplicably, he headed toward the strange dark patch. Some may say it was merely boyhood curiosity that drew him forward. But that was not the case. Treeborne felt a physical attraction to the place.

With his candle refusing to ignite, he had no means of light, but he knew that light was something he no longer needed. He could now see his way clearly. Darkness encircled him and he felt one with it. Unity in ebony.

Reaching the wall, the urge to touch the dark center was so great that his hand lifted as if magnetized. On his touch, the wall melted away like it had never been there in the first place. Its absence revealed a secret compartment.

He wasn't scared. Treeborne felt a strange comfort in the darkness. He edged his hand forward into the secret compartment and rested it on something. Something small, rectangular and ice-cold. Dislodging it from its ancient resting place, he eased out the object and held it. At the same moment, the dark swirled. The air twinkled and oscillated, and then solidified.

Over him towered a giant. A strange twinkling aura outlined the huge man's form. Overwhelmed by omnipotence, Treeborne dropped to his knees and shut his eyes. He remained immobile until the dark god spoke.

"Rise, child, and look upon me."

The giant's voice reverberated around the chamber. As Treeborne listened, the dark god's tone stirred strange feelings. He sensed displacement, and he knew the chamber's sandstone walls didn't surround him anymore.

Treeborne rose and looked upon the man as he was told.

"I see in you a great destiny," said the dark god, known as Aswa-da. "You will be a man of strength, wielding a power unsurpassed."

Then Aswa-da reached out and touched him.

From that point, Treeborne's life would never be the same.

Back in the present, alone, Treeborne looked at the small, rectangular and ice-cold object in his hand. He regarded it as if for the first time. It was just an innocent-looking stone tablet with ancient writing, similar to but smaller than the Rosetta stone. Although it was a piece that would not look out of place in a museum, this tablet was not a relic. It was the center of his success. It was the embodiment of all his successes, past, present and future.

Only he knew of its existence.

Treeborne heard footsteps approaching. He returned the tablet back to his safe, replaced the painting, drew back the curtains and unlocked the door. Seated at his desk, he positioned himself in a posture of command as decreed by the office he carried. Treeborne waited. A knock on the door caused him to speak.

"Come in."

His visitor entered. "Mr. President, do you have a minute?"

Chapter 7

Patsy wasn't a very good cook. She hadn't been brought up that way. Being an army brat, with both parents in the forces, she'd lived by take-out all through her formative years. Yanked from one place to another, friends had been transitional, and life always had a sort of continuous motion about it. She couldn't really settle down anywhere. Home schooling had been the best option for her, and her tutors had been great. She'd eventually landed herself a place at college in Phoenix and graduated in Business Management. Life then took on a steadier pace. She secured a job as an administrator in the Department of Defense, and that's where she met her husband. He'd been ten years her senior. But love, as they say, is love.

Age made no difference.

Within a year of getting married, Zoe had popped up, and seven years later, Peter was born. She gave up work and became a mother. It was a new job she adored, and although take-out was still the principal diet of the family, she was a devoted and loving mother in every other way. Her children were her life and through them she'd experienced a life of stability, something she'd never had as a child herself.

She was to be forty that year, but she didn't look like she'd hit thirty yet. Broad, swaying hips and a well-endowed bosom gave her the typical hourglass figure of the crime noir dames. Her husband had always said he was her gumshoe that would save his damsel in distress.

Goodness knows she could certainly sashay him to distress!

Patsy smiled, thinking about her husband, and pulled open the big bag of MacDonald's take-out. As she reached over to the cupboard for plates, she heard the front door open.

"Zoe, can you put the drink on the table and get Pete out of his room? I'd like us all to have a meal together for a change."

A tall fifteen-year-old with sharp, pale blue eyes and blonde hair entered carrying a bag. Tight, ripped and faded jeans clung to her lithe body and a white diamante Guess sweatshirt with cutaway sections accentuated her youthful breasts.

She heaved the bag up onto the breakfast counter and scowled as her phone pinged. Her attention focused on her phone and she drifted away from the kitchen. Patsy looked up, annoyed, shoveling chips around a quarter pounder.

"I said put the drinks on the table. For once in your life, girl, put that Goddamn phone down!"

Zoe stared sulkily, shrugged and slouched over to grab one of the bottles of coke and put it on the dining table.

"And put some glasses out please, young lady."

"God! I thought slavery had been abolished," muttered Zoe, opening the cupboard.

"Slavery! My girl, you don't know what work is. You got it easy."

"Whatever," said Zoe, placing the glasses on the table. Then she snatched out her phone and started to scroll through it again.

"Go and get Pete down," said Patsy, eyeing her daughter as she chopped up some lettuce and tomatoes. She could just about handle a salad.

"Pete, dinner's ready!" yelled Zoe.

"I said go and get him. God, Zoe. What is wrong with you lately?"

Patsy pushed past her daughter and made for the stairs, but something caught in her peripheral vision. A shadow across the glass crescent at the top of the door. She turned around and peered through the crescent, but nothing was there. She shrugged. Maybe a tree branch.

She alighted the stairs, her mind on getting Pete away from that damn Killzone game he was obsessed with.

Behind her, the front door exploded, shooting glass fragments and wood splinters across the hallway. The force of the blast pushed Patsy forward, and she lay on her stomach across the lower stairs.

She heard Zoe scream.

Her body shook with fear, but she knew she had to pull herself up.

Before she could stand, hands grabbed her from behind and hauled her backwards. She tried to turn around, but as she did, a blindfold was tied tight around her head, cutting off her vision. Her hands were bound by something that immediately dug into her flesh.

Zoe. Peter.

"Mom!"

"Run, Peter. Run!"

Something hard smashed into her stomach, winding her. She gasped.

"What's happen-"

She heard her son momentarily before a whooshing shot past Patsy's ear and cut Pete's voice off. She heard a heavy thump and footsteps raced past her up the stairs.

"Let go of-"

Like her son's, Zoe's voice stopped abruptly.

A piercing pain hit Patsy's neck and the sounds around her faded as her mind cut out.

Chapter 8

The key turned in the lock. By the time it reached a full turn, Ellie was at the door. She opened it wide and stood smiling in her blue satin robe. Her belt, tied tight, sharply outlined her mouthwatering figure. Sam took in the moment to gaze admiringly at his wife from head to foot.

Ellie reached up and slipped her right hand around his neck.

"Darling," Ellie said softly, moving her fingers gently through his short, black hair. Then her hold strengthened, and she pulled him forcefully through the doorway.

Sam smiled, wrapping his arms around her. One hand in the middle of her back and the other around her waist. He drew her in close. Pressed against him, he knew Ellie could feel just how much he'd missed her. Bending down to her lips, Sam kissed her hard.

He moved across her face, kissing her skin.

"God, I need you," he whispered, biting her earlobe. "It's been too long. And I'm starving!"

They fell into the apartment, kissing hard. Sam rammed Ellie against the wall, pinning her tight, and kissed down her neck. Dexterously, he caught the edge of the door with his foot and slammed it shut. Voyeurism was definitely not his thing.

His hands reached up as if to pull down her robe. But Ellie was quicker. Laughing, she slid down the wall out of his hold and maneuvered behind him.

"Well, darling, your dinner is served. Bon appetito!"

Ellie giggled, licking her lips lasciviously, and slipped off her robe, unveiling her delicious naked body.

Sam gazed, his mouth salivating at the á la carte offering before him. Tearing his tie free, getting ready to tuck into the meal on offer, Sam advanced. In unison, Ellie moved forward, plucking at the tiny mother of pearl buttons on his shirt. Parting the expensive woven silk to expose his firm chest, Ellie kissed him and murmured appreciatively. Her fingers deftly smoothed his shirt back from his firm, broad shoulders. The fabric fell to the marble floor beneath.

Sam bent down and kissed her neck. With almost frenzied, full-on passion, Ellie returned his kisses. Her hands drifted down to his belt. She unclasped it and pulled down his zipper. She hooked her thumbs underneath the waistline of his trousers and yanked at them. His boxers dropped in unison, swept down by Ellie's sleight of hand.

Sam breathed deep and grasped her porcelain shoulders. Moving down her body, he savored the peachy, ripe smoothness of her skin beneath his lips.

As Sam's kisses reached her stomach, Ellie arched slightly, breathing hard. She pushed her body, limpet-like, against his lips. His kisses descended lower and Ellie purred. Sam inhaled her fragrance. After twenty-three years, she'd never changed it. An intoxicating mix of sweet honeysuckle, magnolia and vanilla that was still good enough to eat. With his hunger overpowering, Sam consumed her.

Ellie screamed under Sam's exquisite touch and pressed his head harder against her groin. Slowly, Sam lifted her up, cupping her ass and holding her tight as she wrapped her long, slender legs around his neck. The bedroom was light years away. They dropped onto the sofa, panting and gasping, and made love noisily for the rest of the evening.

Like the proverbial cat who got the cream, Ellie's grin hung happily on her face as she drifted into satisfied sleep, curled up in Sam's arms.

Chapter 9

In Washington DC, two men sat in a wood-paneled room and stared at the information flashing up on the laptop positioned between them on a table. The first, a small, squatty man in his late fifties with piercing rat-like eyes and a cruel slit of a mouth was called Godley. He leaned forward, his hands gripping the edge of the desk and he shook his head.

"They're getting better all the time. How did they get to Rikard Allan? You do know what this means?"

The other man was Pedro Russo, third in command in Al Nadir. His strong, angular face was immutable, as if it was carved in rock. Beneath his designer suit rippled the muscles of an athlete. He raised an eyebrow and glared through eyes of ice.

"It means we carry on."

Godley seemed taken aback by Russo's stoic determination.

"But by now they would have discovered our Cambridgeshire cell." His voice had descended to a mutter, and he picked subconsciously at a piece of rough skin alongside his fingernail.

"So? Let them know," replied Russo. "They're helpless. Impotent. Let them rant and rave in their secret little meetings. It makes no difference. We will always be stronger."

The persuasive, powerful tone of Russo forced Godley to nod. His head bobbed up and down in swift agreement.

"Yes, yes. But what about Sam Noor? He's getting to be quite a problem."

Russo sneered. "That won't be a situation that will remain. Believe me."

Hearing this, Godley smiled and lifted his glass. In parallel, Russo did the same.

"For the glory of Al Nadir!" said Russo, and Godley tilted his head in honor of the world's most sadistic terrorists.

Chapter 10

Patsy came around into a solid shield of utter darkness. She tried to orientate herself. The drug they'd given her had knocked her senses. She couldn't see anything. A blindfold still remained tied tight around her head. In the faint distance, she could hear screams.

Bile rose to her throat as she focused long enough to realize the frantic screams were from her own daughter.

"Don't *touch* me!"

Patsy tried to stand, to get to her daughter, but firm hands held her back.

"Zoe!" yelled Patsy, struggling against the hands holding her down.

"Mom, they're-" cried out Zoe.

Then Patsy heard a whack and a dull thud.

"Leave her alone, you bastards!" shouted Patsy.

But she dropped down as a force of iron smashed into her face.

"No. No!" yelled Zoe.

On the floor, Patsy listened to her daughter and her heart pounded.

"Darling, it's going to be ok," slurred Patsy, trying to stay calm. Her face felt like it had been hit by a sledgehammer. Her cheek burned with a thudding pain, and her jaw felt loose like had been dislocated. She tasted coppery blood in her mouth.

"It's gonna be ok, alright," said the captor. His voice was thick like molasses and just as dark. "With a bitch like this, we'll all be ok."

Patsy heard rustling and the ripping of clothes, and Zoe screamed, "Get off me."

"Lovely!" said another captor, his voice higher pitched and spiteful. He started to laugh. Others joined in.

Anger cancelled out fear and Patsy's mother's need to protect rose. Her adrenalin powered up. She pushed hard against her captor then heaved herself to her feet. Still unable to see, but focusing on the sound of her captors, Patsy bent her head down and charged with all her strength like a bull in a ring.

"Leave her alone," screamed Patsy, sounding like a mad banshee.

"What the…"

Patsy heard a loud crash and a third man's voice, tough like a Bronx brawler, howled out, "Crazy fucking bitch. That's my ankle fucked. Get her!"

Hands snatched at her and dragged her along the floor, pulling her by the hair and tearing it from her skull.

Zoe's screams increased. "Please. Please, don't."

"Silence that bitch," said the spiteful voice.

Patsy heard a hefty slap against soft flesh. She twisted and tugged, trying to break free from her captors. They yanked her by the hair and pulled her up to stand. A hand touched her cheek. Sensing it close, Patsy snatched with her teeth, attempting to bite at the fingers that grazed across her skin.

"Feisty mother!" said the molasses voice, and pain shot through Patsy's face. She thought her cheek had been sliced open. Nausea washed through her and she sensed blood on her cheek near her eye. Heavy hands gripped her shoulders and pushed her down. She landed on a soft cushion that she realized was a sofa.

She couldn't hear Zoe anymore and Pete hadn't spoken.

"Zoe? Peter!"

"Shut it, bitch," shouted the Bronx brawler.

Another flash of blinding pain, and Patsy fell against the cushion. She hadn't heard from her children.

"Where are they? What have you done with them? I'll kill you if you've hurt them."

Laughing met her pleas. "Yeah. Kill me. Right!" Molasses voice rang out with incredulity.

Patsy heard a whimpering and heavy crying.

"Zoe?"

The crying closed in on Patsy. The cushion beside her took a weight and she knew her daughter had been pushed down next to her. Patsy turned.

"Zoe," Patsy whispered slowly. "Are you ok?"

"Yeah. Yeah…" answered Zoe, suppressing a sob. Her voice was small and shaking, "I'm…I'm ok."

Patsy's gut twisted. She recognized the truth within Zoe's sobs.

"Bastards!" Patsy screamed, launching herself off the sofa at the voices still laughing cruelly. She collided with something and smashed to the ground amidst more mocking jeers.

"Sit the fuck down, you crazy whore!" said Bronx brawler. His voice was getting rougher.

Savage hands pulled her back and she fell down onto the sofa.

"Mom!"

Peter's voice rang out. Momentary relief surfaced in Patsy.

"Peter." Patsy turned back and forth trying to center in on the sound of her son's voice.

"I'm here, Mom. Next to Zoe."

Patsy could hear her son. Eight-year-old Peter had pushed a commanding tone into his voice. He'd tried to sound grown up. Patsy had drilled in him to always stay strong. That upbringing came through with the courage he now displayed. Patsy felt proud of her son's mettle in the face of such a horrendous situation.

"Are you hurt?" asked Patsy, forcing herself to dial down the panic that threatened to take her over.

"No. I'm ok."

"Can you see?"

"No. I'm blindfolded. Can you, Mom?"

"No. Zoe, darling, can you see?"

Zoe held down a sob as she answered, "No, Mom. They blindfolded me before…before…they…"

"Hush, baby. It's ok."

Patsy purposely interrupted her daughter. She didn't want her to reveal any more in front of young Peter. Zoe moved in to be close to her mother, sniveling, and gently wept.

Patsy's heart crushed.

"Are they still here? I don't hear them."

A force belted Peter in the face and he lunged against Zoe who yelped, terrified.

"Oh, yeah! We're still here. Not going anywhere soon," said the molasses voice with a smile in his tone.

"They hit Pete," called out Zoe, heaving heavier sobs that forced her body to rise and fall against Patsy.

"Leave my children alone," screamed Patsy.

"Leave my children alone," repeated the spiteful voice in a falsetto tone.

"You, sit. And can your yapping. You don't make the orders. We do. And we can do anything we fucking please."

Patsy realized that molasses voice man spoke the truth. She just wanted him to tell her what they wanted. Then, maybe, their nightmare would end.

Chapter 11

Godley watched as Russo slipped out of the door. He was by far the tallest man he had ever seen. Although, given his own diminutive state, most men were taller than him. That's why he found great comfort in his allegiance to Al Nadir.

That's why he'd joined them; they made him *feel* tall. Each meeting he had with Russo made him feel that much taller. Of course, mused Godley, as the door closed quietly, access to money and power was also a major attraction. He wouldn't have been with Al Nadir otherwise. They had approached him. Naturally, his position in government afforded him considerable opportunity to help their operation, and they had seen that he was well rewarded, both financially and in-kind.

The in-kind assistance was often more beneficial. Godley recalled a recent case. He'd been hounded for his nocturnal activities by slimy politicos and heat-seeking journos. The situation had been intolerable, and he requested for his *friends* in Al Nadir to handle it. They wasted no time in nipping that problem in the bud.

He leaned back and rested his head on the wing of the high-backed armchair then sipped slowly at the single malt in his hand. Al Nadir had solved all his problems, bar one: Sam Noor.

What had Russo said? *"That won't be a situation that will remain."*

Godley knew, with or without Russo's help, he was going to change that situation. He couldn't risk Sam Noor finding out about his relationship with Al Nadir.

Chapter 12

The room had been silent for a while.

All Patsy could hear was breathing, her own and her children's. Zoe had gone very still, and Patsy knew she must be in some form of shock. She could feel her daughter's body shaking next to her. She wanted to kill them. If she'd had a gun, she would shoot them. No question. These men were worse than animals. A life sentence was too good for them. The only justice they deserved was a bullet, and she dearly wished she could pull the trigger.

The man with the molasses voice slipped in close. Patsy heard the action slide back on a gun. She knew the sound instantly. Throughout her childhood, that sound had reverberated around her.

"What do you want?" asked Patsy, trembling. "For God's sake. Tell me what you want."

The cold muzzle of the gun pressed against her temple. Patsy swallowed.

"Mom," cried Zoe, hearing the sound of the gun. She huddled close to Patsy. Peter cuddled closer into his sister.

"It's ok, baby."

Patsy wanted to put her arms around her children. She wanted to encase them in her loving protection.

But she couldn't.

Tears welled within her and started to flow, soaking the blindfold.

Peter hadn't said anything and his silence worried Patsy.

"Pete?"

"Yeah, Mom."

Pete's voice was but a whisper and she could hear within his address that he'd been crying without a sound. He was frightened. But he'd still kept his stoic front and remained brave for her sake and his sister's.

"Ok, boys and girls, say hello to Daddy. Patsy, smile for your husband, sweetheart." The man with the molasses voice laughed. "This is your family. If you want them returned to you, alive and unharmed, you do exactly what I tell you."

"Ok." Patsy heard the deadpan timbre of her husband. "Tell me." She detected a slight warble at the end of his short instruction, but she knew her husband and knew he'd try to remain calm.

Molasses voice gave the information to her husband. He added finally, "Involve the police or fail to turn up…"

A volley of shots rang out, and Patsy, Zoe and Peter, unable to see who was being fired at, fearing the worst, all screamed in unison.

"No!" cried out her husband, and Patsy's heart tightened..

"Those were test shots at the floor," returned the molasses voice. "Fail me, and the next ones will be at Zoe's head."

"I'll get it. I'll get you anything. Just don't harm my family."

Patsy could hear the calmness in her husband vanish. He was frantic. Willing to do anything to keep his family safe.

"I know you will. Until tomorrow."

Molasses voice sidled up to Patsy. "You're not a bad looking broad. Not quite like your daughter but…"

Patsy heard salacious sniggers to the left of her and her stomach flipped. She pushed back the feeling and tried to concentrate on escape. She'd counted two men. Plus molasses voice. Three in total. That wasn't an army by a long shot. She'd already wounded one. If she could move the blindfold down, she'd have a chance.

She started to blink hard, causing herself to frown, and moved her shoulder up to try and nudge the blindfold.

"Oh, no you don't," snapped spiteful voiced man, who moved close to her.

Her captor snatched her arm and other hands gripped the blindfold ends, untying it for a second and then tightening with vise-like viciousness. Only absolute darkness was her view.

Molasses voiced man lent in. His breath touched her cheek. He smelt of stale nicotine and beer. Patsy squirmed and flicked her head away. She felt a hand grasp her chin, pressing into her skin, forcing her to face him.

A finger drew down her face, her neck and onto her chest.

"But you're good enough to pass the time."

Chapter 13

The hours fell away, and Sam's arms encased around Ellie like ancient lovers cast in stone. Their legs entwined. Ellie woke and sighed gently. Sam stirred. Lazily, he kissed her hair.

Ellie snuffled amongst the hairs on his chest, exhausted but blissfully happy. The television illuminated the dark lounge, flickering the last scenes of a horror film. Ellie reached over for the remote and switched it to MTV. The heavy bass of club music filled the apartment.

Wired from sex, bursting with party energy and craving more, Ellie jumped up, out of Sam's arms, and started to dance. As Ellie moved, Sam's leg, which had been on top of hers, fell off the sofa. His foot touched the cold marble floor and the sensation sparked Sam's nerves. He woke with a start.

And saw a vision. An incarnation of a male fantasy.

A glorious goddess danced completely naked in front of him.

Her sylphlike but strong body moved in perfect time to the thudding club beat. Hypnotized by her swaying, sultry moves, he lifted off the sofa. Still dancing, Ellie opened her arms wide and flicked her fingers, beckoning Sam to join her.

He felt the rhythm and moved with it into Ellie's arms. His naked body closed in against her and his hands fell instinctively downwards, gripping her hips tight. Ellie writhed against him. Sam closed his eyes, trembling. Ellie's private dancing and the throbbing beat stirred him. Frantically, he pushed Ellie down onto the Qum silk rug. She laughed. He laughed too.

"You sexy little minx!" said Sam, kissing her face, her lips, her neck. All over her body.

They made love fast and hard, their bodies fusing as one. Sam rolled over and fell on his back gasping. Ellie traced his hard stomach muscles with her finger, gradually moving down.

"Oh, God! That was wonderful," Ellie whispered, kissing his stomach. "I think you've just about made up for your absence. Just don't go away again too soon!"

Hearing Ellie's words, Sam pulled up and turned away, his face shadowed with guilt.

"I've got to work tomorrow. I don't want to leave you. But you know I can't let the government down."

"The government! They get more of you than I do," Ellie snapped.

He looked back at Ellie. A scowl was fixed on her beautiful face. It was his duty to remove that expression.

"I wouldn't say that, would you?" said Sam softly, and his chocolate brown eyes twinkled seductively. He pulled Ellie back into his arms, lifted her up and carried her over to their bedroom.

Laying Ellie down, Sam heard her mumble a begrudging, "No."

Sam rewarded her affirmation with delights that replaced her scowl with a beaming smile.

Chapter 14

Ellie gasped. Vise-tight and squeezing hard, massive hands closed around her throat. Her mouth opened and closed as she took great gulps like a guppy fish sucking greedily at food. She snatched any oxygen she could, but his crushing fingers squeezed faster than she could grab air. Her throat burned raw. Scorched by lack of air, her lungs took flame.

I'm dying.

Ellie bricked up the thought. She relegated it to an impenetrable fortress for the weak of spirit. Her heart thundered in her chest. Her eyes closed. She wasn't going to submit to this stranger who wanted to take her life.

Suddenly, she thought of Sam. His face filled her mind, along with memories across the years, and his warm, gentle enveloping of love. A comfort of softness. His touch. Her husband. Her Sam. A love of such power, it coursed through her veins. A love that was embedded in her cells.

A love for which there could be no surrender to the death that called now.

Ellie's mind focused. Sam's eyes, which had seen so much, sparkled so brightly in her mind. A thought blasted into Ellie. Was she to leave those eyes forever, never to see them again? It shattered her to pieces. Then, somehow, the power within her surged, and she scooped those shattered pieces together as one again.

Clarity built. Panic vanished.

But still, the stranger's hands pressed ruthlessly down on her throat. Signals seared deep into her brain.

It wasn't going to end here. Not like this.

Silver shone in her peripheral vision, caught in the glare of car headlights outside. She wrenched her head to the side. Her gun. It still sat to the right of her, where it had fallen. If only she could reach out, maybe, just maybe, she could grab it.

Ellie stretched her right arm and ignored the volcano erupting in her chest. Fingertips touched cold metal. *So close.* She stretched farther; her fingers taut as bones pushed hard against her skin. *Almost there.* The gun was in her grasp.

She lunged. He tightened.

Ellie inhaled but no air came, only overwhelming pain. She pitched forward and carried on dropping, caught in a flat spin that seemed never-ending…

Ellie woke.

She breathed hard and fast. The stranger's hands still imprinted upon her skin. Their heaviness was a visceral pain even out of slumber. They caused a crushing, burning ache. A furnace raging inside her lungs. Ellie swallowed. Muscles seized in her throat. She gagged. Her saliva was poison. It burned, turning her mouth arid and raw.

The silk duvet was wrapped cling-film tight around her. Ellie pushed at the hot, claustrophobic beddings. She needed air. She needed space. She stood. Shaky disorientation hit her. It was like her brain had been starved of oxygen. But how? She knew not what it meant, only that it happened. The floor beneath her slipped away and Ellie slid with it, colliding with the wall. She clung against it, which now provided support not only for the building but for her own frightened frame. Ellie gasped, inhaled and exhaled at length. Each breath was a luxury to be treasured.

Chapter 15

Ellie pulled on her sloppy t-shirt and stumbled across the marble floor. She swallowed, caught her breath and grimaced. Her throat burned. The lining of it had been scoured by sandpaper. Her membranes were stripped. Or such was her imagining, given the desiccated state of her mouth.

She hurried to the kitchen to quench her thirst. A bottle from the fridge served her need. Tipping the cool water down her throat quelled the furnace inside her. She gulped the remainder then took a long breath. *Why did she have that dream again?* Fuzzy thoughts plagued her. She tried to ignore the question. Water was inadequate so early in the morning, and Ellie sought something stronger. The coffee pot: her destination to restore a semblance of order inside her chaotic mind.

Why again? This time, the question stopped her mid-stride. Someone somewhere once told her a reoccurring dream is a sign that something is wrong with your life. The dream was a wakeup call, a notification for life evaluation. Perhaps they were right.

Maybe something *is* wrong with my life, Ellie thought. I work all the time. I've got no social life. Sam is always away. That's a mess for starters. Children: nil. Family: nil. Mum: who knows? Dad: never knew. With all that baggage, no wonder I'm having nightmares.

But Ellie knew she was kidding herself. She was, in fact, very happy with her life.

Ok, Sam wasn't always around, but when he was, it was wonderful. They did everything together. They loved and lived forever in the honeymoon zone, and for her that made their togetherness, however fleeting, complete. True, she didn't have many friends, but the handful she did have were loyal, lasting and helped her whenever she needed. Granted, she was addicted to work. But unlike so many other addictions, this one was good for her. Her addiction brought her independence and, of course, financial freedom. Not having kids or parents didn't come into her life equation. It had neither a positive nor negative effect. It was just a constant with which she'd always lived.

Sam. He was her life. Even when they were apart, they were forever connected. Her favorite times were in bed with him. It wasn't just the sex, although it was awesome, but she liked to watch Sam as he slept. During the day, staring at him would depict her as a soppy romantic type; that was not her nature, and not the reason Sam had fell in love with her. Ellie was pragmatic, down to earth, and didn't look for wine and roses. But at night, she was free to indulge in her romanticized staring. Sam couldn't see her. He couldn't see the doe-eyed wonder taking over her each time his head sank into the pillow.

Her gaze took him in. His skin, golden brown, was tanned akin to those who toiled the land, and like those peasant farmers, he had the muscles to match. Strong and well defined were the contours that graced his face. They alluded to a path to stardom, which he had never followed. High cheekbones, a powerful jaw and squared chin combined to give Sam a dramatic, commanding appearance.

Ellie often ran her fingers along his dark eyebrows. They framed his face and acted as a prelude to the feature Ellie loved most: Sam's striking eyes. Asleep, they were shut, but she could see their sparkle as if they were open. It had been his eyes that first attracted her, the moment she had stepped into that interview room twenty-three years ago. She'd entered with apprehension in her step. Around her were grey oppressive walls and non-descript furnishings. Ellie weighed up her panel of tormentors: a strange motley crew from personnel.

Not daring to hope for anything more than rejection, Ellie sat down.

Then she saw him. Despite inappropriate circumstances, Sam's eyes sparkled almost seductively. They demanded attention, pulling her into him. Ellie remembered his cold, arrogant interviewing technique and his demeanor of stoic professionalism. But throughout the interview, his eyes happily undressed her.

Unnerved and incredibly aroused, Ellie had wanted him. She wanted him at that very moment. Pure self-restraint, the type that keeps one from talking loudly in a library, kept Ellie from leaping out of her chair, grabbing Dr. Noor, as he was known to her then, and devouring his glorious body on the interview room floor.

The memory brought her back to her happy place, and she sighed. Her hand slipped around the mug of coffee she held in her kitchen. Sipping at the hot beverage, Ellie headed for the breakfast bar to sit down.

"Listen to me."

At first, Ellie thought she was hearing things. She shook her head and could almost feel the thoughts rattling around inside. She'd been thinking too much too early, and now, it seemed, her mind was playing games with her sanity. It was definitely time to go back to bed.

"Listen, Ellie."

Ellie span round, expecting to see Sam standing in the kitchen, ready to admonish her for waking too early. But no one was there. This is crazy, she thought. I must be imagining it. She lifted the coffee mug to her lips.

"Listen, Ellie!"

Ellie froze. She heard that alright.

"I'm listening," Ellie responded, half in her mind, half out loud.

As strange as it seemed, she wasn't scared. She was curious. The voice had been deep and strong, like Morgan Freeman, only more resonant and powerful. The echo of his words lingered, ringing in her ears. Ellie smiled and waited to hear more, her curiosity growing.

"Tgonetafaragontootar…ga…bal…ted…sh…sh…ce…al…gof…ar."

What is this? Ellie thought. What is he trying to say?

From beautiful deep sounds of warmth, the booming voice spouted words Ellie couldn't discern. Screwing up her face, she tried to figure out what was being said by the voice. She looked upward at the ceiling. Instinct told her to look to Heaven. Perhaps, somehow, by the grace of God, she would understand what was happening. But no revelation came. Still, the deep voice droned on. But now, not one word made any sense. They came out elongated in one burst as if spoken on a mobile with a weak signal.

"Forgatoogonfarg. Ba…nc…ted…shi…la…go…ta…fa…ted…ce…faa."

Ellie couldn't explain it, but his voice brought a sense of comfort. In not understanding him and recognizing a lack of communication, a sadness infested her soul. She listened to the senseless words fade further from comprehension, and their departure left her vacant.

"Ba go…ted…fa…fa."

Chapter 16

Determined to understand, Ellie locked out all distant sounds around her. Ambient city noises she wouldn't normally have noticed now seemed loud and interruptive. Gradually, she shut out everything and welcomed isolation.

Come back to me, she thought.

But why on Earth she wanted to hear a disembodied voice, she didn't know. By all accounts, it should have terrified her. But it didn't. There was a warm resonance about the voice like a mother's heartbeat; it encapsulated feelings of safety and security.

The voice, unrelenting, kept on its broadcast. Ellie, as if trying to find a radio station, tuned into the incoherent jumble of words, and tried to get a fix on their meaning.

"Too…too…far…far…too…"

It's working, thought Ellie. With her mind focused, she strained to hear the rest. Her hand was the first affected. It gave a slight shiver. The rest of her body followed. The shiver mutated to a stronger vibration, a tremble on a track to signify a train was coming. But what was coming towards her now?

"Too far gone!"

The voice, no longer soft and comforting, came through strong, clear and distinct.

"Balance shifted!"

The words burst through with clarity. The bodiless voice vented its open anger at Ellie. The force of its attack was surging, a truck hurtling headlong into her. Louder and louder, the voice grew as he screamed the words over and over.

"Too far gone. Balance shifted. Too far gone. Balance shifted…"

Ellie, in desperation and now with great fear, for this was not the fatherly voice she'd heard earlier, screamed, "Tell me what you want!" to the open space in her kitchen.

"It's all too far gone…"

The voice, although still angry, was tinged with sadness.

"What is too far gone?" asked Ellie, detecting the desolation in his voice. But the only answer she received was piercing cold and sudden darkness. The morning sun extinguished. No outline or edge could be seen. For all Ellie knew, her kitchen could be dispersed across the universe. Ellie looked into the solid black nothingness, an existence-eroding ebony that infiltrated her soul.

She breathed. The sound of air as it slipped through her slightly parted lips was her only familiarity. It was the only indication that she was still there at all. That she was still alive.

Chapter 17

When Earth children play, they are spiteful. Aswa-da was well aware of this. He had seen enough evidence through the centuries of watching tiny humans. He often found children to have significant layers of darkness for seemingly innocent beings. They became a source of amusement for Aswa-da when he'd wanted to break away from the High Council and the sanctimonious posturing of all those Elders, especially that prick, Aby-od who, somehow, was Leader of Kudamun.

Aswa-da smirked, thinking about his adversary. By-the-*bloody*-book Aby-od. He would never change. But Aswa-da was certain that Aby-od's piety would be his downfall and eventually give Aswa-da his greatest opportunity.

Inside the Observation Room in Kudamun, a place outside of the universal plane and hidden from the universe by a field called the Reality Gap, Aswa-da looked up at the Observation Screen. He recognized the boy of eleven with the small frame and those darting, weasel eyes and a cruel frown of a mouth. Jonathan Donald Treeborne. The boy sat against a dusty river bank with overhanging willows touching the waters. Around him three children, a girl of eight and two boys the same age as him, played. The girl amused herself with her dolls until one of the other boys snatched them and threw them to the edge of the river where the ground was wet, and then ran away laughing.

The girl, upset and annoyed, yelled at the boys. They poked their tongues out at her and made silly faces. Then the boys started to run around between the trees that lined the bank and pretended to shoot each other.

Aswa-da looked at Treeborne still sat alone away from the other children. Aswa-da reached out toward the screen and twirled his finger in a revolving motion. Suddenly, he was standing there on the bank, observing in real Earth time but invisible to all humans around him.

He looked at Treeborne and felt the energies of the sandstone tablet radiate from the boy's rucksack. Nervously, as if sensing Aswa-da's presence, Treeborne pulled the rucksack closer to him and stuck his hand within the folds to touch the artefact. His eyes glinted, revealing a darkness that saturated Aswa-da. The dark god smiled, and then, like starburst from fireworks, his smile faded. Aswa-da saw the same soul of obsidian he'd seen a year before in Treeborne, when the boy had chanced upon the tablet's special resting place in that ziggurat in Uruk.

Aswa-da knew he'd made the right choice.

Treeborne stared across the river, disinterested by the other boys' shows of bravado. But he turned to take in the actions of the girl. She'd wandered back up the bank after collecting her dolls out of the mud. Her hands were messy and dirt had gotten onto her pink polka dot pinafore. She looked with questioning eyes at young Treeborne.

"Don't you wanna join them?"

Treeborne's weasel eyes narrowed and he shook his head. "Nah! Their games are pathetic. They are pathetic. I can easily control them. Watch."

Treeborne took out the object from his rucksack and slipped it into the deep pocket of his shorts. Aswa-da took in the display, delighted that Treeborne was about to use the tablet for a malicious purpose.

"Phil, Neal, can I play cops and robbers with you too?"

Treeborne stood up and maneuvered around the trees to face the two boys. The young girl stood by his side, intrigue on her face, waiting to see what the quiet boy would do.

"No way, JD. You're a weird freak. We don't wanna play with you," said one of the boys.

The other boy nodded and started to chant, "JD's a freaky weirdo. JD's a freaky weirdo!"

Treeborne stared, unmoving, but his hand slithered into his pocket and he started to caress the tablet.

One of the boys noticed his hand movement, and shouted, "Freaky weirdo is playing with himself! Dirty weirdo!"

Still, Treeborne didn't move. But his hand inside his pocket rubbed a little more vigorously. The girl stared at Treeborne, wondering what was happening.

"Phil broke your airplane, Neal," said Treeborne.

Neal swung a glance at his pal Phil. Aswa-da realized from the pained look on Neal's face that the airplane was his treasured toy.

"He broke it on purpose. He was jealous you had one and he didn't," continued the small boy.

"I didn't, Neal. He's lying," said Phil, looking at Neal and then at Treeborne.

Neal turned around to face Phil. His eyes were enlarged and glassy, and his lips drew tight into a pout of anger.

Aswa-da stared at Treeborne, fascinated by his immediate manipulative ability.

"He's not your friend. He talks about you behind your back. You know that bike you lost last summer? Phil took it and sold it."

Neal advanced on Phil, who stepped back. Neal was a taller boy with bigger bones and deep blue eyes that harbored a coldness within them. Phil had a chubbier frame and a lumbering gait. He couldn't move at Neal's speed.

"Neal, I swear. I didn't do that. I didn't do any of it," Phil pleaded, as Neal came in fast on him.

"And Maisie" called Treeborne, "you like her, don't you, Neal? Well Phil likes her too. And he's going to take her away from you."

That last revelation sealed the deal for Neal. He leapt upon Phil, pushing him to the ground, and started to bash in his face with his strong fists.

"He's lying," screamed Phil, as he tried to push Neal off, but the larger boy sat on top, pinning Phil to the dusty ground.

Treeborne watched like an impassive observer.

He'd lit the fuse. Now the fires had started to burn.

Aswa-da crouched down and cocked his head to the side, taking in the hammering Neal was giving to Phil. He looked across at Treeborne and nodded. His experiment was proceeding as planned.

The girl turned to Treeborne as Neal and Phil started to roll down the river bank, screaming, shouting and hitting each other with the total might of their childlike physiques. They splashed into the water, still belting each other.

"Did you do that?" she asked.

"I did," said Treeborne. His inner pride couldn't be hidden.

The girl grinned. From her pleasure, Aswa-da could see she'd been a victim of the boys' pranks one too many times.

"What's your name?" said the girl, sidling closer to Treeborne.

"I'm Jonathan Donald Treeborne. But you can call me JD."

"Hi, JD. I'm Lucy."

The girl's hand sneaked out to grasp Treeborne's hand, and he closed his fingers over hers. Together, silently, they stood on the bank and watched the two boys smash each other to pieces within the murky waters.

Aswa-da swirled his fingers and the crystal walls of the Observation Room in Kudamun encased him. Treeborne was on the Observation Screen, holding hands with the young girl. The two boys who'd been fighting now didn't move. Both faced down in the mud. The river waters rolled over them. Blood trickled down the faces.

From best of friends to best of enemies in minutes.

The powers of manipulation, persuasion and trust all housed in a small sandstone tablet. The tablet emitted a resonance. That tiny vibration needed to align with the resonance inside a human cell, but the cell had to be altered to connect with the resonance. After Aswa-da took Treeborne from the ziggurat in Uruk, he'd brought him into Kudamun and made the minutest of changes to his DNA code that enabled the resonance connection.

Aswa-da was impressed with his handiwork.

He couldn't wait to see the next stage in Treeborne's development.

Chapter 18

The moment the voice screamed, Ellie knew she should've gotten the hell out of the kitchen. But with absolute dark surrounding her, she couldn't even see the door. She strained to peer through the darkness. Her eyes, she hoped, would somehow accustom to their surroundings, but they didn't. It was as if someone had daubed her kitchen with black paint. She held her hand out in front of her but couldn't see even the faintest outline. Reason had vanished. Ellie breathed heavy. Panic built fast. She looked around, searching for understanding as to what she was seeing. Or rather, not seeing.

I must be going mad, she thought. This just can't be happening.

Ellie attempted to step forward. She pulled at her foot but it wouldn't move at all. Frozen to the spot, Ellie stared. The darkness absorbed her desperation. With reluctance, she took in the tricks her mind was turning. Reality, it seemed, like an unwelcome relative, was shut out. It was left hanging on the corner of her consciousness.

Her skin rippled with goose bumps as her senses heightened.

"Change it!"

Through the darkness, the voice came again. It reverberated around and inside her, and took on a cruel insistence, repeating *"change it"* as if the words were on a loop.

Ellie shook. Each word whipped into her like lashes from a leather cord and her body spun, caught in a vortex of thrashing pain.

The darkness that filled her kitchen lifted suddenly and Ellie found herself on a sheer cliff. Below her, the sea churned, ferocious and wild. She looked down and shivered.

Oh my God.

She breathed in.

41

Shit! That's a long way down. How on Earth?
Ellie breathed in staccato bursts.
I've got to focus. All this isn't real. I'm still in my kitchen. All this, it's overwork. And the curry last night. Indigestion and stress. That's all. It'll pass.

But as much as she tried to convince herself, her mind had other ideas. Heavy and confused, it refused to cooperate. She could smell the ozone and taste the salt on her lips. Any notion that she was anywhere else but a sea cliff was rejected by her senses.

Ellie glanced down again and air hit the back of her neck. Her skin tingled. Someone was behind her.

She tried to turn but couldn't move. Whatever had changed her kitchen had left her the same. She was still frozen. Hands were fast upon her.

Please God, thought Ellie. Let me get away!

And suddenly, Ellie was falling. The air rushed through her hair, and she could see, approaching fast, the foamy waters thrashing against the jagged rocks that in seconds would rip her to pieces and obliterate her life.

"Reverse the balance shift!"
The voice exploded behind her and reality shattered around her.

Instinctively, Ellie blinked. In that lid-dropping moment, her kitchen reverted back to normal. She stood rooted to the floor, shaking as another hideous noise whacked into her. Shrieking, painful, tortured shrieking. It was hardly human at all but that of some creature being eviscerated alive. Ellie's ears hurt. She felt dizzy and nauseous.

Trying to get a sense of from where the noise was coming, Ellie reached up to wipe the sweat away from her brow, and realized her mouth was open. That hideous noise was coming from *her*. She looked down and knew why.

The hot coffee she had nestled in her palms now washed over her hand. The mug rested on its side on the breakfast bar. Her screams stopped as if the volume had been muted. The kitchen resumed its graveyard silence.

What the hell just happened?
She looked down at her hand and frowned. Thick, shiny red welts had risen across her knuckles.

God! This hurts.
She headed for the sink but her movements, in haste, were clumsy and chaotic. Disoriented by shock, Ellie collided with the kitchen stool. It teetered back and then gave way to gravity. Chrome hit marble, shattering the quiet.

Chapter 19

Sam's eyes sprung open, alert and focused. Ellie's scream and the stool crashing signaled danger. His training came to the fore. Shooting out of bed, Sam grabbed his Sig Sauer P226 from its concealed compartment in his bag, slipped back the action and ran toward the noise. His senses were acute and primed. With every step, he was analyzing, reflecting and deciding.

Someone was in the apartment. He felt it. Her scream confirmed it.

And that someone had Ellie.

He approached the bedroom wall. On the other side was the kitchen. He listened. Running water. Shuffling against the marble floor. Heavy, fragmented breathing. Cold thoughts rushed through him. His hand tensed. Instinct tightened his finger on the trigger. He strained to hear but no voices came to him. Whoever they were, they were professional. And very, very quiet.

Sam inhaled, slid around the corner with his gun ready to fire, and charged into the room.

"What the *fuck* is happening?" Ellie screamed, thoroughly startled.

Her eyes stared with rigid fascination at Sam's gun.

"What the hell are you doing with that?"

Her incredulous eyes searched his for an explanation. But Sam held his voice and averted Ellie's inspection. What had he been thinking? Charging in there like some maniac. But Sam knew why he had done it. *Instinct.* That deep, raw feeling that told him danger lurked nearby.

Hearing Ellie scream that bone-chilling, gut-wrenching scream had reinforced his initial thought: someone had Ellie and they were hurting her. He'd felt her pain with tangible certainty and had turned on his training to save her.

How could he have been so damn stupid? How could he have misread the signals? Sam realized that if he'd fired…That brutal realization made his blood freeze. His heart thumped as if it was breaking through his body, and he felt sick to the core.

"Have you joined the Territorials or something?"

Ellie failed to master a grip on the situation. Her voice was tinged with sarcasm, but her eyes stared in shock. Blank understanding radiated from her orbs.

Sam shook his head. He de-cocked the gun and laid it down on the worktop. A mug on its side dripped coffee onto the floor. Sam noticed it and nodded to himself.

He could feel Ellie's eyes on him, watching his actions. She'd never seen him with a gun before. Her face paled and she started to shudder.

With the Sig in his hand, he'd turned into a different guy. He wasn't the Sam Noor she'd married.

Her eyes registered a growing fear.

"Sam, what's going on?" Ellie's voice had lost its usually ebullient tone.

"I'm sorry I didn't tell you."

"Didn't tell me what?"

Sam sighed, and then told her something she struggled to believe.

Chapter 20

Early morning light flooded through the gap in the drapes. It lightly tiptoed across the leather topped table in the Cabinet Office in Whitehall. A man walked in and his eyes fixed to the file sitting on the table. The man was six-foot two, very fit, and in his late fifties. He carried a deep golden tan, and his features were attractive, if slightly effeminate. He pushed his fingers nervously through his dark blond hair as he realized to whom the file belonged.

Another man seated at the top of the table read papers that obviously came from the file. Nearing sixty, tall and slim, with dark hair greying in all the right places, his Romanesque features that made him handsome in his younger days now made him look noble. Age had not dulled his superior intellect. His sharp, piercing dark brown eyes were constantly alert. He looked up and greeted the blond man.

"Good morning, Prime Minister."

"Morning, Sir Justin. I hope you have something good to tell me."

Richard Ashton, British PM, knew the moment he said the words that they had been but wishful thinking.

"I am sorry, sir, but this isn't good news."

Sir Justin Maide, Head of MI6 British Intelligence, looked grave.

Ashton glanced back down at the file.

"It's Kinley, isn't it?"

Maide nodded. "Intel says they know. We've got to take him today."

The PM thought deeply. Matthew Kinley was a double agent, an MI6 man on the Al Nadir inside track. He had created smokescreens and misinformation and kept their people safe for four years. But now, the secret was out. Kinley was a hot mark.

"Are we absolutely sure they know?"

Ashton was reticent about taking action that was preemptive. He had to have substantial proof.

"It's conclusive, sir," said Maide. "We have to remove him today."

Ashton understood Maide's anxiety. Al Nadir getting even a sniff of Kinley's double agent status meant Kinley was now a liability.

"You want my authority on this, don't you?" asked Ashton.

He looked back down at the file. Scattered pictures showed Kinley with his wife and young daughter. They were photos of innocence and happiness. Could he risk one more day with Kinley out there?

"What if your intel is wrong?" asked Ashton. "We would be pulling out a perfectly good agent for no reason. Think of what we've achieved, how close we are now to taking down Salim Al Douri. Not to mention the knowledge we've built up, the plans we've foiled. Think about it, Justin. The lives we've saved by having Kinley in there."

"Yes, Prime Minister. But think again about the lives that have been lost just to keep the lie alive. Remember Piccadilly. Remember Operation Snowdrop."

Ashton closed his eyes. Those last two words transported him back. June 28, 2013. Tourist season. People swarmed to London. Piccadilly Circus, the ever-popular meeting point, was at bursting point. Sweaty bodies crammed in like sardines. The trains arrived at the station and waited for the doors to open. But the doors never opened. Explosions ripped through multiple train carriages before the Tannoy announced, "Please mind the gap."

No one stood a chance. Glass and shrapnel blast out in all directions. The ceiling caved. Those who weren't blown to bits or burnt to death were buried alive. Emergency services were quick to respond, but this was the nightmare they'd feared. An explosion in a confined space underground. But above ground, the scene had been even more catastrophic, with fireballs, flames and vehicles smashing into pedestrians and other cars. If people weren't on fire, they were crushed to death. Body parts littered around the fountain that ended up a mass of rubble.

That day, the death toll had been in thousands.

Ashton straightened and suppressed the urge to remember.

"No matter what, lives will always be lost. We are at war, Justin. Don't ever forget that. As long as our body count is less than theirs, we're winning."

The coldness of Ashton's delivery chilled Maide. He knew the prime minister was unscrupulous in politics but the ruthless streak he now displayed caused Maide concern.

"That's one way to look at it."

"It's the *only* way to look at it," replied Ashton.

"So, what you're saying is you want Kinley to remain in the field?"

"Yes." Ashton's adamant tone struck hard in the single word.

Maide was well schooled. He knew when a conversation had ended.

Chapter 21

After Sam had run in like Bourne, Ellie realized that either she was dreaming, or Sam had taken a lot self-defense lessons in secret. She didn't, however, expect to hear the true reason behind his somewhat-crazy actions.

Ellie listened, and then laughed. There was no happiness in the tone. Hysteria creeped in. Her husband's confession was absurd.

"You can't be working for MI6. You're a diplomat."

Sam shook his head.

"It's only a cover, Ellie. That's all it's ever been."

Ellie's laughing halted. Her voice turned shaky. "I…I don't understand. You've been at the Foreign Office for ten years. Haven't you?"

"No, Ellie. I've been in Counter Terrorism Special Operations."

"What?"

"I should've told you sooner. I'm sorry."

"Hang on. Let me get this. You're telling me you're a *spy*?"

"That's the wrong term nowadays. We're field operatives."

"Never mind the terms. That's what you are, isn't it?"

"Yes."

"And you've never actually worked at the Foreign Office at all?"

"I have worked there. But it's not my real job."

"Fuck!"

Ellie's world spun. Questions circled in her mind, caught in the riptide of her thoughts. She remembered how his Foreign Office assignments had been constant and never-ending. Saying 'hello' and 'goodbye' in the same breath had been her life for such a long time. But she'd never suspected anything.

"I don't believe this. I'm in a dream. I'm still asleep and dreaming."

Ellie started to laugh again. But in between the nervous bouts of hollow sound, her eyes clouded with tears. She turned her head away from the reality that faced her. She quivered, not wanting to acknowledge his words. In truth, what she didn't want to believe was the betrayal he'd made of their life together. She didn't want to listen anymore. This was just another nightmare and now she wanted to wake up. She wanted to feel Sam's body next to hers and know that he was good and real and true.

"You're not dreaming. What I've told you is real."

Sam's harsh cold voice brought her back to her senses.

Ellie rubbed away the tears that had started to build up at the corners of her eyes and stared at her husband. Her face was stone and her words came out flint sharp.

"Why didn't you tell me the truth?"

"I wanted to tell you at first. But as time went on, your work kept you so busy, you virtually ignored my work life. You accepted me naturally as a diplomat. It was easier for you not to know."

"But you're my husband. How could you keep this from me? Did you think you couldn't trust me? Is your world so screwed up you couldn't even trust your own wife?"

"Sweetness, of course I trusted you."

"Then why the *hell* did you wait ten years to tell me?"

"They thought it better if you didn't know."

"Who thought that?"

"My superiors."

"And you went along with the lies?"

"I didn't have a choice."

"Everyone has a choice, Sam."

Sam didn't respond. He felt embarrassed and ashamed by his past actions. He hadn't chosen. He'd done nothing, just accepted the route his superiors had laid out for him.

For Ellie, the gun had an inherent magnetism and drew her back to look at it. Sam hadn't seemed fazed or alarmed by the weapon. He'd handled it with such self-assurance, but how, she just couldn't seem to understand, despite his confession.

Ellie replayed how Sam had burst in minutes before. Barely anything about him had resembled her husband. Although he kept himself in good shape, violence was anathema to him and he was a self-proclaimed pacifist. And yet, he'd charged in virtually naked, muscles hardened, ready to fire at anyone unfortunate enough to be in the bullet's line. His eyes flickered with the coldness of a killer's. It was a look she had never seen before. It scared her.

All at once, she felt alone, standing in front of a man she didn't know.

"Where does the truth end and the lie begin? Am I part of your cover too?"

"Ellie, you're just being stupid. You know how much I love you."

"I don't know anything anymore," snapped Ellie.

"Yes, you do. Look at me. I love you, Ellie. You know I'm not lying."

Sam walked over to embrace his wife but the message in her blue-grey eyes told him to stay back.

"I can't take all of this in. I'm trying to, but up here…" She tapped on the side of her head. "It's just not happening."

Ellie's face, always pretty and bubbly, was now ghost-white and showed shock and confusion. Her eyes were crammed full of tears. The tall, statuesque figure he loved had turned small as if her body had caved in. The neckline of her sloppy t-shirt had slipped down her shoulder, exposing a sculptured collarbone and smooth neck.

Sam looked at her. He wanted to kiss that smooth neck and love her and shield her, and make her forget what she'd just seen.

"Why do you do it?" Ellie struggled, trying to understand Sam's rationale for his double life.

"It's just a job,"

His flippant dismissal of the importance of his position fired Ellie, and she bit back. "Don't insult my intelligence. It's much more than that."

"It's not. Don't believe the hype."

With great skill, Sam maneuvered Ellie away from her questioning without her realizing what he'd done.

"There was a time when I was ready to give it all up," he said. "I was going to return to the Ministry of Defense, or even become a diplomat. I'd learnt and done a lot during my cover time and I genuinely like the job."

"So, why didn't you? What changed your mind?"

"Al Nadir. I couldn't leave knowing those fuckers would be calling the shots."

Chapter 22

Kudamun was not a planet. It was a dimension outside of the known universal plane. Kudamun was hidden by the quantum field known as the Reality Gap.

As such Kudamun was outside of time, and those within Kudamun could view a past point in time on any planet across the universe. The only caveat was that no Kudamaz could view a point in time ahead of the current time of that planet. The Kudamaz were explicitly forbidden to view through the Observation Screen into the future of a planet.

Although Aswa-da could see forward into the future of Earth, this future could quickly change by new events on Earth. He could only see a refracted, quantum view of potential possibilities. Until events had solidified, moving from the quantum into the reality plane, the future on Earth that he could view on the Observation Screen was just a quantum view of probabilities.

Of course, it was also strictly against antediluvian law under the Order of Kudamun for any Kudamaz, even if it was the Lord Aby-od, Leader of Kudamun himself to be found viewing a planet's future. This act would be in direct contravention to the Order of Kudamun and that individual would face summary execution by a Harmon wave gun. A device that could literally shatter a body to pieces, but the wave didn't do it quickly. The Harmon wave hit at the quantum level of a body, and worked through the atoms, molecules and cells, eventually causing an earthquake level vibration sending a level of pain of unimaginable magnitude that recipient of the wave passes out. Their body then fades, and finally splinters into fragments of light.

It was also the only way a Kudamaz being could die.

Even Aswa-da, although a rule breaker of the Order of Kudamun in many ways, would never break this law of viewing the future of a planet. He wanted to ensure he avoided such a demise at all costs. Thus, he didn't jump into any planetary future, and certainly not Earth's.

Aswa-da had already seen the impressive impact of the tablet on Jonathan D Treeborne as a child. Now he was interested to see further into Treeborne's life, and how his use of the tablet had changed it.

He flattened his hand, palm down, and moved it backwards and forwards in a fast, shallow elliptical motion. The display on the Observation Screen moved into static as the years of Treeborne's life shot by. The sentient crystals buried within the Observation Screen picked upon on Aswa-da's requirement and the display juddered to a halt. A teenage boy popped up on screen. He was walking through a park, smirking and looking smug.

The teenager was Treeborne eight Earth years after Aswa-da's last viewing of him as a young boy.

Treeborne walked with a group of other boys the same age. But his eyes didn't reflect the playful innocence of youth in the same way. His eyes were dark and menacing, and there was a sense of deadness about them. Like Treeborne had no soul. He swung a glance at his peers that dripped of derision and loathing. Seeing this, Aswa-da nodded and enjoyed his experiment in action.

Aswa-da twirled his finger and the Observation Room melted away. Around him was a park in early summer. A lake with water fowl was to the right and a wide and rolling expanse of grass with slightly burnt patches was to his left. Treeborne strolled with his friends down the tarmac path. Aswa-da watched intently as Treeborne took control.

"Dave, you need to get it tonight," said Treeborne with force, snatching hold of the boy alongside of him. "You know we can't wait any longer."

The teenager, who was a bit on the pudgy side with a stubby nose and doleful, expressive blue eyes, winced, feeling Treeborne's fingers dig in.

"I can't. My pa would kill me if he found out."

"Your pa won't ever find out. Come on. I gotta get into Washington and Lee College. Mom really wants me to get there. I gotta have those exam papers."

The pudgy boy, Dave, stared at Treeborne, clearly worried.

"JD, I really can't. Pa will lose his job as principal if it got out. You know that!"

Treeborne slipped his hand into his pocket. Aswa-da detected a faint outline of the tablet in the folds of his trousers. Aswa-da knew Treeborne was holding the tablet close to his body. He also knew it was now an intrinsic and irremovable part of Treeborne's existence.

"Dave, you need those papers too. Remember your last scores? They're not going to get you into a top college. You won't succeed unless you know what's coming up."

Treeborne glared at Dave, his eyes drilling into his friend, penetrating and flipping Dave's psyche to his bidding. The other boys drifted back a little. By their regard of Treeborne and Dave, Aswa-da recognized that they wanted to stay out of the discussion, which was quickly turning into a heated argument.

"I can't, JD. It's too risky. Don't ask me anymore!" snapped Dave.

Treeborne grabbed Dave brutally by his rounded shoulders.

"It's more risky to leave it to chance. You know that!" hissed Treeborne. "You could lose everything, including the chance to get in with Rachel."

Treeborne stared at Dave as he spoke and raised his eyebrow in a knowing manner. Dave flushed pink as his crush was revealed with blatant enthusiasm. He did a small nod, and then looked down. He seemed scared of the reality of the decision he was about to make. Dave's face rippled through different states, one minute agreeing to Treeborne's demands, the next, back-tracking and refusing.

Treeborne waited. He appeared patient but Aswa-da observed Treeborne's lips flat line and his jaw hardened as his teeth locked tight in his mouth. His eyes took on a sinister glare.

"I can't, JD," said Dave, eventually settling on a final decision. He breathed out and appeared exhausted.

Aswa-da watched, intrigued as to how his subject was going to handle this intransigent attitude from Dave. The teenage boy removed his hand from his pocket and dropped down onto the park bench. Treeborne sat holding his head in his hands.

"It's over for both of us. We may as well just put our names down at K-Mart as checkout boys. Don't think you're ever going to get a shot at Rachel now. You know she's turned on by brainy guys. If you fail, that's it. Bye, bye, Rachel."

Dave stared out across the park. Aswa-da stepped forward to look into Dave's eyes. He was definitely considering Treeborne's last address. He bit his lower lip and carried on chewing it as he sat down slowly, joining Treeborne on the bench.

"You really think so?" Dave asked with a heightened level of caution.

"Yeah. I do," said Treeborne without hesitation. His hand slipped back into his pocket to caress the tablet. "You gotta get the papers tonight. Before you know it, we'll be heading to Wash and Lee College, and you'll have your chance with Rachel. A big chance, Dave. A real big chance. You want that, don't you?"

Dave, still looking across the park, replied in a dreamy voice, "Yeah, JD. I want that. I think I love her. You know that? I really get that feeling."

Aswa-da could see Treeborne holding down a snigger. But Dave was caught up in his emotions.

"Yeah, Dave. I get it. And believe me, you'll get it too. Rachel will bone you like there's no tomorrow. If she hears you're going to Wash and Lee, hell, she'll be onto you like bees around a honey pot. She's yours, buddy. She's yours."

The light of lust shone in Dave's eyes. Aswa-da was impressed. Treeborne knew what to say to manipulate his friend.

"She's mine. Oh, JD. She really could be, couldn't she? She's so beautiful. You think she'll really be mine? I really have a chance?"

Dave's confidence was waning. He slouched his shoulders down, doubting his ability to get the girl of his dreams.

"Dave, get a *fucking* grip!" said Treeborne severely. "You just need to get the papers, nail the exam, and get your acceptance to Wash and Lee. She's as good as in your bed. And if she isn't by then, I'll make sure she is."

Dave snapped his head up with concern. His expressive eyes widened with horror at what he thought Treeborne was implying.

"JD, I ain't going to be forcing her to do anything she doesn't want to do. And neither are you."

"I'm not talking about forcing her or nothing. I mean, I have ways, Dave, to persuade her. She won't get hurt and she'll be willing. But I promise you, if you get those papers tonight, I'll get Rachel in your bed before this week is out."

Dave picked up on the assured statement from Treeborne. Aswa-da notice again the pure lust in his eyes. He licked his lips and rubbed his thighs, getting worked up on Treeborne's last words.

"In my bed. Oh, God, JD. Could you do that?"

"Yep, Dave. But you gotta get those papers from your pa's desk first. After that, you can rock and roll with Rachel."

Dave stared out, his mind floating off as he listened to Treeborne. Then he tilted his head to the side to look at his friend.

"If you promise on your life that you'll get me Rachel, I'll get you the papers." Dave's voice had dropped to a hushed whisper.

"Tonight?" questioned Treeborne, pressing for what he wanted out of the deal.

"Yeah. Tonight," repeated Dave, a little reluctantly. "But you promise to get me Rachel."

"Yeah. I do."

"On your life."

"On my life. Just get me the papers," said Treeborne a little wearily.

Dave nodded. "I will."

Aswa-da performed his shallow elliptical motion. The events around him sped up and scenes changed rapidly. Aswa-da watched Treeborne waiting in his Toyota Camry in a shopping mall car park. The Earth time was 10 p.m. Another car, a Chevy, drew up and flashed its lights twice. Treeborne smiled. What a dick! He thinks he's in a movie.

Treeborne opened his car door slowly, got out, and walked over to the Chevy. At the driver's side, the window wound down and an envelope was thrust through the gap. Snatching it, Treeborne muttered a hurried, "Thanks." Then he tried to depart with haste, but a hand grabbed hold of his.

"Rachel. Remember!" said Dave from the darkness of his car. His voice had a tinge of desperation.

"No sweat," responded Treeborne, pulling his hand away. "Friday. I promise."

Aswa-da ran his shallow elliptical motion with his hand again. Scenes whizzed past as Earth time progressed through seconds, minutes and hours. The Observation Screen targeted Treeborne and Aswa-da watched the scene settle on him in a diner. He sat on his own eating blueberry pancakes and drinking coffee. In Earth time, it was a Thursday, mid-morning.

Treeborne stared through the oblong window as he heard tires on the gravel. An engine switched off outside. A mass of brunette hair emerged from the car. Then long, supple legs inched into tiny khaki shorts stretched out, followed by the young woman's trim waist, toned body and pert, peachy ass. As she turned toward the diner, Treeborne was hit with the full beauty of Rachel Travers. Her body was slender and the white tee she wore showed her full, firm breasts had just the right amount of bounce to insinuate playfulness.

She stepped up, opened the door to the diner and approached Treeborne's table. He took in her face and swallowed. Her graceful neck, high cheekbones, full lips, delicately appointed nose and startling, pale olive eyes promised the delivery of every teenage boy's fantasy. She was a visual incarnation of a siren, and he couldn't wait to dash himself upon her rocks.

"Hi, JD," said Rachel, chewing gum and looking irked. "What's so important you drag me over here?"

Her voice was soft and inquiring with just a flicker of toughness. Her shoulders were pushed back and her deportment was self-assured, and a touch dominant. Treeborne smirked. He liked the balance of soft and hard. It made for a more stimulating experience.

A tingle stirred in his groin. Aswa-da detected this and raised an eyebrow at the new dynamic in play. Treeborne's hand grazed across the sandstone tablet in his pocket and Treeborne concentrated, in the way Aswa-da had taught him.

Persuasion. Manipulation. Trust. His trinity of ability.

"Take a seat, Rachel," stated Treeborne in a strong, confident voice. He stretched out his hand out to welcome Rachel to join him.

Rachel hesitated.

"What do you want?"

The soft lilt had left her voice and Rachel's tone had become quite brittle.

"Sit down and I'll tell you."

His air of mystery piqued Rachel's interest, and she sat down.

"That's better. Would you like some coffee? A donut? Some pancakes? I recommend the pancakes. They're really rather good."

Treeborne signaled to the waitress for another coffee.

"Shut up about the pancakes, JD. I want to know what this is about. You said on the phone that there's an opportunity for me to make some cash."

Treeborne eyed her mischievously, his glance taking in her luscious figure, and then he straightened, and pushed a serious face.

"You know Dave Bateman?"

"Yeah. Principal Bateman's son. So what?"

"He's a traitor. He's working for the other side." Treeborne hung his head and edged toward Rachel's face.

Her beautiful eyes widened. "No way. What? You mean he's a Commie!"

"Yeah. So is the principal. They're both Commie bastards infiltrating our society."

Rachel drew back and stared at Treeborne, her mouth upturned, suspicion in her eyes.

"How do you know this?"

Treeborne moved in closer, reaching across the table, and whispered in Rachel's ear.

"It's a secret operation. My dad's really CIA. He's been watching the Batemans for months. But something's happening. I need your help."

Rachel shook her head. With a grin on her face, she exclaimed loudly,

"Your dad? He does that stuff with rocks. No way is he in the C-"

Treeborne gripped hold of Rachel's hand, squeezing it so her finger tips turned a rosy flush.

"Don't say it, Rachel. This is the truth."

Whilst Treeborne spoke, he held onto the tablet with his other hand. He fixed Rachel with a cold, hard stare. Aswa-da could sense that Treeborne was now able to channel the energies within the tablet. The trinity of his powers were coming to the fore. Treeborne's abilities were intensifying.

Rachel stared into Treeborne's eyes and swallowed deeply.

"God. You really…Oh my God, JD. Is this an operation? Are you…" Rachel lowered her voice, reaching across the table, her lips brushing against Treeborne's ear. "A spy?"

The tingle in his groin increased.

Treeborne, still holding her hand, did a perfunctory nod, and swept a glance around the diner to see if anyone had heard.

Rachel looked around with him, and then giggled.

"Oh my God, JD. This is so cool. Are you like James Bond? Do you have spy stuff?"

Treeborne didn't enter into the humor. His eyes, steely and cold, regarded her with contempt. Rachel sat back, realizing her foolishness.

"This isn't a joke," snapped Treeborne. "We aren't in a movie. Do you want to help your country or not?"

His words were as far removed from teenage japes and jests as they possibly could be. Treeborne watched as Rachel acknowledged his professional efficiency. Her lips moistened and her eyes dilated. She moved her other hand to cover his and pushed her chest forward.

"What can I do to help you?"

Her assuredness had drifted away. In front of Treeborne was a meek and malleable individual.

"It'll be dangerous. Are you ok with that?"

"Yes. Yes, I think so." Her elbows slid forward and her mouth moved close to Treeborne's. "Are you in danger?"

"Often. But I've been trained."

Treeborne gave a surly, arrogant smirk and held the tablet close to him. *Trust me. Trust every word I say is true. Fix the belief. Don't let it leave you.* The mantra rang in his head.

Aswa-da smiled, delighted to see his creation blooming.

Rachel chewed her lip.

Suddenly, unable to hold back, Rachel launched up and planted her lips on Treeborne's. He pulled his hands away and held her face.

She was gorgeous.

Treeborne pulled her up. Putting his arms around her waist, he pulled her into him. The tingle in his groin had turned into a shuddering vibration of want. Her hands wandered down to his trousers. Gripping him, she smiled. She kissed him harder, pushing her tongue into his mouth. He brought his hands to the front of her body, cupping her firm breasts.

"Hey! You guys. Take that someplace else!" yelled the waitress, seeing Treeborne and Rachel's lurid behavior.

"Too damn right," said Treeborne, smirking. He threw down a few dollars for the check then grabbed Rachel's hand, and ran toward the door. "And I got just that someplace!"

Aswa-da observed as Rachel raced out with Treeborne, hand in hand, to his car.

He knew that Treeborne's promise to Dave was just another lie in a lifetime of lies.

Chapter 23

Ellie had no idea who Sam fought against, but logically, of course it had to be Al Nadir. They were a new breed of evil known as a terrorist collective. Initially, their power had been driven by their openness to work and collaborate with other terrorist groups. But the term 'collaborative' could not now be used to describe their current activities. Highly dictatorial, their approach was one of hostile takeover, and whether they wanted to or not, terrorist groups, crime syndicates and even entire rogue states were invaded with rapid and brutally smooth efficiency.

Many years ago, the security agencies had not taken Al Nadir seriously. They saw them as a group of cranks headed by a guy with too much money and a brain fried on too much coke. Then 9/11 hit and all eyes around the world turned to Al Qaeda and Osama bin Laden. The second Gulf War in Iraq and the ensuing battle with the Taliban in Afghanistan kept the intelligence services, the US and the allied troops occupied.

Everyone ignored Salim Al Douri. Assessed by intelligence analysts as not a present threat, Salim and Al Nadir were passed over. Whatever intelligence had been assessed to come to this conclusion had been severely misjudged.

Gradually, the networks Al Nadir formed while the world looked the other way. Rapidly, their reach and capability grew, and in parallel, so did their power. But they were like a building site underneath a tarpaulin cover. The massiveness of the construction couldn't be visualized until the cover was pulled away. One day, early May, six years ago, Al Nadir removed their tarpaulin, and the world was redefined.

Ellie remembered the day. The bloodied faces, the horrific wounds, the global confusion and the calls to blame the security agencies that had failed to protect their people.

Concurrent bombing in thirty major cities.

It was an unprecedented act of terrorism that escalated Al Nadir's position to number one and made Al Qaeda look like playground bullies. Globally connected, Al Nadir's aim was simple: to undermine the economic and social stability of every major country across the world.

Ellie could not begin to comprehend, let alone deal with, the fact that her husband faced such danger. She stared hard at Sam and in a small, soft voice whispered, "They'd kill you if they caught you."

"Eventually, they would."

From Ellie's face, Sam saw that the words had been a step too far.

His wife listened to his unusually cold, matter-of-fact tone, and contemplated the meaning behind his words. Her face drained. The sheer thought of *that* happening to the man she loved made her heart hammer. Bile rose in her throat, forcing her to gag. Sudden stress snapped her head in a vise-like grip and pain sailed through her body. He had risked his life and their future for ten years, and that was unforgivable. At that point, she didn't know whether to love Sam or hate him.

"I'm good, Ellie. I've been trained really well. You have no reason to worry about me. I can take care of myself."

Recalling his impromptu burst of action, she couldn't deny Sam probably could look after himself. But that didn't mean she didn't have reason to worry.

Sam read the anguish on her face and walked over to cuddle her close to him. This time, she didn't signal "back off" in her beautiful eyes. Under his touch, her skin was cold and trembling.

"You know I could lose you?"

As she said it, all Ellie could see in her mind was black. Black clothes she would wear to his funeral. Black she would feel in her heart. Black would be her future without Sam.

Sam stroked her hair and kissed her forehead.

"You're not going to lose me. I'm here."

He tilted her chin up to him and kissed her slowly.

"For how long?" Ellie asked, returning his kiss with growing passion.

"Forever."

"Nobody lives forever."

Ellie kissed him with a fervor he had never seen before. Sam took her hand and led her gently back to bed to show her just how much he really loved her, to eliminate any shred of doubt that still lingered in her confused mind.

Chapter 24

Salim leaned back casually in his chair. He looked at Sabena and smiled broadly. It was all in his grasp. Control of the world. The goal of super-villains from the movies was always thwarted at the last minute by a super-hero coming seemingly from nowhere. But this wasn't the movies. There was no white knight on his faithful charger, nor some dumb prick wearing his pants on the outside of his clothes. No one was going to save the world. It was his for the taking.

Sabena, as if reading his mind, twitched her nose with excitement.

"We're almost there, darling."

Salim nodded, a sexy twinkle in his eye. "Fancy consummating our success?"

Sabena picked up her spoon, skimmed the froth off her cappuccino, brought the spoon to her mouth, and licked down the froth. Salim watched as the tip of her pink tongue licked the last bubble from the cold metal.

"I'll take that as a yes then."

Salim stood up, yanked her head back and kissed her with rough intensity. Sabena breathed heavily, slipped her hands through his hair, softly at first, but then she wound strands around her fingers and tugged him hard towards her.

Another couple seated on a table nearby in the chichi, expensive café on Jumeriah Palm watched their display, disgusted but secretly jealous. Salim, knowing he had an audience, stuck his hand down Sabena's low-cut top, and she in turn groped him with unashamed enthusiasm.

It was only Sabena's mobile ringing that disturbed what would otherwise have been a blatant show of exhibitionism. Disentangling from Salim, Sabena answered with her usual curt, snobby tone.

"What?"

She always made the caller feel uncomfortable, that they had no right to call her, and that she was doing them the utmost honor in answering at all. The fact that this call was to determine her status as the most powerful woman on Earth was neither here nor there. All callers were a nuisance. Especially those who called when she had a gorgeous man in her paws.

"It's done. We have his family," Sabena relayed to Salim.

Her lack of emotion was countered by his ebullience. He clapped his hands together, smiled and then laughed. It was a deep, throaty laugh with almost theatrical overtones as if he was hamming up a part on stage. A few more people turned to stare, but Salim didn't give a shit. If he wanted to be loud, he could. If he wanted to shag Sabena senseless on the table, he could. If he wanted to kill everyone in earshot, he could. He could do anything. And no one could touch him. That's what was all so wonderful.

Of course, the world was looking for him. But his foot soldiers, the millions he'd help rise from the mega-slums around the world, were his eyes and ears. He'd given them life, and in return, they protected him. They served him. They died for him. He was their God. What he asked of them, they did without question.

If they couldn't do what he wanted, he just brought in those who could. He'd never met an intelligence agent from any country who hadn't taken a bite of the cake he'd offered. Oh, yes, they'd pledged their allegiance, their loyalty to their flag and their country, but offer them ten million dollars, and that loyalty got lost in the rush to type the password to their blind account in the Cayman Islands.

Salim knew how to be invisible whilst being as visibly vulgar as possible. It was all down to being connected. Right now, he was surrounded by his minions, watching, waiting, ready and equipped to make a move if they must. They were his perpetual audience and he was playing the lead man. It was a role he had honed to perfection.

Sabena moved forward, rubbing his thigh.

"Weren't we in the middle of consummating our success?"

Chapter 25

Ellie awoke, looked at the clock, and panicked.

"Shit! I'm late."

"Hey, hey. What's happening?"

Sam yawned lazily and made a grab towards Ellie. He fell into the empty space she made as she vacated the bed at speed.

"Why are you up?" he asked. "It's Saturday. Come back to bed."

"Saturday?" Ellie bit her bottom lip and looked sheepishly at Sam. "Oh, bloody hell. I don't know where I am. I thought it was Monday. My head's still not in the right place."

"Get back over here," called Sam, as he beckoned her to bed.

Ellie stared at him, her eyes like daggers, as she realized why she was still so confused.

"After what you told me this morning, I shouldn't stand being anywhere near you!"

Sam's eyes flashed with darkness for a second, and then he reached out, grabbed her and kissed her hungrily. "I doubt I'll be able to stand if we carry on like this."

"Well then, let's build up that stamina of yours." Ellie giggled, and her bright eyes sparkled with naughty playfulness.

Chapter 26

Alexandria, a town of bureaucrats, politicians and servants of the flag, where red brick nineteenth-century townhouses grace the streets and the Potomac River winds through the center, making its way up to Arlington. Just eight miles out of Washington, DC, Alexandria is a place where deals go down and lips stay shut, where a walk through the park to the river can be so quiet, even the birds feel inhibited to chirp. It's a place of unearthly silence as if Mother Nature herself was afraid to talk. Alexandria, a town where secrets are kept and truths are buried.

That morning, someone was intent on burying a certain secret that had gotten out of hand.

Matthew Kinley, Director of Science, Technology, Energy and the Environment (STEE) at the British Embassy in Washington, DC, had risen early. His wife continued to sleep peacefully while he slipped out and got dressed for his morning run. Kinley was heading towards forty-five but his strong, fit physique and face devoid of lines belonged to a man at least a decade younger.

"My elixir is loving myself and loving life!" Kinley told envious middle-aged, stressed out friends. "Shit happens. You deal with it and move on."

His pragmatic, no-nonsense approach to life was one of the traits most admired in him by others. Of course, had they known his secret, they would have held his ability to maintain a deep cover double-agent identity whilst, in the process, saving so many lives in equal regard.

Kinley opened the front door. A faint chill drifted in with the morning heat. He pulled on his jersey and zipped it up tight to his neck. Unlike other joggers, he didn't listen to music. Kinley didn't like distraction. He liked to know what was going on around him. Cocooned in a bubble of music would make him vulnerable. Never in his life had he shown vulnerability, and nothing was going to make him change his number one rule.

Be aware at all times.

Being an agent, Kinley had learnt the power of fear. It heightens the senses. Everything around you shifts into sharper focus and anything out of sync stands out with clarity. For instance, a person who walks slightly slowly. A glint of something metallic and an arm raising could mean someone is answering a mobile or getting ready to fire a gun. Having awareness heightened by fear afforded Kinley vital seconds to determine the difference. Kinley knew to be afraid was to be aware. And to be aware was to be safe.

With this in mind, Kinley picked up a steady jog and breathed in the morning air. He knew he'd soon be leaving. Changes were already happening around him. Invisible wheels were turning and all that he knew to be his life would soon change in an instant. But for now, he had the morning, free and welcoming. Like a lost love, he basked in her warm, soft glow.

Chapter 27

"Want a coffee?" called Ellie into the lounge.

The revelations of early morning were left mostly unmentioned, but their lovemaking had taken on a distinct edge of urgency. It felt as if their time together suddenly mattered again. Sam stepped into the kitchen half dressed in a silk shirt and boxers. His tie dangled unevenly around his neck. He draped his navy trousers over the kitchen stool.

Ellie lifted a mug up in his direction.

"Or do you want something stronger?"

Buttoning his shirt rapidly, Sam walked over, slipped his arms around Ellie's svelte waist and kissed her neck.

"Mmmm, looks like you want something stronger," she said, and bent into him as Sam kissed her.

"Oh, no. Just the coffee, ma'am."

Sam laughed, pulled away and reached for his trousers. Carefully, he stepped into them, pulled them up then smoothed and tucked in his shirt. Each movement was precise. It wasn't the usual fumble that men do when dressing. Sam was exact. His dressing style was an acknowledgement of the life he led. A need for precision and a complete removal of errors. The path of errors led to death, a journey he had no intention of making.

Wandering over to the mirror on the kitchen wall, he swiftly knotted and drew down his tie, which looked flush against his shirt. He looked in the mirror and nodded subconsciously. The tie Ellie had selected looked good. It was a splash of navy blue, pink and purple arranged in a slightly funky, almost modernist way, and it really worked.

"You look gorgeous, stud. Here's your coffee."

Sam smiled smugly. He took the mug from Ellie and sat down on the stool. A slither of coffee was still on the ridge, a remnant from the incident earlier that morning. Somewhere in the confessions and confusions, the reason why she had screamed had been lost. He had thought it was because she'd burnt her hand, but Ellie hadn't disclosed more on the subject.

"Must've been a hell of a shock," said Sam.

He spoke in a casual but affirmative tone, and examined Ellie intently for a reaction. It wasn't just trivial conversation over the breakfast table. Sam was using a tried and tested interrogation technique: open the session with a statement confirming the captive's secret was already known, and before long, they would confess. Sam had often made his prisoners believe that someone else had broken and confessed. Backed against a wall, the game of bluff played out with the inevitable result of the prisoner talking.

Sam knew that the mechanics of this confidence trick, although outwardly appearing easy, were actually founded in complex psychology. In every person, there are two states. One state is the basic instinct to disclose and tell the truth. The other is the conditioned response of lying. The interrogation process worked on the principle of there being a crossover point, a place of intersection where Sam would work to push the hostile into a truth state.

Sam used the technique as if it was second nature and didn't care that the captive, in this case, was his own wife. He expected Ellie to react the same way as anyone else.

"What was a shock?" she asked vaguely.

"When you burned your hand. It must have really hurt you."

Sam's tone was loaded with quiet persistence. His eyes trained on Ellie and read every twitch in her body.

"Hurt me?" muttered Ellie hazily.

Sam watched as Ellie looked out the window pointedly trying to avoid his all-consuming stare.

"That is why you screamed, isn't it?" asked Sam.

He rose off the stool and stood in front of Ellie. With her view blocked, Ellie had no option but to look at him. She shrugged but without conviction.

Then her usually open and expressive gestures turned closed and secretive. Her arms crossed and drew tightly into her body. Her neck went taut, her jaw line turned rigid and her pupils dilated. She looked downwards and to the right, and she blinked slowly. This indicated to Sam that Ellie's brain was in creation mode rather than recall mode.

Very few people were natural-born liars, and even consummate liars had tells. Sam, on the other hand, was a wizard of deception. No matter how hard someone tried to lie, Sam always made them deliver the truth. The ability that had served him so well in MI6 now delivered a truth he didn't want to accept.

His wife was about to lie.

Chapter 28

US President Jonathan D Treeborne flicked through papers on his desk. State business, official engagements and security briefings, they all ran into one long snaking mass of hand-shaking, obligatory thanks and vitriolic denouncements of the CIA's ineptitude. As much as he wanted it to change, he couldn't visualize it happening.

Treeborne smiled as he looked at his watch. The date on his Rolex Oyster showed it was just three weeks ago that he'd met with his merry men: Al Hutchinson, Vice President, Frank Weitz, Defense Secretary and Dave Reiner, Chairman to the Joint Chiefs of Staff.

Then it had been a very different situation. They'd had no way to win against Al Nadir.

3 Weeks Earlier

Al Nadir's onslaught seemed impossible to beat. They had just struck across the Midwest, killing thousands of Americans in packed shopping malls. The bombings had been audacious and cruel. Women and children made up most of the victims. The public backlash had been unforgiving. Distraught family members screaming for Al Nadir's blood openly blamed the government and the president for failing to keep them safe. The president felt they were all stuck in an Iron Maiden with the spikes getting closer.

"What are you saying, Frank? We can't handle this anymore?"

Treeborne squared up to Weitz with an accusatory eye.

Weitz trembled and tried to keep the conviction of his argument, but staring at the president, his courage melted away. Treeborne was an intimidating sight. Hard, cold eyes shouted zero tolerance for anyone who dared cross him.

The US defense secretary had often been on the wrong end of Treeborne's acid tongue, and he didn't fancy another round.

Full defenses on standby, Weitz replied, "Mr. President, we are fighting Al Nadir across the world. We've committed ground forces in seven war zones. Our intelligence services constantly monitor Al Nadir's movements. Some of our agents have infiltrated Al Nadir, but they soon get rooted out and disposed of. Believe me, sir, we have mobilized everything in our power to eradicate Al Nadir. But their powerbase is just too strong."

Weitz stared hopelessly at the president and braced himself for the tirade that he knew would commence.

Treeborne remained silent, hand over his mouth, his expression pensive. No one moved. No one spoke. Anxious glances were shot around the oval office.

A sound of a bird could be heard just outside the window.

"Hear that?"

Treeborne looked around the room at the assembled commanders of his new world peace. Frank Weitz, Dave Reiner and Al Hutchinson listened. They all could discern the faint trill of a bird. With bemused embarrassment, they all subserviently nodded. But each were wondering why the president was referencing bird song in the middle of a security briefing.

"That's what I'm fighting for." Treeborne pointed to the window. "I'm fighting for all life on earth. I want our children to grow up in a world free of war, free of hate and free of terror. Al Nadir must be destroyed, whatever the cost. Do whatever you have to do to achieve this objective. But I want it achieved. I want that little motherfucker, Salim Al Douri, at my feet. I want his alliances crushed. I want his intel dismantled. I want his forces immobilized. I want Al Nadir annihilated. Do I make myself clear?"

The fury poured out of Treeborne as his delivery mutated from calm to frenzy in seconds. He stormed over and grabbed the flag behind his desk.

"What does this represent?" he hollered.

All in the room became mute. They were visibly terrified that any word spoken could be misinterpreted and their career cut short before a second breath was drawn.

"Well, gentlemen? I asked you a question. What does our flag stand for?"

Treeborne had descended into incensed rage. Their silence fueled his ire further. Weitz realized that someone had to intervene to stabilize the president's erratic behavior.

"Mr. President, it stands for truth, justice, liberty and freedom."

Weitz watched cautiously for the president's reaction.

"You bet that's what it stands for. We have a duty to uphold our constitution, to fight for our freedom. And that's why we can't let these little fuckers win. What do you need? More money? Put pressure on our scummy chums south of the border. Let them know the DEA will be up their asses quicker than they can say 'grand felony' if they don't pay up. Hike up the protection money on the towel heads. Rig the markets. Tax the French. I don't know. I don't care. Just do what you must. Just secure me with the capability to obliterate Al Nadir off this planet. *Right?*"

Treeborne's hawk eye scanned his men. What were their thoughts? Would they stand loyal or would they crumble, awash with humanitarian righteousness?

Hutchinson spoke slowly. He thrust forward every syllable resentfully. He knew the consequence of his words, but he was steadfast in his reason to speak.

"Sir, Mr. President, we cannot continue to engage in military conflict with countries on equivocal evidence of Al Nadir having bases and alliances in these countries. It is obvious that Al Nadir has strengthened their alliances in the Middle East, Southeast Asia, South America and Western Russia. But how far these alliances demonstrate a serious threat cannot be determined. Right now, Mr. President, we are facing a situation where Al Nadir is literally in every major country of the world. What are you going to do, sir? Bomb the planet? It's the only way you'll eradicate Al Nadir."

Hutchinson looked hard at the president. Treeborne's face had reddened as he'd heard his vice president's acrimonious account of the real state of play. He was furious at hearing such a reality: Al Nadir was an unstoppable power.

"Can't we just nuke them?" suggested Weitz, vying for points from the president.

But Hutchinson's quick-fire response tore him down. "Nuke who? That's the problem. We're not dealing with a country we can go to war with. We're not facing a traditional dictator, someone who you can plan tactics and strategize against. Al Nadir is an insidious organization that has insinuated itself into zealous factions, terrorist regimes and crime states. Their power and wealth has enabled them to consolidate all terrorist activities so that all terror states are connected under the all-powerful banner of Al Nadir. They are unlike any other threat we have ever faced. Intel predicts that Al Nadir acolytes number tens of millions. Salim Al Douri is an evil, ruthless leader. But he's not a Saddam Hussein. He's not an Osama Bin Laden."

"So who the fuck is he?"

"If we're drawing comparisons, think of Salim Al Douri as the Jack Welch of terrorism."

"Jack would love you for that," growled the president.

"The comparison I'm drawing is not on the man, but his position. Salim is the CEO of Al Nadir. His powerbase and strategy is the same as any CEO in an immensely powerful, global corporation. Growth through acquisition. Diversified to spread the risk. Think about it."

"I'm thinking." Treeborne glared hard at Hutchinson.

"Al Nadir is the crack kids on the streets in downtown Washington. The terrorist insurgencies in South Korea. The child prostitution rings in Russia. The fundamentalist uprisings on the West Bank. Al Nadir is the Coca-Cola of terrorism. Like any global brand, Al Nadir is everywhere. And because of this pervasiveness, they're virtually impervious to attack. Sir, do you see? How can you take out something you can't get a fix on?"

The president didn't respond.

Hutchinson pressed on with his analysis.

"Mr. President, all this conflict is achieving nothing but a collateral body count in six figures and turning us into international pariahs. Our actions aren't bringing down Al Nadir, they're building them up. People across the world hate us. Every attack we deliver, every innocent we kill in the crossfire, gives more credence to the counter-attacks. We're fueling the fires of discontent across the globe and feeding Al Nadir's own recruitment drive."

"So what the fuck do you suggest we do?" Treeborne almost spat the words at Hutchinson.

"I don't know, sir. But I know that exhausting our troops in battles they have little hope of ever winning is not the way to overcome Al Nadir. We need an edge. A few years ago, we were the hyper-power, unstoppable, almighty. But that position has dramatically changed. Al Nadir has weapons and manpower to rival ours. Their intel capability is also on par. We never believed one country had the balls to take us on. And we were right. One country didn't. But the terrorist conglomerate of Al Nadir has turned the tables. We've met our nemesis. Right now, we need to retrench and strategize. We need to find that edge, that something that will make a difference to us in this war."

Remembering his vice president's words, Treeborne had not believed he'd ever find the edge to win the war, but someone, somewhere, had forced the wheels of fate to move in his favor. Change was no more than a week away.

Chapter 29

Sky News ran in the background on a plasma TV inset into a paneled oak fascia. The screen displayed yet another bombing at the hands of Al Nadir. Another son fatherless. Another new widow. Another family ruined.

Ashton balled his fist and hit it on the desk, his face a murderous mask of anger.

"When is this ever going to stop?"

"It'll stop when we take down Salim Al Douri." Maide's voice exposed his despondency. "Al Nadir's a house of cards. Salim's strength is Al Nadir's greatest weakness. Our friends across the waters have come to the same conclusion. That's what Kinley was in there for, but he's run out of time. Intel has confirmed he's been made. I know you wanted to keep him in but now he's a liability. He must be taken out today."

Kinley had been so much more than a double agent. He had been the confidence that gave them the belief they had a fighting chance in this war. Maide shuddered. Where would they go now? No one had survived so long in deep cover before. Kinley had sold them the profile he had carefully developed with his partner, Sam Noor. A British spy worn out by the feckless and ineffectual actions of a government ruled by Russian and Middle Eastern billionaires, who had the morals of a Filipino peasant father on the day he sold his teenage daughter to the village lothario.

Kinley needed to be believed. Lives had been sacrificed.

When Al Nadir knew what they had, a top British Intelligence agent turning of his own accord, they couldn't wait to test him. Piccadilly was the final exam. Barely in with Al Nadir a few months, Kinley had gained access to their top league and had become a global senior lieutenant. He'd divulged secrets that Maide and Ashton agreed British Intelligence could lose, and he'd won favor quickly. Al Nadir could taste the bitterness in Kinley's mouth as he compromised his Foreign Office position and happily provided details on safe houses, black accounts, intel networks, other agents' locations and new technologies. But Al Nadir wanted absolute conviction that Kinley had turned.

A bombing at a major tube station in London. Kinley had the time, date and location. He knew exactly what was going to happen. When Maide received the information, it was precursored with a strict 'take no action'. Like Kinley, Maide knew the future.

Thousands would die. This was the test. British lives on a plate.

If they made any attempt to close the station or stop the bombers, Kinley's double agent mission would be over. He had to be believed. Al Nadir could never suspect Kinley's real purpose.

So, on that day in late June, they had looked away as the bloodied, charred and smashed up bodies rolled out as if on a conveyor belt. Somehow, Maide had managed to sleep through the deafening scream of his conscience that night.

"You'll have to find some other way." Solid determination sounded in Ashton's voice. "This has to finish. Their deaths must mean something."

"You know we'd be slaughtered if the public ever knew." Maide eyed the screen showing bodies being pulled out of the wreckage of a car bombing.

"That will never happen. Kinley will be out. It's only us who know."

"And Sam, of course," said Maide hurriedly.

"Oh, yes…and Sam," mused Ashton.

"But he's a sound man."

Maide stared at Ashton, suddenly not able to read the PM.

"Let's hope so."

Chapter 30

Sam waited for Ellie to respond. As each second passed before she spoke, Sam struggled to understand why his wife was making a conscious decision to lie to him. The more he thought about the fact that Ellie was getting ready to deceive him, the more annoyed he became. He made one last effort to access the truth.

"Ellie, you screamed because you burnt your hand on the coffee, didn't you?"

"Well…I think so," replied Ellie blankly.

She looked away from Sam's piercing stare.

"What do you mean you think so?" snapped Sam. "I don't understand why you can't just tell me what happened."

"Look, Sam, I'm not sure. Something happened in the kitchen but I can't remember."

"Ellie, you woke the whole bloody building when you screamed. You must know why?"

Sam's annoyance melded into worry. Lack of recall was a sign of trauma. Selective amnesia kicks in when the brain is faced with a painful or horrific experience. He had seen it happen many times to operatives in the field. The brain takes over, erases the experiences and creates a void. Operatives had often lied about their actions, but they hadn't done so intentionally or consciously. Their brains had done it for them. Ellie was exhibiting the same traits and this worried him greatly.

"It was a spider, ok!" Ellie flushed with embarrassment.

"You screamed like *that* over a bloody spider?" Sam's voice gave away to Ellie that he didn't buy her excuse. "I thought you feared nothing," he added.

"Well it seems we *both* have things to still learn about each other." Ellie's rebuttal was poignant and biting. Sam was surprised she'd used the moment to take such a low shot.

"I deserved that."

Sam was solemn. He had no right to cast judgement over his wife's lies when he'd lied to her for over ten years.

"No. No, you didn't," replied Ellie softly.

Sam could see the shame flick across her face. She'd used his own guilt against him to deflect his questions.

"Yes, Ellie. I did. I lied to you. I didn't confide in you. I betrayed our trust and openness. But believe me, I did it for you. I did it to protect you."

"Protect me?"

"Yes. What you didn't know couldn't hurt you. You were safe. But that's changed. The balance shifted this morning. Please, darling, you must forget what I've told you. You must never, never repeat what you know to anyone. My life and now yours depends upon your absolute discretion. Can I…"

But Ellie wasn't listening. She had tuned out. *Balance shifted.* That's what Sam had said. Simple words. But they had meaning. They had sparked something deep inside her. She thought hard. Why should they *mean* anything? Unbecoming wrinkles creased across her forehead.

"What did you mean by balance shifted?"

Ellie's words, like a swashbuckler's sword, cut through Sam's with a determined thrust.

"Sorry, what?" Her interruption had distracted him but he answered her question. "Balance shifted. It means you're no longer in the dark as to what I really do. You have come into the light. You know the truth. I no longer have the balance over the information you know. The balance of power has shifted. We're now on an equal footing."

"Could they mean something else, those words?"

"They could mean many things. Why do you care?"

Sam's interest was piqued. He had just revealed he had lied to keep her safe, but she didn't seem to care at all. Ellie appeared more obsessed with two passing words.

"I'm not sure. It's just those words…"

Ellie's voice wandered off and she stared with confused eyes at her husband.

Sam shook his head and replied with terse efficiency.

"Look Ellie, I'd love to discuss this, but I'm going to be late if I don't leave now. My driver has already buzzed up twice and I mustn't keep the PM waiting."

He kissed her swiftly, opened the door and marched down the corridor with a single thought in his mind.

All the years of psych-ops training and he still couldn't read his own wife.

Chapter 31

Justin Maide, unlike the PM, wasn't a great believer in hope. In his world, probabilities weren't good enough. He liked assurances. Better still, he liked certainties. Talking to Sam yesterday, whilst the agent had been still in Oslo, had left him with considerable uncertainty.

"Sam, that's it. We've got to take him out. It's virtually certain they know."

"Sir, you've got to give Kinley time!"

"You know I can't," Maide had said. "Abort is underway."

"Abort? God, sir. I really think you're being preemptive. It's still not conclusive." Sam was exasperated.

"How conclusive do you want it to be? The last operation built on Kinley's intelligence was a bloodbath. They knew everything. They were waiting. It was a setup. You know that, Sam. You saw the report."

"But we've all put so much into this. *You* know that. We can't just throw it all away. Give him one more chance," shouted Sam.

Maide listened. Like Sam, he remembered all the sacrifices that had been made for Operation Snowdrop.

"He's no longer viable. I'm sorry. The decision has been made."

"Change it! You have the authority."

"No."

"You're wrong on this one, sir," said Sam.

"I'm sorry you feel that way," replied Maide.

"You're making a big mistake."

"Time will tell."

"You know, sir, I hope it doesn't."

"What do you mean?"

"Imagine if you are aborting the one man who could bring down Al Nadir. How does that make you feel?"

"Not good," said Maide. "But the decision is final. There is nothing more to discuss."

"And what if he doesn't accept it?"

"Then we'll invoke sign off. You know how these things work."

Sam went quiet. Oh yes, he knew the procedure. Total shut down. Secrets burned along with the truth.

"So you think he's been completely turned. He's not with us anymore?" asked Sam.

"I cannot answer that," responded Maide quietly. "That is why these procedures have to be initiated."

"Tell me, sir. What has it all been for?" Sam gritted his teeth. "If all we're going to do is invoke sign off when things get tough, why the hell did we do anything at all?"

"To make a difference. And for a while, we did. But it didn't last. We have to move on."

"And just forget?"

"If necessary, yes."

"Forget everything?" snapped Sam coldly. "Even Piccadilly?"

Sam had stepped way over the edge and he did it without taking a single beat.

"This conversation is over, Dr. Noor."

Maide knew he had to act fast whilst Sam was in Oslo and Ellie was in Winchester. The couple's absence gave them complete clearance to access the apartment. The call to his people had been just another call. Just another "eyes and ears" operation. He'd made the decision minutes after speaking to Sam.

Perhaps it had been frustration and disappointment on Sam's part, but the discourse had left Maide with intense disquiet. He didn't like his authority being questioned. Even more, he didn't like the way Sam had used Piccadilly as a verbal weapon without hesitation.

Sam was committed and devoted, but he was also a maverick who played by his own rules. Maide always recognized this, but turned a blind eye to his insubordination. It wasn't a concern as long as Sam got the job done.

But when he came close to crossing the line, a line that the four of them, Ashton, Kinley, Sam and himself, had drawn four years ago and agreed would never, ever be crossed, Maide knew he only had one play.

Now, more than ever, he had to know Sam was still with them, that he was still a man to be trusted. He couldn't risk him breaking. He couldn't risk Operation Snowdrop ever being revealed.

Being certain of everything at every stage in the game was the only way to win. Whatever the cost, he had to protect and serve. It was who he was, and no one was going to jeopardize that. He had to know everything. And he would know everything. That was how it worked. That's how he'd made it work for thirty-eight years.

He could not feel anything, should not feel anything. He had to make that call. They were at war. And war demanded extreme measures. He had to be more than certain.

He'd taken the only option open to him. But God help them all if his surveillance found that Sam Noor was now a liability.

Chapter 32

Al Nadir would soon be crushed. Treeborne would listen to their bones crunch as if they were cockroaches. Always the hardest insect to kill, they had to be shown no mercy. Treeborne, as a boy, had enjoyed stepping on them and hearing their hard shells crack under his foot, knowing he'd taken their lives. He would do the same to Al Nadir.

The president had a few minutes before the final demonstration started.

He knew the security briefing that followed would have a very different theme to the meeting three weeks before. Gone would be that utter feeling of hopelessness. The angry despair they had all felt would vanish, for now, he had that wonderful edge. The president smiled complacently as he signed state papers ahead of the meeting. As he signed, the glint of the sleek pen caught his attention. Looking at the pen triggered a memory he cherished as one cherishes a priceless gem.

It only had been a fortnight ago.

2 Weeks Earlier

The president returned to the White House after a particularly uncomfortable state dinner with the president of China. The jibes and pokes at the continually failing US economy and the staggering success of the Chinese one had been transparent. They made Treeborne feel like a trailer park bum asking a loan shark for a tide-over before pay day. Entering his private lounge after snapping viciously at his private secretary, he'd headed for the bottle of bourbon in the corner. He needed something to calm his anger. Catching a glimpse of his face in the mirror behind the bar and seeing how tired and old it had become at fifty-one, he breathed deeply and shook his head. It wasn't supposed to be like this. He looked back at himself. His small head perched on almost square shoulders with dangly arms and a short, rounded body, and he knew he resembled more a chimpanzee than a head of state.

What was going wrong? Where had his power gone?

Not so long ago, he was the one to whom the world answered. Never would presidents have dreamed of targeting snide remarks at him. They would have been far too scared of the repercussions. But now, with Al Nadir ruling at every turn, his power had waned. What Treeborne needed was a booster shot. He needed an edge, something to make them all stand up and respect him again.

Treeborne took his drink and sat down on the sofa. It was then he noticed it: a package in a small brown box. Fearing a bomb, he went to call his secretary, and then stopped. The parcel had no address, only the words, FOR YOUR SUCCESS, in black capital letters. The words gave him courage. Deep inside, he knew it wasn't a bomb, although he didn't understand how.

He edged his chubby hand forward slowly and touched the box. On touching, Treeborne sensed something brush close to his ear, and he thought he heard the rustling of a heavy fabric. It was a familiar sensation, one he'd had before, although he couldn't remember quite when. But when he turned, nothing was there. The room was empty. It was just him, the bourbon and the box.

He looked at the box quizzically and then, with a spurt of courage, he leaned sideways and grasped it with two hands. Lifting it off the sofa, he placed the box in his lap. He stared again at the words, FOR YOUR SUCCESS.

The words were personal. Intimate. As if they were speaking to him directly and answering his call for change. They were urging him to be successful again. Gingerly, he lifted the lid and looked inside. The contents of the box were not what he expected to see.

Chapter 33

President Treeborne was captured in the moment of opening the box. Seeing what was inside, he was surprised and confused as to what he should do. He reached into the molded inner case, picked up one of the two items and held it in his thumb and forefinger. Gradually, he rotated it, examining its structure. It looked like a ball pen, if a slightly up-market, hi-tech-style ball pen, but a ball pen, nonetheless. He returned it to its molded holding and turned his attention to the second item of curiosity: a charcoal plasticine oblong block.

It was more interesting than the pen, for as he looked at it, the center of the block sparkled as if children's glitter had been sprinkled across its surface. He pulled at it with his fingers and then let go, expecting it to remain stretched and floppy. But its inherent elasticity snapped it back into shape. He flattened the block in the palm of his hand like a patty, but as soon as he took the pressure off, the shape sprang back in the middle of his hand as if he hadn't touched it at all. He stared, amazed. It was unlike anything he'd ever seen. But what was it? And what did the pen have to do with it?

He looked at the lettering on the box again. FOR YOUR SUCCESS. How could he possibly succeed with a posh pen and a small block of auto-shaping plasticine?

Treeborne placed the plasticine block on the table and picked up the pen, meaning to write something in his notebook. As the pen came close to the block, the block glowed in the middle like a light was shining through it.

"What the hell?" muttered Treeborne.

He brought the pen, so it touched the block. This time there could be no mistaking the effect. On contact, the middle of the block shone so brightly Treeborne had to cover his eyes.

"Woo, you're some mean little sucker, aren't you?"

Treeborne held the block in his palm and chuckled.

"What in God's name are you?"

Perhaps the words were a trigger. Treeborne suddenly picked up his Dictaphone from his pocket and started to dictate. His eyes glazed over and his voice gave no ounce of emotion. Onto the hard disk drive on the Dictaphone, the president explained slowly how the block and pen worked together. He did so by describing deeply complex mathematics and quantum physics, two subjects he had no knowledge of nor interest in.

When he'd finished the dictation, Treeborne switched off the Dictaphone, stood up and asked his personal secretary to get the chief science officer.

He placed the block and the pen back in the box and waited calmly for his CSO to arrive.

"Yes, Mr. President. How can I help you?" asked the CSO, almost as soon as he was escorted into the private lounge.

"Tell the people at Blacksburg to start testing immediately. All you need to know is in here."

Treeborne indicated to the Dictaphone and he handed it with the box to his CSO.

The CSO was perturbed by the president's ice-cold and calculating behavior. He was used to his homespun ways and brash demeanor, and had expected the obligatory slap on the back, and "How ya doin', Fred?" greeting. But there were no pleasantries, no hand shaking or back slapping, just perfunctory instructions delivered in a crisp tone.

"Is there something else, sir?"

The CSO ventured to know more but the president took him by the elbow and guided him towards the door.

"Yes. I want to hear that the tests are a success."

The CSO had neither time nor opportunity to answer as the president pushed him through the door and closed it briskly behind him.

Treeborne returned to the sofa, put his head on the cushion, and slept.

The US president could never explain how he suddenly knew the intricacies of quantum mechanics, and how he'd instantly forgotten them again after sleeping. But one thing he could remember clearly was the call he'd received from his CSO on site at the Blacksburg labs.

"Mr. President, it worked. It's a success. Your invention is a success."

Chapter 34

22 March, 2017

Matthew Kinley entered his house a little after 9 a.m. The run had been long and satisfying. His heart was beating fast with a healthy thudding rhythm.

Angela Kinley, a slim woman with a small pixie face and brunette bob, prepared pancakes on the stove. She looked around as Kinley unzipped his jersey and grabbed a carton of orange juice from the fridge.

"Please, darling, use a glass," Angela scolded, as she eyed Kinley tipping the pouring spout towards his mouth. "We're not savages yet." Her British Home Counties accent came over more clipped than usual.

Kinley, feeling a dampener on his party, swiped a glass from the cupboard and poured.

"That's better. Now don't you find it tastes nicer in a glass?"

"I suppose so." Kinley conceded begrudgingly to his wife's lesson in etiquette. "But it's not nearly half as fun."

Angela glared at him then laughed. "I'll never tame you, will I?"

She left the stove and moved to Kinley, her arms sneaking around him in a gentle embrace.

"Do you want to?" asked Kinley, rubbing her hair softly.

"Not really," whispered Angela, as she looked at her husband.

His bright blue eyes were vibrant and alive, just like the first day they'd met fifteen years ago at the British Embassy's New Year's Eve party in Athens. Then he'd been just a swirl of blond hair, tanned face and glistening smile. She had been completely enraptured. Hardly a word had passed their lips. Before she knew where she was, Miss 'Shy and Retiring from Frome in Somerset' was making love to the most gorgeous man she'd ever seen. Something about the way they met, the sudden taking of forbidden fruit, and the unfathomable wisp of secrecy that surrounded Kinley, made her feel excited, like she was living her own private movie.

She moved her hand to Kinley's face and pulled him down towards her then kissed him passionately.

"Mummy, do you like my picture?"

A beautiful doll-like child in a pale pink corduroy pinafore dress and crisp white t-shirt stood staring expectantly at Angela in the doorway. She pushed back her lightly curled platinum-blond hair behind her small ear, with an air of assured confidence that was well beyond her years, and waited. When Angela didn't reply immediately, she turned her stunning blue eyes full force towards her mother and repeated the question.

"Mummy, I said do you like my picture?"

Angela stared at the newly painted picture her four-year-old daughter, Charlotte, was holding up. It appeared to be indiscernible blobs of green and blue. She quickly masked her bewilderment with an effusive motherly reply.

"It's lovely, darling. It's…"

"Our house," added Kinley, discerning the painted chaos on the paper and saving his wife from an error of judgement.

"Isn't Lotte clever, Daddy?" said Angela, as she disentangled herself gently from her husband's arms.

"Daddy, I'm going to paint the cat," sang Charlotte, as she skipped out of the kitchen.

Kinley smiled at his wife. "I never did like him as a ginger tom anyway!"

He slipped his arms back around Angela's slim waist. But Charlotte's interruption had changed Angela's mood. Her good Catholic upbringing kicked in and she suddenly felt guilty for her earlier wanton behavior, especially as Lotte had been just next door.

She pulled away from her husband, deep in thought. Kinley noticed.

"Is something wrong, darling?"

"No, no…It's just, with Lotte, we should be more careful. You understand?"

"She's growing up, Angela. Give it a few years and she'll be overtaking us. It won't be weird-looking pictures she'll be showing us, it'll be weird-looking boys."

"Yes, I know, Matt. But I'd like her to savor innocence while she can. You know childhood is the most defining moment of a person's life. I want hers to be wonderful."

"You want to keep the illusion going that life's like a fairy tale and she's the little princess."

"Wouldn't any mother, given the chance?"

Angela remembered her own mother and the way she'd packed Angela off to a bleak boarding school before leaving happily with her father to some far-off destination where he'd been posted. How hard and cold everything had been at the convent. The po-faced nuns and the bullying prefects. She'd grown to be strong in that dark place. It had defined her personality. Even more, it reinforced the resolution that no child of hers would ever suffer from a lack of childhood like she had.

"Lotte is everything to me. You know that," she said.

"Of course I do, as she is to me," replied Kinley.

From the flickers of sadness in his wife's eyes, he knew she was remembering her past. Angela stood up straight, realizing she was giving too much away. The last thing she wanted was pity from Kinley. With a little more sternness than she intended, Angela asked, "Have you chased up that order like I told you to?"

Kinley respected his wife's swift shift to a new subject. He shook his head.

"Sorry, love. I've been bogged down with embassy business. It slipped my mind."

"It's your daughter's birthday present and it slipped your mind? God, Matt, does your work always have to come first? I remember a time when-"

"Look, can we not have this conversation right now? I could really do without it," snapped Kinley, annoyed that the earlier flurry of passion had dissipated. He grabbed his wife's mobile from the worktop.

"It's not a problem. I'll call them right now. I'm sure they'll speed up delivery."

Kinley flicked open the phone and dialed the number of the Massachusetts toy store. A woman came on the line. He gave the order number and requested that the order be expedited as soon as possible as it was his daughter's birthday on Sunday. Instead of excuses, as he'd expected, the woman was courteous, apologized for the delay and confirmed that delivery would be made that day. Pressing the call off, Kinley relayed the outcome to his wife.

"I damn well hope so," she replied. "A handmade Victorian dollhouse is what Lotte wants, and it's what she's going to get. They had better not let us down."

"Well, the woman promised they'd deliver it today, and the way she said it, it was as if her very life depended on it."

Chapter 35

In the car driving to the meeting he'd postponed from the previous night, Sam thought about all that had happened that week. He'd gone to Oslo not just to check out new tech companies worthy of British investment. His principal reason was to capture Rikard Allan, Al Nadir's supposed global lieutenant for Scandinavian operations. He was also an independently wealthy hedge funder and ran a legitimate business. Rikard had dual nationality as both a British and Norwegian citizen.

3 Days Earlier

Sam was aware of playing things coolly. Rikard was highly connected and was the type to ruin careers at the flick of his phone on speed dial to someone of superior authority.

Sam worked with Interpol and the Norwegian Intelligence Service (NIS) following intel that confirmed Rikard was tracking flights. His target was the private airstrip at Gardermoen. Sam linked up access to the Government Communications Headquarters' (GCHQ) latest artificial intelligence system. The AI started running auto-analysis on flight schedules, jet owner history, tail call signs and usage patterns of previous flights against typical corporate flight analytics. The AI searched for any anomalies and these were then cross-correlated with any possible Al Nadir connections, however slim and tenuous.

Sam realized that, in the spy business, making those seemingly random connections delivered the most valuable intelligence.

A connection popped up with a jet owned by a biotech company in Norway where Al Douri had carried a minority shareholding a decade before. Although Al Douri wasn't a visible shareholder anymore, the association was enough to send the alerts through the system. The plane's origin appeared to be from Madrid-Barajas Airport.

Data on flights coming into Barajas fed through into the AI system and the cross-correlating process commenced. A private jet with the same tail call sign was tracked in Lagos and Mumbai. The plane had originally taken off from Beijing Capital International. Intel affirmed the passenger as a high-ranking Ministry of State Security (MSS) official. The AI flagged the MSS official as a potential Al Nadir asset embedded within Chinese Intelligence.

Chatter on the grid confirmed some new EmTech was out there and causing a stir. Sam didn't know what it was, but from the intelligence received, it was something big. Its origin was thought to be China.

Sam knew this wasn't a coincidence.

With his quarry in his sights, Sam had headed down to Gardermoen Airport. He had backup on standby if needed from Interpol and NIS. But he didn't want to spook Rikard nor his target. Even more so, he didn't want to put other agents' lives at risk.

Sam had parked his Merc SLK on the far side of the airport. He ducked down by the hangers and waited. His eyes carried SmartLens contacts, the latest in nano-tech analytics integration. The SmartLens linked directly to GCHQ's AI system. It immediately started to deliver info on the flight arrival. Sam searched the skies and noticed amongst the heavy grey clouds a bright light heading quickly his direction. He watched as the Embraer Phenom plane touched down. Sam scooted around the back of the hanger to the road leading to the exit. He looked through his powerful USCAMEL HD binoculars and saw an Audi R8 driving past the barbwire fence.

Sam recognized the shock of silvery white hair and pale, stern face. The driver was Rikard. SmartLens turned off momentarily, detecting the binoculars use. The R8 stopped at the security gate. The guard tilted his body toward the car's window, but his hand stayed on his gun. Sam watched as a hand from the car flashed something. Maybe a card, thought Sam. But he couldn't see clearly.

Sam ran around to the other side of the hanger, back toward the tarmac and the plane.

The R8 drew up alongside the plane as the steps flipped out and someone emerged. Sam edged closer. An Asian man of medium height with a mass of solid black hair and a round face stepped down from the plane. His eyes searched around as if unsure of what was happening. Even from seven feet away, Sam could see he was jittery. The man headed toward the waiting car.

Sam's SmartLens kicked in the moment he took his binoculars away. The SmartLens app pin pointed the man and intel flashed up in front of Sam's vision.

Dr. Li Wang. Ministry of State Security. Head of Information and Auditing Division, China. Suspected Al Nadir asset. Doctorate in Biochemistry.

Rikard jumped out of the car to greet Dr. Wang. The Chinese gentleman appeared very nervous. He reached inside his pocket and handed a package to Rikard.

Before Sam could react, Dr. Wang suddenly collapsed. Through his binoculars, Sam could clearly make out the blood stains on Dr. Wang's chest. Rikard grinned and leapt back into the R8. He gunned the accelerator as two guys emerged from the hanger. Their guns carried silencers.

A typical Al Nadir move, thought Sam bitterly. He ran at speed back to his car, keeping Rikard in view. SmartLens had already captured the registration of Rikard's car and fed it into the Heads-Up display on his modified SLK. Inside the car, Sam flicked on the HUD and the satellite tracking of Rikard's R8.

From the private airstrip at Gardermoen, Sam tracked Rickard to a house in the luxurious Holmenkollen region on the outskirts of Oslo. The house was on Holms Vei Drive, close to the famous Holmenkollbakken ski ramp.

Rikard parked the car and headed inside. Sam clocked his walk. The man looked self-assured, not giving a damn. He was Al Nadir all over.

Sam ran around the side of the house, looking for a way in. He didn't call for back up immediately. He wanted to handle this himself. Rikard was too risky a target. First, Sam had to neutralize the risk. Sam took out his gun, not his usual Sig but a sedative gun usually used on wild animals.

If he used his Sig, it would be curtains for both Rikard and Sam's career. The hypodermic in his jacket was his only lifeline. Sam knew he was going to need it if Rikard was loaded with the nano-bomb. And if he was an Al Nadir global lieutenant, he most certainly would be.

From the downstairs living room window, Sam could see Rikard talking on the phone and laughing. Sam ran to the back of the house. A door led out onto the garden from the kitchen. Sam whipped out a small object from inside his jacket. It looked like a compass with a sucker on the end. Sam stuck the sucker on the glass near the handle and drew a complete circle, cutting the glass cleanly. He then carefully placed the glass on the floor, put his hand through the hole, flicked the latch to open the door, and ran inside.

Music was playing somewhere. Sam moved fast, keeping against the walls. The music pounded at a greater intensity. It was some sort of Scandinavian hard rock, goth punk mix. Sam grimaced as he listened. In his peripheral vision, he noticed a flash of Rikard's silvery white hair in the doorway. Sam ran across the floor soundlessly and turned the corner.

Rikard was in front of Sam, but with his back to him. Sam didn't hesitate. As Rikard started to turn, Sam fired the sedative gun.

Rikard fell. Sam jumped on him, slamming the hypodermic needle into his neck. Rikard started to shake and his face turned a rosy deep pink. The nano-bomb inside Rikard had recognized the sedative and had begun its initiation sequence. Abruptly, the sequence stopped. Sam breathed out. The agent that had gone into Rikard's body was working.

Sam touched his earpiece. "Get here now!"

"Already here," yelled an Interpol agent.

Sam heard the front door crash open. He snatched the package from inside Rikard's jacket and pocketed it. A number of Interpol and NIS agents stormed into the drawing room and grabbed Rikard's body.

A tall guy with a wry smile looked over at Sam. "We tracked you all the way. But we knew that like the stubborn, brave, little bastard you are, you'd never call for back up."

Sam nodded. "We haven't got much time. That stuff doesn't last long so let's open this fucker up and see what he's got to tell us."

With the UN Peace Summit upon them in just a matter of days, the new intelligence would have serious ramifications on the security of the event. Sam knew it was his responsibility as head of counter-terrorism at British Intelligence MI6 to keep London and the rest of the UK safe from afar. Six's capture of Rikard gave them the intel. But it was down to MI5 to take it and crash Al Nadir's party.

Sam was the first to arrive for the meeting at the Terrace, as the intelligence fraternity called it. Close to Whitehall, the Thames and River Houses, the Terrace was highly favored by all parties as it offered exclusive privacy and excellent convenience. It was also neutral ground, preventing no inherent feelings borne of location that could potentially give an advantage to one party over the others. To outsiders, it was just another bland, white-fronted

Victorian townhouse that London had in abundance.

Sam entered the green-lit cubicle and waited for the biometric analysis. His retina, palm and then full body scan took place in seconds. Upon completion, he was granted access to proceed. He walked down the narrow corridor. With the exception of the sparsely distributed wall lights, the corridor held little illumination. The heavy, burgundy, velvet adorning the walls made it dark and forbidding. It was neither an inviting or happy place. Sam reached the end, opened a heavy oak door and walked into the room.

On entering, he took in his surroundings while he selected a place to sit.

A massive mahogany table overpowered the small room, which had little other furniture except for a slim credenza on the back wall holding a decanter and highball glasses. It was the whiskey platform. The floor was oak and showed signs of wear. Deep indentations and jagged burns suggested it had witnessed a history of conflict. At the window, the curtains were closed. The super tough, laser-resistant glass fitted as standard throughout the Terrace was hidden from view.

Sam glanced up at the ceiling. It was pure white with an attractive coving and a completely ostentatious crystal chandelier that begged for a palatial grand hall. Dark, oak-paneled walls that looked at least a century old surrounded him.

The room was trapped in time. Nothing reflected that it was in the twenty-first century. But Sam knew looks were always deceptive. Behind the antiquated structures, surveillance and biomedical analysis systems silently hummed, running their assigned routines to keep the room's inhabitants safe.

The discovery of Al Nadir's nano-bomb technology had changed the rules on terrorism, and no one was taking any chances. Despite their previous supremacy, the intelligence elite throughout the world knew that the countdown had begun.

Chapter 36

2 Months Earlier

Sam had worked with Jerry, a fellow field agent, on a mission in Rome, Italy to capture a man known only as Palmero who was reputed to be Al Nadir's head of strategic operations for Southern Europe. Sam had a bad feeling in his gut about the ease with which Palmero had allowed himself to be captured. But Jerry had no such qualms.

On capture, he'd thrown Palmero into the back of the van and was preparing to extract some serious talking before they arrived at the secure holding bunker.

"Shit! I think he's ill."

Sam knew the moment Jerry uttered these fateful words that something was seriously wrong. All at once, instinct told Sam what to do.

He screamed at Jerry, "Get the hell away from him!"

But the speed of events swept his words away in the maelstrom that followed.

Sam turned and ran away from the van. But as Jerry tried to pull away, Palmero grabbed his leather jacket. Jerry looked back and caught sight of Palmero's face. With skin of deep purple, eyes bulbous and bloodshot, he smiled sickly at Jerry and mouthed, "Fuck you!" Then promptly exploded.

Diving for cover behind a Peugeot Estate, Sam's heart raced as he tried to piece together what had just happened. Palmero had been searched. He'd had no explosives on him. Sam pushed his head above the bonnet of the car and watched a chain of secondary explosions rip the van apart. Shrapnel hurled in all directions. Flames and acrid smoke billowed out from the vehicle shell that remained on the ground. Sam couldn't see Jerry or Palmero anywhere. As the explosions subsided, Sam rose to his feet to check for survivors.

A dull thud to his right caught his attention. The smell of burning flesh assaulted his senses. Sam whipped his head around to see what had caused the sound and stared straight into Jerry's horror-struck eyes. His head and torso had landed at Sam's feet. The rest of his body parts had been scattered, bloody and burning, around the site. Steel from the van had torn through Jerry when it exploded, ripping him into pieces. Metal shards protruded through Jerry's stomach, now but a grotesque human pincushion.

Sam gagged instinctively. He held his hand over his mouth, and then swallowed hard as his training kicked in. He shuddered ferociously and looked away, forcing down the bile surging in his throat. But his revulsion was overpowered by another emotion. Anger. From that moment, Sam was driven to the point of obsession to find out what had initiated the explosion that killed Jerry.

Chapter 37

After Jerry's death, British Intelligence had been on high alert. Sam knew the meeting at Vauxhall Cross would be decisive. It was a culmination of five weeks spent tracking, interrogating, reviewing and analyzing to discover the cause of the explosion. As is the way in intelligence, Sam uncovered the truth through a combination of good surveillance, opportunity and solid hypothesis.

GCHQ had been doing their job monitoring signals and communications. Essentially everything that could be intercepted was heard by them. They had tracked a rogue signal during a routine frequency sweeping exercise. A few seconds later, an explosion took place at the signal's destination point. Coincidence wasn't a consideration. Immediately, the frequency was locked and automatic scanning assigned on the frequency, along with orders to detect and alert if another signal was broadcast.

The signal GCHQ found was analyzed and discovered to be a carrier for an encoded secondary signal that stored a heavily encrypted software program. Analysts spent hours decrypting and deconstructing the code. The analysts carefully avoided cyber booby-traps and behavioral-based heuristic viruses that, if unleashed, could literally flip algorithmic processes and create backdoors into the heart of the UK's most secure national security data repositories. It was both a painstaking and nerve-wracking process but the analysts worked tirelessly and what they discovered staggered the intelligence community.

Sam took his place at the table. He scanned the room. Around him were leading scientists and engineering experts, but Sam knew they were all waiting on him to contribute his hypothesis on the code's function. His reputation in nano-technology preceded him. A first at Cambridge in physics and a doctorate in micro-engineering took him into IBM as a research scientist for a few years. Post-doctorate research work in intelligent micro-machines attracted the attention of the UK's Ministry of Defense, and they soon came running with an inviting proposition. While at the MoD, Sam had worked on an ultra-secret military reconnaissance project: SWARM (Strategic Wide-scale Assessment and Response Machines). He had led the team that developed prototype nano-agents. The nano-agent's purpose was to collect data on the enemy's position, troop movements and environmental conditions, thus determining the enemy's tactics and strategies for counterattack.

No one around the table doubted that the decrypted code was connected in some way to nano-technology, but they didn't yet know in what capacity Al Nadir was employing it. Sam had studied the code and recognized references to biological structures. Rather than discuss what it couldn't be, Sam decided to go straight for his lead hypothesis.

"This nano-structure works in an organic architecture," stated Sam boldly to the assembled scientists. He pointed to the sections of the code relating to his idea on the LCD screen.

"That's a presumptuous assumption to make, Dr. Noor. It's true that it does appear to need an organic structure to work. This area of the code may even be referencing human DNA, but we need more analysis of the code and, of course, the nano-machine for which the code was written," said the scientist sat closest to Sam.

Ignoring the *presumptuous assumption* snide, Sam grew very suddenly and unexpectedly frustrated. "It's a nano-bomb!" he shouted.

The faces around the table sneered at his unbelievable suggestion.

"Don't be ridiculous," muttered the scientist who had spoken previously.

But Sam wasn't being ridiculous. Throughout the discussion, his mind had gone back to Rome and the Al Nadir agent who had inexplicably exploded.

"Think about the evidence. Look at Rome with Jerry. I personally checked Palmero. I know he had nothing on him. And there's been other examples. Lagos and Chicago this week and Moscow the week before. Face it. Al Nadir operatives have been blowing up, taking our agents with them, and there's nothing that we could do about it. We know Stein-Muller, the hottest man in nano-tech has gone AWOL from his company. And now we have a nano programme that implies in its code use within an organic, maybe even human, DNA structure. Whether you think I'm crazy or not, I don't care. But the evidence shows that somehow Al Nadir is using nano-machines to follow a program to turn a human into a bomb. No explosives. No wires. No failure. The *ultimate* suicide bomber."

The room went very still and very quiet as all those around the table contemplated Sam's words.

"We've got to get our hands on those nano-machines," stated Sir Justin Maide anxiously. "That's the only way we'll know for sure."

Chapter 38

From Sir Justin Maide's voice, Sam knew he was in for a rapid ride. After the meeting, Maide had virtually run him out of the Vauxhall Cross, eager to see him tracking down the origin of the suspected nano-bomb. A recent sighting of Stein-Muller in a Dubai night club coupled with a rogue signal tracked back to a building in the Emirate had Sam in a car hurtling towards RAF Northolt. An hour later, he was in the air and heading towards Dubai.

On the plane, he was brought up to speed on events. A blind account linked to Stein-Muller with an amount of twenty million dollars had been found. Sam knew it was safe to assume it wasn't for work done in developing nano-tubules to reinforce tennis rackets.

An MI6 surveillance agent who had been eyeballing Stein-Muller's movements saw him in a Dubai hotel joined by Al Nadir operatives. After leaving, the operative had trailed Stein-Muller and watched him enter a heavily guarded facility on the outskirts of the city. He stayed in the facility for over an hour, and then departed back to his hotel. The surveillance agent kept close to him, but on instruction, he didn't approach. The surveillance system the agent placed in Stein-Muller's room was sufficient.

"Standby to receive surveillance data."

Sam waited for his laptop to signal safe download. "All received, sir."

"You'll be co-oping with the CIA on this one," said Maide. "I believe you know Ricky Alexander. He knows the facility and has good ground experience. A bird will fly you down to your rendezvous point at Khwaneej. It should be a quick in-out. Good luck, Sam, and Godspeed."

"Thank you, sir."

Sam switched off the transmission and settled in to review the images on his laptop. Unlike a few years ago when spy satellites gave everything away,

Al Nadir's bases were now cloaked by encrypted frequencies that jammed satellite surveillance. So Sam was amazed to see real-time thermal images of the facility in such clarity. He'd have to ask Ricky about that one. Sam smiled. He didn't expect to be working again so soon with Ricky. He hoped it wouldn't be another Cairo.

Chapter 39

The plane touched down at a US military air base, once given by the ruler of Dubai and received with gratitude by the US Air Force. Sam raced from the plane to the waiting bird and gave the thumbs up for the pilot to lift off.

Below him, the landscape changed from box villas in a tight grid to sprawling farmhouses with lush vegetation and wandering livestock. The area of Khwaneej was famed for its rich Emiratis with their weekend homes, places to relax and unwind away from the never-ending hustle of Dubai. Most farms had their own heli-pads as travelling on Dubai's heavily congested roads was not an activity commensurate with rapid relaxation.

Sam's rendezvous point came into sight. A dull, off-white block rising from the sandy floor, with several outbuildings of varying sizes daubed in the same dirty white color, was surrounded by squares of grungy green vegetable patches and date palms.

The helicopter descended onto the pad and Sam ducked as he alighted.

A door at the front of the farmhouse opened and a towering figure emerged. At first, the morning sun reflecting off the windows glared in Sam's eyes and prevented him from discerning the man's features. His hand tensed momentarily on his gun until the man moved closer.

"Good to see you!"

Sam smiled and returned his gun as he heard Ricky's heavy Bronx drawl. Nearing him, Sam glimpsed his blond hair cragged back into a rough ponytail and his confident swagger.

"I really didn't think you'd want to work with me again. Not after Cairo!"

Five Months Earlier

Cairo. August. Hot, sweaty and smelly. Chasing a Spanish Al Nadir senior lieutenant down a cramped alley. All around them, doors suddenly shut and the alley vanished of people. It soon became clear to Sam that Ricky, in his singular tenacity to acquire his target, had led them directly into a rather nasty ambush.

With a gun to Sam's head, courtesy of another Al Nadir agent, and Ricky with his gun trained on his original quarry, all four men were caught in a real game of who blinks first.

"Oh, kill him. I don't care. He means nothing!" shouted Ricky unexpectedly, and he cocked his gun ready to shoot the terrorist.

In return, the terrorist with his gun on Sam cocked his.

"I mean nothing? You bastard. I thought you loved me!" Sam shouted back.

The startling words from the mouth of a towering, tough guy shook the terrorists' machismo, and unbalanced their standing.

"Oh, that's typical. Air your dirty linen in public!" screamed Ricky, making sure he had captured both terrorists' full attention.

"It's alright for you. You're not the one with a gun at his head. How could you do this?" called back Sam in the most fey tone he could muster.

"Oh, kill him. I can't stand his whining."

"You animal!" screamed Sam, looking hurt.

From the corner of his eye, he could see his terrorist captor was no longer watching him, but was fixated by their gay interplay.

"Right back at you, sweetcheeks," retorted Ricky bitchily.

"Even after last night?" questioned Sam, behaving as if the two terrorists didn't exist.

"Especially after last night. I mean your performance…"

"Yes?" Sam feigned anticipation.

"Well, darling," shouted back Ricky. "It was well below par."

"Below par!" yelled back Sam, putting his hands on his waist. "How could you say that?"

"It's simple, darling. You've just lost it."

As Ricky spoke, Sam's hands flew up in the air in an effeminate expressive gesture. "Lost it!" he screamed, and at the same time, he grabbed the terrorist's arm, wrenched it up and locked it behind the terrorist's back.

He howled as Sam's lightning action snapped his bones with stunning ease. Searing pain shot through the nerves of the Al Nadir agent and his fingers let go of the gun. It dropped to the dirty ground, where Sam snatched it quickly and drove it hard into the terrified terrorist.

"Don't fucking move or I'll blow your face off!"

The terrorist, in absolute agony with his arm ripped out of its socket, shattered in a dozen places and twisted the wrong way around, didn't argue.

"Well done, darling." Ricky's face lit up with approval. "I think your performance has improved some."

Chapter 40

Outside the villa in Dubai, Sam looked at Ricky and shook his head. He knew he was a wild card, but he enjoyed their assignments together. And wasn't craziness close to genius? Just what one needs when in a dangerous squeeze.

"So why are you here?" asked Ricky, smiling broadly.

"They bribed me with two weeks extra holiday," called back Sam.

"Yeah, like you'd take it." Ricky gave Sam a knowing wink, threw his arms around his back and bear hugged him. "Don't know why that wife of yours stays. I'm sure she could do better!" Ricky noticed a flicker of sadness in Sam's eyes. Maybe his ribbing was a little close to the bone. "Ah, well, maybe she couldn't," he added, slapping Sam on the back. "Come on in. I'll let you see what's happening down the block."

Ricky led Sam into his office, which was dominated by a fifty-inch screen.

"You got the images ok?" asked Ricky.

Sam nodded. "Yes I did, and I'd be interested to know what you're using."

A conceited expression erupted on Ricky's face. "Al Nadir reckons they can keep us blind. But they're wrong."

He pressed a couple of keys on the keyboard and the screen flickered into focus showing a picture of a large facility with a high wall surrounding it.

"This is where the nano-bomb is being held."

Ricky pointed to the right-hand side of the facility. He pressed a key and the screen segmented into four quarters, showing live thermal feeds from different directions.

"Pin-hole cameras positioned in rocks give us a 360-degree viewpoint. Thermal molecular imaging gives us a clear picture of what's going down," explained Ricky. "And improvements in our scanning technology mean they can be located farther away from the target."

Sam watched the thermal image feed change as each camera switched direction.

"And Al Nadir haven't tapped into the frequency?" asked Sam in disbelief.

"They don't even know we're close. Signal delivered via qubit encryption. The photons take on different properties the moment they're observed. Therefore, the qubits can take on many different values simultaneously. Only the qubit reader back at Langley can strip out the signal, translate it, and send it back here securely. It all happens in a fraction of a second! Apparently, they're using some kind of turbo-charged magnetic field to control the quantum properties. Whatever they are? You've got to hand it to Langley's boffin squad, they sure know how to hide something when they want to."

Sam nodded with sheer admiration as he listened. MI6 had been working on qubit encryption but hadn't managed to keep the quantum entanglement stable enough. When this mission is over, he thought, I'll have to catch up with my techy pals at Blacksburg.

"It's impressive."

Ricky caught the touch of envy in his voice. "Hey, don't feel so bad. You guys got there with the Stealth Suits. That's one hell of an invention."

The Stealth Suit was the latest in camouflage technology, an ingenious British invention that used photo-chromic nano-reflectors embedded into the fabric. All frequencies, including white light, reflected away from the suits giving the impression of invisibility. The suit's photo-chromic nano-reflectors gave a shield across uncovered skin such as hands or face, providing a totally inclusive field of invisibility for the wearer. Although the suits were prototypes, the promise of what they offered was too great for Ricky, and he'd leapt at the opportunity to play guinea pig.

"I can't wait to try them out." Ricky tapped the holdall and then leaned back, smiling, and took a swig of his Budweiser.

"Now to business." Sam's face, now deadly serious, indicated their small talk had finished. "How far is the facility from here?"

"It's just over 25 klicks southwest of here. Once we're done, I'll evacuate with you. This house won't be viable afterwards." Ricky looked around the room. "Can't say I'll miss it."

Sam looked back at the screen. "So we've got ten warm bodies around the two exits, a collection of five in the center, which is probably the clean room area, and a few stragglers on the perimeter facing east. So we'll enter from the west."

"That's about it, Sammy boy."

Sam lifted the bottle to his lips and took a long, deep drink, and then stared at Ricky. His friend, ever the optimist, grinned at him in his crazy, gung-ho way. Sam nodded.

"Ok. So let's get it on."

On Sam's command, Ricky leapt from the chair. He unzipped the holdall and handed Sam one of the gun-metal grey jump suits.

"Sorry it's a bit last season." Ricky slipped into the suit. "But you can accessorize." He held up his Glock.

"No, thanks," said Sam. "My Sig's more than enough."

Sam zipped up the suit.

"Hey, don't forget the specs." Ricky chucked Sam a pair of the purple-lensed glasses. "It's the only way we'll be able to see each other."

"Not that I'm gonna want to see what you're up to!" ribbed Sam, and Ricky laughed.

"Just got to set the detonation sequence and then we're out of here. Take this."

Ricky threw Sam a little blue square, matchbox sized.

"Portable detonation unit," muttered Sam, knowing he had to give it to the pilot in the helicopter outside.

"In case our bird needs to take flight." Ricky programmed the villa's alarm to auto-detonation. "Ok. We're primed. Just need to click this little button." Ricky indicated to the third knob on his Omega watch. "And this place will be Villa Vesuvius."

Sam smiled coldly. "We synch at 06.22."

Ricky nodded, synching his own watch. Sam threw the little blue box in the air and then caught it. "I better get this to the pilot. I'll see you outside."

At the helicopter, Sam handed the blue box to the pilot who held it gingerly as if it were a radioactive isotope.

"Wait here until we report back," said Sam. "ETA 06.50. If we're not back by 07.00, detonate the place and leave. Get word to MI6 Station Head, Greaves. Any sign of trouble, leave and detonate."

The pilot gave a thumbs up to Sam. "Good luck, sir."

Sam heard Ricky behind him and the alarm setting sounded through the villa. A hand slapped him on the back.

"Let's go."

Ricky climbed into the Land Cruiser. Sam got into the passenger side and Ricky shot out of the gates in the direction of Al Nadir's nano facility.

"It's gonna be a cakewalk, sweetcheeks," declared Ricky with plain conceit. "I just, you know, feel it!"

Chapter 41

The thing Ricky had termed a cakewalk soon turned into something very different. The drive took them into a large industrial area. From the images he'd seen at the villa, Sam recognized the ochre-toned wall. Beyond it hid the low-roofed building housing the nano facility.

"That's it."

Ricky parked alongside an adjacent building. Sam pocketed the spare set of keys to the Land Cruiser and got out.

"You reckon this'll work?" questioned Sam, as he fingered the fabric of the Stealth Suit.

"Only one way to find out," answered Ricky.

He put on his purple glasses and charged off in the direction of the facility. Before Sam's eyes, he slipped a switch on the cuff of his suit and literally disappeared.

"Shit!"

Sam watched his hot-headed colleague, true to form, initiate his jump-in-and-think-later modus operandi. Following him, Sam stuffed his Sig into the pocket of his Stealth Suit and flipped the same switch. As he put on the purple glasses, Ricky came into view. He chased and caught up with him at the west side of the facility.

"It works," whispered Sam, somewhat amazed, as he raced past a patrolling guard.

"Of course it does," mumbled Ricky. "You gotta have some faith in those brain-boxes."

Sam smiled. "Keep it down. I was once one of those brain-boxes."

"Explains everything," whispered Ricky.

Sam ignored the bait and snuck in close beside his partner. "The gates are closed."

"Well, aren't you the master of surveillance?" Ricky's sarcasm was in full flow as usual. "All we gotta do is get their attention, and then we can move."

With that, he took out his Glock and fired at the metal gate.

A door inside the bigger metal gate opened and two guards came out, their semi-automatics pointing but a few inches from Sam. He held his breath, edged around the guard and slipped through the open door. Ricky followed quickly behind.

Both kept silent as they ran across the inner courtyard. Sam looked around him, rapidly gaining orientation and reconciling the images he'd seen at the villa with what he saw now. On the left was a set of buildings with dishes and aerials on top. Probably a communications command center, thought Sam, as he sped past. He wished he'd brought explosives. He'd have loved to have created some real mayhem for Al Nadir. But this mission was a 'quick in-out', as Maide had put it. Smooth, surgical strike then leave.

Sam looked to his right and noticed a large dark building with reflective glass. He remembered the thermal images had shown hardly any heat in the building. He shivered. The place felt cold although it was easily edging towards 80 degrees in the morning sun.

Sam tapped Ricky's shoulder. "What do you reckon that is?"

Ricky shrugged as he looked around at the building.

"A weapons store or ammunition pile," muttered Ricky. "God knows. Get with the program. We gotta hit the clean room, not worry about the scenery." He turned and made for the building in the middle that they had identified as the clean room lab area.

"Do you hear that?" Sam looked back at the dark building.

"Hear what?" Ricky turned back, visibly irritated his partner had got side-tracked.

"It sounds like…screaming." Sam pressed against the glass and looked inside.

"I can't hear anything."

"Listen."

"We haven't got time for this kind of shit!"

"Just a second." Sam hesitated. "There's something going on." His instinct as an agent was alert and it told him to investigate. Ignoring the hushed protests from Ricky, he sneaked around into the building, tailgating behind a guard walking inside.

He could hear a woman's voice, icy-cold and cutting with a Sicilian overtone. The woman was talking in bursts of activity, quick and disjointed, interrupted with girlish laughing. The hackles on his neck rose as he heard the laugh.

Sam followed the sound and came to a grey concrete room. The door was ajar. He could see a woman, and although she was facing away from him, he recognized the long black hair and the curvy, gorgeous figure. Sabena Sanantoni, Al Nadir's global second in command. If she was here, something really was going down. He did right to investigate.

In front of her stood another man covered in dust. His body was shaking and he screamed intermittently. Sabena rubbed her hands together and laughed. "This is so good. Hans has exceeded himself."

Hans, thought Sam, she must be referring to Hans Stein-Muller, the rogue nano-technologist. But who was she talking to? Sam moved forward to get a better look. But the person next to Sabena was further inside the room and he couldn't see them without going directly inside. Sam took a step forward and suddenly felt a hand on his shoulder. He stiffened and turned around.

It was Ricky.

He signaled urgently for Sam to leave, but Sam shook his head and pointed at the woman. Ricky's eyes widened as he realized who it was he was watching. At that moment, Sabena turned fully around and stared at Sam straight in the face. Then smiled.

"I'm pleased it's only us seeing this."

Her words and reaction hardened Sam's stomach with fear. He knew he was invisible, but somehow, he felt that Sabena could sense him. Ricky heard her reaction and pulled Sam by the elbow. Reluctantly, he left.

Outside in the courtyard, Sam whispered, "Could she see us?"

Ricky shook his head. "Not possible. We've just gone past three guards and they didn't blink. What makes her so special?"

"I don't know."

Sam looked back at the building and shivered again. What were they doing to that poor man? He wished he could've helped him.

"We've gotta go," said Ricky, and he headed towards the clean room building. Sam knew he couldn't linger, but he was determined to find out more once he had the nano-bomb in his grasp.

Ricky saw their moment as two scientists did their retina scan to enter the facility. He and Sam stepped in behind them, being careful not to touch them.

Sam scanned the glass-walled rooms, and in one, on the right, he could see a row of saline phials. He entered the room and crouched down. Inside the phials he noticed that the coloration of the saline was darker in one area, a sure sign that foreign bodies lurked within the solution. He turned his watch dial, converting it to a magnet, and moved it towards the phials. The coloration followed the path of his watch. Nano-bots were inside. This was what he was looking for. He slipped the phials quickly into the deep pockets of his jump suit.

"Got them?" asked Ricky, sidling up to Sam, who nodded. "Great! Let's go."

Ricky ran out into the corridor with Sam following behind and turned the corner straight into a woman scientist. She screamed as something unseen smashed into her, and Ricky jumped with an audible yelp.

Guards, hearing her scream and Ricky's yelp, looked around to see the imprint of something on her white tunic, and a flickering outline of a figure. They instinctively fired at the outline and carried on firing. Sam and Ricky belted down the corridor at speed, and the guards followed the sound of their footsteps.

Reaching the door, they realized another retina scan was called for permission to exit. Sam shot at the glass and Ricky turned back and fired at the oncoming guards. With the alarm now sounding, Sam and Ricky dived through the shattered glass door. The fragments tore into their suit fabric. Suddenly, Ricky and Sam flickered into view. Their incredible Stealth Suits had one drawback that neither knew: the suit's fabric had to remain unbreached. One tear in the fabric and the collective system of photo-chromic nano-reflectors broke down, rendering the wearer of the suit visible.

The two agents ran like crazy horses, firing over their shoulders and taking out guards as they headed towards the wall. Amid the commotion, Sabena Sanantoni emerged from the dark building and watched their escape. A wry smile sneaked across her beautiful face.

They had been almost free of security when a guard caught in their blind spot saw them climbing the wall and fired. Ricky dropped as the armor-piercing bullets with their heavy tungsten cores sailed through his Kevlar-padded jacket into his back and into his heart. Sam didn't look around. A second taken in sad thought for his dead friend would certainly have killed him too. His focus was to get away.

With cold desperation, Sam scrambled over the wall as bullets flew around him. He leapt to the ground and dived into his car, keeping low in the seat as he started the engine. Slamming the accelerator down hard, the car screamed as he pushed its performance to 60 mph in seconds. He could hear engines revving, and behind him, the metal doors opened. But they were too slow. Sam was already away and heading for the safety of the waiting helicopter.

Chapter 42

22 March, 2017

Sam remembered that after that assignment, so much had been learned about the nano-bomb. Scientists confirmed that Sam's sudden revelation had been spot on. The nano-bots were injected into a person through the saline solution. The moment they were inside the body, they self-replicated rapidly. Although swarming in the operative's bloodstream, the nano-bots were not destroyed by white blood cells. The nano-bots, smaller than a virus, were essentially invisible to a body's defense system. These swarming nano-bots focused on mutating the enzymes. Ironically, these enzymes in their usual operation played a helpful role. They repaired DNA by sending electron charges along sections of a DNA strand. But the nano-bot's mutation process changed the enzyme's iron-sulphur structure at the sub-atomic level. The enzymes were no longer helpful. The change resulted in an increase in acidic concentration. By pushing up the acidic level, the electron charge switched. At that moment of switchover, a completion signal from the principal nano-bot would be sent to an Al Nadir base station. It was this signal that GCHQ had intercepted. The scientists calculated that once the enzyme had polarized, a dramatic catalysis took place, creating a huge electrical current inside the body.

The Al Nadir base station would reply to the completion signal by sending a detonation signal, and the operative would turn into an unseen, undetected bomb.

Having understood the workings of the nano-bomb, British Intelligence scientists had endeavored to find ways to negate its activation. True to form, Al Nadir scientists worked in parallel to develop an even more robust nano-bomb to counter British efforts.

Sam knew the war had already begun, with the world's top nanotechnologists pitched in battle across a landscape created by geometries only visible through an electron microscope. And Sam was well aware that as wars went, it was always the victor who had the right moves to outsmart its opponent.

What had happened with Rikard in Oslo could be the first step in making sure they get the advantage they desperately need.

Chapter 43

The shaping of Treeborne was progressing well. Aswa-da dipped in and out of his life and each time, he was pleased by what was shown. Treeborne used the tablet continuously throughout his days. The energies of the sandstone tool were intrinsically intertwined with Treeborne's DNA.

Without the tablet, Treeborne couldn't exist.

Aswa-da had watched as Treeborne secured his place at Washington and Lee College, just like his tactics with Dave Bateman proved he would. During Treeborne's four-year stint, Aswa-da observed his activities. Treeborne had read Politics. It was an obvious choice, given Treeborne's trinity of abilities. Persuasion. Manipulation. Trust. They were the very ingredients of politics.

But for Treeborne, politics would also ensure his endgame: control.

From the Earth second Aswa-da had given Treeborne the tablet, his understanding of its use and value to his being had gone through several changes. From being a tool to manipulate his friends to play with him, to being a channel to persuade those who'd caught Treeborne's eye to sleep with him, to eventually creating a state of mind in others, those with positions of authority, to trust Treeborne implicitly, to cross the line, and even commit crimes for him.

Aswa-da recognized that Treeborne was a narcissist. He believed he was always right and he expected to have complete control over every situation. For with control, every variable, every outcome, could be predicted and aligned to his exact wishes. So that nothing was left to chance.

His experiment with the human had been more successful than Aswa-da could ever have imagined. Treeborne used the tablet to get through the four years at college and gain his degree in Politics.

Aswa-da jumped into Treeborne's first year at Washington and Lee

College. On screen, Treeborne sat in a rather insalubrious night club. He lounged in an expensive, grey, check, double-breasted suit with wide shoulders that had been made famous by Richard Gere and various GQ models of the late 80's. All around him was curved, red velvet seating. Metal-topped tables strewn with bottles and glasses dotted in front of him, and to his left was a wide dancing area with multicolored lights embedded in the floor.

A typical nightclub of the 80's, thought Aswa-da. But he wondered why Treeborne was there instead of college as it was only mid-afternoon in May, 1987. As Aswa-da watched, the meaning became clearer.

Alongside Treeborne sat another man. He was tall and large-boned with a kindly round face that, Aswa-da was sure, usually carried a smile. Only, at that moment, the man was close to tears. His eyes were full of despair and deep shame. He looked totally broken.

Treeborne moved forward, confidence radiating from him, and he proceeded to leverage the situation the man had unexpectedly found himself in.

Aswa-da smirked and initiated a query on the man via the Observation Screen.

Professor Paul Chambers, President of Washington and Lee College.

Aswa-da nodded subconsciously as he immediately second-guessed what was in play.

Treeborne eyed Chambers with smug superiority as he sipped at his bourbon.

The club owner wandered over.

"Any more drinks, sir?"

Treeborne waved him away with a dismissive hand. The club owner returned back to the bar and shooed his staff into the back to give Treeborne the privacy he desired.

Aswa-da knew, just by one glance at the club owner, that fawning wasn't his modus operandi. He was a tough, callous and hard-hearted individual who did whatever he had to do to keep his business interests profitable. And therein lay the reason for his subservience toward Treeborne. He had obviously assisted the club owner in some way that had involved the use of his trinity of abilities. Aswa-da could hazard a guess that Treeborne had fixed a seemingly immutable problem that the club owner had been unable to resolve. Hence his preferential treatment of the young man.

With the staff and owner in the back and out of earshot, Treeborne turned back to Chambers, complacency oozing from his manner.

"So, we have a deal?"

Chambers remained motionless. He just stared with a mix of horror and revulsion at the photos splayed out on the table.

"Or would you like the College Board to see your holiday snaps?"

Treeborne smirked, picking up one of the photos.

"This one would make an interesting point for the debate on perpetual motion."

Treeborne laughed at Chambers' horrified face.

"I mean just who was pushing and who was pulling?"

The college president looked away, his hand went to his lips and he drew it down, shaking his head.

"I can't. I can't..." he muttered.

Treeborne stopped laughing and glared at Chambers with a stern glint.

"What can't you, President Chambers? Can't believe you had, what do they call it? A sex sandwich with two of your brightest, loveliest students?"

Treeborne watched Chambers shudder, repulsed.

"What did you do?" hissed president Chambers, turning to face Treeborne. Anger burned in his shameful eyes. "I've never done *anything* like this in my entire life!"

"That's amazing because from where I'm standing, those photos show you're quite the expert. I'm sure Jenny and Kyle would agree. Your talents are quite comprehensive and far-reaching!"

Treeborne grinned. He picked up and examined more of the graphic, lurid photos. Every time he looked at one, his eyebrow rose a little higher.

"You dirty, little, blackmailing bastard," whispered President Chambers, shaking with vitriol. He grabbed at some of the photos nearest to him and ripped them apart.

Treeborne revolved slowly to face him.

"For an educated man, President Chambers, you sure are doing some dumb things right now."

Aswa-da, watching in Kudamun, smiled. He was beginning to really relish the moments in Treeborne's life and the unique way Treeborne had taken hold of the opportunities afforded by the tablet.

Aswa-da twirled his finger and the dark walls of the club, replete with floor-to-ceiling mirrors, encased him. He observed as Treeborne decimated the college president with measured precision.

"Ok. This one..." Treeborne selected a photo, the contents of which caused even Aswa-da's eyes to open wider. In the shot, Jenny was on all fours on a massive bed. President Chambers was taking Jenny vigorously whilst Kyle pleasured Chambers with an equally energetic action. Chambers' face was a fusion of intense ecstasy and pain. By the bed, white lines of coke could clearly be seen, and vodka bottles littered the floor.

"…has to be for your Board. And this one…"

Treeborne picked up another photo that carried such an explicit shot Chambers heaved a little.

"…has to be for Mrs. Chambers. Don't you think? I'm sure she'll be completely fascinated to know what her husband gets up to." Treeborne placed an inflection toward the end of the sentence, his eyebrow raised with sardonic enthusiasm. "And with whom."

Chambers shook his head, his face turning a ghostly white. His Adam's apple wobbled. ."I think I'm going to be sick."

"Not on my suit. It's Armani," cried Treeborne, and he maneuvered out of Chambers' vomit range. Treeborne continued to speak as the college president, unable to keep it down, wretched onto the floor next to him. "I'm surprised, President Chambers, by your suddenly squeamish attitude. You are, after all, the star of each shot!"

Chambers took out a tissue from his inside pocket and wiped the residue of sick from his lips.

"As I said earlier," continued Treeborne, "this is a mutual magic trick. You make those God awful E's on my report disappear and I'll see that these photos do a vanishing trick of their own."

Chambers sat immobile, staring at the photos.

Aswa-da ran his eye across the photos, scanning their contents, and he smirked, proud of how corrupt and depraved his creation had become in a few short years of using the tablet. His experiment reflected a human's propensity to gravitate toward the dark. Their innate comfort to remain there was recognizable in their behavior and by their need to lust after the things that shadowed their souls.

Treeborne stared at the college president, who had started to turn the shocking photos over to make them face down. Treeborne knew he was trying to rub out the images in his mind.

"What do you say? Is it a deal, President Chambers?" Treeborne issued a sick smile. He was loving every second of the torment.

"For one year," answered Chambers, swallowing down his fury.

"No! Four years. Not one. Non-negotiable," snapped Treeborne.

"Four years?" yelled Chambers. "You can't really expect me to falsify your marks for the entire duration of the program? That's insane!"

Treeborne shrugged then nodded. "You're right," admitted Treeborne. "It's insane. It's also insane if I don't package up a complete set of these photos, including the ones you've just ripped up, and send them all to the College Board, your wife, the president of the golf club, and, not forgetting, your daughter, Millie. I'm sure she'd be interested to see her father's definition of extracurricular study!"

Chambers' face drained. He hung his head low. "Oh, dear God. No."

"And I'll be generous because I like you." Treeborne tapped Chambers' arm, smiling. "I'll even throw in a movie too."

Chambers' head snapped back up abruptly to face Treeborne.

"Movie?"

"Ah, yes. Didn't I tell you? I got a JVC video camera recently. I've been trying it out, finding decent subjects. You three proved to be subjects," Treeborne sneered. "If not decent."

Treeborne laughed and knocked back his bourbon.

The college president was virtually catatonic.

"So, I say again," said Treeborne. "And for the final time. Do we have ourselves a deal?"

Chambers held himself tight. He shivered and his ghostly white face had now descended into a hue of pale green. Treeborne considered that the man was close to hurling again.

Then he detected the faintest of nods from Chambers.

"Excellent. I'm pleased we've reached a level of understanding commensurate with my needs."

Treeborne reached across and gathered up the photos into a small pile. Then he pocketed them back into his briefcase. He stood up and glared hard at Chambers. Not a shred of a smile graced Treeborne face.

"If you welsh on the deal, or I see any other grade than A's and, of course, a small number of B's to allay suspicions, I will reveal everything. And I do mean everything. Understand? Comprende? Capisce?" said Treeborne with a new level of roughness, and he gripped Chambers' arm tight.

The college president looked down at the hand and then, slowly, he prized open Treeborne's fingers. Then, through gritted teeth, Chambers responded, "I understand."

Treeborne made to leave but Chambers tugged on his jacket. Treeborne clocked the confusion and anguish in the man's eyes.

"I've been a family man and loving husband all my life," said Chambers. "I've never, ever looked at another woman. And as for a man..." He stopped talking as he tried feebly to regain some composure. "Well, the idea is repulsive."

Treeborne stood impatiently. He glanced at his watch and waited for Chambers to center himself.

"So, Jonathan, what I want to know is, how did you do it? How did you turn me into that disgusting, drug-crazed pervert in those pictures? And how can I barely remember it even happening?"

Treeborne smiled broadly. His eyes hooded and his face held a veil of mystery.

"Oh, President Chambers, I'm very sorry. But I can't tell you. Didn't you know a magician never reveals his methods?"

Chapter 44

Kinley always knew it would go one of two ways. He'd come to realize his reason for living: to make sure it went his way. From the moment he had planned his deep cover assignment with Sam, he'd been devoted to bringing down Salim Al Douri. He'd accepted the risks, even welcomed them, if it meant he could pull the pin on Al Nadir's reign. He was so close to the conclusion he'd aimed for over the past four years. That was why he couldn't believe they wanted him out.

A communiqué had come through the innocuous gardening website that had been set up to convey heavily encrypted messages from Sir Justin Maide. Kinley stared at the software app's window, and watched as the powerful software Maide had supplied, pulled in the steganographic encrypted floral images and auto-decoded the message hidden in the binary changes of the image.

ABORT. LEAVE NOW.

Kinley really couldn't believe it. He was *so* close. He selected reluctantly the daffodil graphic, an action that denoted to Maide that Kinley had read the message. The screen instantly refreshed with new overviews of spring flowers. Kinley targeted the central flower, and ran the app again. The software stripped out the binary change hidden in image.

FAILURE TO ABORT WILL INVOKE SIGN OFF.

Kinley understood exactly what "sign-off" meant. MI6 wanted him to leave immediately, otherwise they would take him out. This was total shutdown. After everything he'd worked on, all the risks he'd taken, it had all been for nothing. He couldn't believe the decision that was being made. He recalled Operation Snowdrop. From that moment the state of his soul had been in question. The things he'd done turned his blood to ice. With Sabena and Salim, he'd been sucked into their world of total, uninhibited evil. And he hated himself. Hated every molecule that made up the body of Matt Kinley.

He'd been pleased he'd done the worst things under the moniker of Stuart Kingswood. The name Sabena had crafted with a nano-mask to shield his MI6 known face. Somehow, he'd been able to tell himself that Kingswood and not Kinley had done those things. It had helped his compartmentalization and just about kept his sanity.

But not his soul.

Ashton and Maide had bargained that off the moment they'd agreed to Snowdrop going ahead.

Angrily, Kinley clicked on the snowdrop to register his acknowledgement. How ironic Maide had chosen his flower as the confirmation icon for his agreement to total shutdown.

The screen refreshed again, and this time, a tulip took center stage. Kinley ran the software, and on the screen in the app window was his escape plan.

BOLLINGS. 15M. MX.

A plane had been prepped for him at Bollings Air Force Base. He had fifteen minutes. Maximum. No more time would be given.

He clicked on the bluebell to register his understanding. Maide responded with a final encrypted message in a pansy.

GOOD LUCK. GODSPEED.

Kinley swallowed down the irony of Justin's double standards and clicked on the snowdrop again to confirm acceptance of the conditions. He looked across the hall into the lounge, where he could see Lotte and Angela curled up peacefully together on the sofa. They were watching some kid's program. Angela felt Kinley's eyes on her and turned her head. She caught a look in his eyes for a second, lost and frightened. Usually, she would have just called out, but this time she didn't. Something was bothering her husband. Angela slipped off the sofa and went over to him in his study.

"Is everything alright, darling?"

Kinley flicked off the website and stood up to face Angela.

"We have to leave right now."

"Leave? What do you mean? Why do we have to leave?"

Her astonishment was etched across her worried face. Kinley didn't react with any sentimental additions.

"I can't explain. Just get your things."

Kinley barely looked at his wife as he grabbed his passport and briefcase.

Angela stared dumbstruck, unmoving.

"I'm sorry, but I'm not leaving until you tell me what the hell is happening."

He looked at Angela. Her face was flushed, and her eyes were rimmed with tears. But she was standing straight and strong. As always. Kinley gripped her hands together and held them. He looked directly into her eyes.

"Angela, I can't explain right now. But I need you to trust me. Can you do that for me?"

Angela felt the pressure of his hands around hers. Completely encasing. Protecting. She looked at her husband, his blue eyes full of determination. But she also saw alarm, as much as he tried to shield it from her.

"I need to know more, Matt."

"I know you do, darling." Kinley softened his attitude. "But I can't tell you now. I just need you to do what I tell you."

Angela stiffened instinctively. He had given blind instruction. Do it and don't ask questions. Her life had been full of such moments. One more didn't matter. She nodded her submission.

Kinley let go of her hands. "Thank you."

Angela registered the relief in his face. She turned back to Lotte, who was still caught up in her television program.

"I'd better sort her out. Some birthday, eh?"

"I promise you, darling, I'll make this up to you. And her."

Angela didn't answer. She was already back in the lounge, switching off the television and collecting a protesting daughter.

"Don't turn it off, Mummy. I'm watching!"

"You can see it later."

"Are we going somewhere, Mummy?" asked Lotte, aware of the sudden frenetic activity erupting around her.

"Yes. We're going on a little adventure. You'd like that, wouldn't you?"

Lotte nodded, and then called out, "I need to pee!"

She pulled away from Angela, slipped into the downstairs toilet, and shut the door before Angela could catch her.

Running after her, Angela called out nervously, "Be quick for Mummy, darling. Ok?"

Kinley watched the interaction between his wife and daughter, and then busied himself with wiping his hard drive. The demolish programme he'd invoked was impossible to piece together. Top forensic computing scientists had designed it to be unreconstructable. A swirling vortex like a hurricane appeared on his screen and sucked in all of Kinley's desktop icons, folders and files. And then the screen went blank. Kinley knew his drives had been completely fried. No resurrection programme, no matter how good, would ever bring back what he'd just killed.

"Finished, Mummy," called Lotte, emerging from the toilet.

"Good girl."

Angela snatched at her bag, and spoke to Lotte without looking at her daughter. Lotte was in the hallway, standing by a long window that framed the steps up to their house. Maybe Lotte had said something, but Kinley and Angela were both too caught up in readying themselves to leave to have heard.

Lotte reached up and opened the front door. Kinley heard the latch click, leapt up from his desk and ran into the hall. Angela, in the same moment, turned around and dived into the hall to pull Lotte away from the door.

But both parents were too late.

The door swung open, spurred on by a sudden gust of wind.

To their amazement, Lotte jumped up and down with sheer excitement as the caller proceeded up the steps to their home.

Chapter 45

In the Terrace, Sam came out of his reverie as the door opened and he returned to the present. Quentin Ludlow, the British Foreign Secretary, walked in and nodded at Sam.

"Good afternoon, Sam."

"Afternoon, sir," he replied.

Quentin pulled out the heavy wooden chair and puffed lightly. He eased himself into the gap between the table and chair and withdrew his documents from a leather folder. Quentin was forty-seven going on fifty-seven. Of medium height, with a tiny head and extremely rotund body, he reminded Sam of those double level gourmet Christmas puddings. His steel-blue eyes reflected his unforgiving life. Denied of love, they had a persistent flicker of coldness to them.

Quentin finished inspecting his documents. His eyes locked on the door as it opened. Sir Justin Maide strode into the room. His confident walk announced he was his own man. No one owned him. Or that's what he liked to imagine. He had started in the Service as a junior intelligence analyst after leaving Cambridge with a double first degree thirty-eight years ago. He had dedicated his entire life to The Firm. He'd never married, feeling that the burden of managing the ups and down of a continuous relationship would affect his performance. Instead, when the urge took him, he procured professional services. They served his unusual peccadilloes and somewhat perverted proclivities, and that suited him just fine.

"Afternoon, Quentin, Sam." Maide nodded in his colleagues' direction before taking his seat and scanning through the documents tabled for the meeting.

Quentin looked up and glanced momentarily in Maide's direction. Maide issued a swift almost imperceptible nod. Sam noticed the gesture from the corner of his eye. So much of his life he'd relied on picking up and interpreting non-verbal communication. He'd analyzed the nod before he knew even what he was doing. Was it an acknowledgement, an affirmation or an agreement? Or perhaps, an involuntary head movement with no purpose? Before Sam could dwell further, Quentin turned and spoke to him.

"How are we today? I heard you were a little off last night."

Quentin eyed Sam's reaction. Sam shuffled in his chair with more than a little discomfort. He didn't like Quentin's insinuation. For an agent, the word "off" had a deeper meaning. It was used to cast judgement on ability. Sam pulled himself inwards, rested his elbows on the table and closed in on Quentin, determined to change his line of thinking.

"Hardly 'off,' Quentin. I just needed the love of a good woman."

"Ellie got her welcome home treat then!"

Maide sniggered.

Sam nodded. Naturally, he had triggered the somewhat salacious response to shift focus from questions on his capability. Sam knew he could control a situation just by simple mind games. Maide and Quentin were no different to anyone else. Despite their training, mention sex and the guards come down momentarily. Previous topics get overlooked in favor of sultry images. All at once, the meeting's powerbase shifted. Sam was aware that the uptight, secretive and often dangerous nature of their lives worked well with this approach. The inherent need to think of something fun and free was always on the periphery of their unconsciousness, waiting for a trigger to turn it into real thought. All Sam had to do was supply the trigger.

"You must have been starving last night after your trip back from Oslo. I hear the food's not great over there. But I believe you ate pretty well on your return."

At first, Sam wasn't sure what he'd just heard from Maide's lips.

"Sorry?" said Sam sharply.

"I think what he's saying, Sam, is that you must have been hungry after your trip. I hope your hunger was suitably sated?" asked Quentin smirking as he swiped a sideways glance at Maide.

"And it helped you build up that stamina of yours," added Maide.

Sam looked from Quentin to Maide. Their faces held wry sneers and they shared knowing glances between each other. Sam held his initial smile, but inside, he raged. What they'd said and how they'd said it could only mean one thing.

They had surveillance on him.

Sam seethed, remembering yesterday evening's reunion with Ellie.

How dare they spy on me!

Sam's training kicked in and he bit down on the anger coursing through him. He channeled his anger into something more beneficial. Like finding out why.

Sam rolled through options in his mind. Was it because he'd questioned Maide over Kinley being pulled? Surely not. They'd had heated arguments before with no such repercussions. Sam shifted in his chair as he tried to recall anything else.

Then he remembered the stark and shattering memory of the events of that morning. Ellie screaming, him believing she was in danger, running in with his gun and telling her his true identity. They must have been watching. They must have seen.

Now he was caught in a game where the rules were unknown. He'd broken the code of silence. Such an action would have consequences he'd have to face. But for now, he could only play their game and see where it would lead him.

"Oh, yeah. My hunger certainly was sated! I feasted well. And you *know* I have a big appetite," replied Sam. The smile was hard on his face. His jaw muscles ached from the forced joviality.

The door opened and Dudley Gibbs, Head of MI5, with Paul Weaver, Home Secretary, appeared in the doorway. Gibbs, a dark hulk of a man, ex-army general and an outstanding prop forward in Rugby during his time at Oxford, marched inside. He was talking to Weaver, a tall, bony gent with severe brown eyes, thinly drawn lips and a pale, almost anemic complexion. They took their seats alongside each other at the table and continued speaking, too engrossed in their discussion to recognize the friction in the room between Sam, Maide and Quentin.

In a flash of eyes flicking back and forth, Sam noticed Quentin glancing at Maide. Both carried surreptitious sneers. They had heard Sam's emphasis on 'know'. The message had gotten through.

Sam realized that this was one situation where he couldn't shift the powerbase with just a crude psychological trigger.

Chapter 46

Manipulation of a college president was only the beginning.

Aswa-da always intended Treeborne to achieve a greater goal. He knew it was audacious, but Aswa-da didn't doubt his subject's capacity to achieve what he sought.

Aswa-da delved into Treeborne's life. He'd successfully graduated in Politics from Washington and Lee. His love of the subject matter transcended his studies. Despite the fact he didn't actually study much for anything, Aswa-da recognized in Treeborne a deep thirst for power. A political career was the route to satisfying that thirst.

Treeborne naturally swayed towards Republican values and hated his parents being staunch Democrats. He joined the Republican Party and became a volunteer, supporting them in the campaigns whilst at college, including a presidential election in '89.

Aswa-da, at first, was concerned by Treeborne's blatant use of his trinity of abilities. He wasn't even trying to hide his capabilities. Even the Republican candidate's campaign office recognized his uncanny abilities of manipulation and persuasion.

The chief of staff at the campaign office even said, "People seem to trust you, JD. That's quite something. Trust is hard to earn in anyone. But people naturally believe you. I don't know whether you're an angel or the very devil himself. But right now, I don't care. We're winning in the polls and that's all that matters. Keep doing what you do and there will be a place for you here."

Treeborne stared at the chief of staff. Questioning eyes bore into him. "I could stand for Congress, you mean?"

The chief of staff nodded. "If you can get enough votes behind you to put your name forward, and I'm sure, given what I've already seen of your abilities, that'll be a walk in the park for you. Then yeah, you could stand. I'd back you and I know many more would do the same."

Treeborne smiled. "I'd really love to do that. I could be one hell of a congressman. You know that."

"I most certainly do, JD. I most certainly do."

The chief of staff walked away to handle arrangements for the after-election party, leaving Treeborne to ponder on how quickly he could make it to the House of Representatives.

Aswa-da pushed forward using his shallow elliptical motion and years sped by. Aswa-da watched Treeborne graduate with an MBA from George Mason University in '91. Aswa-da was sure Treeborne had employed similar techniques he'd used on the previous college president. Aswa-da didn't need to see Treeborne's continued descent into depravity. It was enough to know that his descent had picked up in velocity and had a momentum of its own.

Treeborne was dark to the core of his being.

Aswa-da smiled as his subject became ever more obsessed with power and control. Treeborne's activities with the local Republican office integrated completely into his life. He was taken on as a staffer, having been an intern during his MBA.

The chief of staff who'd recognized his abilities, several years earlier, put Treeborne in charge of communications. Whatever Treeborne wrote, any speech, any collateral, seemed to generate incredible results. From a political perspective, Treeborne had the Midas touch, flipping voters and bringing home the Republican vote in a big way. His 10th Congressional District included some of the wealthiest and most educated in Virginia, and remained in Republican hands for many decades.

"Bleeding-heart liberals should be strung up," Treeborne said at one of his party meetings. His compatriots laughed. "We need zero tolerance on everything that is damaging to our society. Anything that changes this glorious country needs to be eradicated."

"True words," muttered the party faithful.

Aswa-da smirked, enjoying Treeborne's engagements. He could see his subject had absolute control of the meeting, whipping up his followers into a seething mass of hate and bigotry.

Aswa-da pushed forward toward the end of the 1990's on Earth. On the screen was a tree-lined street flanked by large houses and immaculate lawns with luxurious cars in all the driveways. Across the street ran banners that read, 'Treeborne for Congress'. On those immaculate lawns stood boards stating, 'Treeborne Delivers'. And on those expensive cars, bumper stickers displayed, 'Trust in Treeborne'.

Inside the campaign office, Treeborne wandered around the room. A sea of bright, young volunteers and interns busily focused on phones and computer screens. Aswa-da was aware that every single face was attractive. Some of the boys and girls giving their all for Treeborne were downright beautiful. He was sure Treeborne had handpicked each one.

The chief of staff who'd always been a supporter of Treeborne remained with him in his campaign. He stood next to a young woman, a twenty-something, stunning specimen who had caught Treeborne's eye. She was on the phone and talking eagerly about Treeborne's manifesto, his values, and what he could do for the recipient of the call when he got to Congress.

She glanced up, blue eyes sparkling, at Treeborne as she realized he was standing over her, watching intently. She smiled warmly and continued her discourse.

Treeborne turned away and grabbed his chief of staff's elbow. "The new girl. Who is she?"

"That's Nancy Reynolds. He father owns Reynolds Real Estate. He's a relatively good-sized donator to the cause too. Why?" said the chief of staff. But by his smirk, Aswa-da knew he was well aware of Treeborne's carnal obsessions.

"I'd like to see her later. Her abilities on the phone, her level of persuasion, it can't be ignored. I think she could benefit from some personal mentoring. See to it."

Treeborne's chief of staff grinned and nodded. "Take it as done, JD."

Aswa-da skipped forward in time to polling day. He looked at the live display in the campaign office. Treeborne had slaughtered his opposition by a massive majority. The straw boaters flew into the air as Treeborne was announced Congressman for the 10th Congressional District of Virginia.

Treeborne smiled across the room and patted the air.

"Thank you. Thank you," he bellowed, confidence radiating from every pore. "Tonight signifies a turning point for us all, not least myself." Treeborne smiled smugly as the room cheered and howled with joy. "But seriously, folks, you've supported me. You've got me to this great moment, and I'll see to it that everything you want and believe in will be made real. I will ensure that the values of this great country are upheld and that we will return to a time where we can hold our heads up high. Proud of our country. Proud of our heritage. Proud to be American. So help me God."

The room descended into a crazy fervor on every word that fell from Treeborne's lips.

Aswa-da laughed. If this was a book, he thought, he couldn't have written Treeborne's chapter better himself. Developments had taken a momentum of their own. Skipping forward, Aswa-da observed the next decade or so of Treeborne's life. He served three two-year terms as Congressman. He'd created a strong name for himself in DC and found favor with many influential individuals, all of whom he eventually managed to control through his unique form of persuasion and manipulation.

During that time, Aswa-da noticed Treeborne had acquired a wife. She was born of old money. Respectable. Immaculate. Beautiful. The expected combination to secure Treeborne's continued political ascendency.

In a hyper-exclusive, not-even-on-the-map club in DC, one of his billionaire industrialist friends turned to him. Knocking back a slug of bourbon and tearing his drunken eyes away from the nearly nude waitresses serving the dark, rose-hued room, he pulled Treeborne over to him.

"You know what, JD? You should run for Senate. It would be a breeze. I'd back you."

Treeborne had already decided to make this change. But he was pleased his powerful friends had recognized his new potential.

Aswa-da moved forward in time to 2004 and Treeborne's last term as Congressman. It was the year he prepared to make the leap to the Senate. New backers came in their droves. Fundraiser events poured funds into the coffers of the campaign office. People of power believed in Treeborne. White- and blue-collar workers believed in Treeborne. Mums, kids and teenagers believed in Treeborne.

They trusted him.

His message, 'Trust in Treeborne', became his political mantra. He was a man who knew instinctively what people wanted and what they needed, and he always delivered.

The trinity of abilities powered his success. In 2006, as Aswa-da shot forward, Treeborne took the crown to be Senator of Virginia. He served one stunning six-year term. Aswa-da could see his positioning was veering toward his end goal. Treeborne was in the fifth year of his term when he cozied up with the governor, and made his play.

"I'm going to run for the presidency. You're going back me, aren't you, George?" Treeborne eyed his friend, searching deep into his soul. "I mean, we've been mates for a long time. We've done a lot together, haven't we?"

Treeborne's eyebrow rose. The governor sitting next to him shifted his significant bulk with more than a little discomfort.

"Yeah. Yeah. We sure have," he replied. The governor's craggy, charming face grew pensive and his eyes hooded as he recalled events he'd rather forget.

"Good times, eh? And more good times to come. Especially if I get in the White House. We can really rock and roll then. So what do you say? You're behind me?"

Treeborne's beady hawk eyes narrowed, searching for confirmation. His hand slipped into his pocket to touch the tablet.

Aswa-da realized that Treeborne had been able to perform his trinity of abilities for many years without much contact with the tablet. As he'd always believed, its powers were now intrinsically part of Treeborne's internal makeup. The powerful resonating energies had intertwined within the nucleotides making up his DNA structural base. They had buried into the genes and chromosomes of each cell in his body.

He was, therefore, surprised by Treeborne's need to revert back to using the tablet manually. Aswa-da pulled himself into the moment. In an instant, he was standing in front of Treeborne and his friend, Governor George Sanderson. Aswa-da examined the governor. He was a colossal guy, very handsome in a rugged way, with brown eyes that hid a slew of secrets.

The man was staring hard at Treeborne but his body language wasn't responding in the correct way. Obviously, he was a powerful man and someone who had conviction and belief. Whatever he'd done in his past, Sanderson was now trying to distance himself from things that could be regarded as unsavory.

He wasn't falling into Treeborne's powers. Treeborne seemed to be holding back. Sanderson was a close friend. Perhaps Treeborne couldn't break him the way he'd broken all his other 'friends'.

Aswa-da was intrigued. How far would Treeborne go? Although he knew the outcome, it was how Treeborne reached it that was important. It confirmed his total immersion into the tablet's powers and Aswa-da's subsequent control of him.

As Aswa-da watched, Treeborne played his ace.

"Of course you are. You've no option. Have you? I mean, that time we…What was she? Fifteen? Fourteen?"

Sanderson swung a look at Treeborne. His handsome face began to crumble. His mouth turned down into a sad scowl displaying hatred of himself. His eyes flickered with disgrace. His huge shoulders slumped forward.

"She said she was eighteen," said Sanderson, sotto voce, so only Treeborne could hear.

"Yeah. Like you really believed her," responded Treeborne, digging into Sanderson's humiliation and shame. "You barely asked the question before you-"

"Yeah. Yeah. I know."

"So, anyway, that's the past. But if we ever want to walk down memory lane, well, it's all here at the press of a button." Treeborne grabbed his phone, invoked his movie app and ran it on mute. He placed it on the table in front of them.

Sanderson's face bled of color. A white mask took over him as his eyes glued to the activities on screen. His mouth pulled back into a stern line and he glared at Treeborne.

"You're supposed to be my friend," Sanderson hissed.

"Yep. I am. The police will never see this and you'll never be charged with statutory rape. So we're all good, aren't we? And you'll back me for the presidency, won't you? You know having me in those hallowed halls will make a massive difference for you. Hell, I'm going to make the rest of your life a party!"

Treeborne bashed his friend on the back with more force than just a friendly hit of comradeship. Sanderson fell forward onto the table and faced the video still running on Treeborne's phone, displaying his performance in explicit detail.

"Yeah. I'll back you," muttered Sanderson. Swallowing down his abhorrence, he pulled himself back onto the seat.

"Good move. The rest of your life as a party is so much better than it being in a prison cell!"

Treeborne grinned. He lent forward and took his phone, switching off the movie app. Then he pocketed it again.

Aswa-da nodded. Treeborne had stepped right over the line. Friends were just there to be used and abused. Loyalty was to be leveraged.

His transformation was complete. Treeborne's soul was completely opaque.

Aswa-da pushed forward to 2013 whilst immersed in the Observation Screen. Treeborne had just been inaugurated as the 44th President of the United States of America. Aswa-da walked with him as he marched up the corridor to the Oval Office.

Treeborne stepped behind the grand desk, staring out at his people.

"Well, guys, we've done it. Let's get this party started!"

The room laughed hard at Treeborne's joke. But little did they know, thought Aswa-da, that the last laugh would be on them.

And the rest of humanity.

Chapter 47

The man Lotte had seen continued up the steps. In his hands was a large cardboard box. His uniform clearly displayed his FedEx courier identity. Kinley and Angela both read the man's badge, and breathed a simultaneous sigh of relief.

"Dr. Kinley?" questioned the courier, looking from husband to the wife. In his job, suggesting the Dr. in question was a man was tantamount to discrimination. He'd heard of colleagues being almost sued for just such a suggestion. He wasn't about to make the same mistake.

"Yes," answered Kinley quickly, his face anxious and very tense.

"I've a delivery for you."

"From?" asked Kinley with uncharacteristic abruptness, and he blocked the courier's entry to the hall.

"The Antique Toy Store, Cambridge, Massachusetts," stated the courier, reading from the label.

"Lotte's doll house," exclaimed Angela.

She regretted her outburst as her daughter jumped up and down screaming, "My present! My present. Open it. Open it!"

The courier held out the box awkwardly and muttered, "Could someone take this? I've got a dozen more deliveries before lunch, and I ain't gonna get them done standing on this doorstep."

Kinley grabbed the box from the courier and maneuvered back from the front door into the hall. Amid the persistent calls from Lotte to open it, Kinley looked at his watch and then at his daughter. He shook his head.

"We haven't got time for this."

But his daughter's smiling face, full of anticipation and blissfully ignorant to the mad dash they were soon going to have to make to stay alive, made him tear open the box.

Lotte cried out, "Show me, Daddy."

Pulling back the flaps of the box, Kinley disturbed a thin layer of dust. He wiped it away and reached inside. As he pulled out the contents, Angela could see the Victorian doll house Kinley had ordered for their daughter's birthday. She smiled at her husband as he placed the doll house on the hall table.

Lotte was now squealing with delight.

"I love it! Let me play with it!"

Kinley touched the toy delicately. He slid his hand down the roof, searching for the catch that would release the front and open the house. He knew they had no time for indulgence of the kind he was engaging in, but he felt sorry for Lotte and her birthday celebrations that would, for now, have to be put on hold. Finding the catch, Kinley flicked it and the front section swung out on its hinges.

"There you are, darling. That's yours. But you can't play with it until Sunday, for that's when your birthday is," explained Angela in a sympathetic but firm voice. She had already realized that the doll house, along with everything else they owned, would have to be left behind. Kinley nodded thanks to his wife for skillfully managing Lotte's emotions.

"We've really got to get going,"

Kinley's tone touched with gentle finality. Angela understood, and grabbed hold of Lotte and her bag. Kinley dropped his hand down to collect his briefcase, and noticed a thin veneer of grey dust across the tips of his fingers.

"They could have cleaned it before sending it," muttered Kinley, almost to himself, and he patted the dust away.

Subconsciously, he checked his hands again, but the dust was still there. As he watched, the few specks on his fingertips seemed to be spreading over his hands. He dropped his briefcase and rubbed nervously against his thighs. But the dust didn't come off. Kinley watched, terrified and fascinated, as the dust moved up to his wrists of its own accord. Frantic to be clean, he rubbed furiously against his jacket, trousers, and finally, the wall. The dust carried on oblivious, working its way up Kinley's arm.

Angela watched his manic behavior. "Darling, what's wrong?"

Kinley ripped open his shirt and saw the grey dust creeping across his shoulders and chest. He looked down, staring deep into the grey that had taken over his torso. It was then that he saw something glittery move quickly within the dust.

"The dust," screamed Kinley, shaking. "There's *something* in the dust."

Chapter 48

"This is going to put us back where we belong. Back on top. Screwing the world again. God, I love that position. Wow-ee, boy! Al Nadir won't know what's hit 'em. And that fucking Chinese president had better show me some decent manners next time we meet."

The US president's words were the culmination of an experiment that had taken over his life. He had followed each test with the diligence of an attentive parent. From the moment his CSO had called, Treeborne had taken a special interest in his new technology. The CSO had been sworn to secrecy as to where the technology had originated. Even if he had revealed it came from the president, no one would have believed him. The CSO didn't even believe it himself and he'd heard the contents of the Dictaphone with his own ears.

The president knew this, but just to make sure the CSO's lips stayed shut, Treeborne put two SS officers on his detail. They shadowed the CSO. Every move he made, they monitored, and once the tests were successful and Project David (as the weapons program was called) had built its own internal momentum, the CSO was removed and disposed of swiftly in the traditional fashion.

No one seemed too concerned by the disappearance of the president's CSO. A resignation letter had been found stating "a need for change," and that was the end of it. Everyone was whipped up in the implications of the new weapon and what it meant for the USA.

After his profound statement, the president looked at Frank Weitz, his defense secretary, who stood next to him for the final test demonstration. Weitz smiled but maintained his mute stance. The two of them stood in silence at the secret location in Blacksburg in Virginia, some four hours away from DC, and watched as a military scientist brought a container with a miniscule deposit of the strange, stretchable compound the president had found in the box.

The scientist took out the pen and aimed it at the small dot in the container. The military scientist nodded to the president, defense secretary and assembled four-star generals, and ran at speed, away from the container. The president and Weitz were at a distance from the container but both could still see the bright flash shining like the birth of a new star for a second in the container.

Within thirty seconds, the ground beneath them shook as if an earthquake happened nearby, and the air around them electrified and sparked, as a charge ripped through the upper atmosphere. The president smiled smugly. He knew what was coming. He turned sideways to watch Weitz's reaction. But his defense secretary remained motionless.

The breeze stilled and a whisper of expectancy wafted through the air, touching their skin. Weitz shivered but held his ground. He stared at the container. As he watched, the reality around him splintered, twisted and fragmented.

"What the hell?" started the defense secretary, stepping back instinctively.

"Don't worry, Frank. It's all part of the demo."

Treeborne barely flinched as the air above the container exploded. A veil of silvery particles spread out across his field of view. The particles reflected bits of ground and sky, and melded both together in a crazy kaleidoscope of shattered color.

"What is this? What am I seeing here?" asked Weitz.

"Our future, Frank. Our beautiful new future," answered Treeborne, smiling.

The particles hung in the air, suspended in the fabric of space-time for a few seconds. Amongst the fragments of sky and ground, the president thought he could see a facet of utter darkness. Deep and cold like the night sky. And in these dark fragments something grew. Treeborne could feel it, an angry storm gathering, its energies building rapidly, an invisible force of immense power.

Around the container, the ground shook violently. The president, defense secretary and small clique of generals and military scientists jumped in unison as a massive clap of thunder broke in the sky above them. It took Treeborne a few seconds of listening before he realized that the thunder wasn't just above them; it was all around them and beneath them. The Earth was howling, a tortured victim screaming out in abject pain.

Weitz listened and shivered. He'd never heard thunder like it before. Although it was just a sound, it possessed a physical connection that touched him. The connection pulled him in. It forced him to feel compassion, to understand injustice, and to know the hurt that his country had caused. Tears pricked his eyes and he refused to wipe them away.

The president watched Weitz's eyes. Such a weak man, he thought. How could he possibly cry at a time when America's new dominance beckoned?

The last thunder strike shrieked, and a huge wave rippled out from the center of the container, catching fragmented particles in its path. On contact with the wave, the particles obliterated, leaving a deep crater where the container had been.

Reality was back to normal. The sky was above. The ground was below. Nothing remained shattered. Except Frank Weitz's mind.

He slowly turned to the president, visibly shaking. His bravado had stripped away as the wave stopped a meter short of him. Visions of his own annihilation brought out a scared humility in him.

"So, Frank, what d'ya say? Now's the time to renegotiate that Chinese loan. Say around zero per cent. What d'ya think?"

Weitz looked out at the blast site, the scorched Earth still strewn with tiny flames flickering in the gentle breeze, and he feared for their "beautiful future."

Chapter 49

Aswa-da recalled the moment two Earth weeks before when he'd left the quantum bomb in Treeborne's private lounge. The box he'd created was simple. It was a brown box, ordinary looking, almost like a shoe box. But the absence of anything other than the three words made it intriguing.

At first, Aswa-da had written 'FOR SUCCESS'. But then he realized it wasn't sufficient. It wasn't anyone's success, but Treeborne's. Aswa-da created the box again and added a personal touch. 'FOR YOUR SUCCESS' was targeted directly to hit Treeborne's psyche.

It was a personal signal that salvation was close.

With the quantum compound bomb inside the box, Aswa-da had shimmered into Treeborne's lounge.

Shimmering was the means of transportation all Kudamaz elders had. It was an ability given to the Kudamaz elders by the Ancient Ones, and involved eleventh-dimensional space-time. Kudamaz elders had only to think of a location, where they wanted to be, then focus their minds and they'd shimmer to that place.

Aswa-da visualized Treeborne's lounge and shimmered into it. Treeborne hadn't returned and Aswa-da solidified into Earth's reality plane completely. He placed the box on the sofa then moved away.

Voices came up quickly outside the door. Aswa-da stepped zero-point-one degrees out of Earth reality and watched Treeborne shout at his private secretary, swearing at the man's incompetence. Then the president lurched himself towards a large bottle of bourbon. Treeborne sat down on the sofa. Aswa-da watched as Treeborne jumped a little, and went for his mobile, and then stopped and stared at the box.

Then Treeborne leant forward and picked up the box. Aswa-da snuck in close to examine his expression, and his long robe touched Treeborne's ear.

Being zero-point-one degree out of Earth's reality plane, Treeborne shouldn't have discerned Aswa-da's movement, but Treeborne turned directly in Aswa-da's direction. On Treeborne's face was complete puzzlement as he tried to figure out what he'd felt.

Watching Treeborne, Aswa-da realized he had to be careful. The man had been changed, albeit slightly, but nevertheless, still changed. He wasn't a simple human anymore. He was attuned to a Kudamaz resonance within the sandstone tablet. Clearly, the change to his DNA had made Treeborne a little more sensitive to Kudamaz encounters, even if those encounters were hidden by being a little out of Earth's reality.

Treeborne sat on the sofa, playing with the contents of the box. Aswa-da was fascinated by his behavior. He observed as Treeborne prodded and pulled at the compound and brought the pen over to touch it.

Better give the idiot some guidance, thought Aswa-da. He touched Treeborne's head and delivered his instructions.

"Pick up the Dictaphone, switch it on, listen to me and repeat it directly."

Aswa-da delivered his knowledge bank packet on how the quantum bomb worked directly to Treeborne, using his mind and mouth as a device to transmit the knowledge to the Dictaphone.

Aswa-da knew that such an engagement would weaken Treeborne greatly. After the president gave the Dictaphone to his CSO, Aswa-da placed Treeborne into a deep and rejuvenating sleep.

Caught up in Treeborne's past, Aswa-da failed to realize when something incredible was happening in his future. He pushed forward to March 22, 2017, the live Earth date, to Blacksburg, Virginia in the US. The scene on the Observation Screen showed Treeborne standing in a field with Defense Secretary Frank Weitz and several military generals.

The field in front of them was vast. Aswa-da watched someone, presumably a military scientist, as he could see his uniform beneath the white coat, stride out into the field holding a transparent container. Inside, he saw a gray small lump of something that he knew to be the quantum compound bomb. Aswa-da twirled his finger and the Observation Room was overwritten with a damp field and greying skies.

Next to him stood the military scientist. He placed the transparent container with the quantum compound bomb onto a high pedestal. Then he stepped away and took out the pen that formed the other half of the bomb's system. The scientist stepped back further as he seemed to know what the effects would be.

Tentatively, he stuck out his hand and aimed the pen at the non-descript gray lump. Inside the gray lump, a light built fast. The scientist nodded and ran away at speed as a bright flash leapt out of the container. Aswa-da marveled at the magnificence of the light. It shone brighter than Earth's sun as the curled-up quantum energies rushed forth into linking mechanism and connected with the reality plane. Aswa-da knew the energies were everywhere at the quantum level. The spark of light was just the initial reaction. It was the unleashing of the energies through the quantum world into the universal reality plane that created the electrified feeling in the atmosphere and made the ground shake.

These energies were part of the makeup of the Earth and should not have been unleashed. Aswa-da smirked. Or that's what the Order of Kudamun demanded.

But he never was one to heed many rules.

Aswa-da watched as the tug of war between the quantum and real worlds resulted in reality fragmenting and splintering, and the Earth howled in pain at this forbidden desecration. Aswa-da could feel the energies building up into a massive crescendo. He smiled, watching the energies as they flooded in a wave from the small gray lump and out across the field in front of Treeborne, Weitz and the generals. The instant the wave touched the reality fragments, it exploded, leaving a jagged crater several meters in diameter.

Aswa-da walked over to Treeborne and looked into his eyes. Hubris and arrogance shone within. He could see the blood-thirsty dominance that radiated through the president. Aswa-da turned to take in the other onlookers with Treeborne. Weitz was a man truly terrified by what he had witnessed. The generals were dumbfounded but grateful. Aswa-da recognized that they knew the power the US now had with the quantum compound bomb.

A unanimous thought rumbled through all the generals' minds and Aswa-da could see it glowing in their rabid eyes.

Soon they would be watching Al Nadir's final days.

Chapter 50

At the Terrace, the banter and innuendo between 'friends' instantly stopped as Richard Ashton, UK Prime Minister, walked into the room. The five men rose to their feet as a sign of respect. The PM patted the air and they returned to their seats.

Ashton scanned the room, detecting a glimmer of tension, and then seated himself at the top of the table.

Intelligent and street-smart, Ashton was also immoral and unscrupulous. The heart of his powerbase was a deep and intricate web of surveillance that infiltrated and investigated everyone around him. That intelligence was then analyzed, and anyone deemed to be a potential threat to him politically or personally was catalogued and kept on hold. Every vice, every secret, every skeleton in the closet of his colleagues, he knew about it. And he used this knowledge when his colleagues became "problematic." Even the media were bullied by his security team to portray him as the ultimate family man, a man balancing the weight of a nation against the pressures of fatherhood. It was an image that made him more vulnerable, and therefore, more accessible to his public. The reality was somewhat different.

Ashton was insatiable, bedding anyone who attracted him. If his bedfellows had thoughts of Sunday paper kiss-and-tell exposes, these ideas were quickly banished, as each one was advised in brutal terms of the consequences of such exposure. So far, none had put the threats to the test.

Chapter 51

Angela Kinley stared at her husband's chest, and then screamed. It was an involuntary reaction. Lotte, on seeing her father's strange grey skin, also started to scream. Angela stopped her outburst immediately and put on a calm voice to comfort her child.

"Lotte, darling, it's ok. Everything's going to be ok."

There was no term of reference for what she was witnessing. No description could explain why grey, household dust had taken over her husband's body. Angela held Lotte close, stroking her hair until the little girl's cries subsided.

"Can you see them?" yelled Kinley, pointing at his body. "Do you see them moving? They're like silver fish. Oh God, Angie. You've got to get them off me."

"I...I don't know what to do. Tell me what to do."

Kinley's mind flipped through possibilities. They had to be some kind of nano-bot, something new Al Nadir hadn't told him about. He knew Sabena would be behind it. Somehow, they must have discovered he was still with MI6. That he hadn't turned at all. That he'd been playing them all this time. He'd read nothing in their faces. He'd only seen Salim a few days before. He'd given nothing away. How long had they known - days, weeks, months? Kinley didn't think it had been any more than a week or so.

In her bed last weekend, Sabena had been her usual nymphomaniac self, full to the brim with her sadistic proclivities, and as per his alter ego Kingswood, he'd obliged her every sick desire and wanton need. Ever since Snowdrop started, her and Kinley had been lovers, if one could call it love. Kinley preferred to regard it as a union of requirement. Operation Snowdrop's objective was to get deep undercover within the terrorist collective, and he'd used Sabena as the 'in' to infiltrate Al Nadir. That's why he had to compartmentalize. Knowing that the hands and lips that touched his innocent, beautiful wife and child had also touched Sabena, and sometimes others in Al Nadir's inner circle, including Salim. The very thought, had he not conditioned his mind completely, could have tipped him over the edge.

Operation Snowdrop had been hailed as a considerable success by the three people who knew about the mission. They'd used the intelligence he'd secured and the incredible access he had into Salim's inner circle to turn parts of Al Nadir's financial castle to rubble. The intel agencies around the world had worked together wiping one hundred billion dollars off Al Nadir's financial capability books.

Only three other people knew of his involvement in Snowdrop: Maide, Ashton and Sam, and all had signed a vow of silence. That had proved necessary as Snowdrop's by product had been innocent deaths by the bucketload. Al Nadir had devised a unique explosive adhesive connected to nano RFIDs embedded within the adhesive mix. They'd had all the posters on the trains replaced with the new adhesive. The bombs behind the posters all simultaneously detonated at eleven hundred hours on June 28, 2013.

On that day, five thousand, eight hundred and twenty people died.

During the four years Kinley had obliterated the lives of tens of thousands.

But he'd also saved tens of millions.

That's the only way he slept at night. Knowing he was still saving lives.

As he looked down at the dust creeping up his body he knew that this was his judgement day.

He'd joked with Sam before Operation Snowdrop started that the job could be the death of him. Now he knew it wasn't a joke.

Kinley pushed back the past and focused.

"Get water! Throw it over me." If they had the same nano-electronics as the previous nano-bomb perhaps he could try and short-circuit them.

Angela let go of Lotte's hand, ran to the kitchen, grabbed a jug, filled it with water and returned to the hallway where she hurled the water over her husband.

"Argh! It's burning!" screamed Kinley, as the water hit the dust. But instead of seeping into his body, the water fizzed to steam. "I'm burning up, Angie. You've got do something. God, you've got to!"

Kinley pleaded to his wife, but Angela was mesmerized by the metamorphosis taking place across her husband's torso. The dust had hardened into a metallic coating.

"Angie, my arms, they feel strange."

Kinley looked down. Both arms, which had been covered in dust, were now shiny silver.

"Oh, God. What's happening? Angie, I'm scared. Angie, help me."

This reaction of a nano-bomb was nothing like he'd ever seen before. Al Nadir had kept this very secret. With the last iteration of the nano-bomb upgraded four weeks ago, Stein-Muller had to have been working on this for a month.

He watched as Angela looked around the hall, trying to find something to help her husband.

She picked up an umbrella. Then a cordless phone. What could she use?

She flicked her head back and forth, dizzy, confused and terrified.

"Mummy! What's wrong with daddy? No, no, Mummy. Mummy, no. No!"

Lotte's loud, penetrating insistence forced Angela to stop her examination of the hall and look back at him. As she stared at Kinley, the sight that greeted her brought out a scream louder than Kinley ever believed she could possibly make.

Chapter 52

Richard Ashton took in his assembled colleagues. Dudley Gibbs looked tired. Paul Weaver looked stunned. Sir Justin Maide looked pensive. Quentin Ludlow looked smug. Dr. Sam Noor looked deeply pissed off. Something was clearly up.

"Good afternoon, gentlemen. What do we have today?"

Ashton glanced through the agenda.

"Al Nadir, and it's not good," replied Maide with solid force, jumping ahead of Gibbs, who scowled.

Ashton glared, his eyes screaming 'When is it ever?'

"Our operations in Oslo proved positive," continued Maide. "Two items of note. The package taken from Rikard by Dr. Noor has been analyzed to be some kind of Ribonucleic Acid (RNA) synaptic inhibitor. Analysis is still on-going. We've also discovered unequivocally that Al Nadir have established a new cell in the UK."

Weaver stared, horrified. "Another one? Oh, good God. Can't we keep our damn borders protected?"

"These are Brits, Home Secretary. No illegal immigrants here," said Gibbs.

Ashton scowled at the comment. He hated that the terrorists were British.

"Gibbs, what the hell is happening with your people?" asked Ashton.

Maide shuffled but knew he couldn't take the lead. This was Five's jurisdiction.

"Prime Minister, we have confirmed a convergence of activity, meetings, money movements, acquisitions and, of course, the usual chatter. Looks like there's a storm brewing. With the summit approaching, we need to be proactive."

Maide leapt in. "Right now, our people are pouring through transcripts of

Rikard's diatribe before he blew."

"Have you identified the cell's location?" Ashton directed the question to Gibbs, who shook his head.

"No, Prime Minister, not exactly. However, we know it's somewhere in Cambridgeshire."

Ashton turned his head sharply to Maide.

"Didn't you learn anything more concrete from Rikard?" shouted the PM.

"Sir, with due respect, Al Nadir operative Rikard Allan was loaded with the nano-bomb. We only had a short interrogation window before the nano-bots in his system sent back his biometric data to Al Nadir confirming his captured status. The signal from them to detonate was sent sooner after, and we had to handle Rikard's demise through a controlled explosion."

Ashton listened and got more irate. "For fuck's sake! Aren't you managing to counter the nano-bomb at all?"

"Of course we are, Prime Minister," responded Gibbs.

But Maide jumped in to finish off the address. "It's just that the complexity of the nano-bomb and the constantly evolving nature of the threat has made progress much slower than we anticipated. Dr. Noor, perhaps you would like to explain further on this."

Sam moved forward with expectancy. Ashton recognized the agent understood his role, and it wasn't to make up the numbers. He had the inside track on Al Nadir's nano-bomb. Ashton stared at Sam as he made a wide scan across the faces at the table. He seemed to be centering himself, but Ashton could discern a pulling of tension at the sides of his lips. The tension increased as his gaze fell upon Quentin and Maide. Ashton took in Quentin's expression. A supercilious mouth up-turned into a condescending sneer. Maide's stance was professional as always, but he could discern a slither of mocking directed at Sam within his intense brown eyes. Ashton watched Sam. He saw him clench his right hand into a fist and his eyes told of an anger he could barely contain. He wanted to rip the men's throats out rather than discuss nano-technology. Ashton knew that look. He'd seen it before, on himself, in the mirror, when someone had pissed him off badly. What on Earth had they done?

"Prime Minister, the nano-bomb is unlike any other threat we've previously faced. To put this into context, three months ago we discovered the nano-bomb, and only five weeks ago, we managed to acquire the technology."

Ashton nodded hurriedly and smiled with gratitude as he remembered that it was down to Sam's endeavors that they had the nano-bomb at all. Sam acknowledged the PM's reaction with a gracious tilt of his head. Ashton noticed Maide straightened up and Ashton could see he was basking with pride. You've got nothing to be proud of, you haven't solved anything, thought Ashton harshly, and looked toward Sam as the agent started to speak.

"Sir, we can expect this model to be upgraded at any moment, if it hasn't been already."

"But tell me, Dr. Noor. What progress has actually been made? What I've heard so far suggests we're still chasing our tails."

Ashton tried to tone down his disdain at British Intelligence's inadequacy. He felt guilty. He didn't mean to target Sam. The agent had done a superb job and it wasn't his fault things weren't moving faster.

Maide and Gibbs needed to come up with the answers he sought.

"Sir, we are progressing. Our success with Rikard Allan was down to our co-op with the CIA to develop the anti-agent. The nano-bomb works like a virus, mutating cells and assimilating them into being part of the nano-bomb. The anti-agent we've developed is a blocking programme that stops assimilation. We managed to block assimilation in Allan for a little over half an hour. That was how we learned of the Cambridge cell. Our scientists are working fourteen-hour shifts to extend the blocking time. Once we get to a permanent block on assimilation, we'll be able to make a real move against Al Nadir."

"Thank you, Dr. Noor. I'm pleased that at least some progress is being made." Ashton's voice, laced with droplets of sarcasm, aggravated Sam.

"Sir, we are doing everything possible," Sam retaliated. "But until we've nailed the nano-bomb, we can't move very far forward."

Ashton placed his hands together as if to pray, and then rested his thumbs underneath his chin and pointed his fingers in Sam's direction.

"Are we absolutely sure that all senior lieutenants have the nano-bomb?" asked Ashton exasperated.

"As far as we know, sir, yes. But Al Nadir is unpredictable. We can't be completely sure of anything," said Sam.

"Talk about feeling impotent," muttered Maide. But he immediately collected himself when the PM glared irritably at him.

"Maide, Gibbs, just tell me. Why Cambridgeshire?" asked Ashton, inwardly confused by the sudden obsession with the previously clean and terrorist-free county.

His security heads stared at the PM, and in their eyes, Ashton could see they had the reason behind Al Nadir's new fixation with the quiet county.

Chapter 53

Salim looked out the window of his luxury helicopter. The cityscape of Jumeriah Palm passed beneath him. Less than a decade ago the place had been just sea. The petrodollar had bought a lot in a very short time, and now the only life that teamed below was of the two-legged kind. He smiled, leaning back and enjoying the sumptuous views of the futuristic, shining towers. The people of Dubai knew what he knew: money could buy anything. For them, it meant culture, class and acceptance. For Salim, money bought freedom.

The myriad alphabet of intel agencies around the world had been carefully bought off. And when the money couldn't talk, interventions from his invisible armies were enough to silence the most avid and tenacious of spies.

Salim knocked back his vodka and poured another as he dived into memories. Those armies had been one of his many masterstrokes. It was such a startlingly obvious idea, he wondered why no one had thought of it before. But, of course, all the terrorist groups preceding Al Nadir had either been driven by an inner cause of religion or revolution, or set up by various government powers to create societies of fear, controlled by propaganda and negative imagery. None had been about the money or sheer domination. Perhaps, that's why they never saw the bigger picture, the connectedness of the world around them. Salim, had taken Al Nadir to the next level.

In truth, it had been Sabena who had made the original suggestion. "Salim, baby, how would you like to really kick start Al Nadir?"

"You know I want to. Bringing together terrorist agencies is one thing, but I want more, much more."

"There are over one point two billion people across the world living in shitholes?"

"So? There are an awful lot of people waking up to interesting aromas?"

Sabena shook her head and smiled at Salim's uncharacteristic naivety. "Let me rephrase it. If we were to harness just five percent of that lot, that's 60 million recruits for Al Nadir."

Salim grasped Sabena's inference immediately. He laughed, grabbed hold of her hair roughly, and pulled her towards him. Sabena's eyes widened with pleasure as the unexpected pain touched her nerves and she moved her lips up towards him.

"Sabena, you are-"

Sabena pushed hard against him, stabbing her tongue violently into his mouth, taking his breath with his words away.

She moved back for a second to speak. "I *know* what I am. Don't you ever forget it!"

Salim prickled uncomfortably at her tone. He pulled her away, his face bloodless and cold. "Baby, I'll remember you when I need to, and I'll forget you when you're no longer needed."

Sabena attempted a smile, trying to playfully suggest her words were just a joke.

"And right now," Salim sneered, his hand edging up her skirt, "you're needed."

Salim enjoyed the memories with pleasure as he fast forwarded from the idea to conception to execution.

After Salim had identified the size of the urban slum population per country, he realized Sabena had really been on to something with her suggestion. Salim's top ten target countries came back with the total slum populations in millions (M):

1. China 191M
2. India 98M
3. Nigeria 42M
4. Brazil 38M
5. Pakistan 32M
6. Indonesia 29M
7. Bangladesh 29M
8. Democratic Republic of Congo 21M
9. Sudan 12M
10. Iraq 11M

Salim knew these were massive figures in terms of people. He wondered how the world had allowed such a level of poverty to persist. These people had been forgotten. The world had turned their backs on the poor. Governments, so-called charities and institutions had made themselves rich on the lives of those invisible ones. Within Salim, he felt a twang of righteousness unbecoming of his persona.

He would give these people what had been stripped from their lives. These people who had lived and scrounged on a rubbish heap twenty-four-seven, who had been forced to put their children into prostitution, who sold their own body parts for money, just to survive.

Al Nadir would give them back their dignity, their identity and, most of all, their sense of respect and pride.

After his initial analysis, Salim pulled together the percentage proportion of the urban population in each country living in slum areas:

1. South Sudan – 95%
2. Central African Republic – 93%
3. Sudan – 91%
4. Chad – 88%
5. Sao Tome and Principe – 86%
6. Guinea-Bissau – 82%
7. Mozambique – 80%
8. Haiti – 74%
9. Niger – 70%
10. Afghanistan – 62%

Salim could see that many countries across the world had urban populations that were almost all comprised of slums. They were all valid targets to be recruited into Al Nadir. The countries that had the highest percentage of the urban population living in slum conditions were most likely to have some form of slum overlord or commander.

In the barrios in Venezuela or favelas in Brazil, the slum overlords were easy to identify. But in the cities where slums were the main urban living profile, which translated to poor access to water and sanitation, no durable housing and insufficient living areas, finding the slum commander may prove a harder activity.

Salim glanced up at Sabena, smirking, as she walked into his office in Al Nadir's private residence, Sanctum, on a tiny island in the Caribbean.

"You know, Sabena, your little idea may just work. Have a look at these figures." Salim pushed the lists in front of Sabena.

"It's a hell of a recruitment opportunity for Al Nadir," she replied. "Do you want me to prime up the global lieutenants in the major countries you've selected?"

"No. I'm going to do a video call to everyone in Al Nadir's senior management team simultaneously across the globe. They need to run the figures and report back to me post-mortem. But I'm giving them the autonomy to make this happen. If we go back and forth like pricks, we'll be no better than their fucking governments."

Sabena nodded, smirking, and slipped forward onto Salim's desk.

"Doesn't this call for a bit of a celebration?" said Sabena, rubbing her thigh against his.

Salim pushed her away roughly. "Not now, babes. I've got to keep my head focused. This is business. We've got time for pleasure later!"

Salim flashed his black eyes. Within them, Sabena detected his seductive intentions. She shivered a little in anticipation and dropped down off the desk.

"Do you want me to set up the conference room?" asked Sabena.

"Now you're thinking my way! Yes. Get it set up on global transmission. I just need to change into something less casual," said Salim, looking down at his t-shirt and shorts.

"Wear Zegna. It makes you look like you own the world," suggested Sabena, heading for the door.

"Babes," called Salim, "that moment isn't far off!"

Sabena peered over her shoulder, raised her eyebrow, and smiled.

After Salim had given his orders to his senior management team (SMT), the Al Nadir machine sprung into activity. On the ground in the countries of the slums, Salim's SMT instructed their global lieutenants. They, in turn, contacted their own intricate and far-reaching networks of Al Nadir staff members. They'd been allocated money to be spent as bribes to slum overlords, cash payments to people, or incentives to the authorities to take whole towns away. Given the amount of fire power coupled with financial strength, removal of people from the slums had been straightforward.

No one wanted to stand against the mighty force of Salim Al Douri and Al Nadir.

Al Nadir teams had gone into the slums with massive trucks, rounded up whole towns and delivered a promise of a real future for their inhabitants. Loading them into the back of the huge trucks, many never spoke. They just looked upon the men and women of Al Nadir as saviors.

Bringers of fresh new lives.

No one refused.

Once operations had commenced in earnest, Salim monitored the satellite feeds. There were thousands of people on screen as black spots like bugs, there to be trained to do his bidding. And train them, Al Nadir did. They trained them in ways of surveillance, combat and sadistic terrorism.

Hidden from the prying eyes of spy satellites by Al Nadir's satellite-image masking technology, new towns were built in the heart of the most isolated jungles and deserts. As they trained and fought, the new recruits pledged their dying allegiance to their savior and God, Salim Al Douri.

After Salim had harnessed the human resource from the slums, Salim's army had swelled to over 70 million. The sheer size of this manpower gave Al Nadir an incredible competitive advantage in the terrorist gameplay. With that number of warm bodies marching to Al Nadir's cause, their strategy of taking over smaller and less powerful terrorist organizations was considerably easier.

It didn't take long before Al Nadir progressed to larger terrorist regimes, and eventually, to entire rogue states.

Although Salim always tried to start his mergers on a diplomatic and amicable footing, more often than not, he didn't finish that way. Once the tens of millions of recruits had been secured and trained to obey his word, Salim focused on vicious and hostile takeovers. In the same way Al Nadir had located and catalogued the slums, the same was done with terrorist organizations across the world.

He knew who owned what. He knew who had control and why. He knew where to push to gain leverage on other partners. And he knew where to eviscerate a crime organization without any consideration of partnership.

Five years on, Salim now had control of seventy-five percent of all terrorist organizations. Such power before Salim's invention of connected terrorism was unheard of. Salim knew he had created a new genre of terror with Al Nadir. And now, he was on the verge of creating another era. Only this time, he was using a weapon very different to anything he'd ever used before.

Chapter 54

Maide moved forward to answer the PM's question and, in unison, Gibbs geared up to respond.

Sam watched the two security chiefs play at brinkmanship. *Like kids in a fucking playground.* Maide leapt in with authority and took the moment from the MI5 chief.

"Prime Minister, the reason for Cambridge is because Salim Al Douri is a Cambridge man with a doctorate in Particle Physics."

Maide stared at each person around the table making sure that all eyes were on him. Sam hated his prima donna tendencies. For God's sake. They were talking about terrorism and he was just sitting there preening and posturing.

"Rikard Allan was also Cambridge alumnus in Political Science. Sabena Sanantoni, Al Nadir's second in command, also received a first at Cambridge in Quantum Physics."

"God, doesn't the university screen before allowing terrorists into their midst?"

"With due respect, sir, I don't think, at the time, they were terrorists. Just wealthy, bright foreign students. And Cambridge isn't accustomed to turning those away," said Gibbs.

Ashton flushed with annoyance. "Yes. I suppose so," he muttered irritably. "But what happened to Bradford or Birmingham? They used to be the hotbeds."

Gibbs stepped in ahead of Maide. His eagerness to restore ground in front of the PM couldn't be hidden.

"If I may, sir, explain. This terrorism we have now is different from what we've ever had before. They aren't Muslim fundamentalists in an Islamic

Jihad. Al Nadir means the 'unique' and that's exactly what they are. They're sharp and slick, and even look good on camera. You won't find covered heads or trailing beards. They're well organized and unbelievably well-funded. Their section leaders are billionaires, well educated, as we've already heard, and most of them are ex-intelligence. Therein lies our biggest problem. They know our moves before we know them. Their collective cause is extortion on a global scale through terror. The nano-bomb has given them even more collateral to do this and succeed. Around the world, once strong governments are now cowering in the face of their connected evil."

Maide nodded, agreeing with Gibbs, but he wanted to take control of the table again. He didn't feel comfortable with Gibbs having too much airplay in front of the PM.

"I believe, sir, what my good colleague is trying to say is twentieth century modes of operation are no longer effective. We need to find alternatives to our usual procedures in capturing terrorists."

"Any suggestions?" asked Ashton, eyeing the table.

Quentin shuffled, avoiding eye contact with Sam, and slithered into the conversation. Sam's back straightened as he heard the foreign secretary's clipped, effeminate tone. He was still smarting from their audacious surveillance. But even more, he was viciously annoyed by Quentin's perverse enjoyment of his discomfort. Sam liked to be in control. But at that moment, he wasn't. And he hated every second.

"By all means, Quentin, go ahead." Ashton outstretched his arm to the foreign secretary.

"Well, perhaps we should consider infiltration. We know they have a cell in Cambridgeshire. Maybe we could get someone inside and ascertain who is, as we now term, 'loaded' and who isn't."

Ashton nodded. Maide and Sam did not respond but stared at each other. Both knew the proposition, although reasonable to hear, was virtually impossible to execute. They should know, having set up the deep cover infiltration of Matthew Kinley. Infiltration always came with loss. It wasn't easy. It wasn't safe. And right now, it wasn't an option.

"Prime Minister, I don't believe the foreign secretary has the full knowledge of Five's operations," said Sam, turning to look at Gibbs, to gain confirmation on his next words. Gibbs moved forward and waited on Sam's delivery.

"Infiltration isn't currently a part of Five's operational strategy due to significant risk of exposure. Al Nadir's bio-scanning, both physiological and psychological, is extremely robust, and roots out spies with thorough efficiency. Procedures at Five and Six are to concentrate on solving the nano-bomb issue completely and monitoring Al Nadir operations as far as we are able."

Gibbs nodded, agreeing with Sam's response.

Quentin sat back, staring between Gibbs and Sam, shaking his head with dismay. By the gentle swaying of his head, he inferred the security service's shortcomings.

"But Six has the capability to infiltrate if they really want to. Don't they?" barked Ashton, staring with apprehension at Maide then Sam. Sam could see that Ashton's question was just a performance. Ashton knew about Kinley as well as him and Maide. It was a means of addressing and dismissing Quentin's suggestion without revealing the reason for their certainty that infiltration was the most dangerous strategy to employ, and one that would undoubtedly lead to failure.

Sam looked at Quentin, who still did not face him directly, preferring to stare at the PM. Sam noticed his smugness. *God would I love to wipe that look off your face.*

For Quentin's benefit, Ashton stared impatiently at Sam for an answer.

"Of course we do," Sam replied. "And I'm sure Five does too."

Sam glanced at Gibbs, who muttered, "We most certainly do."

"It's just that, in the present climate, such action would bring unnecessary risks to the operative. I'm not prepared to sanction any action that would knowingly result in death."

Maide, Ashton and Sam remembered the cost of Kinley getting into Al Nadir and the thousands of lives that had been sacrificed under Operation Snowdrop. Sam caught Ashton's eye and realized the PM was suddenly submerged in the memory of that dreadful day too, for his face went ashen and his eyes darkened. He looked away from Sam. Maide, at the same time, stared at his papers and refrained from direct eye contact. Some people say eyes are windows of the soul. If this was really true, considered Sam, as he looked around the table, Maide and Ashton were doing their level best to pull their curtains tight.

Only Quentin, who had no knowledge of Operation Snowdrop, Matthew Kinley or the impact of his infiltration, remained confident to press ahead with such an idea. He used the pause to take the upper hand.

"Are you sure that's not just an excuse, Dr. Noor?"

Quentin's words tunneled through Sam's composure. They attacked his sense of order and upset his fine balance between peace and war, which constantly raged inside of him. Sam found that he couldn't shield his fierce anger any longer.

"No. It's not an excuse," Sam yelled. "I've told you infiltration won't work right now. I will not put any of my operatives into a situation where I know their chances of survival are less than 50 percent. I am not an executioner!"

Sam remembered the Snowdrop mission. He remembered how the agents in his team had been slaughtered, and he'd just watched, helpless, shielded by a wall from the sniper's laser sights. An executioner was exactly what he'd been made to be.

"I apologize, Dr. Noor. I would never cast doubt on your word," replied Quentin, smiling, dropping the bait.

He didn't need to wait long for Sam to be hooked.

Sam stood up abruptly, scrapping his chair legs against the oak floor.

"Just what is it you're trying to say?"

Sam glared with icy ruthlessness at the foreign secretary. Quentin remained seated. He lifted his eyes up to Sam, the first moment of contact throughout the meeting, and he labored it to the max. With palms open, he stared at Sam and showed ambivalence.

"My dear boy, I'm not trying to say anything. If you think infiltration won't work, so be it. You're the expert. I'm not looking to be your enemy. We are, after all, on the same side. Aren't we Dr. Noor?"

Sam recognized the game as Quentin looked around the room, making sure that his insinuation was clear, that Sam was the troublemaker and perhaps not capable of fulfilling the remit demanded by his current position.

Quentin then shot Sam with his best public-school prefect smile. Sam stiffened.

"Of course we are," said Ashton. "Sam, please be seated. This infiltration discussion is over."

The PM motioned affably to the chair. Sam read the signal and sat down immediately. But inside, he was still seething. This was anything but over.

Chapter 55

Angela had had a relatively sheltered life. She'd experienced a strict convent upbringing forced upon her by parents, who were totally disinterested in her wellbeing and too interested in their own. But until she'd met Matthew Kinley, her life had been dull and boring. She'd left university with a degree in English literature, and had gone to work in the diplomatic service a few days after graduation. She wasn't the type to take a gap year and travel the world. She knew from a young age that she was destined to live an unadventurous existence, and she followed that path. Had she not gone to that party in Athens, she may still have been on that path.

But time and space changed around her the second she set eyes on Kinley. Blue eyes sparkling, laughing, had invited her in. Inviting her to take a chance. To leap into the unknown and hang the consequences. The moment she kissed him, a new destiny was written. A destiny that would have her standing in the middle of a hall in Alexandria, staring at a horrific sight her imagination could never have conjured up.

Her husband, Matthew Kinley, stood semi-naked in front of her with his arms outstretched, palms pointing down to the floor, as if he'd been hit with an electric shock. His veins were prominent, the way they looked when he'd spent too long on the weights. She stared at the veins running through his arms, and realized they were definitely rising.

"Angie, Angie, darling, I love you. I'm sorry. I'm sorry," cried Kinley, as the veins on his arms suddenly split open.

Angela shrieked and turned Lotte's screaming face quickly away from the hideous spectacle. She held her daughter tight against her. Angela knew she had to get away from her husband, but her legs wouldn't move. Her body had frozen through fear into an altered state. Unable to say or do anything, she watched, helpless, as the silver metallic substance that had covered Kinley's arms and chest moved rapidly into his open veins and co-mingled with the flowing blood. Then, bizarrely, the blood pulled back, as if a brake pedal had activated. It ran up Kinley's arms and surged back into his veins along with the silver metallic substance. Within seconds, Kinley's veins had closed, and for an instance, it was like nothing had happened.

"Turn it off, Angie. Please. I can't stand it. Turn it off. *Turn it off now!*"

Kinley's hands shielded his ears and he collapsed onto the floor, huddled and shivering.

Angela swallowed heavily and, still holding Lotte against her, she moved one foot shakily towards her husband.

"Matt?" Her voice was a mere croak. "Matt, are you-"

"*Turn it off!*" yelled Kinley, and he leapt up, shaking, his eyes wild with fear and pain.

Angela fixed a look at his incensed face, and then she looked down and her eyes widened with terror.

"Oh my God, Matthew!"

In the middle of his chest, a heart-shaped silver stain could be seen, and it appeared to be changing color. In front of Angela, the silver turned to purple and then to red.

"Please, Angie, help me. You've got to...to turn it off!" cried Kinley.

"Matt, I'm sorry," whispered Angela. "I don't know what to turn off."

Then Kinley's voice changed from pleading to decisive. "It's over, baby. You've got to run. Just get out!"

Understanding came in a rush and he hated its sudden clarity. The nano-bots inside him were forcing him to mutate.

"I'm not leaving you," cried Angela. "I love you. I don't want to leave you."

"I love you, Angie. I know what's happening. I'm sorry."

"Baby, I love you. I can't leave you!"

Angela's tears took away her vision. As she moved backwards, her daughter's arms wrapped tighter around her. She stretched out her hand and touched Kinley. His skin felt ice cold. Deathly cold. The heart-shaped stain now seemed to pulse strong scarlet. His skin was almost translucent. She could see the veins so clearly.

"Run, baby. Now!" Kinley shouted, his face angry and tired. "Just get away from me!"

Angela let go of her husband, and turned to run. But she had to look at her love one more time. The man who had changed her life. The man who had given her hope and such great happiness. She owed him one last look.

She flicked her head back in her husband's direction and her lips mouthed, "I love you!"

In that moment, Kinley screamed. The hall shone with white heat, a thunderous roaring shook the house, and suddenly, Angela was flying around and around, whipped up in a churning cauldron of smoke and heat.

And then all was dark and silent.

Chapter 56

Project David had been a success. The experiment had demonstrated the new power the US now possessed. Dr. Ross Whyte should have been proud. He was, after all, the project director. President Treeborne himself had given him the role. The name Project David had been Ross' idea in honor of the story of David and Goliath, and how small had triumphed. The president had smiled coldly, appreciating the relevance; the quantum compound was tiny but its power would cut down the Goliath power of Al Nadir.

"A great day, Ross."

The president placed his hand out to shake the scientist's hand. Ross looked down, dazed and not quite collecting what was going on around him.

"A great day for America. Something to tell your grandkids, eh?" said the president, laughing, and he turned to one of his generals. "Yeah, tell them how we whipped Al Nadir's motherfucking ass!"

The generals all joined in the coarse humor.

Ross smiled half-heartedly and nodded, adding, "Yes, we're going to show them who is the boss."

"Too right we'll show them." The president's mouth tightened. "And I'm going to love every goddamn minute of it."

Ross could see the bloodlust in Treeborne's eye, and it caused his bottom lip to tremble slightly. Frank Weitz, who had walked with the president to congratulate Ross, noticed the movement.

"Everything ok, Dr. Whyte?" asked Weitz gently, and eyed Ross' reaction.

Dr. Ross Whyte was a hefty man, tall in stature and big boned, with blond thinning hair and grey sunken eyes. In his late forties, he had spent a lifetime stuck in a lab, and his social skills had taken a beating as a result of such isolation. The only thing that meant anything to him apart from his work was his family. He never cared about anything else.

Ross had known Weitz for some time, and he knew that his colleague's response detected his anxiousness. Ross knew his colleague would want to find the cause of Ross' sudden alarm.

"Yes, yes, sir. Excellent. I'm really delighted with the results," gushed Ross.

Ross was aware his fear was leaking. And that Weitz had picked up on it. He had to dissuade the defense secretary of suspicious thoughts. Weitz stared at Ross thoughtfully, and opened his mouth again to speak, but the president snatched the moment.

"We're all delighted with the results. Now you see that compound gets back safely, Dr. Whyte. We don't want you losing it or nothing. Come on, guys. Let's do the Bourbon some damage." The president laughed again, slapped Dr. Whyte's back, and then walked away with his entourage in tow.

Ross picked up the box containing the compound that they had been using for experimentation purposes. They had only needed a miniscule amount, but he had brought along more in case it had been required. Military personnel came up behind him, and they clicked their heels as he turned.

"Sir, we'll escort you back to the lab."

"Yes, thank you. That would be helpful."

Ross walked down the path back to the lab, accompanied in a diamond formation by the heavily armed officers. He remained silent. The men didn't seem the type for small talk, and anyway, he had three things that occupied his whole mind: his wife, his son and his daughter.

Chapter 57

After Sam's confrontation, the PM decided it was time to wrap up proceedings.

"Dr. Noor, we all concur with your advice regarding infiltration. It is, perhaps, not the best way to use finite resources." Ashton turned to Gibbs and Maide. "Given the existence of this new cell, I'd like a full report from Five and Six on my desk by 9 a.m. tomorrow on increased security measures for the forthcoming UN Peace Summit."

The PM didn't wait for a response. It was a given that Gibbs and Maide had to deliver on this request.

The United Nations Peace Summit would be the world's definitive strike against Al Nadir. Getting the Resolution 8091 Extreme Unreserved Force tabled at the summit had been crucial. Ratification of it was the reason the summit was being held. Ashton knew London, the hosts of the summit would be targeted for all kinds of hell from those terrorist bastards. That meant they had just three days to lock down any security threats, neutralize hostiles, obliterate cells and make the QE2 Conference Center, the venue for the summit, the safest place on the planet.

Ashton stared at Maide and then Gibbs. He wondered if either of them had the ability to deliver what he wanted.

"Right. Well, thank you, gentlemen. I wait to hear good news soon," said Ashton, flicking into his usual mode of address.

Ashton always finished briefings on a positive note. The 'wait to hear good news soon' was his constant belief that things could be turned around. It was a mantra that instilled in him some form of confidence.

Amidst the nodding heads, the PM collected his papers, stood up, and appeared to walk out, but he glanced back and watched as Sam rose, gritted his teeth and glared at Quentin and Maide.

The agent still seemed to be holding down an inner rage.

Ashton didn't want to know. As long the guy did his job and kept the UK safe, he could beat the shit out of Quentin for all he cared.

Chapter 58

Screw this! What the hell am I doing?

Ellie slammed her laptop shut. She'd been Googling "balance shifted" and derivatives of it ever since Sam had left. She'd already blown her appointment at the spa by suddenly obsessing over her laptop, making strange searches. All she'd come up with was nothing but a blistering headache. Catching a glimpse of her pale, drawn face in the mirror, she decided that at least she could get a good workout in the Silent Waters' gym.

An hour later, Ellie arrived back from the gym, knackered, but feeling much more alive than the geeky hermit she was earlier. She sat on the sofa, downed an OJ and flicked on the TV. She grimaced as some hideously cutesy, blonde boys, who looked like they'd been manufactured by a mad Nazi scientist, massacred a golden classic.

"You should be doing homework, not singing harmonies," muttered Ellie enviously, and she flicked to CNN.

Instantly, she was dragged into the scene. A harassed female reporter in her late forties was standing in a tree-lined street. Expensive parked cars either side suggested a wealthy Western country. Behind the reporter, rapid activity signaled something terrible had happened. A man was closing the doors at the back of an ambulance. Exhausted firemen were returning back to their engine. Police cars and darkened people carriers were parked at erratic angles, half on, half off the pavement. Teams in dark clothes and body armor wandered around the street. Several suits did their upmost to stay out of the frame.

Ellie increased the sound.

"…possible assassination of a British Foreign Office official by Al Nadir."

The camera panned to the left of the reporter to show a house. The steps leading up to the front door were intact, but the door had been completely blasted away. The camera zoomed in to show a blackened and smoking hall. Strewn across the pavement was shattered glass and unidentifiable remnants. Water still dripped from the upper walls. Such was the ferocity of the blast, its impact had blown upwards, obliterating the wooden staircase. The inner rooms were in deep shadow. Ellie could discern splinters of wood hanging down from the upper landing like pupae sacks on a branch. At the front of the house, the internal walls had crumbled under a force and were now rubble. A piece of a child's dolls house pointed upwards from the ruins.

Ellie gulped, a lump in her throat rising fast as she looked at the scene. The wreckage she was looking at was once home to a family.

"However, much is still to be known about the explosion that killed the British Senior Foreign Office diplomat, Dr. Matthew Kinley, his wife and their four-year-old daughter. We'll bring you more news as we have it. Now it's back to the studio. This is Susan Davidowitz in Alexandria, Washington DC, for CNN."

Ellie stared dumbstruck at the screen. She knew Matthew Kinley. She had met him and his wife Angela at a Foreign Office Christmas party in Washington DC some years ago. He had been a kind, charming man. She remembered how he'd left Syria when the embassy shut, and how happy he'd been to be the Head of the Science and Technology Section in the Science, Technology, Energy and Environment Department of the British Embassy in Washington DC.

He'd made the comment that it was 'an altogether safer environment for a British official'. Ellie recalled the image of his demolished house.

Yes, she thought, a really safe environment.

Chapter 59

Sabena stared at her phone. Ensconced in her private plane, she curled up on a sofa and slipped her arm leisurely behind her head as she leant back on the cushion. She flicked open the alert that had flashed up on her screen. CNN live started to run. A straight-laced female reporter with a lopsided mouth and dark curly hair gave the run down. Behind her stood a house with the entire front section blown away. Ambulances, petrol cars and blacked-out SUVs littered the area.

Sabena smiled contentedly and pressed pause, keeping a still of the devastated street and obliterated home.

"Teach you to fuck with me, Mr. Kinley!"

Venom dripped from her tongue. Although she tried to quell the hatred, one thought of Kinley and it flowed through her, unrestricted.

He had been everything to her.

It wasn't love. That would have shown weakness.

But it was obsession.

From the moment she'd taken him in January over four years ago, he'd gotten into her mind. He'd tricked his way in with his gorgeous body, sparkling crystal blue eyes…

And his lies.

She believed him from the start. She could read liars. If she'd smelt something wrong, he'd have been sent back to River House in little pieces.

Every word he said about hating the government, MI6 and the establishment, she knew, was true. In his eyes she'd seen the pain and anger. She could feel his absolute hatred.

Salim hadn't trusted him at first. Sabena had rowed over how wrong his judgement had been. She'd vehemently defended Kinley and placed her own credibility on the line to vouch for him. Even when Kinley had killed another

MI6 agent, Dan Carter in Florence, Salim didn't believe him.

"They take out their own. It was a mercy killing. It doesn't mean he's with us, Sabena. I don't trust him."

Sabena could hear Salim's words in her ears. She'd fought with Salim, verbally and, finally, physically.

"I told you, Sabena. He's been too easy. Accepting everything. Doing anything we ask. I don't know but there's something about him that doesn't ring true. I'm going to *speak* to him."

Sabena knew what speak really meant. Salim intended to torture Kinley. She knew he wouldn't survive. She knew that Kinley spoke the truth. He hated MI6. He hated everything about the establishment. He wanted to wreck them. She'd seen it in his eyes. She couldn't let Salim make a terrible mistake, a mistake where she would lose so much.

She watched Salim retreat away from her. He'd made up his mind.

She had to unmake it for him.

Sabena reached out, grabbed Salim's shoulder and wrenched him back, pulling him down toward the floor. Salim was taken by surprise at Sabena's unexpected attack and lost his footing, falling back heavily. Sabena leapt on him and wrapped her hands around his throat. Salim pushed up against her chest with a vicious force and hurled her onto her back. His body came down upon Sabena's and he pelted her body hard. Sabena smashed her fists back at him, and brought her knee up fast into Salim's balls. He grimaced and lifted her body off the floor then slammed it down with a murderous force. Sabena heard a crack, and pain shot across her body.

"What is wrong with you, Sabena?" screamed Salim, as he tried to snatch at her wrists.

"Leave Kinley alone!" Sabena yelled, wincing as she tried to wriggle free of Salim's iron grip. Pain thundered through the left side of her body. She felt shattered inside and knew Salim must have cracked a few ribs.

"He's telling the truth. For once in your fucking life, see what's in front of you. Please, Salim. He's on our side. He's with us. He *is* us. Trust him. You've got to trust him. He'll do anything you say. Anything I say. He just wants to be accepted. We've got the Piccadilly attack planned. Let's bring him in. If suddenly we hear that they find the bombs, we'll know he's MI6 and I'll happily rip him apart. Believe me, Salim. I'm not going soft. But as it stands, he's still our best asset in British Intelligence. Don't burn that."

"Are we done?" said Salim sharply, still holding Sabena's wrists. His eyes flashed with fury.

Sabena nodded with reluctance. Salim released her and she pushed back on her weight. She tried to rise from the floor but couldn't. Salim bent down and allowed Sabena's weight to fall onto him as he helped to pull her up. As she rose, she breathed deeply, suppressing the pain.

"Ok?" asked Salim. A fraction of softness filtered into his tone as he watched Sabena.

"Yeah. I'm ok. But I meant what I said about Kinley," snapped Sabena, shrugging off Salim's hands on her body. "You promise me you'll never consider speaking to him?"

Salim's eyes bore deep inside Sabena. She was in pain and could barely stand upright with her busted ribs. But she faced off against him and wouldn't accept any other response than total agreement to her demands.

"No speaking," agreed Salim grudgingly. Then his head tipped a little to the side. "Need a doctor?"

Sabena touched her ribcage. She'd been right. A couple of her ribs had been broken. But it had been worth it. She'd saved Kinley from being spoken to.

Sabena had never backed down on her complete belief that Kinley had turned. Before the Piccadilly bombing, Kinley had given them access to so much. He'd even revealed a string of safe houses across the world, and after the spies had been captured, Kinley happily took part in their torture and execution.

She'd seen the pleasure on his face. She knew you couldn't fake elation when you're carving someone up.

Kinley was a kindred spirit.

She felt there was a bond between them, a passion for the dark they shared.

When she'd told Kinley about the Piccadilly bombing, she'd seen the joy in his eyes.

"Are you ok with that, Mr. Kinley?"

"Fuck yes! This is what I want. This is *always* what I've wanted!"

She remembered Kinley had been so ecstatic about the prospect of the bombing bringing down the UK government and its security apparatus. He didn't give a shit about the lives that would be taken. He just wanted the establishment to suffer. Kinley didn't care about collateral damage.

Despite Kinley's happy response, Salim had given her strict instructions to monitor everything he did afterwards. Nothing came through. No clandestine meeting. No chatter indicating Six knew the bombing was going to happen.

Kinley had carried on as usual, being an MI6 spy and a diplomat in STEE. After Piccadilly, everything changed.

The dynamic between Salim and Kinley flipped. Salim trusted Kinley implicitly.

Sabena recalled, with a shudder, Barcelona. After they'd watched the devastation on central London, they started to party, and party very, very hard. The three of them, Salim, Kinley and her, had celebrated, enjoying each other's bodies along with copious amounts of champagne and coke.

Inhibition hadn't been a word in their vocabulary.

Over time, they became a sort of weird triumvirate of power in Al Nadir.

Kinley showed he had a love of power and enjoyed dominating those beneath him. He rivaled Salim in his ability for ruthlessness.

That's what drew her closer to him.

Sabena had even crafted an alias, Stuart Kingswood, and designed a special nano-mask for him, to keep his activities from the prying eyes of the intelligence community. She actually cared for his safety. She could hardly remember a time when she cared for anything or anyone before. But Kinley had gotten to her. He had slipped into her psyche and twisted her ability to know what was really happening.

Her ability of perfect recall sometimes tormented her. In Kinley's case, it subtly underlined what an absolute idiot she had let herself become.

"Ok. I'll tell you what I'm going to do. I'm going to tell you what's happening. *Really* happening. Because you don't know. You're in the dark, Sabena. All your mighty intelligence and the most vital intel has evaded you. But I have it," Kinley had said, back four years ago when he'd first told her he wanted to flip and become Al Nadir.

Recalling that conversation back on January 27, 2013, Sabena could see that Kinley had certainly left her in the dark. The vital intel had evaded her, and she didn't know what was really happening. Kinley had kept her in that blinded state for over four years.

It was only by the sarcastic attitude of Godley, their spy in the UK Cabinet, that they discovered the truth just a month ago. She heard it as she scanned the transcripts from Russo's monthly meeting with Godley.

"Seems like Ashton and Maide haven't got anything better to do but look at bloody flower websites. Talk about fiddling while Rome burns."

It had been a passing, seemingly innocent poke at the PM and head of MI6 for their lack of doing anything more substantial than tidying up their gardens. But both Ashton and Maide were interested in the same flower site?

Her hackles shot up. She spared no time in activating an asset Al Nadir had in the IT department within Number 10. A copy of the website code was secured and delivered to Sabena's cryptographic team.

After weeks of searching, one bright analyst suggested steganographic encryption.

Sabena recalled the gawky analyst standing in front of her trying to explain how she and the whole of Al Nadir had been made fools of by MI6.

"It is really most simple," muttered the analyst, using the same excited voice that geeks tend to use when explaining something technical they love.

The analyst pressed on the touch screen and brought up the Forever Flowers website.

"See. Here is the website as normal. They're just a bunch of flowers, roses, tulips, snowdrops etc."

"Yes," snapped Sabena. "I know what the flowers are. Tell me how they hid their fucking messages!"

The analyst shuffled and brought up another window, showing the machine code prompt. He typed in some words and symbols. Sabena recognized the word 'extract' in all that the analyst typed.

Suddenly, the machine code window flashed up with information. Dates and times of operations. Intel about Al Nadir operatives. Account codes. All kinds of information.

"How have they done this? What the fuck did they use?" hissed Sabena, glaring at the information popping up in the window.

The analyst explained to Sabena that there were various techniques to hide secret messages in plain sight. Least Significant Bit (LSB) steganography was a form of steganographic encryption that enabled messages to be encoded into an image by the process of augmenting the image's binary code. The other steganographic technique, the Discrete Cosine Transform Coefficient technique, was one that slightly changed the weights or coefficients of the cosine waves that are used to reconstruct a JPEG image, enabling messages to be encrypted within the image.

"We need to monitor this site constantly and use your steganographic algorithm to overwrite the messages from MI6 with our own little snippets of intel. From now on, we're taking back control."

Sabena patted the analyst on the back, and he nodded, understanding what he had to do.

Sabena turned away and her dangerous eyes glowed with passionate rage. Only one person could possibly have passed on all that information. She vowed that Kinley would never put her in the dark again.

Having the knowledge of Kinley's treacherous double-cross enabled Salim and Sabena to serve up misinformation. As a result, missions built on Kinley's intelligence over the past four weeks were bloodbaths for the Six agents concerned.

But this didn't go anywhere near to appeasing the vicious betrayal felt by both Salim and Sabena. Sabena had wanted to tear him apart. But Salim had calmed her down. She remembered their brief discourse.

"The motherfucker betrayed us, but he's done it all without showing a thing. He's given nothing away. He really is quite an extraordinary spy."

"It sounds like you admire him, Salim!"

"In a way, I do. But we must now be one better. We can't afford to give anything away either. Keep him close. Treat him the same, as I will do. When the times comes, he won't know what's hit him."

Sabena glared at the blasted-out house still on the screen. An evil smirk erupted across her face.

"Did you know what hit you Mr. Kinley?"

Chapter 60

Maide had realized a long time ago it was an "egg-timer" mission. Kinley had used up every last grain of sand to protect and serve, but Maide knew he'd have to take that call one day.

"The whole family…" repeated Maide slowly, remembering the picture of Kinley's daughter laughing, playing in a garden somewhere.

The head of MI6 station in Washington DC reviewed his notes.

"Yes, the whole family. No survivors. TV is already down there. Couldn't blanket in time. Apparently a reporter lives a few doors away and was home at the time of the blast. Didn't take them long to go live."

"Understandable," snapped Maide curtly. "Which channel?"

"CNN."

Maide located the channel, but adverts were running. "Not on yet."

"Keep watching. It'll be on," advised the Washington station head.

"I have to inform the PM."

"Of course. Call me later. We can discuss next steps."

Maide pressed a single number on speed dial.

"I'm sorry, sir. It's over."

At the other end, Ashton's face ran white. Unlike Maide, he had naively believed Kinley was in there to make the final difference. He'd never fully accepted the recent intel that Al Nadir knew Kinley was a mole, despite receiving conclusive proof.

Now his hands shook. It really was over. Al Nadir would never let anyone get that close again. And all those deaths, what did they mean now?

"Do we know how?"

"Bomb. Wiped out everyone."

"I want this chapter re-written. Understand?"

Maide knew what he had to do. "Yes, sir."

Kinley never happened. Operation Snowdrop never happened. Kinley had chosen the name Snowdrop, remaining true to his idealist sensibilities. The snowdrop, the first flower to bud, signals the end of winter. Kinley saw himself as that snowdrop, breaking out of the winter Al Nadir had imposed across the world, to bring a new season of hope and rebirth. A new spring.

Maide swallowed deeply. Just another agent gone. At least if his men had taken him out, it would have been clean. No collateral damage. Wife and daughter would have been unharmed. Angela would have grieved, but she would have eventually moved on and met someone else. Lotte would have had a new dad. Kinley would have been relegated to just a blurred moment, a snapshot in time of someone who had barely registered in her life, and of whom she remembered with love. Yes, mother and daughter would have survived, albeit with a few scars.

Why didn't he act sooner? Maide cursed himself. His clean-up team shouldn't have given Kinley time. Fifteen minutes was fifteen minutes too long. He should have seen it.

"I want Sam on this. He needs to close this investigation."

"And then?" asked Maide, awaiting the kill order on Sam. He was still connected to Snowdrop, and had incendiary information that could bring the whole UK government down.

"No more. This is it. He closes and we close. We now find another way. There are other options. Al Nadir are not indestructible. We'll find another way."

The assured stance the PM had taken reverberated inside Maide. He flicked back to the TV. Breaking news was now on, showing the scene of an Alexandria residential avenue, a visual horror story in the making.

Maide thought darkly about Ashton's words. Those other options had better be found bloody quickly.

Chapter 61

Ellie listened to the rest of the news. *God, everything is so depressing.* What was happening to the world? It seemed to be getting darker and more horrible. Every bulletin was filled with terrorist attacks, murders, rapes, robberies and kidnappings. There never seemed to be any good news. In fact, goodness in general was an extremely scarce commodity.

At first, Ellie had thought it was her view of the world being a little skewed. Then she realized it wasn't just her personal viewpoint. Thinking back over the last few months, people *were* getting more selfish and vacuous. A society already obsessed with celebrity had become even more fanatical about the rich and famous. Society had moved from a culture of "what you are" to a culture of "what you have." And it was clear everybody was looking out for number one.

Ellie noticed that violence, in parallel, had also increased. Every day in London, there seemed to be someone, dead or seriously wounded, hitting the headlines. Spiraling personal debt made money a focal point in everyone's lives. It seemed that friendship, loyalty and trust were words lost to the twentieth century. In the twenty-first century, money talked louder than ever. Everyone had their price.

Ellie shivered. She hated dark thoughts, and always tried to cancel them out before they ingrained into her mind. But now she felt thoroughly melancholy, and was unable to let go of the feeling. It was as if she had somehow been tainted by society's growing darkness. In that instance, Ellie could sense the greed and cruelty in the world, and sensed it gnawing inside her like a lethal disease. With focused determination, Ellie pushed back the feeling and flicked over to another channel. The weather forecast.

"Sunday will be sunny with some scattered showers."

Great, maybe we can go for a drive down south, thought Ellie. She was trying hard to brighten up. But she couldn't help feeling like a misanthrope, angry at a world where love and kindness had been lost to hate and cruelty.

Chapter 62

Sam turned into Grosvenor Road. He couldn't lose those surreptitious glances of Maide and Quentin from his mind. Their words had been disgusting and humiliating. It was clear Maide had seen him and Ellie last night. *Sick fucker!*

He still couldn't understand why they'd put him under surveillance. He wished he'd swept the apartment. But seeing Ellie standing there, waiting, he never had a chance. The truth was sweeping for bugs was furthest from his mind. What did Kinley always drill into him? "Sweeping saves lives!" It would certainly have saved his dignity, if not his life.

Sam shot over the carriage way onto Chelsea Embankment. His mind wandered back to the encounter with Quentin and Maide. He'd read Quentin. It was obvious he hadn't seen anything but was following the signals from Maide to engage. But what was Maide's game? Was it really just because he'd mentioned Piccadilly? Or something else?

Sam knew mentioning Snowdrop had always been strictly off-limits, but Maide had just thrown in the towel by agreeing to remove Kinley. He'd even threatened to invoke 'sign off' if Kinley didn't leave DC, which would place a kill order on Kinley to available wet workers in Alexandria. The whole business infuriated Sam.

It was like Maide didn't value Kinley anymore. He viewed him just as a liability to be eradicated.

After all Kinley had sacrificed. What he'd done. What they'd all done.

Sam didn't know the details of anything beyond what happened that day in Florence, the day Operation Snowdrop started. For operational purposes, Kinley had remained totally dark throughout the four years he'd been in Al Nadir. But Sam had an imagination. He knew what would have been expected of Kinley. He doubted he could have stepped over the line the way his friend had done.

Kinley, running under the alias of Stuart Kingswood, had risen within Al Nadir. Sam learned this through the encrypted comms web channel, Forever Flowers, that Kinley quickly accelerated from his initial position as global senior lieutenant to become the global commander for the Americas and Asia. His positioning meant he was fourth in line to Al Douri himself. As Kingswood, Kinley had secured top-level access. Through his covert work, Kinley had achieved exactly what he'd intended from the beginning. He'd identified money mounds in tens of billions buried within legitimate multinational businesses. One such business was a huge technology company that was directly in the public eye. It had even been given massive lucrative contracts from global governments to manage their data processing and analytics. Kinley's work in uncovering this just over a year ago had enabled a coordinated attack by global intelligence communities on Al Douri's money line, choking off almost a hundred billion dollars.

Governments around the world cancelled contracts. Suppliers put the screws on the company demanding payment. Suspected links to terrorist activities were leaked to Wall Street, affecting the share price as millions of shareholders dumped their shares. The share dump made way for hostile takeover bids, which made the company even more vulnerable. Al Douri had no choice but to put the reserves he'd ring-fenced for terrorist activities into keeping the company afloat, buying shares and bolstering market confidence. The financial attack pushed back his abilities and prevented at least twenty high-profile bombings that would have seen the accumulated death toll in millions.

Sam recalled the mechanics of the operation were ingenious, and all down Kinley's amazing financial business mind. As so many agencies were involved, Al Douri never figured out who was the ringleader. At the time, he believed it had been a big rival tech company. Sam was certain, although he didn't have actual intelligence, that Kinley had fueled that fire of suspicion. Unfortunately, the CEO of the rival firm was found in his Manhattan penthouse, split from head to toe, with a note in the middle between the two halves of his body, which said, *'Thanks for a ripping time! S x'.*

Sam shuddered as the photos of the poor guy leapt into his mind. Without a doubt, Sabena's hand had been on the other end of the machete.

And then there'd been Piccadilly. The lives of innocent citizens, both from the UK and across the world, had been taken that day. It had been state sanctioned murder by any other name. Kinley, Ashton, Maide and him, they'd all been complicit. All knew and accepted the path they were following.

Another memory flashed in.

The road in front of Sam was a blur as images flowed thick and fast. Florence, January 28, 2013. He'd been slammed against the wall between the lounge and bedroom. He'd glanced back and seen the lasers of the snipers. He'd yelled to warn his team. But it was already too late. Greg, Jim and Dan fell as the high-caliber, armor-piercing bullets tore through their Kevlar jackets. His team on the cover mission, Operation Aphrodite, were all massacred by Al Nadir. Only Sam made it out alive.

So much death had enabled Operation Snowdrop to bud. Now that bastard, Maide, wanted to shelve the whole thing.

Burning with anger at the injustice of it all, Sam hit the steering wheel.

He didn't hear the first buzz. His anger blocked out his surroundings. He behaved so unlike his usual demeanor of cool and calculating. He just wasn't keeping it together. He wasn't thinking. Sam knew, where Kinley and Snowdrop were concerned, he possessed virtually no capacity for rational thought.

They'd all gone too far. But lives had been saved.

They'd all done their job.

For the greater good.

Sam's phone buzzed again, and he clocked the caller on his dashboard. DC Station Head Atkins. He swallowed hard. Inside, a prescient flicker of dread rippled through him.

"Yes," said Sam, and his voice recognition system picked up the call immediately.

"Sam?" The moment Sam heard the glimmer of a treble in Atkins' voice, fear surfaced.

"Yes?"

Sam barely wanted to answer. He didn't want to hear the next words.

"Kinley's dead."

Sam gripped the steering wheel so tight his fingers imprinted into the leather like a brand. He breathed deep and tried to focus on the road. He pressed hard on the accelerator and shot down Chelsea Embankment to his apartment.

For an instant, he couldn't speak. Ice replaced his blood and he felt like he'd turned into a glacier. The station head didn't talk either.

Silence loomed within the car.

"Sam," ventured the station head finally. In his tone, he wanted to deliver the news and get the hell off the line. "It was a bomb. It took out him and his family."

Sam listened. He wanted to vomit. Maide had been right all along. Kinley had been made. And Al Nadir had taken their revenge in their usual way.

Annihilation of the entire family.

Sam found his voice, and couldn't, although he tried desperately, suppress a sob.

"Oh, God. Angie. Lotte!"

"My condolences, Sam. I know you guys were close."

Station Head Atkins rang off the line quickly, leaving Sam with the echoing words.

Sam recalled his last meal with the family in Alexandria, some two months earlier. It was just before his operation in Rome. Angie had cooked tagliatelle e funghi porcini con tartufo and they'd drank a fine bottle of Sicilian Fiano. Kinley never spoke about Al Nadir. Their discussions, when in earshot of Angie, were kept to FCO business and any crossover with his work and Kinley's in STEE. Out of earshot, they'd been on Six operations that Kinley, as a top agent, was involved in. Neither broke cover. Any surveillance by Al Nadir would have heard what was expected: two agents talking shop, whether in their cover jobs or on 'the real stuff'.

Sam had been amazed at how Lotte had grown. He'd noticed that, at almost five, she'd become quite precocious, but still remained adorable. Angie had been attentive and lovely as ever during his stay. Kinley had snuggled up with his wife and daughter on the sofa. Sam had taken a large comfy armchair and the four of them watched 'Frozen' on television.

The memory shattered into pieces in Sam's mind as he imagined the explosion taking their lives.

Motherfucking bastards!

Inside, hurt, pain and anger raged. The corners of his eyes pulled as he drove fiercely down the Chelsea Embankment. He tried to concentrate but he knew he wasn't looking. Sam was driving at speed, but he wasn't actually taking in anything at all.

All he could see was Kinley curled up on the sofa with Angie and Lotte, peaceful and happy.

Kinley had given so much for his country. He'd been the absolute patriot. He'd made the ultimate sacrifice.

Sam wasn't going to let Al Nadir get away with it.

He wanted bodies.

And he wanted them falling from his own bloody hands.

Chapter 63

They would be safe.

That's what they'd told him on the video call last night.

He'd arrived home. As he parked the car in his drive, he saw the door blown off its hinges. He'd leapt out the car, grabbing his mobile and about to call 911, when a video call came in.

He stared at his phone. The images he saw were tattooed on his mind.

His wife, Patsy, his daughter, Zoe, and his son, Peter, all blindfolded and held at gun point. He could see they'd been crying. Their dirty faces were tear-stained.

Patsy's face was heavily bruised. Her jaw was swollen and there was a fresh cut just beneath her right eye.

Peter bit his lip. He was trying to stay brave. The left side of his face had a purple bruise snaking down it, and his nose was off center and bleeding badly.

Zoe's sweatshirt was ripped down the front, partially exposing her breasts, and her legs were bare, with her thighs heavily bruised. Her cheek was swollen and cut, and her bottom lip was puffy and bled. Ross shivered on seeing her. He knew what had happened. He had to hold back from thumping the phone or chucking it away.

But most of all, he wanted to kill the barbaric animals who'd done that to his daughter.

Of course, he couldn't do any of those things. He had to endure the transmission until he discovered what the bastards wanted.

A guy with a black balaclava and black T shirt came into view. Two other men, dressed the same, stood at either end of a shabby sofa with guns pointed at his family. Ross thought they were men by how they stood with their legs apart. They had broad shoulders and their automatics cradled a little but the muscles in their arms tensed. They were ready to press the trigger at a second's notice from the head of the gang.

The man in view spoke. "This is your family. If you want them returned to you, alive and unharmed, you do exactly what I tell you."

Ross focused hard. He had to remember everything this man was saying and how he was saying it. His voice was thick like molasses, and Ross had to suppress a shudder. Just the way he sounded, he intoned the very elements of evil.

Ross couldn't believe his family were at the mercy of that man.

"Ok," answered Ross, pushing a quiet calm. But inside, he was breaking apart.

"Take the entire quantum compound and meet me outside Taco Express on 8th off Main at 10 a.m. tomorrow. Involve the police or fail to turn up…"

Ross heard gunfire and the screen went blank. His heart crumbled.

"No!" he screamed.

"Those were tests shot at the floor," returned the molasses-voiced bastard. The picture returned to Ross' family, too terrified to move.

"Fail me and the next ones will be at Zoe's head."

"I'll get it. I'll get you anything. Just don't harm my family." Ross' composure had vanished. He'd seen what they'd already done to his family. He would agree to kill the president at that moment if it brought his family back.

With a smile in his voice, the molasses-voiced bastard answered, "I know you will. Until tomorrow."

The transmission cut out and Ross was left staring traumatized at the screen.

Abruptly, Ross shook the images from his head. He needed to concentrate, and his family's stricken, damaged faces only made him panic. Especially Zoe's.

And right now, he had to focus.

The military officers took up guard outside the lab as Ross walked inside.

He looked at his watch. Less than fifteen minutes to the drop off. He glanced up at the guards outside the room. They appeared to be talking to one another and were not even looking through the glass wall. He was wide enough to position his body as a cover, so neither the camera to the right of him, nor the officers outside, could see his actions. He knew he couldn't waste time thinking about if he could do it. Slipping out the plasticine and silver pen he'd bought from K-

Mart that morning, he quickly switched them with the compound and pen device. Then, he shut the box and walked over to the safe.

Ross was in front of the safe when he felt a sharp tap on his shoulder. That's it, he thought, somehow they've seen me make the switch. Ross knew hesitation would signal guilt. He'd already been sloppy in his reaction with Weitz; he wasn't going to make the same mistake again. He sighed, annoyed at being interrupted, and turned quickly.

"Yes? What is it?"

"Excuse me, Dr. Whyte, I'd like to confirm the contents of the box. Open it please, sir."

Still maintaining the irritable scientist façade, Ross opened the box. His heart was thundering in his throat, so loud he thought the officer might pick up on the vibration. But the officer just peered inside. Satisfied that all the pieces were where they should be, he signaled for Ross to close it.

"Thank you, sir. Please return the box to the safe, Dr. Whyte."

Ross nodded, opened the safe, and placed the box inside it. Closing the safe door, he heard a whirring noise as the time lock activated, a time lock that both he and the officer knew could only be deactivated by the president himself. Ross looked back at the officer.

"All done. Now, if you wouldn't mind…"

"Of course, Dr. Whyte. Please continue with your work."

The officer returned to his team, and together, they dispersed from the lab, leaving Ross to his own business. With the pen and compound deep in his pocket, Ross walked briskly out of the lab. From the tests he'd carried out, he knew both the compound and pen's materials did not register on any periodic table, and therefore, they couldn't be identified by any scanners installed at the Blacksburg facility. Ross swiped his ID through security and left the lab, walking quickly but not hurrying.

He got into his car and drove to the Taco Express on 8th off Main. Parking at the back, Ross shoved the compound into a bag and waited.

He was going to get them back. That was all that mattered. His life didn't count. He knew his career was over. Despite the situation, there would be consequences. The compound was essential to America's future, and the president wouldn't hear any bleating from him about his family being in danger. That his position in all this was intractable didn't mean anything to President Treeborne. Compassion wasn't in his DNA. He was a sociopath, immune to the emotions of others. But Ross didn't care if he rotted in jail for treason. At least he'd have the assurance he'd saved his family.

Chapter 64

Operatives were dying across the world in a variety of painful ways and always at the hands of Al Nadir. Maide knew that. Some he'd even sent to their deaths, but he'd always kept aloof. They were just a combination of letters and numbers, ranks and grades, a string of competencies and capabilities. Nothing more. Single agents were the best, of course. They had no ties. But in a world of equality, he couldn't demand for every operative to be single. Many of them were married with kids. Sometimes the wife or husband knew, but more often than not, they didn't. That's when things had to be handled carefully. Protocols were in place with procedures to ensure financial stability for the remaining partner and continuity of cover for the deceased. This all went on around Maide, and he remained immune to feeling anything. Their lives didn't touch him. He was isolated.

But with Kinley, it had been different.

Perhaps it was because of the incredible risk they'd taken, the lives they had gambled away. Or maybe it was more than that. Maybe it was all just too close to him. Their little team, Ashton, Kinley, Sam and himself, they were going to change the world. They were going to bring down Al Nadir. It sounded ludicrous now. But then, four years ago, they all had the same belief, a true, pure belief, that they could do it.

That was before the deaths started to pile up and the lies started to mount. Now where were they? The team was worn out and tired. Ashton was a showman pandering to the political game. Sam was a rebellious maverick. And Kinley, the man it had all revolved around, was dead. All they had tried to achieve was now, but a wish caught in the wind.

Keeping Operation Snowdrop amongst the four of them had kept the chances of disclosure to a minimum. It had given them free reign to do whatever was necessary for success. But had they been too obsessed with the end game to see what they were really doing?

Maide shuddered. Had they gone too far? Somehow, at the time, when they were in the thick of it, nothing seemed a step too far. It was all for the greater good, the ultimate goal. Bring down Salim Al Douri. No sacrifice was too great if they achieved it. They had all felt the same way. There had been a sense of unity in all of them to walk the dark path. Only now, that unity had gone.

The conversation he'd had with Sam left him with no other option. They had made a pact of silence to never speak of Piccadilly or Snowdrop again. But Sam had broken that vow with cavalier disregard. Maide had to protect his secret and take the appropriate action if Sam was on the verge revealing it to anyone, most of all his wife. The surveillance worried him.

Sam's wife, she was now their biggest problem.

He couldn't discuss this with the PM. He had to keep Ashton clear and able to cry plausible denial. But Maide needed to express his concerns with someone who could take a clear, objective view. So he summoned Quentin Ludlow, the foreign secretary.

As Maide spoke about Sam Noor's insubordinate behavior in general terms, without specifics to Piccadilly, Quentin nodded and sucked on his cigar. It was clear the smoking ban hadn't reached him. In their private location, public bans were meaningless. They were the government. They lived by their own rules.

"But Sam isn't the real problem, despite his recent behavior," said Maide and he tensed momentarily before he composed himself.

"So who is?"

Maide looked pensive. He lit his cigar, puffed out, lent back, reached into his drawer, and took out a slim-line pen drive.

"Remember Sarah Masters?"

Quentin shot a look of fear at Maide as he spoke. That episode had been unbelievable.

Chapter 65

Two Years Earlier

Michael Masters had been with MI6 for over fifteen years. He'd been married to Sarah Masters for twenty-two. They had been just like Sam and Ellie, very much in love. Sarah was the last person in the world to be considered a threat. Michael had been feeling a little under the weather when he'd told her. Just like Sam, he'd had enough of the lying. Michael had wanted Sarah to know. The confession was like a trigger. Something in her snapped. His training couldn't protect him against his own wife. The attack was made even more sadistic by the place of death: their bedroom. Forensics showed they'd had sex minutes before the attack. Sarah's prints were all over him and the murder weapon. She'd smashed his skull repeatedly with an ornate, pewter, bedside lamp. It was a wedding anniversary present to her from Michael.

On the first blow, Michael would have been taken by surprise. Perhaps, he had been looking in the other direction. Shock would have disoriented him. His brain would have told him to react, protect, but the overriding emotions of the heart would have been at odds with taking defensive action against his own wife. He would have been confused for a second. The delay would have given Sarah her second window of attack. By the second blow, his skull would have caved in. By the third he would have been dead.

The path lab report stated Michael had been hit at least twenty times, maybe twenty-two, a blow for every year of his marriage. It was an attack of frenzied insanity. Michael's remains had been more liquid than solid. Hardened agents had retched on the spot. How a woman who claimed to have loved Michael could have done what she did to him, nobody could comprehend. After the murder, Sarah vanished. It was like she'd dropped off the world. All the traces came up negative. She was never brought to justice.

They came to a logical but terrifying conclusion. Al Nadir had gotten to her.

Chapter 66
22 March, 2017

The front door swung open silently, and Sam walked into their apartment. Ellie turned her head towards the door.

"Hello, darling." She leapt up to welcome Sam with a passionate kiss. "How was-"

Sam placed his finger to her lips, silencing her enthusiasm. He daggered her eyes with a raging single look. Ellie stepped back, afraid and full quizzical confusion. Sam grabbed her hand and pulled her roughly over to the desk in the study.

Taking Ellie's jotter pad, he picked up her pen and wrote, *"Don't speak. Flat bugged."*

Ellie looked at Sam, her face drawn and terrified. Shaking slightly, she took the pen from Sam.

"Who?"

Sam took the pen and replied, *"My people. Checking now."*

Ellie watched as Sam reached inside his traveler bag, searched amongst his shirts, and brought out a little device no bigger than a square cigarette lighter. She'd never seen it before. It was silver colored with a plastic strip at the top, which resembled the infrared panel on a TV remote. He depressed two little metal teeth at either side of the device. A front panel lowered to reveal a small row of tiny rectangular buttons with a minute red to green scanning bar underneath. Sam pressed the tiny buttons swiftly and the panel lit up. The scanning bar flickered to green, and Sam began to sweep the apartment.

In a daze, like a programmed automaton, Ellie followed Sam. Standing behind him while he scanned, she could only look on and admire Sam's cool diligence. She didn't know what to do. She was inadequate. Insignificant. His world was so different. She had no experience, no knowledge to help him.

He said nothing, just kept scanning. His concentration was fixed on the little red/green bar. Nothing else mattered, not even her. Nothing detracted his absolute focus. Ellie could see that. She knew she was seeing her husband for the first time. This was the Sam Noor he'd kept hidden.

Ellie opened her mouth to acknowledge her realization. In his peripheral vision, Sam saw the flicker of her mouth move. He grasped her arm tightly and placed his finger up to his lips. The cold anger in his eyes forced her silence. Ellie nodded reluctantly.

Sam left her side and walked quickly into their bedroom. Ellie stepped in behind. She looked around. The unmade bed. Sheets curled and twisted. Faint impressions of their bodies. Evidence of their passionate intensity. It was all before her.

She watched Sam scan with vigorous persistence, his face grave. *What kind of sick bastards play a game like this?* Ellie stared at the bed, and then at her husband sweeping across the air conditioning panels, and she wanted to be sick. Their precious, personal moments had been seen by others. It was nothing less than violation.

Ellie ran to the bathroom, pushed her head into the toilet and retched. Turning on the tap, she cupped her hands and splashed cold water on her face. But her face didn't feel cleansed. Shivering with indignation, Ellie returned to the lounge.

She sat down. Her teeth chattered. Her knees knocked. It was like a force was shaking the life out of her. She couldn't carry on like this. More revelations. More secrets. More lies. This nightmare rollercoaster would never end.

She looked across the lounge. The door beckoned; the rush to leave was physical.

Ellie was on her feet, her bag on her shoulder, before she knew what she was doing. She peered back into the apartment. Sam was still sweeping the bedroom. She turned back and moved slowly towards the door. *One last look.*

Chapter 67

Ross sat in the car with his hands on his thighs, grasping them to quell his panic. He hadn't had any further proof of life, but he hoped the kidnappers would keep to their word.

That's all he had. Hope.

At that moment, sitting in the car, smelling the Mexican fast food wafting out of the ventilator shaft in front of him, and waiting for someone to make contact, he had hardly any hope left.

He thought of Zoe. Bile rose within him. He held down the urge to vomit. Had they done the same to Patsy? Oh my God!

Who were they? How did they know about the quantum compound?

Then, Ross realized, there was only one organization who could do what they'd done.

Al Nadir.

"Dr. Ross Whyte?"

Ross span around on hearing the voice thick like molasses from the video. He cursed himself for being so lax. Ross never even heard the door open. He never felt anyone at all. He must've been so deep in thought to not hear. He felt foolish and exposed.

"You have what I need?"

Ross nodded. "It's here in the bag. All of it."

The man opened the bag and saw the compound. "Where's the pen?"

Ross took the pen from his pocket and handed it to the man.

"Kept them separate. Good thinking. Don't want to attract attention, do we? Al Nadir thanks you for your diligence."

So his theory was right. They were Al Nadir.

Ross took in the man settled beside him. He was an everyday-looking, middle-aged, typically American kind of guy complete with beer gut, Red Sox t-shirt, faded jacket, jeans and a baseball cap. Ross wouldn't have given him a second glance. He didn't look the stereotypical terrorist. But that was always it with Al Nadir. They had broken the mold, and the archetypical terrorist of yesteryear no longer played a role in their new order.

The man smiled and pocketed the pen inside his jacket.

"My family! I've done what you asked. Now return my family."

Ross kept his voice measured and quiet. He didn't want to appear too forceful. Nor did he want to agitate or annoy the terrorist.

"My, you're a demanding guy, aren't you? Surely you expect us to test this first."

Ross looked startled, and then his calmness slipped away as he remembered his family, terrified and in pain. And Zoe. What they'd done. His unbridled anger took over.

"Listen, you bastard! I've done everything you asked. Now give me back my family."

The man listened and smiled, as if a toddler was having a tantrum.

"Just a second."

He waggled his finger with some condescension at Ross. Then, slowly, he brought the compound and pen together. On contact, the compound lit up, shining brilliant light into the car.

"Well, Dr. Whyte, it seems you have, indeed, delivered."

"So, my family? They'll be returned? I'll see them today?" The desperation in his voice couldn't be shielded.

"Why, of course, Dr. Whyte. You'll see your family. You'll see them very soon."

Ross smiled in relief.

"Oh, yeah, I'd say you'll be with them real soon. Look."

The man held up the live feed on his phone to show Dr. Whyte his family. Ross watched as the blindfolds were taken off and they looked into the camera.

"You're all gonna be together," drawled molasses-voiced man.

At that point, a man came into the picture and blasted the son, the daughter and, finally, the wife. Clear, clean shots straight to the head. Ross screamed out and grabbed at the phone.

On the other side of the car, a new man arrived, raised his hand and shot Ross in the head.

"Like I said, all together real soon," repeated molasses-voiced man coldly as he got out of the car.

Chapter 68

It was obvious Treeborne would never be able to keep the quantum compound bomb. His need to tell everyone how wonderful he was, and how he was 'saving the planet', coupled with his insatiable sexual appetite, meant the days of the bomb in Treeborne's hands were going to be very few.

Aswa-da queried the Observation Screen on 'quantum bomb', 'Earth March 22, 2017' and 'President Treeborne'. The inherent analytics within the sentient crystals propelled different instances onto the Screen.

A White House aide that was in the pocket of Al Nadir got wind of the new weapon. Aswa-da watched Salim Al Douri receiving the news. His handsome, chiseled face descended into a homicidal mask of rage. He screamed like an insanely petulant child that he 'had to have the weapon'.

Aswa-da followed Salim's actions. The woman who'd delivered the message slipped into view. Tall with dark hair flowing and bright but menacing black eyes, she tried to placate Salim's ravings. She was Salim's number two, Sabena Sanantoni.

"Babes, we'll find out what it is," said Sabena, adopting a gentle, soothing tone.

"Those motherfuckers in the US can't get the edge on me now. That's not possible. What did our asset say again? A bomb of unthinkable capability. It could take all our bases out in one hit. Is that what that fucker Treeborne is planning to do? Is that prick Ashton behind him? I've got to know, Sabena. I can't be out like this. They're planning to take me down. I'm not going to sit around and watch them do it." Salim was spitting words like bullets. His handsome face reddened, and his eyes grew wide as his anger increased.

"Salim, darling, we'll find out what it is they've got, and we'll take it from them."

Sabena draped her arms around Al Douri's shaking body. Aswa-da watched as she calmed Salim with her words and touch. Her lips dropped down to his neck and she started to kiss him. In parallel, her hands wandered down between his legs and she cupped him with aggressive passion.

"Listen, Salim. No-one fucks with my man. Leave it to me. I'll get you the weapon. I promise."

"I've got to have it, babes. I've got to," muttered Salim impatiently, moving in close to Sabena. Then he grasped her waist tight, staring at her with vicious obsession. "See to it. Use everything you've got. Take it from Treeborne. Bring it to me. I need it. Like I need you."

Salim's lips dropped onto Sabena slightly open mouth and he thrust his tongue inside, fiercely pressing down and almost suffocating her. Sabena's eyes dilated. Far from showing fear, Aswa-da knew, she loved every savage second.

Another instant in the Observation Screen query brought up Sabena on a mission in Dallas. She was in disguise using Hans Stein-Muller's meta-material face cream made of nano-bots that could change her facial structure externally. It effectively created a cloak of her real face and masked it with the newly programmed one.

Aswa-da stared at Sabena as she applied the cream. For Earth technology, it really was incredible. Stein-Muller's biomimetic, programmable, self-reproducing nanocytes could create synthetic skin cells over the top of existing skin. Stein-Muller had used biomimicry to evoke a similar process as the one a chameleon powers up to change its exterior skin to match its surroundings. The difference was that the change was not to match the wearer's environment but instead would match the face on the app program. Aswa-da could see all Sabena had to do was select the identity she wanted on her phone app, smooth the cream into her face and click on 'activate'. The selected face would then be built from the self-reproducing nanocytes that stretched across Sabena's skin in the face cream.

Sabena was literally undercover as the stunningly beautiful Ms. Sara Allesandro-Garcia, a reclusive, extremely wealthy Spanish heiress who now lived in Texas. She exhorted strong patriotism and passionate Republican values. Her sizable donation to the fundraising benefit dinner attended by President Treeborne assured her a position at the top table.

Despite the vigorous vector scans, Stein-Muller's nano-mask held up and Ms. Allesandro-Garcia was greeted warmly by the president's aides, who facilitated her meeting. Sabena turned on her charm. By the end of the evening, the president had fully succumbed to her simple but potent signals. As coffee and liqueurs were served, the president laid a hand on Sabena and suggested, "Further discussion about how she could help the party," with a twinkle in his eye.

Aswa-da observed Treeborne and Sabena enter the Presidential Suite in the hotel. The door slammed after the Secret Services had checked and cleared the room. Before they left, they gave a terse, "We'll be outside, Mr. President."

Treeborne threw Sabena onto the bed, tore her clothes off and mounted her with a brutish disregard. She was no more than a piece of meat for his enjoyment. Aswa-da smirked and moved his hand in his usual elliptical motion to speed up events on screen.

Sabena pulled herself out of Treeborne's clutches and disappeared into the bathroom. Inside, she applied lipstick. She smiled, enjoying the reflection of her gorgeously naked body. She noticed the cuts and bruises caused by the president's violent attentions.

"I'll make you pay, you motherfucker," she sneered.

Aswa-da watched Treeborne grab her and she pushed up her lips to kiss him. His lids fell a little, and Sabena maneuvered him back to the bed, where his eyes closed completely. Aswa-da wondered what she'd given him. The sentient crystals within the Observation Screen delivered directly to his databanks. They revealed that Sabena had used a fast-acting methohexital sedative to place him into lullaby land.

Sabena scooted over to the table and took out her compact from her bag. It was also a bug sweeper. She scanned the room. Aswa-da saw her subconsciously nod, and she pulled out her mascara, turned the bottom, and pulled out what looked like a miniature pen drive. The president's laptop sat on the table.

Sabena flipped up the screen and powered it up. The laptop had been in sleep mode and it popped up with a password page. Sabena inserted the drive. Aswa-da didn't immediately know what she was doing, but the Observation Screen sentient crystals filled his databanks with immediate knowledge. The drive had connected to Al Nadir's super node network and the software that Al Nadir's Japanese scientists had perfected streamed down. The algorithm that used next generation pairing-cryptography broke into the backdoor of the president's laptop. The crypto-analysis function that the software initiated was the equivalent to spoofing the authority of the information system administrator.

Wanting to get closer to see what Sabena was doing, Aswa-da twirled his finger, and he was wrapped in the darkened Presidential Suite. Sabena requested a password reset and entered in her own password. This password would never be seen. Aswa-da knew Sabena would reset it again, after gaining access to default, to its original password.

The desktop screen came up displaying various folders. In the top right-hand corner of the screen, a small red dot appeared. It flashed continuously, signifying its connection to Al Nadir's super node network, and that it was copying the entire contents of the laptop direct to a server thousands of miles away.

Sabena stole a quick look back at the president, who snored peacefully behind her. The dot flashed black, denoting that the server had sucked out all the data. Sabena clicked on the black dot, severing the connection, and initiated the reset of the password back to its original. Her task complete, Sabena withdrew the drive and put the laptop back into sleep mode.

Aswa-da watched as Sabena pressed a small raised area on the pen drive's front and waited. The drive, Aswa-da recognized, had been created from a nano-tech material. As he watched, it suddenly started to break down. Its internal structure imploded until all that was left of the drive was golden glitter. With a swift motion, she delicately collected the glitter into a tissue. Taking another tissue, she wiped off her lipstick, screwed both tissues into a ball, and hurled them into the toilet. She flushed and grinned, watching the tissues float away.

Sabena pulled on her dress. Her panties and bra were in tatters so she left them. Aswa-da turned, following Sabena's eye, as she stared with hatred at Treeborne.

Before Sabena vacated the suite, she scribbled a note beside the telephone.

Thank you, Mr. President, for such a wondrous and enlightening experience. S x.

Aswa-da jumped forward to Salim sitting in front of his laptop, staring at the files taken from Treeborne's computer. He was in his study in Sanctum, the Al Nadir-owned island retreat in the Caribbean, and sun streamed in through the French windows. Salim clicked on Project David. He sped read the information and realized it was the file he'd been searching for. Aswa-da could see his eyes lighting up. His mouth grew wide into a massive smile. He looked across at a tall woman with a strong physique in a cropped top and mini skirt that barely covered her ass.

"Sabena, babes, I've found it! It's a quantum fucking bomb!"

"It's not?" yelled Sabena, running over to see the evidence of this revelation.

"It is and it's gonna be mine."

Sabena leapt into Salim's lap. "What have you got planned, darling? Are you going to steal it?"

Salim pointed to the screen. A big boned guy with white hair was in a photograph in a lab with Treeborne. "Uh, uh. No way. I'm going into the family insurance business. This guy, Dr. Ross Whyte, he's going to be my first client!"

Aswa-da moved his hand in his usual elliptical motion and fast forwarded to March 21, 2017. He watched as Al Nadir operatives, armed with MAC 10's slung across their chests stormed Ross' home. They sedated and snatched his wife, daughter and son. The three men hauled their bodies into the back of a van and sped away. The entire exercise took no more than a minute, and was executed with military precision.

Aswa-da was aware that the intruders were Al Nadir and that the next scenes would be brutal. He didn't need to see them. But, like a kid chewing on a toffee after being told not to eat sweets by his dentist, Aswa-da couldn't help but immerse himself in the sick depravity of the intruders. Throughout the family's ordeal, Aswa-da smirked, enjoying the scenes and reveling in the descent of the human soul.

Aswa-da took the observations forward to Ross sitting in his car. Ross watched his family assassinated and then he was shot almost in parallel.

Cleaning up their mess, thought Aswa-da with a grin.

Red Sox t-shirt man got out of the car and went straight into a black Cadillac SUV with darkened windows with the other shooter. They drove away rapidly.

In the Cadillac, Red Sox t-shirt man made a call.

"Dr. Al Douri, we have it. On our way to the jet now."

Aswa-da switched to observe the recipient of the call, Salim. He lounged on his private sun terrace situated on the roof top of his huge private and heavily secured mansion in Dubai, overlooking crystal waters and sweeping golden sands.

Sabena, in the other lounger, lent over, her slender fingers dancing up his leg in a teasing fashion.

"I reckon someone's going to have a tantrum tonight," purred Sabena.

Al Douri smirked and yanked Sabena onto him. His legs intertwined with hers, gripping and holding her tight against him.

"Yeah. That little fucker, Treeborne. He's going to be crying like a baby!"

Aswa-da twirled his finger again and he was back in the Observation

Room. He stared at Salim and Sabena. He hadn't planned it that way. But he was still satisfied by this new dynamic. He knew his path hadn't been changed.

If anything, the path was more defined now that Salim had come into Aswa-da's playground.

Chapter 69

Quentin had met Ellie on various Foreign Office occasions and evening soirees. He couldn't bring himself to consider, even in the remotest sense, that Ellie was a terrorist. She was so lovely, so bubbly and so enchanting that she couldn't possibly be a threat to national security.

"You can't suspect his wife?" he said.

Maide didn't confirm or deny, only held up the pen drive. "I'm going to show you this."

The MI6 head slipped the drive into a concealed slot in the wood panel of his desk.

The surveillance devices planted in Sam and Ellie's apartment were movement sensitive, only transmitting and recording when movement was detected. On the wide screen plasma tv embedded into an oak alcove situated in front of Maide's desk juddered into life. The scene showed Ellie walking to the door and greeting Sam. Maide raised an eyebrow at Quentin, and pressed fast forward on his laptop. The scenes sped forward. Darkness took over the screen, and then suddenly loud clubbing music burst out. On screen, the first camera view hopped to another camera set at ninety degrees as movement was tracked. The view showed a beautiful, naked woman dancing around a handsome, naked man. Quentin recognized Sam and Ellie immediately.

"Oh, Jesus Christ, Justin. This isn't right."

"Neither was Sarah Masters. Shut up, Quentin. Don't be so wet. I'm not interested in that. Watch what happens later."

Maide pushed the scenes into super-fast forward. Naked bodies melded. Scenes changed. The view switched to static darkness. Then Ellie appeared. The cameras tracked her movement to the kitchen. Quentin looked quizzically at Maide.

"Where are you going with this?"

"Just watch," Maide replied mysteriously, and he turned back to the screen.

Quentin shrugged and did the same. After a few moments of Ellie pouring water from a bottle down her throat and boiling the kettle Quentin asked, "Excuse me Justin, but so far, she doesn't seem to be much of a threat to national security."

"I told you to watch, didn't I? So watch!" snapped Maide, furious.

Quentin looked back at the screen, still preoccupied with Maide's attitude. But he saw that Ellie who had been drinking a cup of coffee, suddenly had started to speak.

"Who's she talking to?

Maide hit pause. "That's what I'd like to know."

"Could it be Sam?"

"No, it's not him. Bedroom surveillance has him still asleep."

"So who?" asked Quentin. "Did they have guests?"

"No, they didn't."

"I don't understand," muttered Quentin.

"Watch the rest. I assure you there will be more questions to ask."

Maide pressed play.

Speaking to an empty kitchen, Ellie looked terrified. Her eyes took on a crazed blankness, and she froze to the spot. Then, without warning, she let forth a blood-chilling scream, and pitched forward as if she was trying to move away from something. The coffee mug she was holding tilted and spilled its boiling contents across her hand.

Maide paused again. Quentin stared at the scream, amazed.

"Our analysts have taken this apart but we can't find out why she screamed."

"Surely it's the coffee." Quentin stared, distracted by Ellie's frozen features. She looked like a woman facing death.

"No, it's not the coffee," said Maide. "She screamed before it spilt."

Quentin rationalized Maide's words. He was right. Ellie had screamed involuntarily. It was as though she could see something unseen by the cameras.

"Could it be an insect? A spider, perhaps?" suggested Quentin, still mesmerized by Ellie's face of fear.

"We thought of that, but our analysis came up with nothing."

"What was it she said? 'I'm listening.' Do you think she was wired up?"

"Why say it otherwise? And then she says, 'Tell me what you want.' It seems to me that someone was giving her instructions."

"But her last words 'What is too far gone?' don't seem to fit. The pattern is wrong," said Quentin, struggling with his own rapid analysis.

"It would fit if Al Nadir was telling her to take action on something that was 'too far gone.' Maybe her relationship with Sam?"

"You think she's a deep cover assassin?" Quentin asked.

"Well, put it like this," said Maide, "a real, loving wife doesn't lie to her husband…"

Quentin finished the thought. "Unless she has something to hide."

Chapter 70

Hours after Sabena heard they had the quantum bomb, she'd disengaged herself from Salim and left the glorious sun terrace in Dubai to head back to her new Cambridgeshire base. Aboard her private Gulfstream jet, heading back to the UK, she smiled to herself as she replayed the call over and over in her head, and let the force of the sparse words sink in. The team she'd hand-picked for the job of acquisition had delivered. Granted, they'd always been a touch psychotic, and often damaged the goods whilst getting to the action, but she couldn't penalize them for that, not when they had a hundred percent success rate.

And anyway, given the opportunity, she always did the same thing. A little damage goes a long way in getting the target to pony up with what they wanted.

Sabena sneered, remembering how things had panned out in life. Salim and Al Nadir would bring her power. Of that, she had always been certain. But what degree of power? That had always been something of an unknown.

Now of course, she knew.

She had met Salim during her time at Cambridge. They'd hit it off immediately, seeing in each other a need to express, experiment and go beyond the boundaries of acceptance.

Sabena smiled playing out in her mind the first time she'd seen Salim.

October 8, 1987. Sabena had just started Cambridge University. She loved being out of Sicily. Free from her cloying parents, always keeping their eye on her, Sabena was determined to have fun, but one look around her on the first day of Semester and Sabena knew she'd have to alter her plans. Surrounded by prissy, public school pricks who only knew one kind of shafting, she reconciled herself to heading down to pub to get a taste of the 'local cuisine'.

But then, he got up and spoke. Sabena had been in a seminar class. His words echoed a defiance of everything, an abject abhorrence to convention. Although his delivery focused on particle physics, the sound of his voice set Sabena alight.

She sat transfixed, in awe of this arrogant, brilliant beast. As beautiful in mind as he was in body.

Sabena knew the guy must have sensed something. With his feral instincts on overdrive, he looked over. His eyes burned into Sabena, captured her and imprisoned her. In one single look. It wasn't like a crush, or even a deep attraction. This was base desire. Animal lust. His eyes sucked Sabena in.

And all she could feel was need. Hot, sticky insatiable need, rising inside her.

The guy was living perfection, and Sabena wanted nothing more than to shatter that exquisiteness to pieces. To feel him lose control, such that he could.

Sabena vowed at that moment, she would ride him until he was broken and belonged totally to her.

The seminar had finished, but Sabena was still caught up in her salacious thoughts.

"It's Salim."

Like spacetime had doubled on itself, he suddenly stood in front of her.

"Sabena."

Her proffered hand was ignored.

He looked at Sabena, his eyes drilling deep to touch the core of her being.

"I will take you so hard you will cry for mercy."

His words left Sabena speechless.

The furnace she'd been stoking throughout the seminar exploded. Sabena was certain Salim could see the reaction in her eyes, for he grabbed her hair roughly and pushed his lips upon hers with a savage intensity. It was unlike anything she'd so far experienced with other guys of his age.

They never made it to the next tutorial.

Salim, she knew, was a creature of the dark. Pain was his ultimate pleasure. And, oh boy, did Sabena scream on that first assignation. He'd been right about that. Though not as a result of his deliciously violent violation. She'd screamed because she'd finally found her match.

Her true soul mate.

A man carved from the very coals of Hell itself. As she was.

After a few months together, it became obvious to Sabena that a one-on-

one relationship for Salim would never be enough. He liked to share and was flexible in his leanings.

Intuitive in the ways of psychology, Sabena realized very quickly the one way to win Salim's eye was to raise the bar further. When word reached Salim of her hedonistic, drug-fueled orgies, his interest piqued. The more salacious and sadistic the sound bites, the more enraptured he became of Sabena.

Sabena understood winning Salim over completely would never be easy.

Whatever way Sabena looked at Salim, he was not your average nineteen-year-old. With his private plane on standby, his speedboat, sports car, in town penthouse, out of town country pile and a string of staff ready to service his every whim, Salim Al Douri even back then had been an industry unto himself.

Sabena soon realized that whatever Salim wanted, he got.

He'd gotten her. That was for sure. But for Salim, Sabena knew she'd never be enough. Salim had an enormous appetite. And he liked to sample a range of dishes from many different places.

So, to ensure the continued arousal of his interest, Sabena devised a new game.

It was all so very easy. Sabena's peers had been so pliable. Effortlessly influenced. With Salim, she'd displayed a lifestyle of sheer excess. And now everyone wanted to be with them. Whatever the association, however tenuous the link, being with Salim and Sabena gave the hanger-on serious credibility. Salim and Sabena, they were the beautiful ones, the brilliant ones.

The ones to be with. The ones to be seen with.

And those fawning fools had done anything she'd asked just to savor the crumbs from their table.

Sabena grinned, remembering.

Oh, those days had been such fun. All she had to say to all those pert young freshers was, "Do you wanna be in our gang?"

Given Salim and Sabena's social positioning, it had been an invitation none could refuse.

April 12, 1988 saw the unveiling of Sabena's game.

Salim had loved theatre. He always saw himself as a showman. The cellar used for the game had been decked out like the set of Caligula, which, given the activities that Sabena had choreographed beneath the hallowed seat of learning, had been very in-keeping.

By partaking in such endeavors, Salim could always enjoy a varied and plentiful menu. And she could continue to reign over Salim's extracurricular life.

Sabena remembered her fellow students walking through the door hidden by a heavy scarlet curtain. On their faces was fear and anticipation in collision. Their skin glowed. Their movements were awkward. They'd been hesitant but at the same time yearning to know more. They'd all heard the stories. The intentionally promulgated snippets of intelligence.

But the truth had been somewhat different.

Once they'd entered, they would never be the same again.

But they all knew to be in with the beautiful people, they had to take the final step.

Sabena mused. It was strange, she thought. None were coerced. None were forced. It was their own freewill that drove them over the threshold into a world beyond that scarlet curtain. In their eyes, everything had been told to her.

Explaining why.

She'd seen the twinkling desperation in their bright innocent eyes. They'd wanted so much to be accepted, to be thought of on par with Salim and her.

Whatever it took, they'd do it.

Sabena knew it was that feeling of knowing they'd follow blind, knowing that she had ultimate control, complete domination over their pathetic lives.

For both Salim and her, complete domination became their greatest high of all.

However, the moment Sabena had Salim eating out of her hand, she knew the chase was over. The spark had gone. The fires were out. Having Salim become a lap dog wasn't what she wanted.

So she dumped him.

It still made Sabena smile, recalling their departure.

"Quite frankly, baby, you haven't got what it takes to keep a girl satisfied," Sabena had said. "I'm gone."

That had been the year she had graduated. Salim, she recalled, had been astonished at first, and then he smiled and gripped her chin.

"As far as you're concerned, nobody has what it takes. Except me. I know that. You know that. You'll be back."

"Don't count on it, babes." Sabena pulled back.

"I know you, Sabena. We were cast in the fires of Hell. Together. We are the same. I will see you again."

Salim turned and walked away, solid confidence in every step. Sabena watched him leave and she bristled, frustrated at him having the last word. But deep down, she knew he was right.

Back in the present, Sabena looked out of her plane. Everything she'd been striving to achieve ever since she'd met Salim, was in her grasp.

The man of her dreams, and perhaps a few of her nightmares, was about to bring her the world.

Chapter 71

Ellie didn't hear Sam behind her. He'd returned to the lounge after scanning the rest of the apartment. Clocking her posture, the bag over her arm, the slight turn of her body towards the front door, he glared. Anger and hurt flickered in his eyes. He knew exactly what she was thinking.

"Where are you going?"

"Out. I won't be gone long," Ellie lied. Tears formed in her eyes.

"I'm clean, Ellie. I'm not working for anyone else but the British government."

Ellie looked at the door, unable to face him. Sam moved in closer, but his hands were by his side. He made no attempt to touch her.

"I know you think I'm lying but I'm not. My allegiance is to Britain." Sam's strong voice sounded so convincing, but then Ellie had been convinced he'd worked for the Foreign Office for ten years.

Still not facing him, she walked softly towards the door. Sam didn't stop her. He was a beyond-expert-trained liar, and he understood her feelings of blatant distrust.

"Go if you don't believe me. I won't stop you. I'll always love you."

Ellie stopped walking. She stood silently. Sam stared at her, willing her to turn around. He noticed movement, slight, but definite movement.

Please turn.

Slowly, Ellie turned. Tears streamed down her face. Her eyes were bloodshot and watery.

"What am I to believe?" she screamed, letting out all the frustration and hurt trapped in her body.

"Believe this, I love you."

It was all Sam could say, and it was the truth.

"Do you? Do you really? I don't know what to believe. One minute you're a diplomat, next minute you're MI6, and now they're checking on you. For all I know you could be a double agent working for that madman Al Douri." Ellie sobbed as her words came through in heaving gasps. "Sam, I'm so confused. I don't know what's real anymore. I just want my husband back."

Ellie's bag slipped down her shoulder and rested on her wrist. Her shoulders shook under the strain of the tears that rocked her body. Ellie had tried to keep it in. She had put on a brave face during the past few hours. But knowing she'd been spied on caused her to let go of her courage. She couldn't hold back anymore.

Sam wrapped his arms around Ellie and kissed her.

"Ellie, I love you more than anything in the world. I never meant for this to happen."

"They had no right!"

"No, they didn't."

"But you've got proof now right? Proof they've been spying us?"

Ellie, wide-eyed and hopeful, waited for Sam to confirm.

Chapter 72

Quentin couldn't believe what he was proposing. Ellie Noor, an Al Nadir spy? It was unbelievable.

Maide continued with his logical relay of the situation. "In the surveillance data, Sam questioned Ellie about why she screamed. Ellie lied. She said it was a spider. He didn't believe a word. You could see it on his face. But he chose not to pursue it. Ellie threw him off base with a highly-targeted emotional hit. Her acting is excellent."

"You think she was acting? That it wasn't just a reflex response?"

"Think about it logically, Quentin. It all adds up."

"Aren't you jumping a bit quickly to that conclusion?"

"I don't believe so. The basis of my assumption is that she lied, and she skillfully obfuscated her husband's questioning. A man who has been trained to interrogate. Is that really the right behavior for a wife?"

It was obvious to Quentin that Maide had thought through his hypothesis and this was a calculated, rather than random, announcement.

"Well, no, it doesn't seem to be," admitted Quentin.

"If she's for real, why should she lie at all?" asked Maide.

"Sam's been lying to her for ten years."

"Yes, but he's a government agent. She's not."

"So why did she lie?"

"Exactly. It doesn't make sense."

"So you think she's a threat?" asked Quentin. "Another Sarah Masters? But we've had taps on her for some time. Her private life is very private. Few friends. Genuine workaholic. Perfect wife for an agent, actually. Too busy with her own life to think about her husband's."

"Until now."

"But why suspect her on just a scream?"

"Gut instinct," said Maide. "I've been in the business a long time, and gut instinct saved my skin more times than I care to imagine."

"And your gut instinct says she's Al Nadir?"

"Yes."

Quentin detected hesitancy. "But you're not sure?"

"Al Nadir have gone beyond what we thought was possible with nanotech, turning operatives into bombs, changing facial structures. Who knows? She could be a new weapon, a sleeping assassin."

"You think the scream was an initiation? That she's somehow activated?"

"Could be."

"But you're not sure?"

"At the moment, I'm in the dark, which is not a place I want to be." Maide turned quiet and thoughtful for a second, his mind seemingly searching to find the next words. "And it's not a place I intend to stay. You know what I need."

Quentin did, and he was very uncomfortable about the whole business.

"I'm not happy about it. Sam is our best agent. But he's also a ruthless killer, and not someone I'd like against me."

"You didn't seem scared of him today. You played him. You made him look the troublemaker."

"That was all political bravado. You know how it works. But this is different, Justin. You don't know what the repercussions could be."

Maide shook his head. "This is national security." He narrowed his eyes. "We have to know beyond any reasonable doubt that Ellie's behavior is completely benign."

Maide pulled open his bottom drawer. He took out a single crystal glass and his bottle of Glen Fiddich, and poured one for himself. Letting the smooth malt slip down his throat, Maide closed his eyes to savor the taste. Then he opened them and turned back to Quentin.

"You know what I want."

Quentin nodded obediently and left the room. Maide poured himself another drink and returned the surveillance video to the beginning. He settled into his chair, lowered the sound and pressed play. Ellie's slow, seductive voice slipped out the speakers.

"Darling."

"God, I need you. It's been too long. And I'm starving!"

"Well, darling, your dinner is served. Bon appetito!"

Chapter 73

On board her plane on the eve of a new era of power, Sabena thought about her life. Her science career had taken her around the world and into a number of laboratories and government research facilities. Quantum physics was extremely hot, and her status had grown fast. She excelled without effort but eventually became bored. Military applications were fun to develop, but no one had the balls to go the distance. Every time she wanted to experiment and tap into the power that lurked in the quantum domain, the four-star generals pulled the rug.

"I don't think we need to be *that* provocative with nature," was their typical response.

Sabena had felt shackled by convention, unable to test her theories, and subservient to the politically correct mode of operation that dominated military research. Angered by the situation, Sabena bit back and earned herself a reputation as a brilliant but spiky scientist. At the end of one of her more venomous walkouts, Sabena found herself in a bar in downtown Washington, DC. She raced through tequilas like water, but they had no effect. She wasn't drunk; she wasn't even a bit tipsy. She was sober, and she was still pissed with the US Department of Defense.

"Drinking away your sorrows?"

The voice came from behind her. Sabena straightened her back as she quickly tried to place the voice. On matching it to memories, a shiver shot through her. She turned.

A man in his mid-forties stood, smiling. He flicked away a curl of jet-black wavy hair as he looked at Sabena through laughing, dark eyes.

"It looks like you need a proper night out, just like the ones we used to have."

Zack was an old squeeze from her crazy Cambridge days, only topped by Salim, both literally and metaphorically.

"So how about it, Beanie Baby?" Zack slipped his hand over Sabena's.

She pulled away stiffly. "I didn't like that name then, and I still don't!"

Zack smiled. "I know something you did like then." He moved his hand over to her thigh. "I hope you haven't changed."

Sabena's lips moistened, her mouth split wide across her face, and she shook her head. Soon after, they left together. For over a week, they spent their time in bed charging up and down memory lane. Sweating, exhausted but exhilarated by their sudden reunion, Sabena felt recharged. Then she thought about returning to work, and her face fell.

It was time to admit the truth.

"Zack, I'm bored. Seeing you again has only reinforced the fact I'm wasting my life. I could be doing anything. But I'm stuck in a lab 24/7 looking at weird spatter patterns of exploding protons and representing them in pages of incomprehensible symbols that only a handful of people in the world can understand. What I really want is something exciting, something edgy, and something dangerous. Right now, I feel I've gone to my own funeral."

"Well, sex and death always seem to go together. You know, those people that get off at funerals." Zack laughed. "You're serious, aren't you?"

Sabena grabbed the wine bottle and took a slug. "Deadly serious. I'm just about ready to walk."

Zack pulled the satin sheets around his hard torso, and gathered them up underneath his arms.

"Feeling cold?" asked Sabena.

But Zack didn't speak. His sudden pensive expression disturbed her. It was strange how she could throw inhibition to the wall and shag with total abandon, and yet one contemplative stare could perturb her enough to feel awkward.

"You want action, don't you?" Zack had reached a decision. He was in for the play. "I can give it to you."

Zack then made a suggestion that turned Sabena Sanantoni's life around and gave her exactly what she wanted.

Chapter 74

As Sam listened to Ellie recall her day, it became painfully obvious that the surveillance in their home had been removed when Ellie went to the gym.

"I really wasn't gone that long," she protested.

"Long enough!"

Sam's fury at the missing evidence flashed in his eyes.

"How do you know about the bugging?"

"It was what a colleague said to me in a meeting," said Sam. "He replayed words I'd said to you, words he couldn't possibly know unless we're under surveillance. And the way he said them left me in no doubt."

"But if you're not a double agent, why bug you? You're on their side."

"They want to keep checks on me. I heard they did it with other agents in the past when they questioned their performance or allegiance. They don't want their prized operatives going off the rails."

"I can't believe they've done this. I just feel so dirty, so angry."

"They may not have had visual. It could have just been audio."

Sam attempted to sweeten the blow. He knew they would have been transmitting audio and visual direct to River house. He'd set up many surveillance missions in the past; he knew the drill. On receipt of transmission, data would be recorded via an encryption program direct to a media file. The file would then be circulated to appropriate section leaders, and Justin Maide.

"Are you sure?"

"No. I'm not sure."

"So somewhere in MI6 there's a tape of us going at it like rabbits. That's really the bottom line, isn't it, Sam?"

"Yes."

Sam didn't know what else to say. It wasn't a tape, but a digitally-encrypted file. But why mince words? Ellie was right. His confession to being an MI6 agent was going to cause him problems. He'd never slipped before, but now – the rules of the game had changed.

"What are you going to do?" asked Ellie. "You can't let them get away with it."

Chapter 75

Sabena toyed with the crayfish salad served by her personal flight assistant, but she was too excited to eat. From the moment she met Zack, her life had been building towards the success she would soon embrace.

"Are you mad? I'd be shot for that!"

Sabena had listened quietly to Zack's proposition and rapidly become incensed by his naivety and stupidity about the level of security that surrounded her work.

"Steal government secrets for you?" confirmed Sabena, her eyes blinking quickly. "You really are quite insane."

Zack stared at her and Sabena knew he was analyzing her response. Outwardly, she showed she was rejecting the idea, but inside she was burning with excitement. Her eyes gave her away. Already dilated, they sparkled with want, and her lips moistened signaling her lust for what was being suggest. She couldn't hide it, she was getting turned on. Just the same way she did when, back in the day, he'd introduced a new sex trick. Outer revulsion, inner fascination.

Sabena jerked up as Zack rubbed her arm slowly.

"Think about it, Sabena. You'll be able to get back at them for keeping you cooped-up like a lab rat. Every time you wanted to test out your theories, they reined you in. For what? Scared of what they'd discover? Terrified to face the truth of your brilliance? I can bring you into a world where they'll not only revere your brilliant mind but they'll pay you well for the pleasure."

Sabena listened. Her face flushed with desire the second Zack mentioned money. But she was nobody's fool. The meeting with Zack in the bar had been no idle reunion. It had been carefully orchestrated and planned.

"How much?" asked Sabena. Her eyes bore into Zack's, drilling into his psyche with an unnatural intensity. Zack swallowed uncomfortably. His employer's profile had been right; Sabena certainly did have a psychotic streak.

"I'm authorized to sanction one million dollars per transaction."

Zack maintained his stare-out game against Sabena. Without showing any sign of responding to the amount offered, Sabena stared at him, motionless and not blinking, for a full minute. Such was the silence between them, Zack wondered whether she'd heard him.

"So what do you say? Is it a deal?"

"Put a zero on the end and I will be your humble servant." Sabena's voice had descended to a whisper. Within a beat, she laughed so loud that Zack felt dizzy by her sudden mood change. She was brilliant. But she was also deeply unstable. Zack was hesitated to continue.

"So what do you say, Zacky-baby? Do we have a deal?"

Zack flipped opened his mobile and spoke to someone, detailing the new offer from Sabena. He heard the instruction, muttered a succinct, "Yes, sir," and closed the phone.

"We have a deal." Sabena whooped loudly. But Zack grabbed hold of her shoulders and shook her roughly. "On one condition, Beanie-Baby. The transaction can be anything."

"It's a deal." Sabena's beautiful eyes grabbed his, drilling into his brain. "But if you screw me over, it will take a microbiologist to identify your remains."

Zack knew Sabena wasn't joking.

It hadn't been immediate, but eventually, having proved her worth in fourteen high-level assassinations, ten multi-agency double-crosses and countless missions involving maiming, torturing and killing at will, Sabena discovered who had been behind her appointment.

In the Buena Vista Cafe, San Francisco, Sabena sat drinking an Irish coffee and savoring the atmosphere. Her career had brought excessive wealth, and with it, the accoutrements of success: a private jet on stand-by, an armor-plated Merc waiting with her driver outside, international designers making one-offs for her alone, and bodyguards by the bucket load. Of course, with her capability, she really didn't need them; they were just another trinket.

There was a tap on her shoulder.

Sabena bristled at the touch and sniffed the air. A single scent brought it all back. Her eyes lit up.

"And here we are again, babe!"

Sabena already knew. As hands turned her around roughly, she reached up. His lips were on hers instantly, his tongue pushing down her throat, almost choking her. Her bodyguards sat by and watched. Releasing her, and allowing her to breathe, Salim smiled.

"How?" started Sabena. Then she realized what a fool she'd been. "For how long?"

"Long enough to know I've made the right decision." Salim smoothed down her hair.

"On what?"

"You. Congratulations! You're my second in command."

"I never expected anything less."

Sabena lifted the Irish coffee, licked the froth off the top, and laughed as Salim moved in for a second round of breathlessness. Remembering that moment, Sabena smiled again. Love and hate in equal measure. But she couldn't deny he brought out the best in her. From her seat high in the clouds, she looked down on the world. It was the position she had been born to take.

Chapter 76

Ellie was hard and defiant, but listening to her words, Sam knew she was also very naïve. Yes, she was a good businesswoman. Yes, she was witty, sharp and clever. But she was a baby when it came to the intelligence business. Unless he could prove with real, physical evidence that MI6 had acted incongruously towards him, he could do nothing. He just had to accept it, take it on the chin, and continue with his job.

He'd been in MI6 for over a decade, but never before had he encountered such blatant abuse of power *against* him. He'd stepped over the line a million times. He'd done things no man should ever have to do. But he'd done it all in the name of his country, to keep Britain safe from hostile warriors, fanaticals and mercenary opportunists. Sam had never given them cause for concern, and certainly not cause for putting him under surveillance.

He'd considered the possibility initially that it was because he'd mentioned Piccadilly to Maide. Was Maide really that paranoid? Did Maide really believe he was going to break? Ready to blow all their secrets? Was that why they'd put him under the lens?

Sam couldn't work it out. It wasn't a first for Maide and him to argue. Sam tolerated the yes sir/no sir politics of the job, but he also gave as good as he got. Maide always knew Sam was a maverick who went by his own rules. Since he'd recruited him, Sam had taken his own chances and was answerable only to himself. It was a package Maide had signed up to without complaint.

It didn't make sense that now, after one sharp disagreement, with a few choice words on both sides, that Maide felt the need to put Sam under surveillance.

Didn't Maide know he'd never reveal Snowdrop outside the quartet. He wasn't into committing suicide. It would be as much the end for him, as it would be for MI6 and the UK government. Despite what they'd achieved with Operation Snowdrop, those lives that had been taken at Piccadilly would be brought into question, Sam, Maide and Ashton, they'd all face trial if they were lucky. Or just be executed as traitors of the state, if they weren't. Whatever way, their lives would be over.

Maide must realize he'd never be that crazy.

But surveilling him meant that his loyalty and allegiance was in question. His confession to Ellie wasn't going to make matters any easier.

"Well, Sam? What are you going to do about it?"

Sam had been quiet whilst he recollected his thoughts. Ellie stared impatiently at him, her anger overflowing. She had her honor at stake. She expected her husband to do the chivalrous thing and demand the tape back from MI6.

"Well?"

"I can't do anything about it."

Ellie's jaw dropped. "Excuse me? You're going to do *nothing* about it? The great Dr. Sam Noor, Foreign Office Golden Boy and MI6 Super Spy, is going to do nothing about it?"

"Oh for fuck's sake, Ellie. Get real," Sam snapped, his anger rising at his wife's lack of understanding. "Why do you think I scanned the flat? I needed evidence. They've taken it. Of course. They wouldn't have said anything if the bugs had still been here."

"God, they must have been quick. I went to the gym about quarter to two. Your meeting was quarter past, wasn't it?"

"Yeah." Sam nodded. "The meeting wouldn't even have begun, and the bugs would have been out."

"What would have happened if I hadn't gone out?"

"Nothing. They wouldn't have risked it."

"So what are you going to do?"

"I can't do anything. I needed the devices. Without them, everything's hearsay, nothing more. My word against theirs. They'll say I'm paranoid, and they'll have me under psyche-eval before you can say the word liability. All I can do is just do my job. Better than ever, in fact, to prove that I'm not breaking or losing it, as they obviously think I am."

"That's it then? I'm the Kim Kardashian of the spy set."

"It doesn't work like that. It'll just be part of a security dossier on me. It'll be logged and filed."

"You really think?"

"I know how this works. You're safe."

"But they won't like me knowing."

"No, they won't."

"What's going to happen?"

Sam looked at his wife. What could he tell her? He didn't know the truth to that question.

"I don't know. But you mustn't ever tell anyone about me. You understand?"

Sam's strict, hard voice sounded alien to Ellie. She nodded, but once again, she was frightened. Sam looked at Ellie. All the anger and indignation erased from her face, leaving a timid child trapped in a woman's body.

"I'm scared," she whispered.

"There's nothing to worry about. You're safe."

Sam pulled Ellie close to him.

"You're safe," he echoed, as if the repetition might help him believe his own words.

Chapter 77

On answering her phone, Sabena was uncharacteristically polite. Her usually curt tone was replaced with a soft, seductive and breathy lilt. This sudden change in Sabena did not mean she'd finally seen the error of her ways. It was that the caller was Salim Al Douri, a man she loathed and loved in equal measure.

"The tests have confirmed the capability. The power is now with us." Salim's voice was calm and calculating. Sabena imagined the voice as that of an accountant explaining a tax return. It was bland to the point of being boring. She was amazed, considering the wonderful news.

"Is everything…" Sabena started the sentence hesitantly, but Salim chewed up her words before she could finish.

"No, it's not! You should not have employed the second level. It was too early!"

Salim was referring to Kinley's assassination that morning.

"But I thought you wanted to send them a message. Let them know that we're still the leaders in the game. Despite that motherfucker Kinley. We still make the rules. I thought second level would be the right approach. It was what we had agreed," explained Sabena, her originally defensive posturing descending into crawling.

"We never agreed on second level deployment. It's still too early. There's too many cracks. Frequencies need to be cleared up. Better masking needs to be employed."

"I apologize, Salim. I really thought it was an action you'd have wanted taken."

"The action, yes. The execution of it, no." Salim paused before the final volley. "You may be brilliant, Sabena, but sometimes you can be a fucking idiot!"

Sabena flushed red with embarrassment, and was grateful he hadn't used the video satcomm to call. She still couldn't see what she'd done wrong. The experiments had been thoroughly checked and second level deployment of the new nano-bomb was absolutely locked down where frequencies were concerned. No one would be able to intercept. Salim was being totally unreasonable.

"I don't think-"

"No, you don't. That's your problem. Did you check with your assets? Did you know they had invoked sign-off? It was just a matter of time. It needed no intervention at all, just a delay tactic."

Sabena was ashamed. She'd been so eager to use the second level nano-bomb on that double-crossing fucker Kinley she hadn't realized MI6 had him down for assassination.

"Another stunt like the one pulled this morning..."

She didn't need to hear the rest. "I understand, Salim. No more stunts."

"Now." A happier tone slithered into Salim's voice. "It's time to congratulate ourselves. How does First Lady of the World sound to you?"

Chapter 78

The restaurant was typically Italian. There was little light except for the Chianti-bottled candles on the tables. The mood was intimate and romantic. Sam stretched his hands over the small table and clasped Ellie's. Her skin was soft and silken. He brought one of her hands up to his lips and kissed it. Raising his head, he looked at Ellie. Her eyes sparkled in the candlelight. Ellie reached over and kissed him. He wished it could always be like this.

Sam had made the decision to eat out. Neither felt like spending much time in the flat. Although Sam claimed no devices were there, he could see in Ellie's eyes the deep hurt. Her privacy and her life had been ruthlessly violated for no clear reason.

Sam wanted to be feel alive. Kinley's death reinforced the fact he could be easily next on Salim's shopping list. He needed to spend as much time with Ellie as he possibly could.

To know, just for a moment, what real happiness could feel like.

Before dinner, they took a walk by the riverside. Ellie's hand encased in his; he tightened it. Keeping her close. Since his confession to working in Six, he'd started to hate himself. What had possessed him to take such risks for so long. When she'd been ignorant, somehow it had all been ok. It was like he'd been living a lie himself. One he'd convinced himself was true.

He'd not wanted to face the truth. Ellie trusted him. And he'd betrayed her. He could have died, and she'd never have known, and that's what ripped him apart inside. Yes, he was patriot. Yes, he loved his country. He wanted to protect and serve, and had done so for over a decade.

But at what cost?

Sam stopped abruptly. He turned Ellie around to face him. Her eyes widened, expectant and filled with love, despite what he'd put her through.

It was turning dusk. The early evening was cool. But the nights were starting to draw out, welcoming the summer. Overcome with emotions, the Kinley bombing, Ellie's unexplained scream, his confession and the bugging, it all came crashing down upon him.

He needed Ellie, like he needed oxygen to breathe. He needed her completely. Suppressing the pain inside him, Sam pushed Ellie against the railings and kissed her hard. Out in the open, he felt freer than inside their apartment.

Under his lips he noticed Ellie quiver, and she opened her mouth letting his tongue caress and intertwine with hers. His arms slipped around her waist and Sam pulled Ellie closer to him.

"You know I love you, don't you sweetness?"

Ellie's eyes glittered as he spoke. She nodded but didn't return with her usual 'love you too sweetness'.

Sam swallowed, and his hand drifted up to touch her face.

Ellie's hand gripped his and pulled his hand down. Her expression unreadable to Sam. A feat he couldn't help but wonder about, as Ellie took his hand in hers and made to walk along the riverside.

"We'd better get going." Ellie had said, glancing at her Longines watch. "We don't want them to let the table go."

"They won't," Sam muttered, kissing behind her ear. He detected a slight stiffening, but he put it down to the chill of the evening air.

"They will. It's almost nine o'clock."

"Oh, come on then."

Sam had resigned to Ellie's nagging, dropped his arm around her shoulder, and they walked towards the restaurant. The table had been perfect, secluded and out of the way of others. Sam and Ellie kissed, cuddled and fondled like newlyweds. In the candlelight, they could forget everything. They could be the Sam and Ellie that existed before unwanted knowledge almost pushed them both over the edge.

As Sam kissed Ellie, he wanted to make the moment last forever.

Chapter 79

In the heart of the Cambridgeshire countryside, Sabena's sleek Gulfstream III landed silently on the tarmac strip, off radar thanks to their cloaking technology. Sometimes, she felt Al Nadir had taken the fun out of the hunt. Those poor intel guys didn't even get a sniff. They couldn't see anything at all.

The area showed itself as a food processing plant with lorries running back and forth. But walking inside through the dull double-doors, Sabena saw a different scene. Sophisticated laboratories spawning nano-chaos, communications centers constantly buzzing with encrypted messages and operatives being trained into keen and willing killers were all housed within the boring brickwork and corrugated roofing.

Sabena strode through the corridors. With every step, people stopped what they were doing and immediately looked to the floor. They didn't salute her; that would have given her military status, which Sabena hated. She knew she was far greater than all that regimental bullshit. No, instead, they averted their eyes through fear and respect. Sabena was terrorist royalty. Everyone knew the code and heeded the way.

Sabena's second in command and occasional lover, Pedro Russo, stood patiently at her side as she entered her command station. She took to her leather chair and flicked a switch to broadcast on an internal comms channel.

"Is the Stealth Runner ready?"

"Yes, ma'am. The Runner is ready and charged. Transparency at maximum capacity."

Sabena listened to her engineering manager's account and smiled.

"Excellent!" She switched off the comms and turned to Russo. "Evacuation measures?"

"All in operation. We've already evacuated all but essential personnel. All other cells have assured one hundred percent evacuation to their pre-assigned destinations. Essential personnel evacuate Q-Day plus 3."

"Again, excellent! Well, it seems all is in order."

Sabena turned to the screen behind her to contact Salim with the details of progress.

"Excuse me, ma'am. There is something you should know," said Russo.

Sabena turned. "What is it? What should I know?"

"We've been listening in on the communiqués, you know, the grid chatter and so forth-"

"Yes, I know," interrupted Sabena.

"It seems London may be changed. It may no longer be the venue for the UN Peace Summit."

"Our assets, what do they say?"

"To them, no change. But certain wavelengths are discussing change strategies."

"Your take on this?" asked Sabena, her eyes steely and cold as they absorbed his every gesture.

Russo felt she had the ability to pull into those dark eyes his very being. Unsettled, he shifted from one foot to the other before replying.

"I believe we have to be ready for any contingency. We can't risk a wrong move at this stage."

"I agree. So what do you suggest?"

"Perhaps absolute confirmation as to exactly where the location will be."

"Exactly what I was thinking, Russo."

Sabena scanned in her mind, and decided that Godley would be the best asset to use in the British government.

Chapter 80

They were walking home along the road to their apartment when it happened.

Ellie had been talking loudly about what they were going to do tomorrow.

"...and the weather forecast looks good, so maybe we could go down south, stop in Charmouth. We haven't done that in ages..."

A single beep sounded from Sam's pocket. He stopped walking, pulled away from Ellie, and turned his face to the wall.

"You know about Kinley?"

Sam recognized the voice as Sir Justin Maide. He pressed his fingers hard into his palm and desperately tried to control the anger that had started to surface. The cold fury he'd felt when he'd heard earlier about his friend's death was returning. His body shook, and he had to focus himself to lock down the pounding pain of loss before he could answer Maide.

"Yes, I heard."

"He was the longest in there. It's a shame. Such an agent to lose."

"But we did," Sam replied through gritted teeth.

Kinley had been undercover in Al Nadir for over four years. MI6 knew before the first nano-bomb exploded that Al Nadir had been working on a leading-edge weapons technology, but at that time, it had been thought to be a virulent biological agent.

"Any idea how?" asked Sam.

"Insider informant." Maide's tone did not change or waver, just remained cold and bland.

"One of ours?" Sam kept an equally emotionless delivery.

"Had to be. Kinley was watertight over there."

"Any suggestions?"

"We're still looking."

"It makes me nervous we could be compromised from that high up," said Sam.

"Nobody has confirmed anything. It's all speculative."

"Still, it makes our position vulnerable, and I don't like that."

"Neither do I," replied Maide. "But this is Al Nadir. We need to expect and deal with absolutely anything."

"I don't like being reactive in this war, sir."

"I understand. None of us do. But it's a situation that has been forced on us."

"Not anymore. They struck a raw nerve with Kinley. They're gonna pay!"

"No personal vendettas, Sam. You know the code."

Sam went silent. If necessary, he was going to take this war right to Al Nadir's doorstep. In the past, Sam's combination of technical know-how, brilliance and sheer brute strength meant that answers, in some shape or form, were always forthcoming. How he came by the answers was sometimes not documented officially, but his boss always knew the facts. Sam had seen it in Maide's face too many times, his fear that Sam could one day turn of his own accord or be coerced into turning. It was Maide's greatest nightmare.

Sam knew another of Maide's nightmares was Sam going off on a revenge drive. Maide's next words said it all.

"We need you on this one, and we need you *clear*. Understand?"

"Of course I understand," said Sam pushing down the furious heat of rage inside him.

"What do you want from me?"

"Get to the truth, the way you always do. I know what the Company is like these days. They've got too much to handle. This will be brushed over, and I don't want that. No one here wants that. Kinley was worth more than a second-rate CSI doing the onceover."

"I agree. Send me all the crime scene data you've got. I'll pick through it on the plane."

"The Americans have already combed it and come up with nothing but the C4 in a parcel."

"Did they find anything about the courier?"

"Legit. All records check out."

"And that's it? They're leaving it?" Sam swallowed hard, amazed at how quickly events could be pigeonholed and loose ends tied.

"Yes, that's it. They say it was a simple explosion. C4. Legit courier. Case closed."

"It would be different if it was one of theirs on our soil."

"I know. It gets in your throat, doesn't it? Their double bloody standards."

"I'll close this properly. You can rely on me, sir."

"A plane is being prepped. Wheels up at zero one hundred hours from Northolt. I hope you didn't have any plans this weekend."

Sam stared at Ellie, who was standing a little away from him, arms folded and glaring with annoyance.

"Nothing that can't wait until I get to the truth."

"Good man."

"And I will get to it." Sam was responding to Maide but also reinforcing his commitment to himself.

"I know you will. We wouldn't be speaking if I thought you couldn't. Good luck Sam, and God speed."

Sam rang off. Kinley had been a good agent and an even better friend. They'd looked out for each other on missions and his intel and unselfish actions had saved Sam's life on numerous occasions. So much he'd owed to Kinley.

They all did.

The Firm wouldn't have had the successes they did over the past four years if Kinley hadn't sacrificed his soul to the dark side. He'd bring Kinley's killers in, and he'd spare no mercy doing it.

Ellie had watched Sam turn away to talk on the phone. She had been standing close by and had heard snippets of his conversation.

"Sam, what's happening?"

"Come on. We've got to walk faster. I need to get my stuff," hissed Sam with ice cold authority.

Ellie was dumbstruck. This couldn't be happening.

"No!" She stood still.

Sam marched forward and then turned around to look at her.

"Ellie, please. Not now. You know how important my job is."

Sam glared at her, furious.

"This isn't fair," started Ellie.

Sam shot a look at her. 'Not here', he stated firmly. He turned and marched quickly away. He didn't want to talk. He heard Ellie's footsteps quickening as she ran to keep up with him. He took her elbow and the two of them walked with haste back to the apartment in silence.

Chapter 81

Sam punched in the access code to the apartment. The double doors slid open. As Sam and Ellie stepped into the reception area, Harold, the doorman, smiled at them.

"Good evening."

His genial demeanor was perfect for pandering to the elite who lived at Silent Waters apartment complex.

"Evening, Harold."

Sam ushered Ellie into the lift. The doors closed. Ellie whipped around, staring hard at Sam.

"I don't believe this. You're going to leave me!"

"Do I have a choice?"

"Yes. You could say you were taking your wife to the seaside."

Sam didn't dignify Ellie's ridiculous suggestion with a response. Instead, he remained quiet until they reached the seventh floor. Ellie also remained silent. She knew she'd reacted stupidly. But the truth was, she was afraid. She'd learnt so much so fast, and now she couldn't contemplate being alone.

The moment they were inside their apartment, Ellie's verbal backlash hit Sam in the face.

"You can't just leave me. I can sort of understand why you can't get the tape back, not having the evidence and such, but you can't leave me. Not now. Please, love. Be by my side. I need you."

"I've left you before. What's the big deal?"

"Sam, how can you say that? For one, I didn't know you were an agent when you left before. And two, they bugged our flat. Did you hear what I said? They came into our home and bugged our bloody flat. If they can do that, they can do anything. I'm frightened, Sam. Don't you get that? I'm *fucking* frightened!"

"Ellie, you're being neurotic. You're my wife. They wouldn't dare touch you. I'd kill them."

"Please, Sam. Don't go."

Ellie had never begged in her life. Her voice was small and shaking. Sam felt cruel ignoring her pleas.

"I have to."

"Why?"

"Matthew Kinley, a friend of mine, has been assassinated."

"I know. I saw it on the news. I didn't know he was that much of a friend."

"Well, he was. A really good one. I've been asked to sort out his affairs in the US."

Ellie nodded. She could hear the annoyance in Sam's voice. He really didn't want to tell her anything. She recalled in the past, when she'd asked him about his work. "Oh, it's boring bureaucratic stuff, darling. You wouldn't be interested." Ellie had believed him.

"I'm sorry. I've got to go. I would have loved to have gone to the seaside tomorrow." Sam found himself meaning it. He would have delighted in spending the day with Ellie bumming around the south coast. "Maybe next week."

"You're going to be gone a week?"

"Could be. I don't know. It depends how soon I can wrap things up over there. Maybe two, at the most."

"Oh, God. No!"

Ellie's voice reverberated with despondency and desperation. A fortnight was too long.

"Can't you just tell them to shove the job?"

It was a totally illogical thing to say but her desperation had driven her to say it.

"Ellie, darling, please be sensible. Lots of people rely on me doing my job. If I throw in the towel now, questions will be asked. I have to prove to them I've still got it. I'm sorry, sweetness. But while I'm gone, you're going to have to be strong."

Ellie looked at Sam mournfully, her bottom lip gradually turning up in a slight quiver. Sam bent his head down and kissed her.

"I'm so sorry I brought you into all this," said Sam. "I really am."

He kissed her harder. Ellie pulled away. But determination shone in her eyes. If they were to have a future, she had to see this through.

"Come with me," said Sam. "There's something I want to show you."

Enigmatically, Sam led Ellie into the bedroom and closed the door.

Chapter 82

A sharp rap on his hotel door startled Godley, who was preparing for a crucial policy meeting in Washington DC, with his US counterpart. He heard a scraping noise on the carpet as something was slid under his door. Cautiously, he stood up and noticed a small brown envelope rather like a wage packet had been thrust beneath into the room. He shook his head, amazed. How did they always know where he was?

Inside the envelope was a SIM card, as usual. Simple and effective. He took out his burner phone, slipped in the SIM chip, turned it on, and waited.

It howled almost instantly in his hand.

He couldn't believe it. *She* never called. It was normally his handler, an Oxford bedfellow of his old acquaintance. Or Pedro Russo. But never her. Clearly his work that lead to revealing Kinley as a double agent had elevated his position.

As UK Secretary of State for Defense, he had sight of the most sensitive military information, but he always had to be extremely circumspect as to what intel ended up in Al Nadir's hands. He couldn't have any backdraft from his activities. He didn't want to burn politically or literally.

Godley was a realist. He knew he was only valuable to his masters all the time he could deliver, but the moment he couldn't, they'd think nothing of wiping him out. It didn't matter a damn about him being a government minister.

For now though, Godley knew he was very valuable.

Godley recalled how he'd been the catalyst to eventually making Kinley.

One Month Earlier

Ashton trusted Godley with secrets.

He was the PM's Mr. Fix-it and, therefore, had a greater level of access to the PM than his other Cabinet colleagues. He'd delivered results and won Ashton's trust through many years of political problem-solving.

It had been during one of those problem-solving visits that Godley first clocked the horticulture website on Ashton's laptop.

Godley had been requested by Ashton as a matter of urgency. At the request, he'd walked around from Whitehall at speed. He'd marched forward, past Cumberford, the prime minister's parliamentary private secretary (PPS). The man barely raised a glance, except to issue a curt, "Good Afternoon Minister."

Opening the door, Godley could see Ashton sat on his sofa with his laptop on his thighs. Godley noticed the website immediately. Its name, *Forever Flowers*, registered a slight smirk. The PM was probably trying to get on his wife's good side, thought Godley wryly, knowing Ashton's propensity for salacious escapades.

"Prime Minister, you wanted to see me?"

Ashton clicked off the site, shut the laptop swiftly, and flicked a look at Godley. For a mere second, Godley detected a shadow of concern. Then Ashton slipped his laptop onto the coffee table and leapt up, effusive and smirking in his indomitable way.

"Ah, yes. Godley, my friend. We have an issue with that troublesome shit backbencher Boris Jacobs. He's causing more than a little stirring with his insinuations about my ability to keep the UK safe from Al Nadir attacks. With the Peace Summit coming up on March 25, I can't afford any ripples. Use whatever you need to and silence him."

Ashton delivered his demand with brutal efficiency. Godley nodded.

"Of course, Prime Minister. Take it as done," said Godley.

His beady, black rat-like eyes narrowed as he ran down options in his mind on how he could keep Jacobs' loose and increasingly vicious tongue in check. From the dangerous look Ashton shot him, it appeared the option that the PM really wanted was for Jacobs to have some tongue action with a scalpel. Naturally, Godley couldn't undertake such an option. But just its consideration gave him a delightful image of backbencher Jacobs in unbelievable agony as his mischievous muscle was permanently removed.

The second time Godley spied the Forever Flowers site was at Maide's residence in Godalming.

Ashton picked him up in his Jag, saying, "Trouble in Turkey. Get in. We need to be on-point if things get hot."

Godley ducked into the car and realized that Ashton wasn't alone. Sam Noor sat in the front. He turned as Godley squeezed himself into the seat beside the PM.

"Evening, Minister," said Sam with his usual ice-cold, sinister tone.

Godley shivered at Sam's voice. He always felt the agent was just keeping down a riotous anger. He'd heard that Six referred to Sam as the 'go-to guy' if all else fails. He had a ruthless but impressive reputation.

And he always delivered the required results.

"So, we have a situation in Turkey," Sam continued. "One of our covert operatives in Millî İstihbarat Teşkilatı (MİT), better known to you and me as the National Intelligence Organization in Ankara, has been killed. We believe an MİT official working for Al Nadir could be behind it. Our operative was inside MİT to uncover Al Nadir double-agents. But it's all brewing into a major diplomatic incident. MİT are claiming we were stealing documents of national security. They said it was their right to execute a foreign spy."

"Difficult situation," said Godley. "Do they have evidence of the theft?"

"They're claiming evidence, but they aren't being forthcoming. Trouble is, we've more than one guy in MİT. If the others are exposed, it may look like a hostile act against the Turks. We have to be ready to counter any reprisals," explained Ashton.

"How many are we talking about?" said Godley, looking at Sam, instinctively knowing he had more intel.

"It's a few," responded Sam. On his face, Godley read wariness. He was deliberately vague.

"I'll ensure our bases at Akrotiri and Dhekelia are ready," said Godley quickly.

"I hope it won't get to that," said Ashton. "But that's why you're here."

Godley nodded.

The rest of the journey was taken up with Sam giving a debrief on the position of Al Nadir in Turkey, their alliances and current known operations and cells.

The Jag turned into the gravel driveway and someone within the Andalusian mansion beyond opened the gates. The driver brought the car to the entrance and got out to open the door for the PM. Sam stepped out simultaneously with the driver. Godley opened his side.

Maide was at the door. He welcomed them in with a sweeping hand.

Godley didn't like Maide much. He always had a sense of unease around him. Maide often sidelined Godley, using the excuse that UK defense need not be involved as it was an 'out of country intelligence issue'. Or, of course, the old chestnut, 'not a domestic security concern'. Godley had retaliated by stating that the majority of the wars currently fought were 'out of the country' and were very much a 'domestic security concern', as the success or failure of those wars directly correlated to the level of terrorism perpetrated on UK soil.

Godley walked through the hallway and was dumbstruck. It was the first time he'd been to Maide's place. He'd heard murmurs about how Maide had replicated the Moorish mansion in Cordoba where he'd stayed decades ago. But Godley never believed it to be true.

He did his best to suppress a gasp. The floor was shining white marble with turquoise interlocking Ayyubid star patterns. Above him, a vaulted and coffered cedar ceiling was carved with more elaborate geometric Moorish designs. An alcove with tilework, which Godley recognized as zellige, housed an extraordinary vase constructed from a kaleidoscope of pieces of pottery.

Godley swept a look to the right of him. A door stood wide open. From the bookshelf wall unit stretching to the ceiling and the desk in front of the window, he deduced it was Maide's study. Maide's laptop was open. The drapes hadn't been pulled and the garden was dark. The bright screen of Maide's computer reflected clearly in the glass as Godley walked past.

Just a glance, but he recognized the page immediately, having seen the same on Ashton's computer a few days before.

Forever Flowers.

Godley wondered why both Ashton and Maide suddenly showed a passion for horticulture.

In his monthly debrief with his Al Nadir handler, he happened to mention that strange occurrence.

Pedro Russo took the meeting. They met at the Holiday Inn, Slough, just off junction six on the M4. The location changed monthly, and intel came via a chat room that focused on movie talk about the latest films. Godley's moniker in the chatroom was Ratman. Russo's was Shadowman. The comms protocols on Godley's private laptop ran on Al Nadir's cloaked private satellite network.

Godley gave his run down on events. He had to give enough juicy titbits to warrant payment. His retainer with Al Nadir was fifty thousand a month. But he knew if they terminated the contract, they'd terminate him too. So he had more than enough incentive to keep them sweet.

He'd mentioned the strange sight of Forever Flowers almost in passing at the end of their one-hour meeting.

"Seems like Ashton and Maide haven't got anything better to do but look at bloody flower websites. Talk about fiddling while Rome burns."

Godley smirked but Pedro's face was stern. He ringed around the occurrence.

"Do you know the name of the website?" asked Pedro, his pen poised.

"Yes, I do. It was Forever Flowers. You know those terribly corny sites with balloons and love hearts in the corners? Must be a coincidence, both of them looking. Obviously trying to impress the women in their lives. Clearly been naughty boys."

Pedro wrote down the name.

"Thank you, Godley. You may have delivered more than you know."

Godley didn't realize at the time, but his horticulture coincidence turned out to be the biggest revelation to Al Nadir, and more importantly, to Sabena Sanantoni.

His throwaway words resulted in taking away the lives of three people: Kinley, Angie and little Lotte.

Chapter 83

23 March, 2017

Sam rested back in the leather seats and sipped his gin and tonic. God, he felt bad about leaving Ellie. He knew she was bright, but this was a whole new world for her. It wasn't something you could learn overnight. That's why he'd given her the gun. He hoped he'd done the right thing.

Her handling of it had been excellent. She'd always been a rapid assimilator of anything, and her understanding was very quick tonight, despite how stressed she was. She would know what to do if the time ever came to use it. He prayed to God that day would never come. But like any good agent, he had to be prepared and know when to act. All he had done was give Ellie the tools to secure survival. Her survival was everything to him.

He pulled aside the curtains and looked outside. People milled around on the streets. Saturday night was erupting in a blaze of neon lights, speeding cars and scantily-clad clubbers. The car weaved its way through the drugged-up throng. Sam watched people having fun. Pure envy stabbed him, not because he wanted to run around acting crazy, but because they had the freedom to do so. If he had his time over, he would have turned down Maide's offer. He would *never* have made that decision had he foreseen the consequences.

All the time Ellie had been blinded to the truth, everything had been acceptable. He had arranged with MI6 that, should anything happen to him on a mission, Ellie would be told nothing of his life as an agent. His life cover was substantial. Ellie would have been comfortable. Thinking back on this arrangement, Sam despised himself. Although it placed both of them in danger, revealing the truth to Ellie had been cathartic, like he was released from something that'd been suffocating him for over a decade. But he knew the truth had been difficult for Ellie to accept, and he knew that the events of the past twenty-four hours had almost resulted in him losing her.

Sam loved Ellie so much, but he couldn't even carry her photo with him, for fear it may fall into hostile hands. Imagining Ellie, her bright smile, her sensual smoky, blue eyes, and her voice that constantly reflected strength and kindness, made him feel whole.

Sam snapped open his eyes and picked up his mobile.

"Hello."

"Hello, sweetness."

"Oh, Sam. I couldn't see the caller ID. Are you ok?"

"It's like Stevie Wonder sang, 'I just called to say I love you.'"

"Oh, darling." Ellie was choked. "I love you too."

"I'll call you when I arrive. It may be early in the morning. Is that ok?"

"Call whenever you want. I'll be waiting."

"Love you, sweetness."

"Love you too."

Sam felt better for talking to Ellie; she made everything real in his world of unreality.

Chapter 84

Godley brought himself back to the present. He stopped his pride at scoring big time for Al Nadir ruining the next few minutes of his life. It would've happened if he'd kept Sabena Sanantoni waiting on the phone any longer.

"Are you there? Concentrate, alright! We have reason to believe there are changes a-foot. Anything to vindicate this rumor?"

He listened to Sabena's crisp, efficient tones and imagined her as a cool, ice maiden in a white leather bikini brandishing a silver riding crop. The vision was very sudden and graphic. He had to shake his head to maintain control of the current situation.

"I believe this is a misnomer," Godley replied. "Put out in desperation to create misinformation and smokescreens. It will be the initial location."

"But what if it's not? I can't afford a fuck-up!"

"No, quite. That's not what anyone would want," replied Godley curtly. He never liked ladies to swear. It made them cheap and tacky. His vision of Sabena as the unapproachable ice queen splintered into pieces and what remained had her as a tough-talking streetwalker.

"So you're going to do your job. Find out what's happening, if the chatter is misdirection or new information," snapped Sabena.

"That won't be easy. Security is at its tightest, even for someone like me. I'll only know hours before the start."

"That's not good enough," rasped Sabena. "I need to know now. It's what you're there for. It's what we fucking pay you for, you little shit. Just ask Ashton. He'll tell you."

"But what if he doesn't?" whined Godley, ignoring the direct insult.

"Make him. You're good at that. You're his Mr. Fix-it. Otherwise, I'll have to fix you." Godley shivered slightly. Before he had a chance to reply, Sabena suddenly started giggling. "Oh, my darling, don't worry. Just get the confirmation of exactly where the venue is and everybody's happy."

"Yes. Alright," acquiesced Godley. He knew Sabena's demented mood swings and attraction to sadistic violence. He never wanted to be in a situation where she was 'fixing him'.

"Excellent. I knew we could rely on you. You're such a sound man," Sabena said breezily. "Naturally, you'll be recompensed well for your troubles."

Godley smiled to himself. 'Recompensed well', the phrase that made it easier for him to put up with Sabena's foul mouth and psychotic behavior.

"I await your call, darling." Sabena's voice was breathy, reminiscent of a coy teenage girl. Unexpectedly, she flipped personality. Her laugh hit a shrill, determined pitch. "By tomorrow!"

Godley listened, but before he could protest, Sabena rung off.

Now he had spoken to *her*, Godley wondered when he would speak to *him*.

Chapter 85

The light above the screen in front of him flickered on. A satcomm transmission on a secure frequency was coming through. Sam sighed. This was his life; he'd better accept it. Sam depressed the button on his armrest and Justin Maide shivered onto the screen. His face was bellicose, a man facing war.

"I'm sending you the data you requested."

Sam watched the status bar zoom across the screen as his laptop gorged up the bytes being transmitted. It flashed at one hundred percent. Sam turned back to the satcomm screen.

"All received, sir. What's the latest from Langley?"

"They still believe the standard explosives story."

"They don't think it was anything else?" Sam was amazed by the CIA's myopia.

"Why should they? There was no recognized signal for nano-bomb detonation at the time of the blast."

"Have they scanned all frequencies?"

"Of course. That's standard procedure. There have been a lot of signals we've not seen before. I've sent you all the monitoring files so you can review." Maide stopped abruptly, half wanting to carry on, but not sure whether to.

Sam picked up on it. "Something else?"

"Yes. But it could make things difficult for Greene politically if we start poking."

"Well, I'm not shy of a good poke." Sam smirked. "Tell me, sir."

"Greene's team monitored a signal three days ago. They tracked it back to a garage, but when they arrived, the place was deserted. The signal appeared to have the same properties as a nano-bomb signal, but it was on a different frequency. Further deconstruction showed it wasn't a nano-bomb signal at all. It had no internal carrier, so it couldn't deliver anything."

"Just dead hold?" suggested Sam.

"Exactly." Maide nodded. "And they ignored it."

"Big mistake. Not having an internal carrier didn't mean it wasn't connected to Kinley's death." Sam was suddenly deeply annoyed. There was much more to his friend's demise than just C4. "What's your take on this, sir?"

"I know anomalies make me nervous. Anything out of step, like that signal, puts me instantly on guard."

Anomalies made Sam nervous too. "So Greene has closed the book on this?"

Maide scowled and nodded his head. "Seems that way."

"So, we're on our own on this." Sam couldn't remember how many times he'd repeated those words where the CIA was concerned.

"Looks like it. Greene finalized the report on the signal as innocent."

"Innocent? It was hardly that to begin with!" shouted Sam, his ire rising as he learnt more about the stunning incompetence of his US colleagues.

"They're putting it down to tech malfunction," explained Maide.

"Was there anything from the scene that stuck out? Forensics was there first. Did their report identify anything unusual, however small or insignificant?" asked Sam.

Maide flicked through the forensic report again. "First on the scene described the hall area covered in a thin film of grey, silver dust. The investigator didn't think much of it, as it was a bomb site, and later reports don't mention any dust at all."

Sam stared hard at the screen as he listened to the report. "Dust?" he repeated. Then his blood ran inexplicably cold at the four-letter word. He was transported back to Dubai, the dark building and Sabena's shrill laugh as a man screamed in abject agony.

"Yes, Sam. Are you on to something?"

"Maybe, sir. Pull up my report on the nano-bomb mission five weeks ago."

Maide brought up the report and sped read through it.

"Review the field surveillance section, sir," said Sam. "The part about the dark building in Al Nadir's enclosure."

Maide read the section aloud. "Three persons. Two visible. One unidentified male. One identified female, Sabena Sanantoni. And one unknown person. Male unidentified covered in grey, silver dust, screaming and shaking." Sam could still hear the man's terrified howl in his ears; it was as if he was being electrocuted. "You think Kinley was attacked by dust?"

"Not by the dust but something in the dust," stated Sam. Suddenly, everything fell into place. As the connections started to roll, Sam couldn't stop. "Sir, it's next gen nano-tech. You mentioned there had been a lot of signal activity this morning. It could be a long shot, but run a signals check around the time of the blast and cross correlate to find a match with any signals broadcast at the exact same time as I was at the building in Dubai."

"That's more a leap of faith than a long shot, Sam. But let's give it a try."

Maide turned to his IT surveillance whiz. Out of earshot, he issued him with the same instructions Sam had given. The whiz went to work immediately on checking signals for cross correlation points. Maide turned back to Sam.

"If what I saw was next gen nano, then they've been laughing at us all this time."

Sam's anger was justified. From the corner of his eye, Sam could still see Ricky falling back as he scrambled over the wall to survive. Bringing back the nano-bomb had come at a terrible price, but they thought they had the edge by acquiring it. Now, it seemed, all they had were goods past their sell-by date, earlier versions without the upgrades. Sam felt cheated.

The whiz pointed to his monitor screen. Maide nodded. "Sam, we do have a correlation. Identical wave patterns on both accounts."

"That proves it, sir. They've gone to the next level. We can't waste time. There must have been a point of origin. Track the signal back and get our US 'friends' to raid the location."

"That won't be easy." The second he questioned Greene, Maide would start a political maelstrom.

"Nobody ever said our job was, sir."

"Quite."

Maide nudged back from the screen. Sam noticed the movement, and the edginess in Maide's voice; he wanted removal from the task.

"Do you want me to broach it?"

"It would be better, don't you think? Keep my powder and all that."

Sam could see the relief in Maide's face.

"No problem. Greene did wrong by closing the book so soon. He'll have to eat a bit of humble pecan pie and like it."

"Go easy Sam. They're called friends for a reason."

"Noted, sir."

"But, do what you have to do. Kinley was a damn good man. See justice is done."

"I intend to, sir."

"Good luck and Godspeed, Sam."

"Thank you sir. Goodbye."

Chapter 86

Although the blast had only happened that morning, the CIA had sent their teams in and every aspect, it seemed, had been thoroughly processed. The courier company confirmed a scheduled delivery. According to the consignment note on their system, the parcel had been from Anna Bennoit at Sentury Selections, Cambridge, Massachusetts. But the courier who had delivered the parcel felt sure it had been from The Antique Toy Company.

Greene's men took the system consignment note to be the accurate one, and reworked a rather crude and obvious anagram revealing the name of Sabena Sanantoni, second to the infamous Salim Al Douri himself.

Sam dialed into Morgan Greene's vid-phone. As he waited for it to be answered, he realized just what a political pickle he was heading for. In basic terms, Greene and his team hadn't done their job. They had taken the easy way out and swept further opportunities for investigation away.

A bad-tempered, dark-skinned man in his early sixties came online. "Yeah? What?" He then added a little more convivially, "Sam, hi. How are you? En route, I hope?"

Greene's face took up the screen in a massive, powerful ensemble of arrogance and petulance. Sam felt his jet-black eyes drill into him as if he knew what he was going to say and was attempting to subvert him before Sam could strike. Sam swallowed.

"Yeah, I'm winging my way over. Did your people check on rogue signals at the time of the blast?"

"Of course. We're not playing at this, Sam."

Already Greene's hackles were rising at the innocent question.

"Notice anything unusual?" Sam held back from divulging everything too quickly.

"No. Why? You got something?" Greene shuffled uncomfortably.

"Yes. It's next gen nano-tech."

"Explain." Greene deliberately failed to react to the discovery.

"During the nano-bomb mission five weeks ago, and at the time of the blast today, the same rogue signal was broadcast. We've tracked the signal back to three possible originator locations. I need you to authorize a raid on each location. I'm sending you the locations now."

Sam sent a live secure text to Greene as he spoke. Greene received the three locations and snorted.

"I can't do that. Sorry, Sam. But that parcel was sent by Sabena Sanantoni. It was C4. No way was this a nano-bomb hit."

"Read the mission report. I was there, Greene. I saw that man covered in grey, silver dust, the same grey, silver dust they found at the blast today. No one has looked into it, but I know it is next gen nano. Sabena was there in Dubai. She referenced Stein-Muller. Believe me, it's not a long shot. We've already cross-correlated the two signals. It's not a coincidence. Make the raid and you'll score gold."

Greene growled, "It was C4, Sam."

Sam protested vehemently, but Greene was not interested.

"Are you absolutely sure it was a standard bomb?" asked Sam finally. Greene stared at Sam, annoyed he doubted his team's judgement and capability.

"Sam, we've done all the checks. It was the Sanantoni SWALK, sealed with a loving kiss. End of story."

"Yes, but-"

"No buts, Sam. We're done on this one."

"Isn't our job to look at all possibilities? Can we afford to pigeonhole this? What if it *is* next gen nano? What if a new weapon is about to be released on an unsuspecting world, and we had a trailer of what is to come, and we did nothing about it? What does that make us?"

Greene moved uneasily, and then grunted, "You want me to authorize further resources for this?"

He spoke as if Sam asked for him to fork out for financing the raid from his own pocket.

"Well, you wouldn't want anyone to say you hadn't been thorough."

Sam was persistent and determined. He wasn't going to let Greene close and sweep things under the carpet. Greene's face reddened as he acknowledged Sam's blatant inference that the way he'd handled the investigation was less than perfect.

"I can't sanction any raids, not with the evidence as it stands. There's not enough."

"Even with the signal correlation?"

"Still not enough, Sam."

"Can you give me anything?"

Greene thought for a moment. The last thing he wanted was for his men to have missed something. It was his record and reputation at stake. He couldn't be seen to have failed.

"What do you need?" asked Greene wearily.

Sam flashed a wry smile. He knew Greene would hedge his bets.

"Give me eyeballs at each of the locations."

Greene nodded. "Ok Sam. But only for twenty-four hours. If nothing turns up, that's it. It's over."

Chapter 87

Greene was as good as his word. Minutes after his talk with Sam, he sanctioned surveillance on the three locations. Much of the success of surveillance is down to dogged tenacity. But there is a small proportion that is down to luck. Someone must have dealt Sam a good hand of the L-word that day. The agent assigned to the surveillance of one of the three locations, a DIY store, had only been parked in a back street for a few minutes when a tall, youngish man stuck his head out the back door of the shop. He looked around furtively, and then emerged fully into the yard. The agent watched as the man placed a case in the back of a car.

Maybe it was the man's shady movements, but something about his behavior appeared odd to the agent. He called back to Greene and recorded his suspicions. Everything he saw was being captured through his camera in real time and being sent back for analysis. It didn't take long for a sudden burst of activity.

Although the agent didn't know it, the man he had seen had been positively identified as Hans Stein-Muller, a rogue nano-technologist in Al Nadir's employment. Despite his disguise to make him look younger, the CIA's powerful artificial intelligence system had analyzed the various vector points on his face, and had run analytics on possible hostiles in systems databases. The AI system had given a probability factor of the man being Stein-Muller. It was over ninety-percent probability, and this was more than enough to secure a hit.

Soon after, a raid followed. After a brief gunfight, the operatives were captured. There had been six in all. Three had been shot and the other three had been tranquilized with a fast-acting sedative.

Greene swallowed down his pride and rang Sam back with the news.

"We got them all. They behaved as if the location was lilywhite."

Sam detected the tension in Greene's voice. He would have loved to have said to Sam, 'Well that was a non-starter. You've just wasted a whole bunch of tax dollars.' But instead, he had to admit that Sam's intuition had been right. There had been a new nano-bomb, activated by a secondary signal sent at the point of detonation, and his people had almost been duped into believing otherwise. "We've scanned all three and none were loaded."

"As we say here in Blighty, 'they got caught with their trousers down.'" Sam laughed at his own humor, and Greene issued an awkward smile. This was a score to MI6, and he knew it. Sam could see Greene was uncomfortable, so he pulled back on the hubris. "Have the interrogations begun?"

"Not yet. We've isolated them. Make them sweat a bit."

"I wouldn't count on that. Al Nadir operatives are hard fuckers. They won't break easily. If they're not loaded, they'll have other defenses."

Greene stiffened his back. He glared back at Sam. Who the hell did that hotshot think he was? "You may be good, Sam, but I have still been in this game longer than you. I still have a few tricks up my sleeve."

Sam knew he'd pissed off Greene. He backed down several notches. "I learnt what I know from the best. You've been a good teacher."

Greene harrumphed a little at the praise. "Yeah, well, right!"

"All I'm saying is watch them. These guys aren't clean."

"When are terrorists ever clean?"

Sam nodded in agreement.

"We will start with sodium pentothal," said Greene, "and if that doesn't yield any meaningful breakthroughs, we'll initiate neural magnified stimuli. A little NMS and they'll sing like birds."

"And if not, they'll be dead," added Sam darkly.

Greene severed the connection on a brief goodbye. Sam poured himself a brandy and sat back. A small conceited grin formed on his face as the warm liquid slipped down his throat.

Chapter 88

Neural Magnified Stimuli, NightMareScene, or simply NMS, was regarded as a godsend in the intelligence community. Engineered by brilliant scientists at the cutting edge of genetic manipulation, NMS was a highly-effective drug that recreated and played out a captive's darkest fear with absolute clarity. Forced to experience what they had banished to the deepest recesses of their mind, the captive always talked. On divulging their treasured secrets, a trap door that had been built into the drug instantly brought the captive back to reality.

It was, however, the drug's customization that made it so special. During an interrogation, a sample of blood was taken from the captive and used as raw material for the drug's synthesis. The sample was then analyzed using genetic-sensing technology and the genes that will be augmented are identified.

First, the gene that works on the hippocampus and handles memory was removed. Second, the gene that drives the amygdala, the area of the brain responsible for fear, was also taken out. These genes are treated with protein super-enhancers, and then incorporated into a biotech compound with a hallucinogenic base.

Without fail, when administered, the drug reaped the desired results. It was often remarked, amongst the intelligence elite, that if there was a temple built to NMS, agents around the world would probably make a pilgrimage there to pray.

Chapter 89

Ellie tossed and turned, but she couldn't sleep. Every few minutes, her eyes opened to stare at the red LED of her alarm clock. The minutes were edging closer to Sunday morning. Ellie watched television until late. Sam had called twice. When he got on the plane, he promised he'd call her on touchdown in Washington.

Ellie had been drowsy after watching a late-night film, but when she'd switched off the TV, her drowsiness faded like the picture on the screen. She was, at once, alert. She couldn't help but stare at the lights embedded in the ceiling. Although Sam had swept the apartment again, at her behest, before he left and had confirmed no devices were in the apartment, she still had the feeling of being under surveillance. Ellie had even changed for bed in the bathroom with the lights out. Stepping into the bedroom, she felt exposed. She pulled the hem of her sloppy t-shirt down farther to cover her thighs, and crawled into bed, snatching the duvet cover tightly around herself.

Ellie knew her sudden insomnia was due to the feeling of being watched. She never believed she could feel so awkward in her own home. Eventually, after a fitful, restless few hours, Ellie drifted into an agitated sleep.

Chapter 90

Salim was the first to know. He threw down his phone on receiving the news. Then he stared into space for a minute or two, and seemed not to register his surroundings. His faithful acolytes around him ventured to speak, but with no reaction from Salim. Then, like his personality had carved in two, from the silence came an insane roar. He flipped open the satcomm channel and the massive screen buzzed into life in front of him.

In her office, back in the Cambridgeshire plant, Sabena saw the light on the satcomm channel flash. She flicked a switch to receive the transmission. Salim's face greeted her, seething and angry.

"Sabena, you know what's fucking happened?"

Sabena didn't. But she didn't want to admit she didn't know. "I'm sorry, the channel cut out. What did you need, Salim?"

"Don't fucking give me that, you stupid fucking bitch. They're caught. All of them. Stein-Muller. Lupez. Even my fucking cousin, Rasheed."

Sabena's eyes widened and her lips trembled. "How did this happen?"

"How? Because of you, you fucking idiot. You and your second level deployment. I told you it wasn't fucking ready. I warned you the fucking frequencies weren't locked down. But no, you knew best. And now because of your incompetence, my cousin is in their fucking hands."

"I don't understand how they could possibly have..." Sabena was bemused. Had the CIA really upped their intelligence capability?

"I'll tell you how, Sam Noor, nano-tech scientist turned agent. He was at the R and D facility in Dubai. Remember, you told me. He must have seen the demo you and Rasheed were doing with the test subject. He made the connections. He's behind their incarceration."

Salim put his hands together, closed his eyes, and raised his head to heaven as if to pray. No one moved. The world was silent, joining Salim in his impromptu meditation. Then he opened his eyes and screamed his command at Sabena.

"I want Sam Noor dead!"

Chapter 91

The debrief had begun. Morgan Greene ran through the identities of the subjects that had been captured. Agent Jonson sat on his right. Fellow agents, Bergman and Taylor, who took part in the raid, sat on his left. They all encircled the table and watched the faces of the three Al Nadir operatives flash up on the main screen with their background intel.

"All three are known terrorists," Greene began.

He positioned his light pointer to the first face.

"Sacha Lupez. Graduate from MIT. Top explosives expert. A really nasty little guy. Killed his own brother over a woman. After MIT, he went back and joined Carlos Penla's crew. He did most of his military training in Columbia. He's thought to be the mastermind behind the mall bombing campaign of Al Nadir a couple of months back. Lupez graduated north of the border when Al Nadir took over the drug cartel from Penla three years ago."

Greene moved his pointer to the right-hand image.

"Hans Stein-Muller. Graduate of Stanford. Area of expertise is nano-technology. Worked as a legitimate scientist until five years ago. We believe Al Nadir bought him. He's thought to be one of the team who built the first nano-bomb."

Greene stopped speaking. He had reached the third image. He turned to face the table.

"This guy, if the rumors are right, could lead us straight to Salim Al Douri."

The agents around the table raised their eyes in amazement. The notorious and highly illusive Salim Al Douri was the global leader of Al Nadir. He, and only he, had been responsible for architecting the strategies that enabled the unbelievable rise of Al Nadir over the past five years. He was the most wanted man on the planet.

"We only know him as Rasheed. Rumor says he's Salim's first cousin. Little is known about him except that he has been sighted at some of the most vicious bombings the world has ever seen. Middle East origin. If he *is* Salim's cousin, he could either be Syrian or Iraqi, depending upon which mother he has. Of course, nationality makes no difference. He's a terrorist, that overrides everything, and we have him. He's free of cyanide and he's not loaded. We couldn't ask for more."

"Why didn't anyone grab them at control?" asked Agent Taylor, amazed that immigration security hadn't picked them up. Greene laughed rudely in his face. Taylor reddened.

"Jesus, Taylor, we don't know how they got in, but we do know they weren't standing in line to get their passport stamped. What do you think? They're day trippers?"

Taylor shuffled his papers uncomfortably and didn't make eye contact with anyone.

"We've got solid gold assets, thanks to Sam Noor's quick thinking," Greene muttered begrudgingly. "So let's get this show on the road."

Chapter 92

The prisoners were removed from their individual cells and escorted to the interrogation rooms. Blood samples were taken from each and NMS was synthesized. The agents tried interrogating with sodium pentothal, but the captives remained infuriatingly silent. All three were schooled in the art of avoiding interrogation. NMS was administered. The agents sat back in their respective rooms and waited for the painful illusions to manifest. They commenced questioning. No answers came forward. They persisted. NMS was not having any effect at all. The three Al Nadir operatives glared back at the agents, their expressions surly and smug. Whatever the terrorists were seeing through their eyes, it certainly wasn't their darkest fear.

Agent Bergman was the first to notice there was a problem. He'd been interrogating Stein-Muller and was only getting a face of full-blown arrogance. He got up, ran out of the interrogation room and contacted Morgan Greene.

"Sir, we have a problem. NMS is not working. These guys have a tolerance to it. They're not making a beep."

"Shit!" Greene was crestfallen. NMS was their white knight in the war against terrorism. If Al Nadir had found a way around NMS, they really were screwed. "Bergman, take them back to their cells until we work out how to proceed."

Greene dialed Sam's satcomm. Although he hated to admit it, and would never, ever tell him publicly, but the British agent was a great sounding board at times like this.

"We got ourselves a problem." Greene's face was grave.

Sam moved forward, his eyes sharp and focused. "What is it?"

"Those guys we caught, you were right about other defenses. They've got a tolerance to NMS."

"It has to be that RNA synaptic inhibitor."

"What RNA synaptic inhibitor?" snarled Greene, piercing Sam with his dark eyes.

"Rikard, the Al Nadir lieutenant we caught in Oslo, had a phial of something. The full analysis has only just come through. It's an anti-agent that uses genetically modified RNA proteins on a bioengineered base. The anti-agent appears to inhibit synapse functions in hippocampal neurons. As RNA is responsible for activity-dependent changes in synaptic transmission in hippocampal neurons, a genetically engineered RNA-based inhibitor drug does the opposite. The fact that the amygdala, the center for fear in the brain exhibits theta-oscillation activity that phase-locks with hippocampal theta-oscillation during retrieval of some memories, gave the creators of this new anti-agent the link-in between the hippocampus and the amygdala that they needed. You see, interneurons in the amygdala are able to entrain rhythms and, therefore, can facilitate interactions of the brain's nuclei with other parts of the brain during the retrieval of fear memory. The Chinese cracked this neurological code, forging the connection through the theta phase-lock, and developed an RNA synaptic inhibitor that stops an operative's darkest fears from being brought to the fore and visualized around them."

"I'd appreciate that in plain English some time, Sam. But I get the gist. You're basically saying that as far as NMS goes, we're fucked!"

"Yes, I'm afraid so. If Rikard had the anti-agent delivered to him, other lieutenants and high net worth operatives like Stein-Muller would already have been injected with it."

Maddened that Al Nadir had found an anti-agent to their star drug, Sam thumped the seat.

NMS was politically correct. Human rights protestors couldn't say the captives' rights had been violated, and this gave security agencies in the West carte blanche to get away with horrific interrogations. NMS wasn't deemed torture because physically, they weren't *touching* the captives. But everyone on the inner track knew what the drug produced was ten times worse than water-boarding or electrode stimulation. And it never failed to deliver results.

But if Al Nadir really had cracked its neurological key, they'd have to go back to their old ways. It was something, Sam wasn't averse to. To hell with the PC brigade.

"We knew it was going to happen soon enough," said Greene. "It's a miracle we kept it going for so long. Now we'll have to get the lab boys working on a new alternative."

"But what about now, Morgan? We need answers," said Sam.

"I know we do. But you know we have to tread carefully, Sam. We don't want to annoy anyone unnecessarily. You know the boys on the Hill are always watching."

Sam couldn't believe what he was hearing. He whipped around to confront him. "For fuck's sake, Morgan. Are you an agent or a politician? Because you sure as hell can't be both."

"Sam, you know what it's like." Greene was ashamed. Sam was right. Recently, he was more a politician than an agent. His integrity had slipped.

"You want answers, yes or no?" Sam stared with coldness at Greene. His mentor's nod barely registered. "Then when I arrive, let me do my job."

"We have to keep it in line with protocol," Greene reminded Sam.

"Fuck protocol. These guys are terrorists. You want answers. I'll get you answers."

"Now, Sam…" Greene began. But one look at Sam and he knew his words were pointless. "I'll email you the headlines so you can be ready to roll when you arrive."

"Good. See you later."

It was going to be a long night. He'd better snatch some shuteye before he arrived. Sam had to be his very best for Al Nadir's boys.

Chapter 93

The plane touched down on time. Sam sped down the steps towards the waiting helicopter. He ducked his head to avoid the blades, climbed in, settled into the seat and strapped himself in. He pulled the door shut and gave the pilot the thumbs up. The helicopter lifted swiftly off the ground. Sam dug into his bag and removed the papers he'd printed out on the plane. He scanned the operatives' details. He lingered on Rasheed's file. So this was Salim's cousin. The interrogation was going to be very interesting.

Sam stepped out of the helicopter and ran towards the back entrance of Langley. Greene was waiting for him by the toughened glass and metal double doors. Sam shook his hand hurriedly and continued walking with Greene through the doors. The foyer was yawning, bright and clinical. White walls, devoid of pictures or any paraphernalia, grey granite flooring and gleaming stainless steel combined to create an air of elitist, secretive superiority. Further inside, Sam could see a sheet of seemingly unbroken glass stretching across from one side of the foyer to the other.

On approach, Greene placed his right hand on the glass. A pale turquoise light appeared from inside the glass and scanned Greene's hand, moving up, down, left, and right, then finally diagonally from corner to corner. An image of Greene's hand was imprinted on the glass by a violet light. No message came up. No "cleared" or "access permitted." Greene waited for a few seconds. The solid sheet of glass gently and silently slid apart to allow Greene to enter, and then rapidly closed just as silently behind him. Sam placed his right hand on the glass and awaited the scan. The glass opened to allow him passage. He looked over his shoulder. The glass slotted back into place, once again giving the appearance of a single pane. Sam was impressed. The cut down the middle couldn't be detected. He hadn't seen that at Langley before. They were obviously increasing their security measures, given that the US was on constant orange alert for terrorist attacks.

"Is that new?" asked Sam, pointing to the glass.

"Yeah. Good, isn't it?"

"It is."

Sam stopped talking. Greene was suddenly bathed in a series of blue laser lights crossing over his body. Their movement was intricate, complex and rapid. In front of him was another pane of glass with no visible entrance. Inside, a faint red glow could be seen and a few seconds later, the glass parted.

From the foyer, Sam hadn't realized there were two panes of glass with just a meter in between. He stared out at Greene on the other side of the glass while the blue lasers danced over him. The glass in front infused with a red light and the glass opened. Sam stepped through.

"What is that? I know it's for security, but I've not seen anything like it before. What happened to the cubicles?"

"Cubicles weren't safe enough. These scanners work at the molecular level. They can detect nano-agents used for changing facial appearances, surveillance and munitions applications."

Sam nodded. "Incredible. How does the glass work?"

"I'll let you into a secret. It's not glass at all. It's a special crystalline mix developed using nano-technology. Inside are trillions of nano-bots. The crystal nano-bot's program ensures they remain linked together giving the appearance of the glass being solid. They send a signal to each other to open when a scan has been affirmative."

Greene continued to walk. Sam followed at his side.

"Intelligent glass. That's cool."

"It's more than that, Sam. It's virtually unbreakable. The scientists say a cruise missile could hit and it wouldn't break. It's something to do with the oscillation frequency inside each of the crystal's nano-bot pitching automatically to the vibration of the blast. So, in Einstein's theory of relativity, if both the blast vibration and the bots oscillation frequencies are the same, the glass remains static and is thus unbreakable. We've already encased the Oval Office in it from the inside, and some parts of the Pentagon are going to be installing it soon."

"My God, that's amazing, Morgan. Unbreakable, intelligent glass. Who thought of that one?"

"Sorry, Sam. Protocol prevents me from disclosing that."

"You mean you nicked the technology?"

Sam knew when words like 'protocol prevents me' were used, it invariably meant that the CIA had procured it from unofficial sources.

Greene deftly avoided Sam's insinuation. "Hadn't we better get back to business?"

"I was going to, but that glass blew me away. You know how I'm a sucker for technology. So, the prisoners, are they talking yet?"

"Nothing. With their tolerance to NMS, it's going to be difficult getting anything from them. Unless we use other means."

"So use them." Sam headed with speed down a stark white corridor in the direction of the interrogation cells.

"You know what I said." Greene was concerned with Sam's maverick approach to interrogation. It may work in MI6, but he was on US turf now, and out of his jurisdiction.

"And you know what I said," interjected Sam. "If you want answers, I'll get them my way."

Greene nodded reluctantly. "Right. You do it your way. But make sure, Sam, you get those answers. Who do you want first?"

"Rasheed."

"He's down here."

Greene led Sam down to one of the small cells on the left. Sam stopped outside.

"I think it would be better if you left now."

Sam's meaning to Greene was clear. If it got complicated, he wouldn't be implicated. MI6 could take the can.

"Yes, I think you're right."

Greene turned to leave. He didn't like it, not one bit. But they needed answers, and Sam was a solutions man. Whatever way he arrived at the solution, he never failed.

"Remember, Sam, get those answers."

Greene walked with haste up the corridor, away from the breach of human rights that Sam was about to commit.

Chapter 94

Sam opened the little window in the cell door and stared at Rasheed. He was wearing a CIA standard issue orange jumpsuit. He was cuffed, but his legs were free. Sitting on the metal bench, Rasheed looked fiercely back at Sam. He certainly had presence and was clearly powerful. In his late twenties, very tall, at least six feet three inches, extremely muscular, with black-brown eyes and handsome, swarthy features, he looked arrogant and rock hard. And he was going to take some breaking.

"Get anything from him?" asked Sam to Taylor and the other agent. Taylor shook his head.

"Not a peep." His drawn face echoed his despondence.

"Strip him." Sam added with callous determination, "And get the cage."

"We need authority to-" Taylor muttered nervously.

The cage in question was a flat metal lattice cube, no more than three-feet square in size. The metal strips were five centimeters in width with a rough, sharp edge, thereby exacerbating the pain a captive would experience from being in such a confined space. Taylor thought the cage was inhumane and barbaric. Sam, however, had no qualms and was not going to accept any protestations to the contrary.

"I'm your authority," Sam shouted, glaring at the nervous agent. "Greene has green lighted it. You want answers? Do it."

Taylor and his colleague entered Rasheed's cell. Sam stood behind them, watching, his hand resting on his Sig. They approached Rasheed. He snarled and backed against the wall. Taylor reached up and pulled apart the poppers on his jumpsuit. The other agent unlocked the cuffs for a second to remove his sleeves. Sam brought his gun up level with Rasheed's face. He stared at the gun. Sam cocked it. Rasheed read Sam's eyes. *No tricks.* Rasheed smirked into the barrel.

Taylor pulled down Rasheed's jumpsuit. The moment the material was clear of his arms, the other agent swiftly re-cuffed him. The jumpsuit dropped to the floor. Rasheed stumbled over the rough cotton material and out of the cell. He stared ahead indignantly. Taylor pushed him into the interrogation room. Sam followed behind. The cage was in the room. Rasheed looked down at it. Sam poked him in the back with his Sig.

"Get in!" Sam pointed to the cage.

Rasheed didn't move.

"I said, get in."

Rasheed still did not move. His eyes stared hard at Sam. He grinned.

"Fine, we'll play it your way." Sam motioned to the agents. "Get him in there."

The two agents pulled Rasheed down to the height of the cage, removed the cuffs and pushed his huge naked body into the tiny space. The metal strips sliced into his skin like a cheese cutter. Rasheed grimaced but didn't scream. He curled himself to accommodate his massive body into the miniature space, his neck muscles stretched, and deep pain shot through his spine. Rasheed's hair poked through the lattice. His head, with nowhere to go but down, pushed into his chest, virtually restricting his breathing. His chin stuck deep into the socket of his breastbone. Thoroughbred legs pushed tight against his head. His knees slammed into his ears. The backs of his heels touched his testicles. His thick, powerful arms circled around him like a shield. In silence, Rasheed took in all the stunning discomfort. From the outside, he looked like he belonged to a contortionist's act.

Rasheed had not been given any food or drink since he'd been captured. Sam knew he would be hungry and thirsty. He would stay that way. The light in the interrogation room was switched off. Complete sensory deprivation. Cramped in, hunched up, and in complete darkness, Sam left him.

Chapter 95

Inside the Observation Room, Aswa-da was fascinated to watch Treeborne. He wanted to know if the president knew about the theft of the quantum bomb. He focused on querying 'President Treeborne current activities' and stated March 22, 2017.

The Screen lurched and images flowed of Treeborne sitting at a table in an opulent dining room. He was at the White House, entertaining influential business guests. Around him, people fawned and crawled, wanting to gain favor with the leader of the free world.

Treeborne put down his knife and fork and took a gulp of wine.

"I tell you now," the president started, and he looked up and down the table, eyeing everyone. All his table guests held their cutlery poised, waiting on his word. "I've got a way to annihilate those Al Nadir bastards for good!"

The entire room gasped.

Treeborne moved his ass around on the beige leather covered chairs, getting comfortable, and lent forward, placing his big elbows firmly on the table. He pursed his lips and narrowed his eyes as he picked up his knife. A piece of meat from his beef medallion hung desperately to the blade, as he pointed it in Weitz's direction.

"They're as good as dead, aren't they, Frank?"

Weitz shuffled awkwardly, aware that now the room had captured him in their eyes. "Yes, Mr. President," he muttered.

"What is it that you've got?" asked a billionaire arms manufacturer to the left of Weitz. On his face was immediate worry that his company's number one position was about to be toppled.

"Can't say yet, boys and girls. But you're gonna know soon enough. Testing's all done. Just gotta get the UN's approval under Resolution 8091.

That's happening at the Peace Summit in London in a few days' time. Then we're good to go."

Treeborne returned back to his unfinished plate and began shoveling the rest of his food into his mouth. Aswa-da smirked, deeply amused by the president's posturing, especially knowing that the quantum bomb was in Salim's hands.

Another dinner guest, an investment banker, asked, "Mr. President, what is UN Resolution 8091? I haven't heard of it before."

"Sure you haven't. I just drafted it a few days before with my secretary of state, Dick Cowl. But this is gonna change everything. Trust me. Al Nadir are over."

"But, Mr. President, you haven't-" began the investment banker, but one of the president's security services officers pushed on his shoulder. The banker looked around sharply and read the message in the officer's face. He pulled his shoulder away from the officer's touch, but refrained from further enquiry.

Treeborne clocked the move and sneered. Then he moved back so that the serving staff could remove his plate and glanced across the room.

"Lovely dinner, huh?" exclaimed Treeborne to his guests.

His gaze fell upon a gorgeous red-headed woman sitting next to the annoying banker. She was petite but perfectly formed. The wide belt she wore attenuated her waist, making her appear waif-like. He wondered if just his single hand could encase around her. Or would he need both?

He signaled to his aide, who jumped to his attention.

"The red head next to the prick banker. Who is she?" Treeborne asked directly into his ear.

"That's the prick banker Cuthbert Jones' wife, Emily. Would you like to speak to her?"

"Yeah," whispered Treeborne, staring hard at the woman, willing her to react. He couldn't help licking his lips as he watched her slender frame move like human harmony.

The aide edged up to Emily and murmured in her ear. Her prick banker husband was engrossed in conversation with a bald-headed guy. He'd virtually ignored his beautiful wife all evening, who regarded the rest of the table with disinterest. She swept her soft blue eyes across the room and sipped her wine with languid ease. On her face, Treeborne recognized utter boredom.

Immediately, on Treeborne's aide giving her the message, she looked up in his direction and smiled. Gently, she pushed her chair back, slipped out between the other diners and walked with the president's aide. Treeborne was aware her husband hadn't even noticed she'd gone.

Another aide came to Treeborne's side.

"Excuse me, Mr. President, but there's something that needs your attention."

Aswa-da watched on and laughed, knowing what was happening.

Treeborne stood up, making his apologies swiftly about 'state business' and the fact that he 'never has a moment's rest'.

He followed his aide, walking hastily and holding down a smile of exhilaration.

The aide directed Treeborne into one of the side rooms. He opened the door, and saw, sat demurely on the white chaise long, Emily.

Treeborne grinned then closed and locked the door.

"I saw you looked bored earlier. I reckon I've got something to raise your interest."

Chapter 96

Sam entered with the two agents, switched on the light, opened the cage and pulled out Rasheed. Four hours had passed since Sam had left him in the cage, but his surly expression remained unchanged. The experience hadn't even dented Rasheed's formidable stamina. A small metal-topped table and two metal chairs stood to the right of the cage.

Sam hurled Rasheed into one chair and sat down in the other. He glared at his captive. The steel table was cold to touch, but Sam's words were colder.

"It's going to get harder from here. You know that. We know about the new nano-bomb, how it works, and who it was targeting."

Rasheed looked scornfully at Sam.

"Kinley was a good friend. I suggest you talk and save yourself a lot of pain."

Rasheed stared at Sam. Then he spat at him from across the table. The spit landed on Sam's cheek as a hot, stale fluid. Sam took a tissue from his pocket, reached up and wiped the spit away. He looked back at Rasheed.

"Now that wasn't very nice. You're going to get another four hours in the cage for that."

Sam stood up, walked behind Rasheed, grabbed his arm and wrenched it back with a savage force. A click indicated that Rasheed's shoulder had dislocated. Rasheed bit down hard on his lip to stop from screaming. Sam thrust him back down on the table. Sandwiching Rasheed's cheek between his hands and the cold steel table, Sam pulled his dislocated shoulder back further. Rasheed didn't make a sound. One tough son of bitch, thought Sam. His arm came down tight and heavy on Rasheed's neck. In parallel, he pushed his knee into the small of his back, forcing him to arch painfully.

He spoke in Rasheed's ear. "The new nano-bomb. Tell me!"

"Kiss um muk," Rasheed snarled. *I fuck your mother.*

"Ibn el gha'bar," Sam answered instinctively. *You son of a bitch.*

"Kiss um muk," Rasheed repeated and spat again at Sam.

"Oh, fuck you," said Sam, pulling Rasheed off the table. He wasn't going to get any answers from the bastard yet. He needed more treatment.

Sam kicked him hard in the back of his knees, forcing Rasheed to the ground. He dragged Rasheed like a ragdoll by his arm across the floor. His dislocated shoulder stuck outwards grotesquely, translucent skin pulling taut like cling-film over the dislodged bone. Sam signaled at the two agents to return Rasheed to the cage. They pushed him inside and his body coiled into an uncomfortably tight ball. The agents could see Rasheed's shoulder was still out. They knew he must be in pain, but he didn't scream at all. He was silent. His head turned slightly as it buried in his chest and he displayed one insolent eye at Sam. The agents locked the cage door.

They felt out of their depth engaging in such barbaric torture. Although Rasheed was a terrorist, they were ashamed at the way he was being treated. He was, after all, a human being. They doubted they could have treated an animal the way that Sam was treating Rasheed.

"See you in four hours. By that time, you may feel like talking. And if you don't, well, we'll try something new. Maybe an amp or two up your ass will do it. Think about it, fuck head." Sam laughed, and moved away to turn the light off.

"Your friend Kinley," began Rasheed.

Sam flinched at the mention of Kinley, his finger resting on the light switch. But he didn't turn around.

Rasheed's voice, muffled and wheezing, continued, "We knew about him. We played him. We played your intelligence agency. We fed him shit and, like the dog he was, he ate it greedily."

Rasheed's one eye stared cruelly at Sam's back and he let forth a muted laugh. Sam whirled round, his anger burning. Rasheed's face, although buried in his torso, was full of impudence and disdain.

"You fucker," hissed Sam, and he kicked the cage hard.

But Rasheed continued his strained laugh.

"That's good," said Sam. "You carry on laughing until I come back. Then we'll see who laughs."

Sam hit the switch and darkness prevailed again.

Chapter 97

One thing, two words, that's all Salim ever wanted in life. He kept it simple.

Except those two words were: the world.

It wasn't a dream or a fanciful notion. He was Salim Al Douri, and he didn't even know what a fanciful notion was. No, wanting the world was a future reality Salim knew he could shape. It was all down to the right combination of people, resource and opportunity. Bringing those components together meant Salim would soon be on the right trajectory to achieve his goal.

After an outstanding array of academic accolades from Eton, Cambridge and Harvard, Salim was approached by the CIA, who made him an offer. Salim accepted. Eight years in, Salim could see it wasn't working. The Company was losing more often than winning. And Salim wanted to be a winner. Counter-intelligence taught Salim a crucial lesson. Everything is connected. Only very, very few step back far enough to see the bigger picture.

Salim, even then, was already several miles out of the earth's atmosphere. The bigger picture was seared on his eyeballs.

A globally connected terrorist collective. That's what was needed. No more agency constructs, nut jobs or religionist fundamentalists. Just a dose of good old fashioned, no-holds-barred evil.

When the revelation hit Salim, he was still stuck in the middle of Langley. He'd just got back from a mission and was in debrief. The mission hadn't gone well. Salim witnessed his fellow agents gunned down in front of him. It was the fifth mission in as many months that had gone southwards. Salim knew he was lucky to escape with his life. Salim's CO had been concerned about what this latest episode would do to him. She'd mentioned trauma and stress. The truth was, Salim had watched as his colleagues, or those he regarded endearingly as 'total imbeciles' die in front of him, and felt no sadness. Salim knew it was inevitable. They had it coming. They'd been too slow, never read situations properly and never listened, believing they knew everything. They'd paid for their narcissism with their lives.

But Salim recognized this was his easy out, making it seem his nerves were shattered, that he was on the ledge with nothing to stop him from tipping over.

Salim smirked into his hand. He peered out the window of his private plane as it flew over the Zagros mountain range near the Iraq/Iran border, and he recalled how he'd played the Company.

His CO had come over to his desk corner. She'd flopped down in a chair opposite him. Looking Salim up and down, she scowled.

"I'm not happy about you, Salim. You're going through a psyche-eval tomorrow."

Salim's CO was a woman. She was pretty but verged on the tom-boyish. He'd assessed her within minutes of her initial taking command of his assignments. With short auburn hair, a pixie face, tall and with a firm, muscular body, Salim recognized that she leant more to the girls than the boys, but would, at a push, flip either way.

Salim CO stared at him and he looked up, eyes full of tears.

"I don't think I can take this anymore."

She put her hand out to grasp Salim's hand. *Stupid bitch!*

"Salim you're the best. I know. I recruited you. I knew what you were the minute I set eyes on you at Harvard. You've been in this business eight years. Some don't last half that long. I know what it can do to a person. You've done great things. But right now, you're useless to me. Go home, get some rest, and let the psyche-eval do its job tomorrow."

Before his psyche-eval, Salim snorted up a line of cocaine. By the time the CIA appointed psychologist called him, Salim was so strung out he could hardly hold a syllable. The psychologist sat in the chair, but Salim sat on an ant hill. Or so it would seem. Jumpy didn't even begin to describe it.

Half-way through, Salim got up, screaming, "That's it. I'm through." He tore off his CIA badge, laid down his gun and walked out.

Salim grinned as he remembered the psychologist look over at his CO. She had just shrugged halfheartedly, and said, "Let him go."

Within an hour of walking, Salim was back in the air flying to Dubai. He'd rang his pilot who had his plane on stand-by.

It was October 10, 2000. The day Al Nadir was formed. The genesis of a corporation that would give Salim what he wanted.

Having worked in the CIA, Salim knew what triggered them, and thus, he knew what to avoid. He architected it for Al Nadir to be wacky and over-the-top, and therefore off the CIA's radar as it wouldn't have been considered a threat.

Al Nadir became a cult. Its focus: the worship of ancient aliens. Its membership: the brats of the rich and famous, billionaire playboys wanting something different and gorgeous beauties wanting an 'in' to top level eligible bachelors. For them, Al Nadir equaled hedonistic, naked 'alien prayer' parties, total craziness and drug-fueled excess.

For a while.

After 9/11 hit, alerts were everywhere. Suspicion lingered. But the Company was too fixed on Al Qaeda and their own vendetta wars. They weren't interested in Salim or his crazy world.

But he still threw them a curve ball. Just in case.

The family's yearly sojourn to Europe delivered the tactical advantage Salim had needed. His parents' allowance had started to run slightly dry, and although he still had more money than most people would see in an entire lifetime, it wasn't enough. His parents' pocket money just wasn't sufficient for Salim's plans.

Contacts he'd made during his 'black ops' days handled everything.

All loose ends were tied.

Salim's family's flight to Marbella was their swan song. He felt nothing. It was a requirement, that was all. Salim needed their billions and his parents' deaths were the most efficient way to get his hands on them. His brother and sister's demise, he regarded as a considerable bonus. He hated them anyway. Always trying to change him when he was younger. Always jealous of who he became.

Salim was pleased to be shot of them.

The Agency got wind of his family disaster. Through back channels, Salim's old CO contacted him. She stood in front of him, wringing out her hands as she tried to figure out what to say.

Salim lifted the glass to his lips and savored the taste of the malt whisky. He laughed into his glass as he recalled his CO's pathetic face, covered in sorrow for his loss.

"Salim, what can I say? I'm so, so sorry. We'll do everything we can. We'll catch the bastards."

"Thank you. But this is it for me. I'm quitting. I just can't live another day without my family. I loved them so much."

In front of his old CO, Salim played the suicidal son to the hilt. He remembered her whittling on about it being Al Qaeda. They'd bombed his father's plane. Intel pointed at it being down to pipelines.

"I'll get you justice for your family, Salim. I promise you. I give my solemn word."

Solemn word, thought Salim. What does that even mean for someone in the Company? They've never been able to keep a promise in their life.

He thanked her. Then he added with a morbid inference, "It's the last time you'll ever see or speak to me again."

Salim turned and walked away quickly, as his CO shouted desperately, "Salim, what do you mean? Tell me. Please, for God's sake, don't do anything crazy!"

At the time, Salim's new-found mega-wealth had been heavily bolstered by some strategic investments. He still had his playboy billionaires on speed dial. They were always good for insider tips. It didn't take long for Salim to multiply the billions. Playing the markets judiciously and buoyed by inside track intel, in a year, he'd amassed close to half a trillion.

That level of wealth gave Salim the leverage he needed to make things happen.

Word was out in the markets that a financial guru was betting against the markets and winning. But no one knew who. In the Agency, Salim had learnt how to hide money flows. His training paid off.

With the money secured, it was time to change again. Another metamorphosis for Salim beckoned.

He picked up what he had and made it clear to anyone who knew him that he was going into the wilderness to find himself. Gone was the party prince. He would live as a hermit.

Salim walked out of his penthouse and out of the 21st Century.

With no electronic communication, Salim fell off the grid completely.

Of course, in reality, Salim hadn't fallen anywhere. He'd just bought a string of Low Earth Orbiting (LEOs) satellites and set up his own advanced telecoms system, working on protocols beyond the knowledge or reach of the intelligence agencies, or anyone else.

Except Salim.

He smiled, recalling the ease of everything.

He'd gone to work, acquiring a whole host of companies covering everything from nano-tech and biotech to advanced weapons and chemical processing.

Nothing was in his name. Nothing could be traced to him.

But he owned everything.

Salim was the architect in this new world of his own creation.

And the irony of the entire plan was that it was all done in plain sight of everyone. Al Nadir was hatched in those faceless buildings, those massive corporations, and those industrial plants across the world. The places where legitimate business was conducted, where taxes were paid, where governments even gave the companies lucrative contracts.

Salim's staff worked on projects and plans completely blind to the bigger picture.

By that time, Salim had recruited tens of thousands of people to Al Nadir through those bona fide commercial activities. And every single one marched to Salim's tune.

Gradually, over time, Salim's network of capability across the globe grew until, finally, the day arrived when he decided to unveil his true intentions.

It was the day when, Salim Al Douri, their religious, harmless irritant, had said, "I'm back!"

Salim still remembered, with considerable affection, walking down those plane steps in Dubai as he received calls from his global lieutenants confirming the concurrent detonation of multiple bombs in thirty cities around the world.

That day everyone stood up and listened to Salim Al Douri.

Now they would bow down to him.

On his plane in the present moment, Salim stared at the box in his lap holding the quantum bomb components. Those whimpering governments had planned, through their Peace Summit and UN Resolution 8091, to destroy everything he had built.

They would pay a price for their actions.

And the price would be the world.

Chapter 98

Sir Justin Maide stared at the screen on his tablet. Ellie's image was frozen, and she was caught in a scream. If only she'd explained something to Sam, explained why she'd screamed.

Instead of lie flatly to his face.

He didn't want to institute an extraction and interrogation, but Sam Noor knew more secrets than most of the operatives in River House. And he knew the biggest and most damaging secret of all.

Operation Snowdrop.

Now Ellie knew the truth about Sam's life, Maide couldn't risk for her to be an Al Nadir sleeper agent. He couldn't risk her knowing about Snowdrop even if she was just an ordinary woman.

Sam may already have told her, thought Maide, and scratched his chin absently. He raised the high ball glass to his lips. The Glenfiddich wasn't having quite the same calming effect as it usually did. He tipped another three fingers worth and knocked it back.

Perhaps he'd been impulsive about rubbing Sam's face in it with his surveillance. He'd just been so furious about Sam questioning his judgement when he'd decided to pull Kinley. He couldn't help making Sam pay for his insubordinate behavior. He also wanted to let him know what would happen if he ever broached the Snowdrop subject ever again.

But Maide wished he'd kept the surveillance on Sam and Ellie. Then he'd have known for certain what Ellie was really about. But, of course, he'd also have run the risk of Sam's constant sweeping habit. If he'd found Six's bugs in his apartment, Sam would have raised hell. The PM would have gotten involved and it could have turned very bloody for everyone.

Maide looked at the folder next to his tablet. It was a precis of Ellie Noor's life.

EYES ONLY SECURITY BRIEF

Subject: Ellie Noor
Maiden Name: Vale

DOB: 02.05.1974
Place: Fulham, London
Home: Silent Waters, Chelsea, London and Red Rose Lodge, Winchester
Occupation: Managing Director, Cloud Nine Tech, Winchester

Family History

Husband: Dr Sam Noor ████████████████████████

Father: Stardust Traveller (real name Tim Jones)
DOB: 21 December 1942
Place of Birth: Dover
Current Status: Deceased: 27/11/1982. Reason: OD Heroin

Mother: Athena Marguerite Blaketon-Royce
DOB: 18.03.1959
Place of Birth: Chelsea
Current Status: Married: Senator Alan Bohlen-Curtis, Republican.
Location: Houston, Texas
Estranged relationship with daughter

Great Aunt: Lillian Joan Wilson
DOB: 11 May 1902
Place of Birth: Fulham
Current Status: Deceased: 12 January 1990 Reason: Cardiac infarction
Great Aunt responsible for Ellie's upbringing until aged 16. Ellie was talent
spotted in London and became a model with Models One. She stayed in the
company's accommodation in London with other young models but did not
like the lifestyle and left to join IBM.

Background to Relationship

First met Sam Noor: August 4, 1994. Location: IBM Hursley Park, Winchester.
Interviewed for a position as Executive Secretary.
Love interest of Dr Sam Noor almost immediately.
Relationship commenced: 18 August 1994
Married: 20 December 1994, Winchester
Children: None

Surveillance Snapshot

Security Risk Assessment (as at 21 March 2017): Low
Link to: Transcript A115_2
SurvID: Log8880_14_UDE_771_Y

Exhibited irrational behaviour, outside of psyche-range.
Spoke to an empty kitchen.
Appeared to communicate with someone not visible on surveillance.
Screamed for no reason.
Did not provide reason to husband.
When pressed by husband for a reason, subject lied explicitly and directly.

Revision of Risk Assessment: High.

Further Action

Identify cause of the scream.
Verify level of national security threat (ascertain whether she is a Category A hostile).

As a result of what he'd seen on the surveillance, Maide had revised the risk assessment to high. He knew that Ellie appeared, at least externally, to be no threat at all. She lived her life almost entirely to do two things: building her company and worshiping the ground that Sam walked on.

But something didn't ring true.

Maide played the video surveillance again. The tech analyst had marked the points where Ellie had spoken to an open, empty kitchen.

"I'm listening."

Ellie's face showed she was listening intently to something. Maide was sure she was getting her orders from someone.

Then her face changed. It became crumpled with fear and desperation. She looked up and yelled, "Tell me what you want."

In her response, it was plain to Maide. Ellie was asking what the other side wanted. That was a definite confirmation someone was talking to her.

Maide clicked on the indicated point on the timeline to hear her last words.

"What is too far gone?"

Ellie was asking someone a question. It wasn't Sam, and they had no guests. Maide had been in the field a considerable time and he knew when an operative was being given their orders.

Instinctively, he knew Ellie was being told to do something that didn't align with what she wanted to do. Maide could see her body freeze and she didn't move at all. She was pensive. In listening mode. Still. Her face was getting more contorted and frightened, and then suddenly she started to thrash around, screaming like a mad woman. Her face became ingrained with unimaginable fear. It was like someone was trying to kill her. In the midst of her wreathing and blood-curdling howls, she tipped over the coffee onto her hand. Although it burnt her, Maide noticed the pain seemed to bring her back from whatever state she was in before. Maybe the endorphins flooding her system overwrote whatever created Ellie's induced state. Or maybe it was time dependent.

Maide felt he was falling into a labyrinth of maybes. He'd never felt so confused in his life.

He resumed viewing the surveillance and watched as Sam rushed in brandishing his gun. From the scene, Ellie was deeply terrified. Sam confessed as to who he really was, and Ellie was stunned.

Maide brought the tablet up close and re-ran the moment of Sam's confession. He zoomed in on Ellie and inspected how she reacted to the news that her husband worked for MI6.

There was no avoiding the truth of what the camera had picked up. She genuinely didn't know. Maide could read her surprise and see how shattered the news of Sam's deceit made her feel. She virtually collapsed in front of him.

Either she was an incredible actress and liar, or Ellie really didn't know anything of her husband's job. It was all a conundrum. If she didn't know about Sam, who was giving her orders? And why?

He couldn't have Sam living with an unknown and potentially hostile entity. He had to verify completely just who the hell Sam's wife was.

The actions he'd just green lighted could be vindicated by this need. He had to protect and serve. His agents. His country. Himself.

Maide knew, whatever happened, he had to uncover the mystery that was Ellie Noor.

Chapter 99

The next morning, Ellie rose late. She showered quickly, changed into her short denim skirt, pale green cashmere jumper and wool/silk jacket, and started to work on her laptop. She tried to remain sanguine about Sam's departure and her own safety. Having the gun helped. But it was no replacement for Sam.

Around mid-morning, Ellie's stomach grumbled. She wandered into the kitchen and rummaged in the fridge. There was virtually nothing to eat, bar cheese and juices. The lethal combination of stunning revelation and burning passion had resulted in her failure to engage in domestic duties. As a housewife, Ellie failed abysmally.

She grabbed her car keys and headed for the nearest supermarket.

In the car, her music was blasting. The sun was out. Although she wasn't exactly happy, Ellie was gradually coming to terms with the weird life she now lived.

Deep in thought, Ellie didn't notice the jet-black BMW draw up behind her at the lights. With the high number of car-jackings, Ellie usually made a point of having autolock enabled in the car's system as she drove, but the function had been acting up. Annoyed by this, and in one of her more impulsive moments, Ellie had gone into the car system and toggled autolock off. She'd meant to call the garage about it, but with work pressures, that call had been forgotten.

The moment was swift. Ellie stopped at the lights. The streets were empty. People were resting, enjoying their Sunday morning lie-in and shaking off their hangovers from Saturday night. She slipped the car into neutral, brought up the handbrake and waited for the notoriously long lights to change.

Suddenly, everything was happening.

The car door opened. Before Ellie had a chance to react, she felt a sharp pain. She looked to the right. A man in a balaclava had thrust a needle into her neck. The effect of the chloral hydrate hit Ellie's system. She slumped forward.

The passenger door flung open. A second man reached in and unlocked the safety belt. Placing one arm behind Ellie's back and the other beneath her knees, he skillfully pulled her over to the passenger side. He fixed her seatbelt and positioned her head against the window to make it look like she was sleeping. Then he got into the back seat.

The first man whipped off his balaclava and slid into the driver's seat. The lights changed to green. He pushed the car into drive and released the handbrake.

The black BMW followed behind. Quentin sat in the back and watched nervously Ellie's capture. Admiring their smooth synchronization, he snapped open his phone and spoke coldly.

"Extraction complete."

TO BE CONTINUED … IN THE DOMINANT

* END OF BOOK THINGS *

The Dominant
Part Two * Book Two

Chapter 1

23 March 2017

Ellie Noor lifted her head groggily. The bag covering her head had robbed her sight completely. She focused hard to look through the bag, but the tightly packed weave made it impossible. She realized uncomfortably that most of her clothes had been removed. But, thankfully, her underwear still remained. Cold inspired by fear shuddered through her. Instinctively, she tried to move, to cover herself and preserve her modesty, but as she tried to pull her hand, it was as though a knife carved through her arm and she whimpered.

Why was she in pain?

Ellie moved her hips, as if to turn, and that slicing feeling caught her again. She swung back and forth, and waves of agony washed through her.

The cutting sensation didn't appear when she didn't move. Only when she tried to use her limbs did the hurt surface. She reasoned that it had to be something they'd given her. Maybe it was something affecting her muscles, forcing agony to prevent her movement.

Amongst the pain, Ellie felt metal around her wrists and ankles. Someone was set on her being as inanimate as possible.

Hooded, nearly naked and chained to a chair, overwhelming panic swept through her.

Despite her intractable situation, Ellie swallowed hard and forced herself to be calm. She breathed slowly and fell into the rhythm.

She was a managing director of a top EmTech business. She'd handled presentations and negotiations with many multibillion-dollar companies.

She never panicked once. She'd just got on and done what was needed.

But what did she rely on then?

Logic.

Common sense.

Understanding the environment and making her play.

Her thought processes had started to quell her panic.

She couldn't see, but she could hear. Without sight, her listening naturally became more acute and Ellie attempted to define her surroundings according to what she could hear. She listened but couldn't hear anything, just the sound of her own breathing.

Then, suddenly, footsteps approached. The footsteps were light. If the owner was a man, he wasn't large, or else he'd been trained to push the weight off his tread like in stealth combat. The owner may even be a woman. Ellie sniffed the air for any scent, but apart from the sterile, chemical smell ingrained in the hood, she smelled nothing.

Her analytical mind took over, lessening her fear as she began to 'see' through her other senses.

Ellie sensed that it was a man. She couldn't figure why she thought this. Maybe the way in which the person walked. Although light, the step still sounded manly.

She forgot she couldn't move and made to turn to face her captor, but that sharp cutting feeling once again shot through her body. She inhaled sharply.

The footsteps stopped.

Arrival.

Ellie breathed out.

She tried again to focus, but her mind was cloudy and heavy like a great weight was upon it. She couldn't remember anything. She couldn't even remember her clothes being removed. That fact disturbed her. How could she not remember that?

Ellie was terrified. She was more terrified than she ever believed she was capable of feeling. In fact, the feeling of being terrified, so often spoken about by people that had been kidnapped, was a totally physical manifestation.

Ellie's brain frazzled with stimuli and backstory. What had already happened to her? What was going to happen to her? It was all conjecture. But such was its power, it could easily have sent Ellie into an absolute internal frenzy, a hysterical madness, as she waited for her captors to commence whatever they intended to do.

She didn't have to wait long for her captors to get to work.

Sharp pain shot up her arm. A needle had been inserted. Ellie tried to turn her head but couldn't. Again, she concentrated but whatever they'd given her was too quick and too powerful.

The room began to spin and slide. It was like she was very drunk. Ellie felt nauseous. She wanted to vomit but couldn't move.

"We know you're activated, but not in the same way as the nano-bomb. I wouldn't be standing here if you were loaded."

Someone gripped her hood and pulled it away.

A light came on, shattering her vision. Brilliant white everywhere, burning like a laser in her eyes. She desperately wanted to shut out the painful whiteness, but she couldn't lift her arm. It was chained to the chair.

"Sam Noor's your target, isn't he?"

The words came from behind her. They sounded like the perpetrator was underneath water. Ellie couldn't believe what she was hearing. Her husband was her target. What the hell was he talking about?

Ellie tried to turn, but sharp pain caught her. Whatever they'd given her was working at full strength. Any movement Ellie tried to make instantly caused her severe agony.

"I said, Sam Noor's your target. We know all about it. No point in denying it."

Ellie didn't say anything. The whole idea that Sam was her target. It was insane.

The person whose footsteps Ellie had heard eventually came into her eye line.

Tall and gaunt, with blond hair and dark grey eyes of steel, he walked softly. He had a slightly effeminate element about him, which, somehow, made him more sinister. He tipped his head to the side and stared at Ellie, eyeing her body slowly. He reached in and placed a finger to her cheek. Ellie trembled.

"Hello, sweetie. Let's see what you're about."

The interrogator walked around the chair Ellie was chained to. Ellie tried to follow him, but a sharp, jagged burning sensation cut like a lathe through her body. Ellie caught her breath. Her body ached. She breathed in and out in long gasps and struggled bravely to cope with the violent torment.

"Oh, now I wouldn't move if I were you," the interrogator sneered, as he watched Ellie grimace. "It could get very painful if you do. Just stay still, listen to me, and answer my questions."

Ellie looked in front of her and not at the interrogator. This stance annoyed him and he pulled at her shoulder, forcing Ellie to face him. Ellie cried out as the quick twist brought a wave of agony within her muscles, and she held her breath as the deep, cutting hurt surged through her.

"That's better. Now keep your face on me. I don't want to hurt you."

Ellie stared at him. His smirking, sly mouth and steel ice eyes did not reflect his words.

Defiance stormed within her.

She wasn't going to give him the satisfaction of seeing her fear. She wasn't going to give him the satisfaction of getting anything from her.

Somehow, the drug they'd given her had brought clarity. A fog lifted in her mind. Fear had been her enemy. But she wasn't filled with fear now.

She was filled with hate.

Ellie glared at her interrogator and did not utter a word.

"We saw you talking in your kitchen yesterday morning. But no one was there. Who were you talking to?"

Ellie remained silent. Her eyes glazed over, and she ignored her interrogator.

"Did you know that Sam Noor was MI6 before yesterday?" he asked.

"Are you with Al Nadir?" the interviewer continued.

"We saw you scream. We know that was the initiation, wasn't it?" The bland emotionless voice persisted.

"The Sleeping Assassin technology. We know all about it?"

Ellie, ignoring all questions, pulled frantically at her clamps. Pain cut through her mercilessly and her beautiful face mutated into a horrible grimace.

"Who is Sam Noor?"

"Who are you with?"

"Why did you scream?"

"Who were you talking to in your kitchen?"

The interrogator spoke pointedly. He wanted answers.

He stood in front of Ellie, and then dropped down. He grasped her legs and moved up, stroking her thighs. Ellie swallowed but forced herself to stay strong. He nudged up close so that Ellie could feel his breath on her stomach. She recoiled.

"Listen, darling, Guantanamo Bay is heartbeat away, and we all know how they'll treat a pretty thing like you."

Ellie flinched at the words, understanding the inference, but retained her silence.

The interrogator scowled, rose to his feet, and looked straight down at Ellie with impatience.

"I will continue to ask you questions all day and all night. I'll be replaced with another person just like me. But we're gonna keep you in that chair until you speak. No toilet breaks. No food. No water. No sleep. You will speak to me. Sooner or later, you'll have to. So let's avoid all this unnecessary stress and tell me what I want to know."

The interrogator walked around, and then came in close to Ellie, sneering.

"Your friend, Rikard, fessed up just before he blew in Oslo. He told us everything. Keeping silent isn't going to help you."

Ellie stared ahead and said nothing.

Infuriated by Ellie's silence, the interrogator continued with the same drill over and over. Ellie knew he wanted to break her, but his monosyllabic interrogation technique was having no effect on her at all. She sat silent, every so often pulling or trying to rise from the chair, only to be dissuaded by the painful cutting sensation that ravaged her body every time she moved.

Ellie was aware of time passing but she could not be sure how many hours she'd spent in the white room. Closing her eyes, she tried to block out the interrogator's persistent, penetrating mantra. But his voice broke through, invading her place of solace.

"Oh, no you don't! You're not going to sleep," said the interrogator sharply, and he shook Ellie awake. As he shook her, vibrations of pain cut into her body. Her head was splitting with a new headache, and nausea had returned full blast.

"Are you with…" The interrogator never had chance to finish his incessant questioning. Ellie interrupted, screaming:

"Oh! Go fuck yourself!"

Ellie's somewhat ill-advised words of courage ejected from her shaking lips. She'd had enough of his boring bloody voice. She felt like shit. Her head was splitting and if she heard another word from the fucker's lips, she'd puke.

Yes, it was a reckless thing to say. But sometimes Ellie spoke first and thought later. The droning, debilitating voice had pushed Ellie beyond caring.

With her customary impulsiveness on overdrive, at that moment, caution was not in her vocabulary.

Hearing her words, and the only words she'd said in the entire interrogation session, the interrogator yanked her arm to the side. As he pulled, the chains dug deep into her wrist.

Ellie felt a sudden stabbing.

Yet another needle was driven with naked brutality into her skin.

Ellie winced and tried to look round. Her neck shook with pain by the simple movement. But she withstood it long enough to see, in her peripheral vision, the hands of the interrogator taking a blood sample.

Ellie broke into a sweat. Who the hell were these people? Why did they need her blood? Somehow, she had to get out, but her body from the head down was completely immobile. The drugs delivered total paralysis.

Imprisoned in her own body, she could do nothing.

The interrogator smiled at Ellie in a way that made her stomach flip, and the vicious whiteness of the room extinguished as the room was absorbed again into the dark.

READY TO CONTINUE THE RIDE?

Dear Reader

Ellie has found out her husband Sam works for MI6. After a diet of lies for ten years, Ellie agrees to stay, and although hurt by Sam's betrayal, love keeps them together. Sam has discovered an upgrade to the nanobomb he stole from Al Nadir. Those responsible for Kinley's death have been captured.

Are you ready for the next instalment?

Ellie has been abducted. Sam is in the States, unaware of her plight. Maide wants answers. How far will he go to find them? The quantum bomb has been stolen. What will President Treeborne do when he finds out? And what will be Salim's next move?

If you enjoyed the first book in the series, you will love The Dominant. The action ratchets up as secrets unravel. The plotline will blast your mind and will have you reading all night. Get ready for the ride of your life.

Continue with the adventure
https://geni.us/AfPzq52

GET OPERATION SNOWDROP FOR FREE

You heard about Operation Snowdrop a lot in The Trusted. Now is your chance to get the inside track on what really happened. You can get access to Operation Snowdrop and get the truth behind the mission that crossed the line.

If you want to get insider intelligence on Sam and Ellie next adventures, early bird discounts on all future releases in *The Trusted Thriller* series, access to competitions or instant access to me, Michelle Medhat, then subscribe by hitting the link below and we can continue this journey together.

GET ACCESS TO OPERATION SNOWDROP
https://dl.bookfunnel.com/nz69zq8lp2

ENJOY THIS BOOK?
YOU CAN MAKE A DIFFERENCE

You have probably heard this before, but for an author, reviews really do make a difference. They are our lifeblood and we live and die by them. Honest reviews help others to find out about books they wouldn't have heard of before.

If you have enjoyed this book, I would be very grateful if you could spend a few minutes to leave a review on the book's Amazon page. You can jump straight to the review page by hitting the link below.

LEAVE A REVIEW HERE
https://geni.us/BcQhS

Learn more about Michelle Medhat

www.forever-connected.com
michelle@forever-connected.com

THE TRUSTED THRILLER SERIES

This Thriller Series is an edge-of-your-seat, ruthless, non-stop ride packed with gripping spy action, provocative sci-fi suspense, sex, political intrigue and amazing sci-tech to push Bond into the background! If you're searching for something that's nail-biting to the very end - you've found it in this extraordinary Thriller Series.

If you've read this book first, and haven't discovered the rest of the series yet, you need to read these books. Don't miss out, get them now and get the full story!

The Trusted (Book One – Part One)

He's a husband, a killer, and the only man who can save the world…

Sam Noor keeps his double lives separate with expert precision. But when the MI6 agent's wife discovers the lie, he fears that both his worlds may shatter. Distraught and conflicted, Noor concentrates on his latest mission and discovers a weapon that could cause a global catastrophe…

Drawn into the fight against a sinister terrorist group with powerful connections, Noor must uncover the faction's secrets by any means necessary. Even if it puts the woman he loves in the line of fire.

But Noor has no way of knowing that a supernatural war rages within his nation. And the winner could take charge of humanity's very soul.

Against forces that defy his reality, can Noor protect millions of innocents from a bloody end?

The Dominant (Book Two – Part Two)

One spy's war on terror could decide the fate of humanity...

MI6 agent Sam Noor isn't afraid to get his hands dirty to protect his homeland. While overseas interrogating an enemy terrorist, he's horrified to learn his beloved wife suffered the same brutal tactics from his own men. Determined to expose the betrayal and extract bloody justice, Noor uncovers an unbelievable fact: his wife died and somehow came back to life...

Swept up in an international power struggle, Noor goes rogue to uncover the eye-opening truth. The fallout from Sam's revenge ripples from the Oval Office through the CIA and MI6. As he fights tooth and nail to turn back the doomsday clock, cosmic forces wage their own battle for Earth's future. And Noor fears that preventing nuclear destruction may sacrifice the love of his life.

Can the maverick agent protect his wife and save his world from annihilation?

The Resonance (Book Three – Part Three)

World War III rages. What can she do to protect the innocent?

Ellie Noor's hope hangs by a thread. Tortured to within an inch of her life by sadistic terrorists, she's horrified to learn her husband's efforts to free her cost a half-a-million lives. But grief must wait as Ellie is swept up in an interdimensional attempt to stop all-out nuclear destruction.

Shocked to discover the key to saving the universe lies inside her, she becomes a potent instrument to respawn Earth's lost protector. But with the world's atomic arsenals locked and loaded, and sinister beings on the attack, she fears only an unfathomable miracle can halt humanity's extinction.

Can Ellie unleash her hidden power and prevent her planet's annihilation?

A WORD FROM THE AUTHOR

The Trusted is part one – book one of a thriller series that is very special to me. The series has been born out of extraordinary experiences I've had around the world, throughout my career. My background in science, technology and innovation has given me incredible insight, and thus, the technologies explored throughout the series have their foundations in real science.

The aspect of energies, vibrations and what is reality has always intrigued me, and it was my desire to weave these into a high-octane spy story based in our current times. Maybe some of you reading this will have doubts about how metaphysical things have any place at all in a fast-moving spy novel, but as in my work, I tend to explore and push the envelope on the art of the possible.

I urge you to take a leap.

You may just love where you land.

Michelle Medhat

Find out more
www.forever-connected.com
michelle@forever-connected.com

Twitter @theconnected1   Facebook @michellemedhat

The Playlists of *The Trusted Thriller Series*

The Trusted
Everlasting – Take That
Secrets – One Republic
Have I Told You Lately that I Love You – Rod Stewart
Rock You Like a Hurricane – Scorpions
Khalina Lewahdina (Let's stay alone together) – Amr Diab
E.T. – Katy Perry
Solsbury Hill – Peter Gabriel
Angel with a Shotgun – The Cab
Only Love can Hurt Like This – Paloma Faith
Who Wants to Live Forever – Queen
Rule the World – Take That
Fighting Suspicions – Rebecca Ferguson
The Architect – Paloma Faith
Rewrite the Stars – Zac Efron & Zendaya
The Last of the Secret Agents – Nancy Sinatra
New Divide – Linkin Park
Army of Two – Olly Murs
Demons – Imagine Dragons
Shine a Light – Bryan Adams
Don't Stop Believin' – Journey
What Part of my Body Hurts the Most – Rob Fowler & Sharon Sexton
Please Don't Leave Me – P!nk
Set Fire to the Rain – Adele
Guilty – Paloma Faith
Almeno Stavolta (At Least this Time…) – Nek
Candlelight – Jack Savoretti
I Belong to you – Caro Emerald
Try – P!nk
Redemption – The Strange Familiar
Nothing Breaks Like a Heart – Mark Ronson (Feat. Miley Cyrus)
Many Shades of Black – Adele & The Raconteurs
See Who I am – Within Temptation

The Dominant

Secrets – P!nk
La Tortura (The Torture)– Shakira
L'Altra Dimensione (The Other Dimension) – Måneskin
Amor Eterno (Eternal Love) – Fonseca
My Immortal – Evanescence
Revenge – P!nk with Eminem
Killer Queen - Queen
So Am I – Ava Max
Any Way You Want It – Journey
Me – Taylor Swift & Brendon Urie
Lucy in the Sky with Diamonds – The Beatles
Some Guys Have All the Luck – Rod Stewart
Perfetto (Perfect)– Gianna Nannini
Half the World Away – Aurora
Raise Hell – Brandi Carlisle
The Pretender – Foo Fighters
Too Good to Lose - Rebecca Ferguson
Maybe – Lewis Capaldi
Something's Gotta Give – One Republic
Torna a Casa (Come Back Home) – Måneskin
I Want to Break Free – Queen
Amo Soltanto Te (I Only Love You)– Andrea Bocelli & Ed Sheeran
Love at First Sight – Kylie
Whisky Tango – Jack Savoretti
Wonder – Naughty Boy with Emeli Sandé
Retribution – Jeff Scott Soto
Ayami Beek (My Days With You) - Elissa
Wasted – Jack Savoretti
Light My Fire – The Doors
We Share the Same Sun – Stereophonics
Surrender – Paloma Faith
What Have You Done – Within Temptation
Out of the Frying Pan and Into the Fire – Meatloaf
Rockstar (Salim's Theme) – Nickelback
Radioactive – Imagine Dragons
Back for Good – Take That
Danger Zone – Kenny Loggins

What Doesn't Kill You (Stronger) – Kelly Clarkson
Sweet But Psycho – Ava Max
Welcome to The Jungle – Guns and Roses

The Resonance
Strong - Mark Kingswood
Hiding – Florence + The Machine
The Sound of Sunshine – Michael Franti & Spearhead
All of My Heart - ABC
Toxic – Britney Spears
Burn it to the Ground - Nickelback
On Top of the World – Imagine Dragons
The Scientist - Coldplay
Blood on My Hands – Jack Savoretti
Music's Too Sad Without You – Kylie Minogue & Jack Savoretti
Suspicious Minds – Elvis Presley
Girls Just Wanna Have Fun – Cyndi Lauper
Traitor - Daughtry
Torn – Natalie Imbruglia
Dear Mr. President – P!nk
The Prayer – Celine Dion & Andrea Bocelli
The Winner Takes It All - ABBA
Guilty – Paloma Faith
Strip Me – Natasha Bedingfield
Won't Get Fooled Again – The Who
Changing – Paloma Faith
Drops of Jupiter – Train
Liar – Camila Cabello
Bring Me To Life – Evanescence
Venus – Bananarama
WW3 – Paloma Faith
Find U Again – Mark Ronson (feat. Camila Cabello)
Get Lucky – Daft Punk (feat. Pharrell Williams & Nile Rodgers)
Dancing in the Dark – Bruce Springsteen
Rescue Me – One Republic
Superheroes – The Script
Get Outta My Way – Kylie Minogue
Set Fire to the Rain – Adele

Who's Crying Now – Journey
Pain is So Close to Pleasure – Queen
Dark Night of the Soul – Van Morrison
Maybe Tomorrow – The Stereophonics
One Last Kiss – Kylie Minogue
Any Other Way – Jack Savoretti
Truth Hurts – Bullet for My Valentine
Stuck in the Middle with You – Stealers Wheel
Firework – Katy Perry
Red Light Spells Danger – Billy Ocean
Breaking Your Own Heart – Kelly Clarkson
Everything is Broken – Bob Dylan
Simples Corazones (Simple Hearts) – Fonseca
Greatest Mistake – Jack Savoretti
When Love Takes Over – David Guetta (feat. Kelly Rowland)
Shine – Emeli Sandè
I Saved the World Today – Eurythmics
Cold – James Blunt
Hold Me Close – David Essex
We Are Bound – Jack Savoretti
The Power of Love – Huey Lewis & The News

ACKNOWLEDGEMENTS

The name that has made this book a reality is Sam Medhat, my husband. He is my inspiration, and without him this book, and the series that follows, would never have been created. He is the one who listens to every word written. He is the one who endures my frustrations when I have writer's block. He is the one who is constantly woken up by my unsuccessful attempts at creeping into bed in the wee small hours, after I've become lost in my writing world.

Without Sam, no writing would have happened.

Whilst writing this series, I lost my brother, father and mother. None of them lived to see this in print, however their love is embodied within the words, and I hope, somewhere, they can see the result of the faith they had in me to achieve.

I would like to thank my fabulous editor Ceri Savage, who has been with me on this journey, and who has been incredible in her support and advice.

Michelle Medhat

Made in United States
Orlando, FL
11 January 2022